ZAR

I live in deepest Cheshire surrounded by horses, dogs, cats and amazing countryside. When I'm not visiting wine bars, artisan markets or admiring the scenery in sexy high heels or green wellies, I can be found in flip flops on the beach in Barcelona, or more likely sampling the tapas!

I write hot romance and bonkbusters. My most recent release, 'Stable Mates', is a fun romp through the Cheshire country-side and combines some of my greatest loves – horses, dogs, hot men and strong women (and not forgetting champagne and fast cars)!

You can find out more about me, and all my contact details at www.ZaraStoneley.com.

Stable Mates

ZARA STONELEY

HarperImpulse an imprint of
HarperCollins*Publishers* Ltd
77–85 Fulham Palace Road
Hammersmith, London W6 8JB

www.harpercollins.co.uk

A Paperback Original 2014

First published in Great Britain in ebook format by HarperImpulse 2014

Cover Images © Shutterstock.com

Zara Stoneley asserts the moral right to
be identified as the author of this work

A catalogue record for this book is
available from the British Library

ISBN: 9780008106409

t

Au

permission of the publishers.

This one is for you, Mum! xx

Tippermere

Welcome to tranquil Tippermere, set deep in the Cheshire country-side. Home to lords and ladies, horsemen and farmers.

Set on the highest hill, keeping a close eye on the village and its inhabit-ants, lies Tipping House Estate. In pride of place is the grand Elizabethan-style mansion, sweeping down in front of her are immaculate gardens, well-kept parkland and rolling acres that spread as far as the eye can see.

Follow the stream down to the flat below, and nestling between copses and lakes, you find Folly Lake Manor and the sprawling grounds of the bustling Equestrian Centre. The country lane in front wends its way between high hedges to the village green, the church and two village pubs. It then fans out into tributaries. Follow them further and you find a small eventing yard, a scat-tering of country cottages and rambling working farms.

Take the road north eastwards, travel on a few short miles and soon the elegant village of Kitterly Heath unfolds before you - a village whose origins were recorded in the Domesday Book. At one end of the ancient high street a solid 14th-century church stands sentry, with an imposing school at the other, and all around sprawl the mansions, old and new, that house the rich and famous...

The Residents of Tippermere

Marcus James – *millionaire businessman owner of Folly Lake Manor and the Equestrian Centre at Tippermere. Recently deceased.*

Amanda James – *the grieving widow. Elegant and understated, delicate and demure.*

Charlotte 'Lottie' Brinkley – *disorganised but lovable daughter of Billy. Desperately seeking something, if only she knew what.*

Rory Steel – *devilishly daring and sexy three-day eventer, owner of a small eventing yard in Tippermere.*

Tilly – *head of the terrier trio that accompanies Rory everywhere.*

Billy Brinkley – *Lottie's father. Former superstar showjumper, based at the equestrian centre.*

Victoria 'Tiggy' Stafford – *dog groomer and sometime groom for Billy. As friendly, shaggy and eternally optimistic as a spaniel.*

*

Philippa 'Pip' Keelan – headline hunting journalist. Trim, sophisticated and slightly scary. Recently moved to Tippermere from London, in search of real life and real men.

Mick O'Neal – expert farrier, Irish charmer, dangerously attractive.

Lady Elizabeth Stanthorpe – owner of Tipping House Estate, lover of strong gin and tonics. Meddler and mischief-maker. Lottie's gran, Dominic's mother.

Bertie & Holmes – Elizabeth's black labradors.

Dominic Stanthorpe – dressage rider extraordinaire. Uncle to Lottie, son of Elizabeth, slightly bemused and frustrated by both.

Tom Strachan – sexy ex-underwear model. Divorced, devastated but amazingly dishy. Recently made his 'escape to the country' with his goth daughter.

Tabatha Strachan – teenage daughter of Tom. Horse-mad, but suitably unimpressed by most other things.

*

David Simcock – England goalkeeper, resident of the neighbouring Kitterly Heath.

Sam – partner of David. Lover of dogs, diamonds and designer delights.

Anthony Simcock – property developer father of David.

*

The horses – too numerous to list

Chapter 1

'I think he's dead.'

Rory Steel had been enjoying, in his semi-conscious state, a particularly gratifying dream, in which he was just about to clear the last cross-country hurdle that stood between him and the gallop down the home straight, when his mobile had started to buzz like an irritated hornet inches from his ear. He'd picked it up automatically, horse suspended mid-leap.

'Shit, you're kidding.' The horse dissolved, along with his dream of a perfect round, as he sat bolt upright. Something he instantly regretted as a sledgehammer came into contact with his skull and church bells started ringing in his ears. 'Fucking hell.' As he sank back on to a soft pillow, clutching his throbbing head, Rory briefly wondered if the caller had been making a pronouncement of his own demise, then decided that was rubbish. It hurt too much.

And he could see faint outlines in the dark that surrounded him, and surely death was a total blackout? He prodded his temples experimentally and decided his head probably wasn't about to disintegrate in a bloody mess. But, where the hell was he?

From somewhere in the general direction of his feet came an indignant disembodied voice, which meant he hadn't flung the phone far. Now all he had to do was find it, without causing himself grievous bodily harm.

Rory put an exploratory hand out and came into contact with skin; soft, warm skin that definitely wasn't his own. And it all came flooding back with clarity. He was in a horsebox, crammed into the bulkhead bed, with a tin roof only a foot or so above him. Which explained the ringing in his ears. And he was with Lottie.

'Bugger off.' She pushed his hand away, her voice groggy with sleep.

'I was trying to find the light switch.'

'Not heard it called that before.'

The phone was squawking, more desperate by the second, from its mystery location.

'What's that funny noise?' The words came out on a yawn as Lottie stretched, groaning as her foot came into contact with the wall.

'My mobile.'

'Well bloody answer it.' She rolled over and buried her head under the pillow, and his hand shifted to the dip in her waist before drifting down to her hip. He liked Lottie's hips.

'Proper child-bearing hips these.' His fingers tightened, in sympathy with other parts of his body.

'Huh, you mean big.' She didn't sound as drowsy now, as she swatted at his hand again and shifted onto her back. 'And don't you dare go back to playing with my boobs. Answer the phone.'

'I can't find the bloody thing in the dark, can I?' He groped further down her body, which earned him a slap, and finally his fingers closed around the lump of hard plastic, just as Lottie flicked the light on. She was shaking her head at him.

'You're hopeless.'

'And you're just so fuckable.' He blew her a kiss and stared openly at her naked body. He'd missed a lot of things about Lottie while she'd been gone, but that glorious body had been his first thought when he'd heard she was heading back.

In fact, Lottie's uninhibited nakedness had probably been what he had fallen in love with in the first place. Sometimes he found it

2

hard to believe that he'd found someone even more disorganised than he was, and he'd found her need to flee the country even more incomprehensible. But when it came to bed and her body, her complete lack of hang-ups made her irresistible.

'Who is that? Who's there?' The voice in his ear had moved on from hysterics to a mix of suspicion and brittle annoyance and he half wished he'd prolonged his 'find the phone' game. Who knew what it might have led to?

'It's me of course, who the hell do you think it is? Who's that?'

'There is a chance, darling…' Lottie straddled him, which was no mean feat given the headspace, and his cock hardened in anticipation. He could ditch the phone right now, straight out of the window. She reached forward, those perfect breasts bobbing against him; he could already taste her kiss. Except he couldn't. She'd grabbed the phone and was waggling it in front of his face.

'Hang on, that isn't my bloody phone.'

'Exactly.' She giggled and fell sideways.

'Hello? Hello? You're not—'

'Pip.' Rory stared at the bright-pink phone in disgust. 'Hell, I'd forgotten I'd ended up with bloody Pip's phone again. Why the fuck does she keep walking off with my mobile?' Pip was lovely, Pip was totally, one hundred per cent organised when it came to work and a shambling mess when it came to everything else. And this was the third time in a week she'd picked up his mobile by mistake and walked off with it. Which left him with hers.

'Why don't you keep it in your pocket, like everyone else?' Lottie was regarding him through big green eyes, her head cradled in her hand. Mussed-up hair in a tangle round her face. A very kissable face, and he just knew that mouth would taste of sex. He leaned forward, just as she put a hand out to his chest. 'Rory, you're on the phone, remember?'

He sighed. 'I'd rather be on you.'

'Shush,' she giggled, 'she can hear you.' He made a move to chuck the phone back down the bed, but she grabbed it from him before he had chance.

'Hello?'

He trailed a finger over her slightly rounded stomach and was rewarded with a slap. 'Stop it.'

'I can't. You're irresistible, especially when you're cross.'

'You're not Pip, either.' He could hear the voice, sharp, on the other end of the line.

'Nope. It's Lottie. Pip has got Rory's mobile, her number—'

'I know what the number is, thank you.'

'Hey, is that Amanda? Hello? Amanda?' Lottie dropped the phone on his chest and flopped back. 'Well thanks to you too. She's bloody hung up on me.'

'I'm hung up on you.' He stroked a finger down one of the forbidden breasts, over the peak of a nipple. 'So, fancy a bit of mounting practice?'

'What time is it?'

Rory sighed and held his wrist up so she could see his watch. 'I really don't know why you haven't got a watch.'

'I lose them, or drop them in water buckets. And they leave tan lines.' She stretched perfectly bronzed, unmarked arms out in front of her and squinted again at his watch. 'You do know your class starts in an hour?'

Oh yeah, that was what he was doing shacked up in the crummiest horsebox that Billy Brinkley owned. With the man's daughter. They'd got to the showground and hit the whiskey and an uncomfortable, cramped bed with the long-legged shapely Charlotte had, in his drunken haze, seemed a far better bet than the comfort of the hotel that the horse's owner had booked for him half a mile up the road.

'And Flashy needs a good half-hour work-in unless you want to exit over the judge's car like she did last time.'

'Well you'd better shift your arse, hadn't you gorgeous?' He gave the bum he quite fancied fondling a shove with his foot. 'I can't exit anywhere with you in the way.'

4

Three minutes later the horsebox door was open and Rory Steel stood in nothing more than breeches and boots, surveying the showground. There was an early-morning spring nip in the air that did nothing to clear his head, nor did the sight of already gleaming horses being walked out.

His two least-favourite aspects of the world of eventing he competed in were dressage and small events like this. Unfortunately, Flash didn't approve of dressage either, so he'd been forced to take the sensible route and bring her to a smaller dressage competition. The other competitors would hate him because they knew who he was and considered it jolly bad form to compete at a lower level. And he'd hate every minute because there was a good chance the stroppy little mare would play up like the prima donna she was and make him look a prize dick.

Hot Flash had been named well, though as far as he was concerned it was more like Hot Flush; she was as temperamental as a menopausal woman. Not that he'd known that many, but the image of his mum at fifty stuck in his mind. She'd developed a temper worse than his dad's had ever been. Which was going some.

'Are you going to just stand there showing the world your abs or let me get past so I can get her ready?'

'I'd rather have just lain there, actually.' He ran his fingers through his hair and could swear his head was literally throbbing. 'Christ, was that whiskey you were plying me with last night bootleggers' stuff?'

'Probably. You know me, anything to get you into bed.' She grinned, which made her even more shaggable, and he couldn't resist kissing those full lips, sliding his hand round onto her firm bum so he could pull her closer.

Lottie wriggled her way past him. 'Are you going to ride dressed like that? Try distraction techniques so no one notices what a crap test you've done? I can see the headlines now,' she waved her hands in the air 'Rory Steel, the fearless eventer, beaten by a bunch of Cheshire WAGs.'

'Piss off.' His foot missed her bum by inches as she jumped down the steps laughing. It beat him how she managed to get up so bright-eyed and bushy-tailed when they'd spent the evening getting slaughtered and the night getting shagged.

***

It wasn't until Lottie was grooming the laid-back Flash that she remembered the phone call. If Pip had been calling first thing in the morning, it wouldn't have seemed strange. Pip had been shadowing Rory's every move lately. But it was Amanda. And that was just weird. Pip did horses, didn't think anything of getting up before the birds had started tweeting to get a horse ready for a show. But Amanda was a lady of leisure; well at least that's how the rest of Tippermere saw her. Marcus made the millions and his beautiful wife spent them. His extravagance had been to buy Folly Lake Equestrian Centre and sponsor one or two of the riders who frequented it, but his lovely wife had zero interest in the centre, the horses or even the riders, which was a constant source of amazement to Lottie. If she'd been married to the slightly portly and very bossy Marcus, she'd have felt entitled to eye up every single fit horseman at close quarters as a consolation prize, but the only time she'd ever spotted Amanda down at the stables was when she'd been searching out her errant husband – who had no qualms about mentally undressing every groom and female rider on the yard. Lottie reckoned he was totally shameless; he'd have shagged anything with a pulse, even the podgy dishevelled Tiggy or the bad-tempered Fliss.

Maybe Amanda was frigid. But she didn't seem like that; she'd been a bit of a laugh at the parties they'd held in Folly Lake Manor, or Follyfoot funny farm as Rory and his mates often referred to it. To them it was a majestic home for misfits. To others, like Billy, her father, it was a necessary evil in the village.

Either way, Marcus and Amanda were regarded with amused

suspicion by some, and as generous benefactors by others. But everyone agreed they threw a bloody good party.

Maybe, Lottie thought, Amanda had married Marcus for his money, and he'd married her for her looks and that was it. A shiver ran down her spine as Flash nibbled at her collar.

'Now you are going to behave for Rory, aren't you?' She knew how much he hated events like this, but Flash desperately needed some smaller venues to persuade her that dressage arenas weren't inhabited by lions. The mare was a dream in the stable, and had a jump as big and brave as her heart on the cross-country course, with flicking heels that respected the flimsy show jumps, but in the vast emptiness of the dressage arena she was like a firecracker about to go off. Lottie knew how she felt. It was like being dropped on a fashion runway in uncomfortable shoes and being told not to trip up, not that she knew much about fashion shows, but she imagined it was the same. Hushed silence, everyone watching and an acre of space poised to make a fool of you.

But in the few three-day events Rory had entered her, the cricket score of the dressage section had meant any hope of being on the leader board was doomed, even when the fiery, fearless chestnut jumped out of her skin in the other two phases of the competition.

Lottie dropped the white pad and elegant black saddle onto the mare's iridescent back just as an out-of-tune whistle announced Rory's arrival.

'Some of those plaits look like a poodle's topknot.'

'You're very lucky you didn't have to do them yourself, mate.' She bent down to tighten the girth and took the time to admire his toned thighs on her way back up. 'I'm only here because there wasn't anything else to do, and if I'd stayed on dad's yard for another five minutes I'd have screamed and hightailed it back to Barcelona.'

'Why go all the way to Spain when I'm here?' His lazy gaze drifted over her body as the soft drawl made its way straight between her thighs. Charlotte loved Rory for many reasons: his

7

sense of humour, easy-going nature, fit-toned body, but most of all because he didn't mean a word he said. No expectations. Just fun. Which was exactly what, she'd decided she needed after leaving her shit of a boyfriend on a Spanish beach and heading reluctantly back to Cheshire, because she had nowhere else to go. When Lottie had left Tippermere one of the reasons (and there had been several) had been Rory and his complete inability to take anything, including relationships, seriously. But now she was back she'd concluded that it was actually a bonus.

'Because it's sunny there and no one gives a damn about Billy bloody Brinkley, and,' she paused in her list of some of the other reasons as she got to the crux of the matter, 'there aren't any horses.' Which was, she told herself, why she'd run first of all to Australia, then somehow ended up in Barcelona after hooking up with an adventurer who had itchier feet than she had. Todd.

It was slightly ironic that in the search for a soul mate who didn't want to be tied down or committed to anyone or anything, she'd managed to end up with a serial adulterer who also happened to be a bigamist. Spreading it around was bad enough, but the arrival of a platoon of police armed to the teeth, on the beach of all places, had been the ultimate in humiliation. It wasn't like she'd even had her best bikini on. Todd the hunter could, as far as she was concerned, go screw himself. Which might be the only option left if he got deported from Spain and stuck in the slammer.

'How boring.' Rory grinned and ran a large, capable hand through his messy curls before checking the girth. 'What the fuck do you do then, apart from drink?' He didn't wait for an answer. 'Now, do I risk working her in and scaring all the other riders out of the warm-up area, or shall I just enter at A?'

Knowing Rory as she did, she guessed it was probably a rhetorical question, but answered it anyway. 'And exit three seconds later?' She patted the docile Flash, who was looking like a tired donkey. 'I suppose it might give you a chance of getting in the top twenty if you manage to scare all the others off.' She worked on keeping a thoughtful face, but one glance of the sexily frustrated look Rory shot at her tickled her somewhere deep down and brought a grin to her face. It was hard to stay serious with him around; you either laughed with him, or, as he was so funny when he got angry, you had to laugh at him. 'I don't know what your problem is, call yourself a horseman, you could put a baby on her.' She gave the mare a dig in the ribs as the horse was now resting a leg, and leaning half a ton of horseflesh against her. 'Come on you old nag, let's go bust some balls.'

'That's what I'm worried about, busting mine.' Rory gave the mare a hearty slap on the rump as they walked out of the stall past him and flicked some shavings out of the long tail. 'Call yourself a groom.'

'No, I don't actually. Remind me not to come to your rescue again you ungrateful sod.'

Lottie watched as he buttoned up his jacket and straightened the cravat. He was the type of man she couldn't resist coming to the rescue of. One flash of that wicked grin and she came running like a bloody lapdog, well like his army of terriers. Which reminded her... 'Are the dogs okay in the back of the lorry?'

'They were trying to dig a hole in the floor when I left them, hope the floorboards are more solid than the rest of that rust bucket.'

'At least that rust bucket,' Lottie tried to look haughty and was pretty sure she'd failed, 'is one up on your posh purple passion wagon, which wouldn't even start.' The wagon was nothing like the lorry that had been gifted to Rory by one of his rich owners, who liked only the best for their darling horse. But it was the only thing Billy would lend her. This one didn't have shiny livery, full kitchen area, shower and double bed. It had space for three horses at the back, a narrow tack room with just enough room to swing a very small cat in the middle, and an 'almost' double bed squashed above the cab.

'I suppose well used and dirty,' he winked at her, 'but in full working order is better than immaculate and good-looking but can't rise to the occasion.'

She followed his line of sight straight to the upright and correct figure of her uncle, Dominic Stanthorpe. Dressage rider extraordinaire, or so a certain gushing woman's mag had once labelled him. 'Are you having a go at Uncle Dom again? And how do you know he can't rise to the occasion?' She raised an eyebrow, then held up a hand as he opened his mouth to answer. 'No, on second thoughts, don't go there. I don't want to know what the latest trailer-trash gossip is. I *like* Uncle Dom.'

'You like everyone, darling. Which is why you call so many shits your friends.'

'And are you one of those many shits?' She checked Flash's bridle as she spoke, straightening the bit, running a finger along the curb, trying not to be concerned whether he answered or not. 'Maybe you should try her in a hackamore?'

'Maybe I should put my name on the suicide watch.' His tone was dry. 'And no, Charlott-ie,' his firm, dry lips came down lightly over hers, 'I try not to shit on my own doorstep.' He pulled down the stirrup leathers and Flash, who'd gone back to resting a leg, nearly fell over as he landed lightly in the saddle.

Lottie grinned as they staggered sideways. 'Never seen a half pass performed half-mounted before. Can you do them when you're in the saddle too?'

'Smart-arse.' Rory gave her the finger and straightened his hat. 'Maybe you should let the dogs out; might be a good distraction.'

She smiled and dropped a kiss on the mare's velvet soft nose, breathing in the horsey smell. 'Try and stay in the ring this time darling.' Flash snorted in response, not a good sign, her nostrils flaring until she could see the pink lining.

'What the fuck is he doing here in this backwater, anyway?' Rory was still staring suspiciously over in Dom's direction.

Lottie shrugged. 'Gran probably told him, so he could keep an eye on us.'

'Oh great, so we trek all the way out here where nobody can witness my death and Elizabeth goes and spreads the word to the whole county. I wondered why it was so bloody busy.'

'You're exaggerating, about the whole county and about your death. Stop being such a prima donna.'

***

Rory and Flash were early in the running, which was a bonus as the patch of grass set aside for warming up was quiet. If they were jumping, it didn't matter how many other horses were around, Flash had the poles to concentrate on and everything else faded into insignificance. Given an obstacle-free area, though, and the horse seemed to think someone was waiting to plan a surprise, suspicion traced its way through every muscle in her body and anything from another horse to a spectator's hat was guaranteed to wind her up.

However much she teased him, Lottie knew Rory was a good rider, and so did he. He was strong from eventing, a sport not for the faint-hearted or weak-bodied, but his muscle tone was long and lean rather than the short, compact build that her show-jumping father sported. And he didn't seek to dominate, which was a saving grace when it came to a horse like Flash. He sat quietly, confidently, long legs wrapped around her – holding her in a safe embrace. When Flash spooked, he didn't react, his body going with her, his hands giving but firm.

Lottie's gaze was locked onto him. She couldn't help but watch him. He might not portray quite the picture of elegance and control that Dom did, but it was almost like he was part of the horse. His body adapted, flowed in response, shifting like he had to do during the wild cross-country rollercoaster of twists and turns, ups and downs. She flicked her gaze from Rory to Dom and back again, so different and yet so the same. And yeah, Dom was so controlled, so distant almost, in contrast to the fiery ball

11

of energy that was Rory, that she could see why each regarded the other with suspicion.

To Dom, Rory was a wild child with no respect for his own safety, and no style. The latter probably being the most injurious to his fine sensibilities. He distrusted the man's apparent casual attitude to women, was wary of his easy sense of humour and cavalier approach to life. And to Rory, Dom was too prim and proper, totally unbending and most likely gay, which was quite an accomplishment given his parentage and upbringing.

Lottie grinned as Flash fly-bucked and Rory did a good imitation of a rodeo rider, waving one arm in the air. She could almost feel the waves of disapproval emanating from Dom on the other side of the area. But whatever they said, she was pretty sure they admired each other in some weird, indefinable way.

The judge's car horn went and Lottie checked the running order. She signalled at Rory, next in, and saw Flash's ears flicker in what could have been warning or anticipation.

Enter at C, working trot was the official first line of the dressage test. The fact that Flash entered was in fact a bonus, but there was nothing that suggested 'working' and only a smattering of 'trot' in what followed. She danced in a zigzag combination that involved trot, canter and an amazingly good pirouette. Lottie could have sworn Rory closed his eyes briefly as he silently willed the horse down the centre line.

The next few instructions on the test would have been a mystery to even an experienced onlooker. The ten-metre circle resembled a broken egg and the extended trot, which should have been a thing of controlled beauty, would have been brilliant put to music – the type of music that is played as background to firework displays. Lottie realised she was humming the 1812 Overture in time to the fly bucks and heel kicks, whilst Rory sat strangely calm on top of Flash, resigned to his fate, as if he was hacking out the quiet nag she'd appeared in the stable. They really excelled when they came to the flying change, for a moment they seemed suspended in the air as Flash decided whether to paddle desperately in an attempt to fly into hyperspace, or give up and come back to terra firma.

Lottie covered her eyes and peered through her fingers, half expecting them to come crashing down in a heap of tangled legs, and then, miraculously, as the mare's hooves hit the ground, she seemed to calm down. Maybe it was because she'd had that sensation of jumping, and it had switched her mad chestnut brain on to automatic, but something happened. She flew through the next few movements, finished the test with the kind of perfection that instilled silent awe, and then carried on flying – straight out of the ring, narrowly missing the judge's car and scattering the onlookers who'd come for a quiet day out to watch the horse world's answer to ballet.

Rory grinned and dropped the reins as the steward jumped out of the way, clipboard flying straight at the judge's secretary whose hat went one way and cup of coffee the other, splashing a passing great dane, who, with a yelp of surprise, headed off in the opposite direction, towing his surprised teenage owner, baseball cap askew, with him.

Lottie started giggling, then glanced up to find Dom had ridden over and was in front of her, staring disapprovingly down his elegant long nose. Even his horse looked like it took a dim view of the situation. 'That man really doesn't do the dressage world any favours at all.' He gave an exaggerated sigh. 'Airs above the ground aren't normally performed at this level, which even a numbskull eventer like Rory should know.' He tutted, the horse gave a discreet snort. She tried to keep the laughter in, she really did, but it hurt. Her ribs hurt, her eyes started streaming and suddenly she couldn't help herself anymore. She let it all out, howling with laughter until she was doubled up and could hardly breathe.

She paused, aware that Dom and his mount were still standing motionless in front of her. Tiny equine hooves oiled and polished so she could see a whisper of her reflection in them. She took a calming breath and wiped the tears away with the back of her hand. 'He's not that bad, and you know it.'

Dom shook his head slowly. 'I think you better go and catch them, don't you?'

'They'll be at the horsebox; Flash always heads for home when she's upset.' She blew her nose, which helped a little at calming the hysterics that had been bubbling around in her chest. 'Christ, I hope she hasn't actually headed for the main gate, she might really want to get home this time.'

Dom raised an eyebrow even further.

'Kidding. Honest. They'll be fine. Oh, good luck.'

'Thank you, Charlotte.' She half expected him to add, 'but there is no luck involved', but he didn't. He just nodded, although she could have sworn there was a glimmer of a smile chasing across his perfect features as he nudged his horse into a walk. 'Oh, Charlie,' he turned in the saddle, almost as an afterthought. 'Don't let him break your heart, will you? Men like him are never worth it, believe me.' Then he gathered his reins and trotted back across the arena.

'No heart left to break, Uncle Dom.'

***

Flash was, as Lottie had expected, by the horsebox when she got there; tied to a piece of twine and tugging lazily at a hay net, happy as an old-age pensioner on a day trip to Brighton.

Rory was sitting on the ramp, smoking a cigarette. His jacket had been discarded beside him, the cravat on top of it, his dark curls damp and flattened from the hat. He grinned. 'What kept you?'

'Couldn't keep up.' She sank down beside him, took a draw on his cigarette and handed it back. 'I'm not one hundred per cent sure, but I'd say you were probably eliminated.'

'I don't believe in doing things by halves.'

'Nope. Balls still intact then?'

'I might have to check on that one, unless you want to do it for me?'

14

'It's a bit public here.'

'True.' He took another long draw on the cigarette, blew a smoke ring. 'I'd sell that horse if she wasn't such a bloody good jumper.'

'Maybe next time you should warm her up in the show-jumping ring?'

'Hmm.' He stood up, ground out the cigarette butt with his boot and picked up his jacket.

'Or maybe you should just use her as a showjumper?'

'And let some idiot like your dad get his heavy-handed mitts on her?'

'Or maybe you should ask Dom to have a look at her?'

He gave her a look, which she guessed equated to something like, when hell freezes over. Then paused. 'You can, if you want.' Which was the closest he was going to get to a yes. He liked the horse, she knew he did. She could be the best on his yard, if she'd do even an average test. And she would be wasted just doing show-jumping. Cross-country was her forte. And the way she'd flown today, even Lottie could see she had paces to die for. Though 'to die for' probably weren't the right words to use where she was concerned.

'You want to check out these balls, then?'

She grinned. 'Could do, I'm good at medical things like that.'

'Right, you sort out the Menopausal Madonna and I'll give the dogs a run before we head back for a full inspection.'

He stepped off the ramp, then held out a hand and hauled her to her feet.

'Yes sir, Mr Bossy Boots.'

'Do as you're told for once.'

'Hey, don't forget this.' She picked up the bright-pink mobile phone, which he'd dropped on the ramp next to his packet of fags. 'You never said, what was Amanda calling about this morning?'

Rory dropped the phone into his pocket, his brow wrinkled as he tried to remember and she fought the impulse to stroke the lines away. 'Oh, she said he was dead.' He stared into the distance, still deep in thought. 'I presume she was talking about Marcus.'

'Marcus, dead?'

He shrugged, threw open the door of the box and stood back as the three terriers tumbled out.

'She said Marcus was dead?'

'Dunno, don't worry about it, I probably misheard. Be back in a bit, darling. Come on gang.' And he whistled the dogs up and headed off, surrounded by a whirlwind of brown and white yappiness, leaving a gobsmacked Lottie staring after him, mouth open.

Chapter 2

Philippa Keelan put the brush down and watched as the wagon pulled into the yard. Rory, as male-chauvinistic as ever, was behind the steering wheel; Lottie had her long legs stretched out on the dashboard with a terrier balanced precariously on her thighs. The second, older, terrier was sitting sensibly between driver and passenger, and the third one was galloping back and forth along the back of the seat, trying to peer out of the windows and barking with excitement at being home.

Pip felt the broad smile spread across her face and knew, deep in her heart, that coming here had been good for her. She'd never thought of herself as a country girl. By the age of fifteen she'd been screaming to get out of the small Welsh village where she'd been unceremoniously 'dragged up'. But after years of city life, here she was, stuck deep in the Cheshire countryside with a mix of horsey heroes, grumpy farmers and a smattering of WAGs.

From the first day her mother had shoved pencils and crayons in her direction, to keep her out of mischief, she'd been hooked. From the moment she'd learned that the hieroglyphics spread before her made up words, and the words made up a magical mystery story, she'd become an addict. Words and make-believe were far more interesting than the rolling Welsh hills and dirty sheep. Her wellies had been tossed aside in favour of a good book or, as she hit her teens, a girlie magazine. Pip was born to be a journalist, and a damned good one she'd become.

Her move to study in London had been the start of a new life, and apart from returning to Wales for the occasional daughterly duties of birthdays and Christmas, she'd never looked, or stepped, back.

Success had not come cheaply, social life was an enigma as she'd kept her head down and chased every lead and story she'd been offered until she hit the top, her dream job, interviewing the stars and travelling the world. Pip didn't want a desk job, an editor's position, she wanted to write. And write she did. Until she met Lottie on a Spanish beach.

She'd finished an assignment and was spending a couple of days 'chilling' as her editor had suggested, well, told her to. But it was a foreign concept and after three hours she'd been champing at the bit to get back to what she thought of as real life, until she'd hooked up with Lottie and her boyfriend. Until she'd listened to the self-deprecating stories that Lottie told about her famous father and her frequent spills from the saddles of his top horses. All of a sudden Pip felt jaded, lost in a sea of words. She needed a reality check. A kick up the arse. Some real people, rather than the endless stream of sycophants and stars.

And so, with the promise that Lottie would find her some work 'no probs as long as you don't mind some shit-shovelling', she told her editor she was taking a sabbatical. She agreed to work freelance. And now she was here. With a curly-haired lovable rogue called Rory, the madcap, irresponsible Lottie, who she was sure was desperately seeking security, and a bunch of horses that were more than one step up the ladder from the Welsh ponies she'd been brought up on. Although, as she well knew from past bruises, a Section D cob could be just as hot-headed as a thoroughbred, when it could be bothered to put the effort in.

'Well, is it true?' Lottie was out of the cab, pushing the gates shut before the lorry had halted, with the dogs tumbling out after her and fanning across the yard like an army patrol on search duty.

'Hi, to you too.' Pip waggled the bottom of her polo shirt to let some air in and wished she had shorts on like Lottie, minus the red-wealed thighs from a wobbling terrier. It had been cool when she'd started work, but now it was surprisingly close for an April day.

She cut a striking figure, but didn't quite realise the impact she'd had on the men or the place since landing in Tippermere a few months previously. Her neat bob of blonde hair was almost permanently pulled back into a severe ponytail, but it showed off her fine cheekbones and bright-blue eyes, and to the onlooker she was the picture of London sophistication, not a Welsh country girl. Which was exactly the image she'd set out to project. Pip always achieved what she wanted, even if her soft tone and seemingly laid-back approach belied it. She had an iron will and the determination of one of Rory's terriers. Which was how she'd got to the top of her career path and how she kept her trim figure and perfect complexion. Pip worked hard at whatever she did. Quietly. Which scared men off. Completely. Until she'd come here and found that the horsemen that Lottie shared her life with were a hundred miles from the city slickers she'd been sharing her bed and brain with for the last God knows how many years. She hadn't decided yet if that was a good thing or bad. Here, taking a gentle hint was an alien concept; 'no' had to be articulated very loudly, accompanied by something bordering on GBH. And when they got it, they just laughed and moved on. No fragile egos and over-sensitivity here.

'Pip, you can be so bloody annoying when you want to be.' Lottie started to lower the ramp of the lorry with the ease of someone who'd done it a billion times.

'Says the girl who stood me up last night so she could lorry-hop.'

Lottie coloured up. 'I only went with him because you said you couldn't. You're the one who grooms for him, not me.'

'Touché. Yes, then.'

'Yes, what?'

19

Pip jumped as Rory grabbed her from behind and landed a loud smacker of a kiss on her bare neck. 'Yuk. That is so gross, can't you keep him under control, Lottie?' Lottie shrugged, with a grin flickering briefly across her worried features. Control wasn't something she was overly bothered about. Out of control was much more fun. But Pip took a much more serious and regulated view of life. 'How did the little firecracker go, then?'

'You got it in one.' He made a gesture like an explosion and grinned. 'I need consoling, proof that my manhood has not been tarnished.'

'I don't do consolation, betcha Lottie does, though.'

'I thought you could both try.' He tipped his head on one side and Pip laughed.

'In your dreams, you dirty boy.'

'Can't blame a man for trying.'

'PIP.'

They both stared at the explosion from Lottie, who obviously couldn't wait any longer for an answer to her question.

'Looks like she's getting impatient, bit like me.' Rory pulled her closer, until the sandpaper roughness of his unshaved cheek brushed lightly against hers and the teasing tawny eyes offered an invitation that she'd been tempted by more than once.

Pip nudged him away. 'You two deserve each other. Anyhow, what were you doing with my bloody phone again?'

'It was you that picked up mine. Again.'

'No, Rory. You were the one who left the yard in such a hurry last night to go off on your magical mystery tour with Lottie and the ginger wonder. I mean, how can anyone confuse this,' she waggled the bright-pink phone in front of him, 'with this?' And handed over his black one. 'I'm surprised you even managed to load the right horse.'

He grinned and gave her a peck on the cheek. 'I never mix up my horses. Or my women.'

'For fuck's sake, will you two stop talking bollocks and tell me if someone has fucking died?'

Pip sighed. 'What on earth has got in to you?'

'Please, just answer the question.'

'Marcus. Amanda woke up in the early hours to find him stone-cold dead next to her. Well I'm not sure if he was actually cold, but—'

'Pip.'

'Okay, okay. She panicked and rang the first person she could think of, which was me. Or, in this case, you, Rory.' She shook her head slowly. 'I take it you weren't exactly helpful or consolatory.'

'She woke me up.'

'Sure.'

'And then I lost the phone when I sat up and hit my head, and all I could find were Lottie's boobs.'

'Stop. You're not helping your case.'

'Marcus is dead? He died?' Lottie was trying not to jump from one foot to the other in agitation.

'Yes, Lottie. He's dead, died, the two tend to be linked.'

'Christ, Dad will go apeshit.' Lottie sank down on the ramp of the lorry and cradled her head in her hands. Oblivious to the now-stamping Flash who had been expecting release from the confines of the horsebox and to be let out to grass. She looked up, a glimmer of hope still stirring. 'You're absolutely sure he's dead?'

'Well the funeral is in a week, so someone has seriously cocked up if he isn't.' Pip strode up the ramp past the dazed Lottie and started to untie the mare, who knew that the competition ordeal was over and she was home. 'I don't get what the issue is. Your dad didn't even like him anyway, did he? None of them did, apart from Amanda of course. Shift over or you might get one of Flash's specials.'

Lottie slid off the ramp and stood up slowly in front of the bemused Rory. 'She'll sell up, she hates horses.'

'She might not actually hate them, poppet.'

'You're right, that's worse. She doesn't give a monkey's.'

'I don't get you pair at all.' With a clatter of hooves and an ear-shrieking whinny that threatened to burst Lottie's eardrums, Flash came down the ramp and headed for her stable, coming to an abrupt halt when she reached the end of the lead rope, which still had Pip attached. A Pip who had stopped by the anguished-looking Lottie. 'What's the problem? Neither of you liked him, did you?' She looked from one to the other. 'I mean, you hardly knew him.'

'I did know him. I saw him at the centre all the time. I used to bloody live there, remember?' Lottie peered through her fingers. Liking him wasn't the issue.

'Well, to be fair, I don't remember, because I wasn't here then. But you weren't pals, were you? You hardly even know Amanda, do you? But you look like one of your nearest and dearest has popped their clogs.'

'But what if she sells up?'

'So?' Pip shrugged, and hauled back on the rope as the mare made a new dash for freedom. 'Someone will buy it, I mean how many places like that come on the market? That equestrian centre must be worth an absolute fortune.'

'Exactly. To a property developer.' Rory caught hold of Flash's headcollar to avoid her spinning round and knocking the already wavering Lottie to the floor. He understood the look on Lottie's face, even if Pip hadn't caught on. 'If she sells to the first person who knocks on the door, then Billy has lost his yard and facilities, the pony club lose their venue, and the winter dressage and show-jumping competitions are gone forever. The place will be bulldozed and turned into a chavvy housing estate or a country theme park.'

'Very succinct appraisal. You're such a snob, Rory.'

'But what about Dad?' Lottie's wail got lost as Rory's defensive streak kicked in. To Tippermere, the Equestrian Centre was the heart of the village, to Billy it was something far more important. It was his life, and always had been, as far as Lottie could gather,

22

since the death of the one person that had mattered most to him. Her mother.

'This is Cheshire not bloody Essex, we wouldn't even be able to hack down the lanes because they'd be snarled up with petrol fumes from 4x4s that are only used for the school run, and The Bull's Head would be renamed The Rampant Cow and serve mojitos and turkey twizzlers to the masses.'

Pip laughed. 'Don't exaggerate, you sound a right nobby nimby. Anyhow, I'm sure Amanda wouldn't do anything like that. And aren't you being a bit selfish? Neither of you have asked how she is, or anything.'

'How is she?' Lottie looked up from the piece of hay she'd been frantically tying in knots, her mind still on Billy and what he'd do when he found out. If he hadn't already.

'That sounds so insincere Lots, she's in bits, I mean how would you take it if you woke up and found the love of your life stiff at the side of you? And I mean stiff all over, not just where it matters.'

'You're calling *me* for being insincere and say something like that?' Lottie dropped the wisp of hay and stuck her hands in her pockets. 'Do you think he was the love of her life?'

'Well she was very fond of him, it wasn't just his wallet, though I'm sure that helped. It was a massive heart attack, apparently.'

'They weren't? I mean, you know, at it? Do you remember that film where they were and the guy had a heart attack?'

'I'm off if you're going to talk films. Here, I'll take her.' Rory tugged the lead rope from Pip's hand.

'Goldie Hawn, wasn't it?' Pip grinned. 'On your way to comfort the grieving widow are you Rory, offer your services?'

'Well, neither of you are interested.' He gave her ponytail a tug. 'Maybe she needs a manly shoulder to cry on.'

'You better shower first, you stink of eau de horse.'

'Oh, God, you don't think every man in the village will be making up to her now, do you?' Lottie was gnawing at the inside of her cheek and looking even more worried than ever, her gaze fixed on Rory, who laughed. 'It's not bloody funny.'

'As neither of you think she likes horses, then I think falling for a man who permanently stinks of manure, is covered in horse or dog hair and spends every waking hour either talking about the four-legged wonders or riding them is not on her bucket list. She'd probably prefer a nice, rich city wanker. Sorry to have to say this, but I think every man that I've met in this place falls into that smelly category. Well, every single man within a twenty, no make that thirty, mile radius.' Pip looked from one to the other and wondered what really worried Lottie more, the fact that Rory might go off to woo the stricken widow, or that her dad could find himself without stables and a yard. But, as seriously sexy and fit as Rory was, she couldn't imagine the immaculate Amanda falling for his charms.

'Thank you for the ego boost, darling Pippa.' Rory gave her a smacker straight on the lips. 'We can rely on you to bring us down to earth. Love the artistic muck heap by the way.'

'You noticed.' Despite herself, Pip grinned. It had taken her half the afternoon to coax the spilling muck heap into some kind of order. And climbing on top of it had left her stinking from sweat as well as horseshit.

'I thought you were going to see your mum?' Lottie was staring at her, suspicion lacing the normally clear gaze. 'Which is why you couldn't go to the dressage with Rory.'

'Well…' She paused. 'She rang to tell me she was too busy and could I make it next week.' Which was half true, she had been invited next week, but not instead of today. Today she'd wanted to check out the new arrivals in the village, partly for work and partly because she was curious. And it had been worth missing the sight of Rory being carted unceremoniously through a novice dressage test. Just.

'So, how did it go?' She looked at Lottie.

'You know that Morecambe and Wise sketch—'

'I'm not that old.'

24

'Nor am I, but there are repeats. Every Christmas. The one with the piano, where he says he's playing all the right notes but not necessarily in the right order? It was like that. Every step, every transition, but not necessarily in the right order. And some of them combined.' Lottie was fighting to keep her face straight, but gave up the battle when Pip started to giggle. 'That horse has paces to die for apparently, and Rory nearly did.' A full giggle attack hit. 'Honestly, I nearly wet myself, especially when Uncle Dom came up to pass comment.'

'Shit, wow.' Pip glanced at Rory and the look on his face set her off again.

'You pair are so immature, such giggly girls, aren't you?'

'Yup.'

He headed across the yard, the docile Flash keeping step as the terriers circled them at a safe distance.

'Oh, Christ, it wasn't really that bad was it? Seriously?'

'Seriously.' Lottie sobered up. 'She was a complete cow for the first half, did a brilliant second part and then spotted a hat she didn't like and left the arena without using the marked exit. Just missed the judge's car, but nearly annihilated the secretary.'

'He's taken it reasonably well, though, hasn't he?'

'Reasonably, but no way was I going to argue with him over who drove the lorry back. Good job dad didn't spot him as we drove through the village.' Lottie grimaced and tried not to think about the fact that they'd had a very close encounter with a large group of ramblers (which Billy wouldn't have cared about, as he viewed them in a similar light as he did rabbits: destructive and a waste of space), and an even closer shave with a Lycra-clad trio of cyclists who had made a grab for the wing mirror in retaliation (which he would have been bothered about, as it resulted in a swerve that nearly put a scrape down the other side of the lorry).

'Talking about to die for, I have just got to tell you who I saw today. I mean after I tidied the yard, exercised all the horses and sorted the muck heap, you know, in the ten minutes left.' Lottie

25

just looked at her. 'Well ask then.'

'Amaze me, who did you see, Pip?'

'Tom Strachan.'

'Tom Strachan?'

'You know, you do, you have to. Gosh Lottie you really are buried in this place aren't you? It's like being on another planet. Tom. He's a model, and I don't mean some airy-fairy gay boy, he is hot. Seriously hot. To die for, even by my standards.'

'And?'

'He's moved in; he's the guy who has rented Blake House. Thomas Strachan is your new neighbour, Lottie, and,' she put a hand on Lottie's arm, 'he's just got divorced. I'm telling you, while the guys are consoling Amanda, the girls are going to be hot-footing it over to console the man distraught after his wife cleared him out and cleared off. Get your sexy knickers on girl, because we are going to go on a Tom hunt.'

'But if his wife left him, then he can't be that hot, can he? Pip?'

But Pip was already heading off across the yard towards her bright-pink moped, which was nearly as striking as her mobile phone cover, and with a sigh, Lottie lifted the ramp of the box back up and with a backwards wave clambered up into the cab.

Chapter 3

Lottie had decided, as she rifled through her drawers, scattering undergarments, that she hadn't actually got any sexy knickers. There were the lacy white ones that had looked very sexy, in an untouched kind of way, when she'd bought them. But now they looked thoroughly touched, well, pawed, and a very unfetching shade of pale grey after being thrown in the wash with her jeans. Which left the mum pants or the bright-red thong, which she didn't often wear as she was pretty sure you could see it through the clinging cream show jodhpurs that she'd had on for its last outing. Well, at least that was the theory after she'd had her bum ogled by more than the normal quota of randy riders.

Exactly why Pip had insisted she accompany her along on the 'date' she'd arranged with the 'to die for' Tom, she wasn't quite sure, until she pushed open the door of the rustic bar/restaurant and spotted the willowy figure, bob of blonde hair now perfectly arranged around her elfin features, smiling beguilingly at a tall man and a teenage girl. Or rather, she was smiling at the man, and the teenager was scowling at both of them.

She really must get that appointment at the opticians for a sight test organised, Lottie thought as she squinted, trying to bring him into sharper focus. At this distance he just looked like a normal man, which was vaguely disappointing when she'd spent ten minutes wriggling about on the floor trying to get the two sides of the flies of her jeans to at least approach each other so she could force the zip up. She'd been promised a demi-god and been delivered a half-decent human as far as she could see. And she'd spent another frustrating twenty minutes smothering her hair with anti-frizz products, and more time than she should have trying to work out which of her tops was sexy but not too tarty. Which, by her reckoning, was an hour wasted that could have been spent on doing something else. Like working out whether it was worth joining in with the exercise DVD she'd been watching or whether it should be consigned to the maybe drawer, or shagging Rory in a proper bed. Shagging in the horsebox could be fun, if you were pissed, or desperate, or both. But after the sixth time of banging an elbow or knee it lost a bit of its shine. She must be getting old or boring, or both.

Pip was waving wildly at her, even with her suspect sight she could work that one out. She took a deep breath and headed over to them, holding her stomach in (just in case Tom was in fact better looking from touching distance) and trying to avoid the teenager's gimlet stare.

Close up, Tom looked like he had from the door; nice but slightly disappointing after the build-up. And his daughter, Tabatha, sent out waves of disapproval and boredom as she studied Lottie's hair, make-up and clothes and dismissed her as not worth another glance.

'Tom, meet Lottie, she knows absolutely everything there is to know about horses. Her dad is Billy Brinkley, the famous showjumper.'

Teenage Tabatha had a slightly more interested look on her face now, which could have been down to the way Lottie was squirming with embarrassment, or the mention of her father, who'd been known for jumping more than just poles. In fact she could vividly remember one particularly cringeworthy headline that had caused even the mild-mannered Tiggy to explode, and left him with the

28

label Billy 'the bonk' Brinkley for quite a while after. 'Star rider jumps Poles, Germans and Swedes in bid to win gold' had met her at the breakfast table after someone had posted a picture on Twitter of three naked female riders, and Billy in the middle, celebrating success in a Jacuzzi, wearing nothing more than his birthday suit. And then there had, of course, been a rival rag which had tried to go one better with a 'Bonko Billy' cartoon involving a medal around his neck and Stetson on his head as he straddled what Tiggy had termed (none too fondly) a 'big-boobed babe'.

During her painful adolescence her father's name had hung heavy round her neck. He was everything you didn't want in a parent: over the top, in the newspapers and available to any long-legged blonde who wanted a man to drape herself over. In other words, famous…or infamous. Billy believed in the work hard, play hard philosophy. Luckily, her stern grandmother, Elizabeth, had been a stabilising influence, assuring herself, and everyone else in earshot, that it was just a bit of fun and was what athletes did. The word athlete still made Lottie cringe.

'And,' Pip paused for effect, 'her Uncle is Dominic Stanthorpe, the dressage rider.'

Tabatha looked almost impressed.

'And she helps Rory Steel out.' Pip finished her triple whammy introduction and sat back, looking very pleased with herself.

'You know Rory?' Tabatha couldn't disguise the sudden interest in her voice. Rory was definitely more poster-boy material than the other pair, who were positively ancient in the world of teen-agedom. Lottie nodded, raised an eyebrow at Pip and sat down.

'So she'd be the absolutely perfect person to help you out and give Tabatha some riding lessons. Wouldn't you, Lots?'

Lottie looked from one to the other and wished, not for the first time in her life, that she'd insisted on some facts before agreeing to something. Or at least listened if there had been any kind of explanation.

'Can you excuse us?' She'd only just sat down, and not had a sip of drink or bite of food, but the ladies loos were calling.

***

'But I am not a riding instructor,' Lottie hissed, hoping that no one could overhear, and that the word *not* had been loud enough.

'You do the pony club camp sessions.' Pip was flicking her hair and admiring the effect in the mirror, which was most unlike her. Although the way she was doing it looked practised, so Lottie concluded that it was just a side to her that nobody in Tippermere had been treated to before.

'That's different.'

'How?' Flick, twirl.

'Will you stop that?' Lottie was finding it distracting, and funny. Pip stopped.

'One, they can all ride.'

'Tab can ride a bit.' Pout at her reflection. 'Tom said so.'

'Two, I only do it because I did a deal with Dad – I take it off his hands and then I can use the horsebox whenever I want.'

'And for *whatever* you want. Does he know you've turned it into a passion wagon? Talk about pimp my ride.'

Lottie ignored her. 'And three, you've only done it to get in his good books. What are you up to, Pippa? I mean he's not really your type is he? I thought you'd done all that, I thought you said you were sick of primping pretty boys and wanted a down-to-earth man. Or else why did you come here?'

'I have and I am, but he is pretty.' Pip sounded wistful. 'And rich, and caring. Do you know he's involved in this dog rescue thing?'

'No, I didn't.' She sighed and wondered what else she didn't know. 'But you seem to know an awful lot about him.' And you fancy him.

'I did an interview with him last year, which is why my ed gave me a nudge when she heard he was moving here. He needs a friend, Lottie, and I have decided to nominate myself. We've got

30

common ground, know the same people.'

'What if he moved here to get away from "common ground"? Like you supposedly did? He might just want to be with his daughter and desperate dogs. Or he might have more in common with Tiggy.'

'What would a well-groomed model have in common with tatty Tiggy?'

'You can be so mean, I'm sure she's got a very attractive side.' Lottie grinned. 'Dogs. That's what they have in common.'

Pip, sure that the grin meant Lottie was weakening, pushed on. 'Oh, go on, give it a go. I bet she's a lovely girl underneath all that black eyeliner.'

'She's a bored teenager.'

'She is horse mad, Tom said. Which is partly why he came here. He is so keen to get her into the pony club and all that, he wants to give her some stability, and I think he's loaded, you know. He's so successful, and,' she moved closer so if there had been anyone in the toilet cubicles they couldn't hear, 'the rumour is that he comes from a mega-rich family, apparently. He'll probably buy her a pony and sponsor you as well.'

'You're like a hound moving in for the kill.'

'Thank you.' Pip grinned. 'So, it's agreed?'

'No, Pip. Nothing is agreed. I'll think about it. Now, didn't you promise me champagne and a pizza?'

'Look, it's not really for me, it's not that I'm after him, but he's a lovely guy and I reckon I can spin a whole load of work out of this.'

'So, it's business, not pleasure?'

'Well, there's no harm in mixing it a bit, is there?' Pip linked her elegant, long-fingered hand through Lottie's arm and more or less dragged her from the safety of the ladies washroom.

'And he's too old for you.'

'He looks very well maintained to me.'

***

31

Tom loved his daughter with a strength that was a constant cause of amazement. He'd been brought up in a household where a father considered his duty was done when he paid for the food on the table and showed up at weekends to eat it. The fact that he'd been genuinely interested in his daughter since the day she'd whimpered her way into his life was a totally unexpected bonus.

When he'd married the heartbreakingly beautiful Tamara (as the press coined her), there had been a flicker of hope in his life that had outshone everything to date. Someone finally loved him, cared about the same things that he did; he finally had someone to share his life and future with. And then he'd found out that 'breaking' was the key word in Tam's life, not 'heart'.

The spectacular wedding that she had orchestrated had been bank-breaking, but he'd agreed. After all, whereas for him, constantly in the spotlight, a quiet wedding in an idyllic location would have been perfect, he appreciated that for her the wedding was a highlight, her moment of glory. And how could he refuse? She was like a beautiful pedigree cat, gorgeous, demanding but loving and cajoling to the point of suffocation. Tamara wanted to be pampered and adored, naively he'd thought that was temporary, not an integral part of her make-up.

The wedding was just the start. When Tam had said 'I do', she was launching herself into what she'd always desired – a glamorous lifestyle. The unspoiled beauty wanted to be spoiled, big time. After all, Tom was a sought-after model, he was sent designer clothes daily, and tickets for every movie premiere, theatre performance and nightclub opening. He should have been perfect. They were the most attractive, in-demand couple of the decade. They would live a jet-set life and have fun. Or so Tamara had assumed.

He couldn't blame her for getting frustrated by the reclusive bore he longed to be. Whatever his father had failed to give him in terms of time and loving, he couldn't avoid passing on his genes. He was a banker, he thought things out logically and planned for the future. And that DNA was passed on to his son, along with his wife's attractive features and willingness to please. Tom wanted to please his adorable wife, but he couldn't keep up with the demands. Away from his work he needed downtime, needed to slow down and imbue his life with structure. He wasn't a rich, good-looking playboy, he was a guy who rescued sick animals and liked a long country walk to help him unwind.

No, Tom couldn't blame Tamara for falling out of love with him, but he could blame her for hitching up with his manager, fleecing him and then disappearing off to Spain. But out of the whole fiasco there had been a divine gift. Their daughter. And the fact that her mother, his ex-wife, was as disinterested in Tab as his father had been disinterested in him was, as far as he could see, a bonus. True, he did believe that a child needed its mother, but Tamara was no more mature than a sixteen-year-old herself, and her lifestyle choices were not ones he'd want inflicted on any daughter, let alone his. He would never stand in their way if they wanted to spend more time together, but at the moment, from his perspective, the fact that they were in different countries was more of an advantage than a disadvantage.

Coming to Tippermere had been a move he had not consulted his daughter about, and so far she had not been impressed, but he knew he could win her over. The village could be good for both of them. No, not could, would. And whilst he had some misgivings about the media-happy Philippa, he was convinced she was the answer to many of the current questions life posed. The main one being, how to convince his daughter that this backwater was a taste of heaven?

He watched the two girls make their way back to the table. The slim, well-groomed, efficient-looking Pippa, who would have blended in effortlessly on one of his shoots. Confident of her own abilities, the type who would manage your diary, massage your ego and add an efficient dose of sex into the mix if you both needed some stress relief. Lottie looked an altogether different cup of tea. She had the toned body of an athlete and the bronze sheen of a sun-lover – he found himself wondering about the presence or absence of tan lines. Sex with Lottie, he'd hazard a guess, would be messy and fun, not that he was going to get involved with anyone out here. And the sudden image of her tapping a whip against her strong thigh brought a shudder that he couldn't quite place. Formidable and fun were not two words he'd ever put together before, but from the look in her eye, Lottie was the type of girl who could take control easier than she could give it away.

'Are we going to be hanging here much longer, Dad?'

'That depends on whether you want to meet some world-class riders or just plod along with the pony-clubbers I guess, Tabby. Up to you.'

'She doesn't look like a world-class rider.'

Tom bit back the response with a smile. She smiled back. 'Everything okay, ladies? I ordered that bottle of champagne, hope you don't mind?'

'Mind? I could murder a drink right now. You have got no idea what kind of a day I've had.' Lottie had the glass to her lips and had taken a greedy mouthful before she had even sat down properly. 'You're a lifesaver, but if you really want to win my heart, tell me you've ordered food as well. Rory was in such a bad mood he wouldn't even let us stop to get a burger.'

'You've been with Rory today?' Tabatha uncrossed her arms. 'What's he like? I mean, is he really that fit?'

'This was before the class.' Lottie knew she probably shouldn't, but couldn't resist flashing her mobile in front of Tabatha, revealing a shot of Rory when he'd been posing on the wagon steps with his toned abs on display. 'I did make him put a shirt and jacket on, though.' She flicked onto the next picture, which was Rory nonchalantly sitting astride Flash, long legs stretched at her sides, feet dangling free of the stirrups, one hand on the buckle end of the reins, the other grasping a cigarette. His last request, he'd called it. Lottie actually preferred the picture of him with his clothes on, which worried her a bit. The sun was behind him and his hatless

34

head was a mass of curls. He looked a bit like a swashbuckling hero – minus the sword.

'Can I see the first one again?'

Lottie reluctantly flicked back to the first picture. He *was* so gorgeous, and although he played to the crowd, she had a feeling that deep down he wanted to be loved. Properly. But it just didn't seem to be by her. Not that she wanted that now, of course. She was independent, wanted fun and freedom. Definitely.

But she was back in Tippermere. And his bed. She tried to supress the sigh.

Lottie had fancied Rory for as long as she could remember. Forever. And he did fancy her (although of course it had taken him a bit longer to realise), but it had been a jokey, easy-going relationship. Not a 'maybe this could be forever' type of thing.

After her disastrous 'world tour' as her father called it, she had told herself that Rory was the perfect antidote to her humiliation of being conned by a serial adulterer, but looking at the photo now she had a horrible feeling that she'd never actually managed to fall out of lust and love with him. And never would. God, who in their right mind preferred to ogle a picture of a man like Rory more *with* his clothes on?

She glanced up and Tom was studying her with a very slightly disapproving air. He was probably deciding that she wouldn't be a good influence on his daughter, that she was more likely to be sharing pictures of semi-nude men than teaching how to do a collected trot.

'Sorry.' She could feel a blush spread across her cheeks.

'No problem. Who am I to say anything about looking at men without their clothes on?' He smiled, the first genuine smile that the Tippermere residents had seen from him, and Pip, Lottie, and every female member of the restaurant staff that was in range were left in no doubt as to why he made a fortune in front of the camera.

Lottie put the phone down. 'Why have you come here? I mean it's not exactly commuter belt is it, if you're working?' Mild

35

embarrassment made her voice the questions she would have normally kept politely to herself.

Tom shifted in his seat. 'Well, you're here for one.' As the words came out, he could tell that flattery wasn't going to get him anywhere. 'You've got excellent facilities here for Tabby to really progress; it is what she wants to do. Isn't it?' Tab shrugged, like only a teenager can. 'And it is commuter belt. I can get on a plane in half an hour, or jump in the car and be on the M6 in seconds. And, no one notices me here. I mean the area is plastered with premiership footballers and soap stars, so I'm just another face.' He gave what he hoped was a casual shrug. There were a hundred reasons he could give for picking this particular area of the country, but one in particular right now he was reluctant to voice.

Chapter 4

Elizabeth Stanthorpe had been born in Tipping House and fully intended to die there. After she'd ensured that her family would continue running the estate in the way it deserved to be.

'I imagine that young Rory thinks Dominic is gay.' She raised an eyebrow as Lottie spluttered a shower of gin and tonic over one of the black Labradors and then hastily tried to rub it in with the back of her hand.

'I'm not sure that's why they don't like each other, not that I think Uncle Dom is gay, of course.'

'Well, I did.' She took another swig of her own drink.

'Gran, you can't say that.'

'Well he can be so bloody prissy at times; not a bit like his father was. If it hadn't been a home birth I would have thought there had been a mix up at some point. No one would have ever have accused your grandfather of batting for the other side, although those private schools can bring out the worst in boys.' She focused back on her only granddaughter, only grandchild, who was going a funny shade of pink. 'Well, you did bring it up, darling. Pour me another drink whilst you're up, there's a good girl.'

Lottie had been about to say she wasn't actually up, but knew it was useless to argue with her grandmother, who had what she referred to as 'backbone'.

As she sloshed a good measure of Bombay Sapphire gin into the chipped crystal, she decided that it was a good job they didn't make them like that anymore. Although the matriarch could be more fun than the rest of the family put together when it suited her. Nothing stopped Elizabeth when she got the bit between her teeth, and Lottie secretly thought that her grandmother wasn't as batty, forgetful and deaf as she liked to make out.

'All I said,' she passed the drink to Elizabeth, who sniffed it as though she suspected it might be laced with something, or more likely not strong enough, 'was that Rory thought it was strange when Uncle Dom turned up at the dressage. Did you have anything to do with that?'

'I may have mentioned it.' She tapped a long nail against the side of the glass, piercing blue eyes fixed on Lottie. 'You could do a lot better than that man, Charlotte.' She shook her head slowly. 'You are so like your mother in some ways.'

When Elizabeth had borne two children for Charles Stanthorpe, she had, in her usual manner, carried out her duties exactly as could have been expected. Their eldest child, Dominic, was a fair-haired, blue-eyed, easy-going child, who was always keen to please, courteous, but precise to the point of obsession. More than once, Elizabeth had been filled with an irrational desire to rearrange his meticulously organised toys, and then Alexandra had arrived and done it for her.

Alexa was as beautiful and wild as Dom was pretty and controlled. Her dark eyes would glint with mischievousness and her long curls bob as she dashed around the large house, causing chaos. With the family Labs in her wake, Alexa would tear around like a mini tornado, leaving a trail of destruction behind her. But with her ready grin, infectious giggle and affable nature, remonstrating with her was something that was easier left to others. So everybody did. Everyone forgave and forgot, with the result that, by the time she hit her teens, the fun-loving little girl had turned into an irresistible challenge that scared the living daylights out of many of her chosen suitors.

So Elizabeth found, as her children hit puberty, that she was hit with an unexpected problem. Her son showed no apparent interest in the female form, funnelling all his efforts into the pursuit of equine excellence, and her hitherto perfect daughter, Alexa, showed too much interest in horsemen. At twenty-two she was smitten with the very dashing, but totally unsuitable, William Brinkley; at twenty-three she was pregnant with his child. The day after her twenty-fifth birthday she died in a tragic accident.

Lottie knew with the 'just like your mother comment' exactly where this conversation was going and did her best to head it off with the skill of someone who'd had to do it many times before. Her mother, Alexandra, had been destined to marry someone befitting her breeding, until she fell for Billy Brinkley. A sportsman, who was as competent in the sack as the saddle, if the headlines and stable tittle-tattle were to be believed. Lottie had never known her mother; losing her when she was just a toddler had meant she had never felt the real pang of loving and losing, but as she grew up she felt like there was an element of her life missing. The bossy, but well-meaning, Elizabeth had considered it her duty to support her only granddaughter and give her all the information she could ever need, drip-feeding it to her from the day she was old enough to understand.

'Grandma, I don't need watching.'

'I do wish you wouldn't call me Grandma, it makes me sound ancient.'

'And I like Rory. He's fun.'

'Hmm, I bet he is.' The sharp eyes gave her an uncomfortable once-over. 'Life isn't just about fun though, is it? I mean it is fine for men to sow their wild oats, but even these days it isn't good form for a lady. And nor are those plimsolls.' The slight twitch could have been a suppressed smile, Lottie reckoned, or a warning there was more to come.

She groaned inwardly. 'Converses, Gran.' She knew she couldn't win any kind of discussion with Elizabeth. And why were 'plim-solls', as she termed them, any worse than the green wellies that her grandmother stomped out in, whatever the weather, along with the ancient, waxed Barbour jacket that must be nearly as old as she was?

'So, are you going to tell me about that young man?'

'Sorry?'

'Oh, Bertie, you really shouldn't.' Lottie cringed as her grand-mother tugged determinedly at her knickers, which, for some strange reason, were visible at the waistband of her tweed skirt, then heaved a sigh of relief as Elizabeth triumphantly pulled out a handkerchief, which she wafted in front of her nose. Bertie had stood up at the sound of his name and was now swishing his tail around as only a fat Labrador can, his big brown eyes fixed unerringly on his owner. 'These bloody dogs know exactly how to get what they want. I'm sure he can pass wind at will. Worse than children. Come on you smelly bugger.' Lottie shifted back so that the whip-like tail didn't catch her on the shins. She'd got enough bruises and scratches from Rory's terriers; any more and she'd be looking like a badly patched quilt in shades of purple.

Whatever Elizabeth said, though, there was a definite family resemblance between Dominic and his mother. They were both slim, upright and had the type of striking long noses and piercing gazes that left you feeling like you were being told off by a particu-larly stern schoolteacher. Lottie hadn't a clue how old her grand-mother actually was, but she didn't act or look it. And she didn't move at all like a geriatric when she wanted something. She was already marching out of the room, her words echoing in the cavernous, wood-panelled hallway, Bertie and his half-brother, Holmes, hurtling after her, nails tip-tapping on the hard floor in her wake, as Lottie put her drink down and scrambled after them. She was still trying to catch her breath as a welcome rush of fresh air hit her.

Elizabeth didn't believe in central heating, it was just for softies who liked to burn money, which meant the house was freezing all year round. Even in summer.

'You were telling me about this man?'

'Was I?'

Elizabeth tut-tutted and waved the dogs on in front. 'You were out with Philippa?'

'Ah, that man.' It suddenly simultaneously dawned on her who she was being interrogated about and worried her as to why. Elizabeth never made casual enquiries; there had to be a reason. 'Tom.'

Her grandmother was waiting for more.

'Tom Strachan. He's a model.' She absentmindedly picked up the stick that Bertie had dropped at her feet and flung it as far as she could across the manicured lawn, which wasn't far. The bounding Bertie soon came back, his head held high, Labrador smile across his happy face as he stopped in front of them. Dropping   his prize, his whole body wagged in wobbly ecstasy.

'Pretty boy, isn't he? Bertie NO.'

Just in time, before she grabbed it, Lottie realised that Bertie had deposited a decomposed rabbit at her feet this time, not a stick. She wiped her hand down the front of her top, even though she hadn't actually touched it.

'Er, yes.'

'Charles always did say one should never trust a man with long hair. He's either an artist and waster or a scoundrel.'

'He's a model, Gran, and it's not that long, his hair.' Lottie tried to remember exactly how long his hair was, but however much she screwed up her eyes and mouth the image didn't come.

'Don't do that, darling, it will give you frown lines.'

'Anyway, Gramps only said that because he was in the army. He thought anything that wasn't a short back and sides was long.'

Elizabeth waved a dismissive hand. 'I suppose he will at least dress well, if he's a model.'

'I don't know really. He models underwear, y-fronts, you know, pants.' Were pristine pants the equivalent of dressing well?

'I do know what pants are Charlotte, and I know you mean pants not trousers. Just because I'm old doesn't mean I've lost my marbles. But what's his proper job? Standing around in your pants isn't a job for a real man.' Modelling obviously wasn't going to cut it.

'I think.' Oh, God, why hadn't she been concentrating on what Pip had said? She should have known the all-seeing Elizabeth would want answers. It suddenly came to her, and she almost shouted it out triumphantly. 'He runs a rescue home for dogs as well.' Or something like that. Bertie barked, impatient at the delay, and Elizabeth made a huffing noise.

'And there's obviously a huge demand for that type of thing here.' Elizabeth's tone was laden heavy with sarcasm.

Okay, dog rescue wasn't going to cut it either. 'I think he came here because his wife left him, and his daughter likes horses, so…' She shrugged and threw the stick, which hit the sunbathing Holmes squarely on the rump, followed closely by the full weight of Bertie, who was going too fast to stop and didn't believe in swerving. Holmes leapt up with a snarl, as his seniority demanded in times of attack.

'Boys, stop that.' Even Lottie jumped as the full force of Elizabeth's bellow stopped them dead. 'And do *you* think he's gay?'

'Gay? I never said I thought he was gay. Well, no, I mean he's married, and then his daughter—'

'No, not Thomas, Dominic.'

'Well, I—'

'He's not dear.' Elizabeth patted her arm. 'I must admit I did wonder, but I'd say he's just very careful. Right, hadn't you better be off?' She glanced at her watch. 'I'm supposed to be playing golf this afternoon, although why on earth that woman can't get up early like normal people do and get a round in before breakfast is a mystery. Come along dear, you can give me a lift to Christine's and I will get Dominic to pick me up later.'

Elizabeth turned on her heel and set off back towards the house,

Lottie and the dogs getting tangled up in the scramble to follow her.

***

It was only when Lottie got to her car, luckily in advance of Elizabeth, that it dawned on her that it was even more of a mess than it normally was. Which was down to too much time spent trying to fit visits to Rory in, in between running around after her father.

Lottie sighed as she opened the passenger door of her car and a crisp packet drifted out. She stared at the mess. Brushing the car seat with the old pair of jodhpurs she found on the backseat didn't seem to help matters at all; in fact it left a very nasty brown smear on the seat, which just had to be chocolate. And when she opened the glove compartment to shove the empty drinks can and sandwich box in, several empty Minstrel packets, along with a Snickers packet (empty) and a Mars wrapper (full) tumbled out. She took a bite of the chocolate bar and then started to stuff things under the seat with her spare hand. Elizabeth had no qualms about climbing into a Land Rover full of muddy boots and dog hair, but food wrappers of any kind were worthy of a sniff. One just didn't buy things in wrappers, well at least Elizabeth didn't. The housekeeper did, then she unwrapped everything, burned the paper and pretended that everything was cooked from raw ingredients that she'd more or less grown with her own hands. The operative word being 'less.'

Driving her grandmother the handful of miles to her friend's house was the normal ordeal. Lottie honestly didn't know anyone who made her quite so nervous. She was more than capable of handling a horsebox, and had been driving her father's tractor since her legs had been long enough for her feet to reach the pedals, but with Elizabeth in the passenger seat her nerves were shot to bits. It was always the same; she started with a routine inspection of the interior, then she moved onto comments about speed ('doesn't this car go any faster?'), cornering ('do you really need to brake every time?'), overtaking ('just because the stupid man wants to go at that speed doesn't mean we all need to, dear, in my day he'd have been run off the road') and ended with parking (where she just opened the door and stared pointedly at the kerb, 'shall I call a cab dear?' being the normal comment, if she bothered with one).

'Maybe your father needs to get you a better car. That might help,' was always her parting comment before she slammed the door hard enough to check for rust damage, and after dusting herself down, she headed off.

It took most of the drive back, with the window down and the radio turned up full blast, sending the echoes of a defiant Pink into the countryside, before Lottie had relaxed her jaw enough to stop her teeth aching. By the time she drew up outside Rory's cottage, she could almost, almost see the funny side.

***

Lottie walked on to Rory's yard just as a man she'd never seen before stripped his t-shirt over his head and displayed a very attractive six-pack. She counted. It was definitely a six-pack. And she was pretty sure that if she had seen it before she would have remembered. Bodies like that tended to make a lasting impression.

Driving back from Tipping House, she'd had two things on her mind. One, what was her grandmother up to? Because she was definitely up to something as far as Tom and Uncle Dom went. And two, why was Tom here, in Tippermere? Why here, exactly? There was something he wasn't saying, and she had a horrible feeling there was something Elizabeth knew. Or why would she have been so interested?

Both thoughts were swiftly relegated to the back of her mind though as the beautiful naked torso, or was that naked beautiful torso, grabbed every inch of her attention. As he had his top fixed firmly over his head, and so couldn't see, there didn't seem to be

44

a problem in taking advantage and staring. So she did. Until she realised he'd thrown the clothing to one side and she was staring open-mouthed at a guy who was staring straight back at her. He wasn't open-mouthed, though, he looked slightly concerned, as if she might be a deranged mad woman escaped from the nearest loony bin. She shut her mouth.

'Sorry.' And went red. 'I, er, have you seen Rory, or er Pip?'

'You must be Lottie.' Now that was the type of deep, dark, sexy voice she thought only existed in her imagination. She'd always had a thing for a nice accent, and Irish just shot straight to the top of the hit parade. Lottie resisted the fleeting urge to shut her eyes and ask him to keep talking. Then it registered that he knew her name. And she didn't know his; she really would have remembered if she'd met him before. With or without clothes. Definitely.

Rory had a lot of friends; no one she would have ever called close, but lots of drinking buddies, eventing buddies, hunting buddies. Ever since they'd fallen into dating, he'd been surrounded by people, and at every party you could find the entertaining Rory in the thick of things, which at times could be bloody annoying. This included most of the times when she'd had a few drinks and was starting to feel either mildly randy and in need of attention, or well-oiled enough for her chatterbox mode to have kicked in and she just needed to talk. To him. But, even though they'd spent a lot of drunken evenings together (and drunken nights), she was pretty sure she would have spotted this guy, even if she did only have eyes for Rory.

'Are you okay?'

'Fine.' Lottie squeaked, cleared her throat and tried again. She had been quite happy ogling him, now the tables were turned she felt more than a little bit uncomfortable. Like an eavesdropper who'd been caught out with a glass to the wall, not that she'd stoop to that kind of thing.

Mick O'Neal repressed the smile, put his hands on his hips and took the time to drink in the vision that had materialised before his eyes. She wasn't at all how he'd expected her from the sketchy descriptions Rory had laced into their conversations. For one, he'd translated the 'plenty to grab hold of' as fat, whereas Charlotte was as shapely as she was toned.

'Are they in?'

'They are indeed. Last I heard, Rory was trying to blame Pip for not entering his horse in some event, and she was giving him a bollocking back. She threw his phone at him, along with a few other things from the sound of it. I'm Mick by the way.'

He held out a hand and she stared at it with suspicion. Then regretted it when he placed it back on his hip. And then decided that the safest place to be was as far away from him as possible. Contact might be a mistake.

'Great, thanks, so you are.' Feeling mildly stupid, which was nothing new, Lottie made a dash for the safety of the kitchen and Rory, only to find a battlefield. The small kitchen table was normally piled high with entry forms, schedules, directions, vets bills and every other conceivable bit of information that an eventer might ever need. Today they'd been scattered in all directions. She teased one out of the corner of a terrier's mouth and then gave it back to the dog when she realised it was only a phone bill. A second terrier lay forlornly in her small basket, sheets of paper still slowly floating down, her chin on her paws and her eyes darting anxiously between her master and the arm-flailing Pip.

'I pay you to send in the fucking entries on time.'

'You don't bloody pay me, and even if you did, what am I supposed to be? A bloody mind-reader?'

'I do pay you.'

'Not to be your bloody cleaner, housemaid or secretary. I,' she waved her arms towards the still-open door, 'work out there, you moron. You said you wanted a bloody groom, not a nanny.'

Rory, who was sitting on one of the chairs at the kitchen table, dumped his muddy boots on the chair opposite and crossed his arms rebelliously. Which Lottie was sure was because he just knew his attitude would wind Pip up even more.

'What are you two arguing about now?' She pulled out a spare chair and sank back onto it, a dog landing on her lap for reassurance almost before her bum was settled on the seat. When Lottie had suggested Pip come and work for Rory, it had never occurred to her how the sparks might fly. Lottie and Rory thought along the same lines, they were both slightly disorganised, both more interested in play than work and neither of them took much seriously, apart from, of course, horses. Pip was different. Pip took everything seriously and ran her life with military precision when she was on duty. And when she was at the yard, it was business not pleasure. And Rory drove her round the bend. Neither of them would give an inch, one because of his male pride, the other because she was never, ever wrong and wasn't prepared to pretend she was. The fact that she was quite happy to throw things if it got her point across made life interesting. She'd only been here a matter of months, but already Rory had found out that if he was wrong he was damned well going to be told. Repeatedly. Until he admitted it. The only problem was, Rory was never, in his eyes, wrong.

'He's lost his entry for next weekend.' Pip glanced at her briefly, then fixed an accusing glare back on Rory.

'*I've* lost?' He ran his hand through his curls, eyes wide with the injustice of it all.

'You've lost. You did not ask me to send that entry in, Rory Steel, and we both know it.'

'It's not the one in the wagon is it? For Rio?' Lottie tried to sound casual and hide the note of guilt in her voice. She distinctly remembered Rory picking up his post on the way out last weekend, and reading it in the cab as they took Flash to the dressage. And when he'd left it on the seat, she'd glanced briefly then stuffed it all in the glove compartment to stop the terriers chewing it to shreds. Then forgotten all about it. Until now. She kept her gaze fixed on the terrier and rubbed the silky ear between thumb and finger.

'You are kidding?' Pip had reached the hands-on-hips stage.

47

The terrier yelped as she rubbed a bit too hard. Rory frowned. 'Oh, yeah I remember now. I did enter, that was the confirmation.' He grinned. 'Brilliant. Glad we got that sorted.'

'Sorted? You call that sorted? You bastard, I just knew it was nothing to do with me.' Pip was almost stamping her foot.

'So,' Lottie coughed to get their attention as they were back to a stand-off, 'who is that guy on the yard?'

'Oh, shit, I was supposed to be helping him, he said he'd sort Kis for me.'

Rory laughed as Pip shot out of the kitchen. 'Come here gorgeous, I need some TLC after that battering.'

'It's your own fault.' Lottie stood up, tipping the terrier onto the floor, and moving over to sit on his knee, shivering as his fingers rubbed exactly the right spot between her shoulder blades. 'You know she's not going to take it lying down if you blame her for things that aren't her fault.'

'Will you take it lying down?'

'You're being rude again, aren't you? Anyway, who is he?'

'Why, do you fancy him?' He didn't wait for an answer, but stood up and unceremoniously dumped her off his knee. 'Come on, I thought you knew him. Or maybe he arrived when you were off on your world tour.'

For a moment Lottie thought she heard a note of censure in his voice, then dismissed it. He didn't care that she'd gone off in search of freedom and wide open spaces, he hadn't even seemed that pleased when she'd got back. After a brief period of awkward side-stepping and enquiries about each other's health and welfare, they'd just fallen back into step and carried on where they'd left off.

Mick was holding a hoof between his firm, denim-clad thighs and pointing at bits to Pippa, their heads close together, her blonde shiny bob and his unruly dark hair a stark contrast. To Lottie it just looked like a hoof; how could anyone be that interested?

'He's into this barefoot trimming crap.' Rory lit up a cigarette and leaned against the stable door to watch him. 'Aren't you, mate?'

Mick ignored him and flicked a large bit of hoof off with his trimming knife, which the smallest and nippiest of the terriers leapt on and carried off like a trophy. When he looked up, his dark gaze met Lottie's and she didn't know whether to squirm or melt. Or just feel guilty. 'You're a farrier?' And state the obvious.

'I am. And for my sins I'm staying here, with that heathen.' He dropped the hoof, straightened up and waved the knife in Rory's direction. 'I had to go back to Ireland for a bit to sort some business, so I missed the homecoming,' he smiled straight at her, 'I got back last night.'

Mick had been brought up by a traditional Irish farrier and was trimming feet by the time he could hold a knife. The fact that it wasn't safe or probably legal was by the by. He only hit a problem when he started experimenting with something other than traditional shoeing and his father termed him an 'eejit who should know better'. But it had left one of his terminally lame horses sound enough to compete again, which was good enough to make him consider that maybe his father didn't know everything. Mick was wise enough, though, to keep the fact to himself, continue to shoe in the way he'd been taught and to spread the word only to the few who sought him out. He rubbed out the kinks in his spine and watched as Pip trotted the horse up the yard for him.

His move to Cheshire had been totally unplanned. But it had stopped him dissolving into a bottle of whiskey and self-pity after Niamh had waved an airline ticket in his face and told him the time for 'fecking about' was over. He could put a ring on her finger and fly with her, or rot in Ireland on his own. He'd chosen Ireland and his horses. And then, after a week of drinking too much, and a day out hunting with Rory, he'd booked a one-way ticket of his own and taken the boat over to Liverpool. He'd been fond of his girlfriend in a way he'd never been fond of anyone before. But ultimatums didn't do it for him. And the thrill of setting foot on foreign soil could never beat the adrenalin rush of galloping across country on nearly half a ton of barely controlled horseflesh. And

Rory had some very attractive horseflesh on his yard.

Mick tore his gaze back from the easy-to-look-at Lottie onto the challenge that was Pip. The girl was attractive enough, except she never stopped asking questions long enough for you to appreciate it, and she was the bossiest female he'd come across in his life, with the possible expectation of his very Irish, very interfering, mother. Now she was staring at him expectantly and all but tapping her foot.

'I'd stop that, unless you want me to nail it to the floor, treasure. She trotted up fine, but no haring about the countryside or we'll be back to square one. And don't you go taking her to the last drag hunt meeting of the season.'

'I don't believe in hunting. It's an archaic tradition.'

'It's not hunting, it's drag hunting.' His tone was mild, as though talking to a child, but Lottie suspected that any minute now Pip was going to launch into a tirade. 'And it's a test of courage.'

Pip narrowed her eyes and glared at him, obviously torn between the desire to say something and the need to keep on his good side. She might not have been around horses much, but she already knew that good farriers were few and far between, and good farriers who could be bothered to turn up on time were even rarer. She bit down on her bottom lip and scowled, which brought a lazy, and to Lottie's eye, very sexy smile to his face.

'I bet you enjoy a rough ride across country, don't you Lottie?' He winked.

Lottie opened and closed her mouth, not wanting the thoughts that he'd conjured up in her head to come tumbling out. She didn't quite know how to take this sex god that had been dropped in their midst. Did he have some weird kind of Irish sense of humour that she didn't quite understand?

'She does, the rougher the better, don't you?' Rory pulled her into a bear hug of possession. Observing Mick from a position of safety, Lottie decided he was probably dangerous. He was making her nervous without even doing anything, and he was intent on winding Pip up, as though he needed some kind of stimulation or danger, which figured if he was a draghunt enthusiast or game-player. It would really have been better if she hadn't been dying to find out more about him.

'So, you'll both be riding out on Sunday, then?' He was swinging the heavy metal file from side to side and the youngest of the terriers stood transfixed, her eyes following its route. A route to being brained if she wasn't careful. Then abruptly he stopped the motion with a swift toss in the air before he caught it and dropped it in the heavy wooden tool box at his feet. 'Both of you?'

Lottie nodded nervously and looked up at Rory, wondering why she was asking him. She never did normally. 'I think so.'

'Yup, if you've not lamed all the horses with your fancy new ideas. Isn't it beer time yet?'

Lottie glanced at her watch. She'd already had gin and tonic time with her gran, whose idea of a weak drink was a double gin with a waft of tonic, and was feeling slightly off-centre. Carrying on drinking, mid-afternoon, with no food in her was probably a bad idea.

'Well…' There was a sudden outbreak of 'Your Sex is on Fire' from somewhere in the region of Lottie's knickers, and Mick gave her a smouldering look that nearly ignited other parts of her, or that could just have been because part of her brain had taken off on a fantasy she couldn't control. 'Shit, oh, hang on.' The burn hit her face, he must think she was so immature…or up for it with absolutely anyone. Maybe he thought it was an open invite? 'It's my phone.' State the obvious. Which was firmly stuck deep in a pocket that didn't really have room for a hand, let alone a phone. Lottie could feel herself slowly incinerating as she fought against the fabric. The phone stopped ringing. Then started again, 'Sex on Fire' gradually increasing in volume to match face on fire.

'Dad?' She was shocked to see his number; Billy seldom, if ever, rang her.

'You need to get over here. Now.' Billy was normally as

51

easy-going as they came, but if he was ever going to be short-tempered it was with his daughter. Plus he was bossy and said exactly what was on his mind.

'But I'm—'

'It doesn't matter what you're doing. You sent them here, so you can damned well come and entertain them. What do you think I am, a children's entertainer?' He was hissing, his voice low, as though he didn't want to be overheard.

'Sorry? Dad I—' But Lottie had been left with a ringtone in her ear, which was less embarrassing than 'Sex on Fire'. Marginally. They were all staring at her.

'So, that was Daddy, was it? I take it you're not allowed out to play?'

God, that Irish burr was having a funny effect on her. She clung on to Rory's arms, which were still draped around her, with one hand, and her phone with the other.

'He's hung up.' What was it with people hanging up on her while she was in the middle of saying stuff? Was she really getting that boring?

'So what did old Billy the goat want then?' Rory rested his chin on her head.

'I haven't a clue, he was jabbering on about kids and my fault, and stuff.' She paused and looked at Pip. 'Do you think he's lost it? You know, the whole Amanda thing? I mean, he must be stressed, even if he's not saying anything.'

'Billy boy, stressed?' Rory was smiling; she could hear it in his voice. 'Now that'll be the day. About as likely as Dom getting his leg over with one of the WAGs from Kitterly, I'd say.'

'Nah.' Pip grinned back. 'He's made of sterner stuff than that. So what's with calling him a goat?'

'Billy goat gruff?' Mick seemed amused, but still managed to sound like he was issuing an invite to bed.

'Nothing that deep. Eats anything, shags anything and jumps anything.' Rory was definitely grinning now, well, pretty much chortling.

'Don't talk about my dad like that.' He knew she didn't like it. She'd had too many years of jokes about her dad to find them funny; shame everyone else did.

'So, this Amanda is his latest shag?'

Pip burst out laughing, and Kis, her horse, threw her head up, nearly dragging her arm from its socket. 'Shit, stop that, you stupid mare.'

'She's not stupid, that one.' Mick cast his eye over the horse. He'd seen the mare out with Rory in the past; she was talented but lame more often than she was sound. So she'd been out at grass when Pip had arrived and announced that she would look after her. Looking after her was one thing, but everyone, including Pip, knew that she was seriously outclassed by the horse and was as likely to take her to a drag hunt as she was to take a vow of celibacy.

'And nor is Amanda. We've decided she needs a new man, but I'm not sure she'll fancy Billy, she thinks horses smell, and Billy spends most of his life on one.' Kismet bit her shoulder, and Pip, who believed in a non-punishment regime, tried her best not to retaliate.

'Sex on Fire' set off again and Lottie stared at it resignedly before jabbing at the answer call button.

'If you're not here in five minutes, girl, Marcus won't be the only one they'll be burying next week.'

Chapter 5

Lottie spotted the brand-new Jaguar F-type the moment she got through the imposing gates that flanked the entrance to Folly Lake Equestrian Centre. It was yellow. As in bright canary yellow. Which in her eyes was a gross travesty of a car that (a) was sleek and gorgeous and (b) was named after a cat. It was the type of car that should have said old money, or at least new money with a modicum of taste, but she'd never particularly liked yellow – unless it was daffodils.

The sudden indigestion-like pain in her chest didn't have anything to do with the half baguette that she had crammed down in two minutes flat as she drove the short distance from Rory's, because she was starving and needed to soak up Gran's gin. It was panic. What if it was someone who'd already heard that Marcus was dead? Who was here to buy the place, or sell the place, or… Crumbs, she tried to park her car as far as she could from the other one, knowing it made her old banger look even older. Surely Amanda couldn't have moved that fast. And her father had said it was her fault. Which was a bit confusing. No way could she have arranged for a developer to visit the place and then forgotten about it.

She made a move out of the car, nearly strangling herself in the process, and realised she still had her seatbelt on. Calm, she had

54

to be calm. It wasn't her fault Marcus was dead, and she couldn't be blamed for telling anyone. She hadn't, had she? What if she'd said something when she was drunk? What if she'd told someone to come round and buy the place when she was at the dressage? Or after that bottle of bubbly with Tom? What if she'd danced on the table and announced it to the whole restaurant?

No, she couldn't have. Could she? No, no way. Definitely no way. And Billy had been ranting on about not being a children's entertainer, she definitely wouldn't have sent someone who wanted to open a kids' theme park.

The arena doors were wide open, and she raced through and practically fell over... Tom.

'Hi.'

'Err, hi.' She threw an apologetic smile and an arm out to stop herself falling and nearly collided with the floppy fringe. 'Sorry, I just... Dad?'

Billy was sitting astride a horse and had obviously been in the middle of a schooling session when Tom and Tabatha had turned up. The horse had a sheen of sweat on its coat, the bay turned almost to black, the froth around its bit flecked with the deep green of new spring grass. Billy still had his phone in his hand, no doubt so he could call her again if she didn't turn up in the allotted five-minute window.

'Here she is. Well, it was nice to meet you, after all I'd heard.' And he'd launched the horse from stand still into a trot, then within a stride into a canter and straight at the nearest poles.

Here she is. Who? What? Lottie glanced over her shoulder at the bemused Tom, then back the other way to his daughter, who appeared as star-struck as she was dumbstruck.

Tabatha gazed after Billy with the look of adoration that Lottie had grown up with. 'Gosh, he really is your dad, really your dad, so cool.'

'And being a model is old hat?' Tom spoke offhandedly, obviously used to being dismissed as useless by his daughter.

'Being a model is so gay.' She threw him an assessing glance. 'Not that you are, but, you know, when I tell people you're a model, well, they just assume.'

'Thanks for the vote of confidence, love you too.'

'Well, y'know.' She shrugged. 'Billy is just SO cool. Do you think he'd let me ride his horse, Charlotte?'

'Lottie.' She corrected her automatically, then stared blankly over in Billy's direction. 'No, I'm pretty sure he wouldn't let you ride that one, and believe me, you wouldn't want to. So?' She looked from one to the other. It had been a relief to see them here, and not some money-waving developer with a contract and pen in his hand. Not that the equestrian centre was Billy's to sell, of course. But… Billy seemed to think she'd invited Tom and Tabatha here, so what had given him that idea? She folded her arms and frowned, at a complete loss as to why she was there.

'You said we could pop down and arrange some lessons, for Tab?'

'Did I?' It should have been becoming clear, but it wasn't. 'Sorry, er I did, of course I did. Yes…' She must have done, at some point over that meal, when he'd been pouring the champagne for her and Pip as though everyone drank it by the magnum.

'Great place here.' Obviously he wasn't going to be put off.

***

Tom gazed around the indoor arena and couldn't believe his luck. Fate had brought him to exactly the right place. Tabatha actually looked interested for the first time in weeks. He wasn't quite sure why, as he watched Billy canter around the arena. I mean the man was portly, to put it politely. Or was stout more the word? He was all short arms and legs, though he undoubtedly knew how to stay on a horse. Even if at take-off he looked like he was going to get to the other side before the horse. And he'd been nice enough, but keener on riding than passing pleasantries. When he'd lifted his hat, it was to show off a mop of unruly sandy curls, damp with sweat and flattened to his skull, with the first trace of a thinning patch in the middle. His face was weathered, the crinkle around his eyes had to be from squinting not smiling, and the way he grunted at the horse reminded Tom of a grumpy farmer herding cows. But Tabby had said he was a medal winner, one of the best, so who was he to argue?

'I'll, er, show you round, shall I?' Lottie was still looking at them as though she hadn't got a clue why they were there.

'Can I stay here?' Tab looked hopeful and Tom wavered. 'And watch? That would be cool, wouldn't it, Lottie?'

'Lazy cow.' Billy cantered a tight circle in front of them, scattering rubber as the horse fly-bucked bad-temperedly. He gave her a swift crack behind the saddle, which made Tom flinch. 'Put that pole back, Lots.' Lottie clambered over the small wall and put the pole back in its cup. 'Now you'll fucking do as I say and pick those feet up, you bloody donkey. Jesus Christ.'

Tom looked slightly alarmed. 'Maybe not. Better if you come with us, darling. I think Billy is busy.'

He felt better when he got his daughter away from the slightly alarming, very sweaty and profusely swearing Billy, and back on a par, when Lottie led the way into the calm and orderly yard. It was a pleasant surprise. After watching the gung-ho Billy, scruffy polo shirt flapping with every jump and saddle soap-stains on his breeches, he'd half imagined that the yard would be in disarray, with startled horses in every corner. But it was an oasis of calm, which reminded him that, whatever his appearance had suggested to the contrary, the man was a world-beater. A champion. And Tab instantly looked grumpy with boredom, until Lottie started to introduce them to the horses.

'This is Monty Jack.' She stroked the velvet nose of a dark bay horse, the soft wicker echoing around the silent yard.

'Gosh,' Tab had her mouth open, 'not the, not, this isn't Monty as in…?'

Lottie laughed, and Tom felt himself smiling with her. 'Yup, it's *the* Monty.'

'Wow, awesome. I saw him at Olympia, do you remember, Dad? Wow, when he did that last jump he was so amazing.'

Tom shrugged, trying to avoid saying no, Olympia had just been another day out, but Tab wasn't listening anyway. 'He was so brilliant in the Puissance. I mean, I was way back in the stands, but he's here now. Mega, just, he's… can I stroke him?'

They'd lost him, but his daughter was back to being interested again, which was good enough for him.

'And this is Monty's Mistake.' Lottie had strode on to the next stable, obviously in tour mode, and got much the same reaction as before from Tabatha.

'This place is just so cool.'

Who'd have thought anyone could be so interested in something four-legged that had big teeth at one end, hard hooves at the other, and excreted great piles of waste and smelly air constantly? But his daughter was transformed, so mission accomplished, even if it was easier than even he, with a bucketload of optimism, could ever have expected. Lord, if he could only keep her in this mood all the time. His concentration lapsed, a horse was a horse, all the same except they came in a variety of colours and sizes.

Apart from the odd wisp of hay in front of the stables, where horses had stood to chew and watch their neighbours, the concrete was as clean and tidy as if it had been constantly brushed, but there was no one in sight. The soft rays of spring sunshine filtered over the low roofs of the stable blocks, burnishing the old red tiles, dancing over the fading daffodils and the jaunty primroses and pansies. For some strange reason, Tom felt at peace. At home. Like he hadn't felt since he'd walked out of the house they'd lived in since Tab had been born.

Even Lottie was relaxed here; she wasn't looking at him like he was some alien that she was expecting to grope her with a third arm at every turn. In cut-off denim shorts, a faded polo shirt that had seen better days and her hair pulled through the back of a baseball cap, she looked the picture of health and a thousand times sexier than any woman he'd seen in a long, long time. She was also young, he reminded himself. And he wasn't going to get involved with anyone. And definitely not the girl he was courting into taking his daughter in hand. Even if, with horse slobber on her shoulder, she still looked good enough to make him feel the first stirrings in his groin he'd felt in a long time. It must be all this bloody country air; he must have overdosed on oxygen and it was making him light-headed.

'The thing is.' The woman in question was staring at him with a clear and unnerving gaze, and biting the inside of her cheek. 'Well, I don't usually give lessons.' She sounded apologetic, like a doctor forced to give bad news. 'I don't know what Pip told you, but all these horses are, well...'

'Unsuitable?' Tom spoke gently, sinking down on to the worn bench outside the stable. He crossed his ankles and tried not to stare at her long legs, at the perfect dip of a waist, which led to softly rounded breasts. 'I could close my eyes.'

'Sorry?'

She was staring, wide-eyed with a hint of alarm. Shit, he'd said it out loud. 'Nothing, sorry, just thinking out loud.' If he'd been smarter he could have thought of something witty that sounded the same, but he'd need a week and a thesaurus.

'Oh, right. Well. It's not that I'm not saying Tabatha isn't a good rider, well I don't know, but, well, even if she was really good... Well, the thing is, Dad won't let anyone on his horses unless he's seen them ride, and I've only got the one horse and she's very green.'

Tom held a hand up. 'It's fine. Honestly. We've arranged to get a horse on loan for the summer, from the stables that Tab used to go to. It's arriving tomorrow. Actually, I was wondering if you had a spare stable.' He glanced around; there seemed lots of empty stables.

'It's not a bleeding livery stables.' The gruff tone announced Billy's arrival and dispersed that last lingering of Tom's erotic musings.

Tom had heard, on good authority, well, from Pip, that Billy was as easy-going as they came. 'He's a right laugh; everyone loves Billy' had been her exact words, he remembered. Either they'd caught the man on an off day, or his idea of a right laugh and Pip's were on different planets. And he had thought, or hoped, he could trust Pip's judgement.

'She is, like, totally amazing.' Tab was staring at the horse that Billy was perched on, and for a moment Tom thought he saw a softening of the man's features.

'She needs taking in hand, like a lot of females.' There was a hint of a crooked smile, which Tom wasn't that keen on. 'So, you're not here to put in an offer, then?' The question came out abruptly.

'Sorry?'

Billy took that as a no. 'Well, that's okay, then. Lottie be a darling and get her untacked, Tiggy seems to have gone AWOL.'

'Dad, I need—' But he'd jumped off the horse and strode off, tapping his crop against his boot. Lottie grabbed the horse's reins, just as she started to wander after Billy, which was an annoying habit most of his horses developed. The need to follow him.

She needed to talk to Tom, then she needed to get home and changed so that she could get to the pub before Rory, Pip and Mick were too drunk to miss her. The last thing she wanted to do was run round after her dad just because the vague and unreliable Tiggy had wandered off again. Why her father had employed the woman, Lottie really didn't know.

'You have got spare stables, though?' Tom found that the further away the man was, the more relaxed he became.

'I, er...' Lottie stared at him. If she didn't get rid of them soon she wouldn't have time for a shower before she headed to the pub, and all of a sudden she didn't want to be smelly.

'Great, I knew it. How about we just try it for a week or two? I'm happy to pay the going rate. I mean you've got everything here.' He named an amount that made Lottie's stomach jolt. Was that monthly or weekly? 'Then, how about a lesson next week so you can assess Tab?' She felt her head nodding, which it really wasn't supposed to be doing. Amazing what the need to get rid of someone could do to your common sense.

'Brilliant, see you tomorrow. Come on Tabby, I can see Lottie's busy.'

He winked, put a fatherly arm around his daughter and was heading for the eyesore of a car before Lottie got the chance to ask what was supposed to be happening tomorrow.

***

Amanda James stood, a picture of restrained elegance, and stared out of the window at the vast expanse of immaculate lawn and felt a sudden pang for a vision of concrete. It wasn't that she didn't like it here; she loved it. But everything was so raw, animal-like. Even Lady Stanthorpe was as sharp, assessing and brusque as they come. These ladies might play golf and have afternoon tea, but their homes were freezing and their furniture passed on down so many years that each piece had its own ten generation pedigree.

And an Aga was fine, when it bloody worked. That was the trouble; everything was such damned hard work. Even the talking, unless you had a degree in equine studies. God, how she hated horses sometimes; they were impossible to escape. Totally impossible.

It hadn't bothered Marcus; he had a totally unshakeable self-belief that carried him through life untouched by the scathing comments and put-downs. He had loved being a part of the 'country set', as he termed his neighbours. And he didn't care that he'd just bought his way in, that he was as much a part of it as a palm tree in a park. He had been there, and that was all that mattered.

Amanda missed him. She missed his confidence, missed the way he bellowed for more sugar in his tea, despite the fact that the

61

sugar bowl had been a matter of inches from his cup, missed the fact that he looked after her in his loud, brash way, like a father.

She was being stupid.

Amanda just sometimes longed for convenience, for a meaningless chat about the latest fashion. She didn't understand most of the people here, apart from Pippa. She picked up her mobile, paused for a moment with the contact list open. A flash of yellow down by the yard caught her eye and the tall slim figure caught her attention even more firmly. Whoever had been visiting Billy Brinkley was far different to the normal, scruffy, bow-legged characters, and the car was enough to make her feel her prayers had been answered. She hadn't realised until now just how much she'd started to loathe the sight of 4X4s and long for leather and sleek. She needed a distraction, and she needed one now. Before she made the biggest mistake of her life.

She pressed the call button. Forget fashion, Pippa knew everything. Pippa would know exactly who the visitor was. And Pippa would know precisely how to fix the nightmare that the funeral was just about to turn into.

Chapter 6

'You can't go like that.'

Rory shrugged, the boyish grin spreading over his features. 'Why not? It's my best jacket.' Infectious, but oh so wrong.

'It's a hunting jacket, and we're going to a funeral. Remember?' Lottie, who had been under strict instructions (via her invite, if you called it an invite where funerals where concerned) not to wear black, and on the verge of rebelling out of a sense of decorum, had found it hard enough to find something suitable for herself. But Rory was going too far. And they were running out of time. And she was about to start giggling, which was so wrong. 'It's a bit disrespectful, I know the invite said not to wear black, but…' She bit down on her lip, to stop the smile that Rory was doing his best to draw out of her.

'It's what he wanted, look.' Rory dug his own card out from the pile of papers on the table and waved it roughly in her direction.

'I don't want to look. I know what it says, but it feels wrong.' One of the dogs, which had taken Rory's dig through the paperwork as an invite to jump on the table, put her paws up on Lottie's chest and grinned a terrier grin, tongue lolling. 'Don't you dare lick me.' It sank down on its haunches, paws leaving a snagged trail down her best satin shirt as sharp nails dragged from her boobs down to her stomach. 'Oh, Christ.' She already felt a mess. The dog yapped and she was very tempted to pick it up, sit on the sofa and bury herself, not Marcus, for the rest of the day. She rubbed absentmindedly at the scratch mark instead, hoping it would go away. 'I don't get it.'

'Maybe he's having a last laugh at the country yokels. Well, it will be a laugh with your dad as pall-bearer at one end of his bloody coffin, and me and Dom at the other. He'll be sliding from one end of the coffin to the other.' The grin had broadened. 'Knock some bloody sense into him.'

Lottie shut her eyes against the image of the lopsided coffin and bit the inside of her cheek harder, to stop the hysteria bubbling out. It was true. Rory and Dom had to be at least eight inches taller apiece than Billy. 'Maybe it was a joke. I mean he didn't expect to drop dead did he? He must have written it when he was drunk and meant to change it when he was expecting—'

'To die? He must have been well pissed; well it's his own bloody fault then. And if this is his last request, well, who are we to deny the man?'

'You're enjoying this.'

'I bloody am. Look, why should we all be in black and miserable as sin just because he's pegged it?'

'Well, Dad is.' She suddenly remembered just what Marcus's death could mean, did mean. 'Miserable I mean.' The equestrian centre had never been like a real family home to her, no more than the place she rented now (which she was never in long enough to add any homely touches to). She had no particular attachment to either place, but it was her father's livelihood. And it was more. After her mother had died, he'd initially moved out of the farmhouse, which had only been rented, and moved in to the impersonal environment of the groom's quarters above the stables at Folly Lake equestrian centre, which suited him perfectly. During his waking hours he could shut out the pain and immerse himself in his horses, with every need on tap. But as the nightmares had softened he'd realised that his daughter needed more. They had moved back in to the house that bordered the yard, but his work obsession hadn't eased. And so Lottie's early childhood had been spent surrounded by horses and riders, grooms who could keep an eye on her, and on-off nannies who loved horses and dogs. And riders. Not that she had ever thought it unconventional, or felt herself hard done by. But nor had it given her any roots. Which, Elizabeth was sure, was why she still had the urge to wander. To find what she was missing.

Now, if the centre was sold, Billy could find the refuge he had buried himself in following Alexa's death dragged from his grasp. And Lottie was old and wise enough to be scared. For both of them. If he lost that, what was left?

'At least one of us will keep a straight face, then. I rely on you, darling.' Rory blew her a kiss and raised an eyebrow in his best devil-may-care manner. 'Do you reckon he'd want me to take the hunting horn?' He picked up the horn, which she hadn't spotted, and gave an experimental blow, which sent the terrier, startled, into her arms, scrabbling long red weals down her chest.

'Shit.' The muscled-up body of the little dog went over her shoulder and hit the floor running. 'Don't you dare, Rory Steel. Go away Tilly, in your bed.' Instead, the little dog started haring around the kitchen like a minor whirlwind, barking excitedly, sending papers flying from the table in her flight over and under everything that was in her way. Lottie knew better than to move. 'The invite definitely didn't mention hunting horns.'

'It did say hunting jacket, though, so, like it or not, that's what I'm wearing.'

'Without the breeches?' She looked at his legs pointedly, and wondered, not for the first time, why even the sexiest legs in the world had knobbly knees in the middle.

'Bugger. It's your fault for knocking when I was half dressed.' Rory strode out of the kitchen, all three dogs at his heels, shirt tails sadly covering his well-muscled, but decidedly naked, thighs. 'Just polish my boots, will you?'

Lottie stared at the boots, still decorated with mud from his last ride out. The smell of leather pricked at her nostrils as she picked one up and wondered whether it would be quicker to drop it in the sink, or scrub it with a brush.

***

It was colder inside the church than out. Lottie wondered if that was a tactical thing to make you feel sad and remorseful. Or just a lack of money. Or stinginess. The church, like her gran, had been around a long time and knew how to spend its pennies on what it wanted and not what the rest of the world might appreciate.

Elizabeth had embraced the theme of the funeral in her normal fashion. Wearing black, because it was what she considered right and proper, and to hell with what the bereaved or deceased might want. 'Great Expectations' was the first thought that hit Lottie, followed quickly by 'Addams Family' when she saw the dramatic make-up and newly manicured nails. It just wasn't fair how her gran, who let's face it didn't need perfect nails, could have them that length and unchipped when her own looked exactly how nails tended to look when you spent most of your time mucking out stables and moving jump poles.

***

Amanda sat bolt upright, because otherwise she was sure she'd crumple in a heap, and felt strangely detached as she stared at the coffin. So, this was it. It hadn't been a nightmare when she'd woken up to find his arm pressed cold against her. And it seemed surreal, and somehow wrong, to be sharing his last moments with the group of people he'd wanted here. In life they'd been such different people, and in death they were too. They'd grown apart because they were so different, but stayed together because maybe they were the same, deep down.

For one ghastly moment she imagined the coffin lid coming up and his great guffaw of a laugh ringing out into the silent cavernous interior of the church. But it didn't. Just like he hadn't turned around one day and asked forgiveness for all the women he'd laid and promised to be faithful to until the end of his days. No, some things were as improbable as landing on Mars and discovering it actually was inhabited by a race that understood every word you said to them.

The last time she'd sat in a church had been their wedding. Which was bad; maybe she didn't deserve to be happy? All the trimmings: a horse and carriage, a white satin gown, enough flowers to finish off a hay-fever sufferer. The façade of a fairy tale, turning her into the princess he wanted to live with. Well, maybe not live with the person he wanted to put on a pedestal and use as a symbol of what you could achieve if you worked hard. Which was a bit ironic, as Amanda had worked bloody hard to turn herself into that type of person. From the geeky, unfashionable teenager brought up in the suburbs, she'd made a career out of self-improvement. 'Self' being the operative word. If she hadn't bothered, maybe she'd have found a man who truly loved her, and who was faithful. Maybe not.

'I'll be good to you, Mandy. You'll never want for anything, I promise.' And he had been, and she hadn't been left wanting. Whatever everybody thought. Which would have been fine if she'd been a pampered pet poodle.

She'd forgiven his affairs at first, but then she'd realised that he had to shag everything that had a pulse and she knew if she'd thought the tip of the iceberg had been bad enough, the rest that was hidden underwater would end up drowning her. And it was the fact that everyone knew; that was what really hurt her.

He'd been in her bed the night he died, for a reason. He'd wanted to explain all the reasons she didn't want a divorce. Quietly, patiently, like you'd explain to a five-year-old with learning diffi-culties. Marcus was good, was believable, and was lovable in his

67

own way. He knew how to persuade her, knew every weak spot, and knew that she didn't really want to go through with it. He wanted to find a compromise that would suit both of them, and she was so close to saying yes to him. So close, because it was next to impossible for her to deny him, whatever he did. But the one thing that any compromise could never give her was what she needed most. Freedom. Freedom and her self-respect back.

The stained-glass window blurred, so she glanced down at the coffin, then down further to her cold hands clasped so tightly in her lap that the fingertips had gone from pinkish to white and were heading for blue.

And she fucking missed the stupid bastard. A drop of water splashed down onto her thumb. Shit, she couldn't cry. She just mustn't. But tensing her jaw didn't seem to work, nor did biting her bottom lip. A second and third tear found their way out. Although someone had to mourn his passing, he was, had been, a good man, deep down. That was why she'd married him. He'd spent a whole life changing himself, like she had, into a symbol of success. But she'd recognised that kernel of the original man that still remained, as though he'd winkled out the bits of her that hung on from the past. And that was what tied them together. Until the reality of who they'd become had been too heavy to ignore. Why the hell did things have to change? What was wrong with just being happy?

She surreptitiously wiped across her cheek with the back of her hand and glanced around the packed pews. How many of these people knew Marcus? Really knew who he was. Had been. At a guess, none of them knew and none of them cared. They'd come because he was a success, and even in death some of that might rub off onto them.

If she could just march out now and tell them all to go to hell, she would. The old Amanda might have done, his Mandy. But she couldn't. Marcus would have wanted it this way; he *had* wanted it this way. The circus, that didn't respect him at all, but did celebrate his achievements. The attendance alone did that. You couldn't count love by numbers, but you could count respect. Or envy. Now all she needed was the whole fiasco to pass as quickly as possible and then she could go to bed with a bottle of wine and flannelette pyjamas and mourn in her own way. He'd have laughed at that: ditching the satin nightwear to mourn him. And he'd have hugged her. Shit, she was going to start blubbing again if she wasn't careful. She just had to concentrate. On the crowd, on being polite. On forgetting why they were there, like everyone else would soon do. God, she'd kill for a drink right now.

***

'There was water in the bottom of my boot.' Rory slid into the pew next to Lottie and hissed in her ear. The warmth of his thigh welcome in more ways than the normal ones.

'Don't wriggle, dear, sit still.'

Lottie had thought she'd only shifted a small, unnoticeable, amount, and in Rory's direction. But eagle-eyed Elizabeth had noticed it.

'I know. Accident with the tap.' She'd gone for the sink option and the tap had spurted cold water out uncontrollably when she'd turned it the wrong way. 'It isn't much.'

'That's easy for you to say.' He squeezed her own thigh, how the hell was she supposed not to wriggle when he did that? 'He didn't roll about too much, think old Billy must have put risers in his heels.'

'I thought he looked taller.' Elizabeth's tone was dry.

And how did her gran hear whispered words when she played deaf most of the time? Obviously, she decided, there must be a gap between her ears and the words had gone straight through.

***

Mercifully the service was short, sweet and not too sycophantic. And the congregation sighed a collective sigh of relief when they got out of the cold, dark gloom of the ancient church and into the soft warmth of the spring sunshine.

Marcus had opted for cremation, which meant that although he didn't go out with a bang, nor did he go with a thud. As Pip put it, 'A ball of fire just has to be better than a clod of earth, doesn't it?'

'Sex on fire is even better.'

Lottie would have been pleased if she could have hung onto the urge to stamp on Mick's foot, or put his own sex on fire, when the Irish burr cut into the conversation. But, annoyingly, the need went quickly when she looked up, straight into those dancing Irish eyes. She just wanted to gaze at him, like an adoring Spaniel might, and wag her tail, except now she was going from the ridiculous to the faintly obscene. 'You're not going to let me forget that, are you?'

'I haven't decided yet.' The toe-curling smile made her want to spin the banter out, but Elizabeth was hot on her heels.

'You and Rupert can come with me.'

'Rory. You know he's called Rory, Gran.'

'Sorry, what was that, Roger?'

'I've got my own car here, thanks.'

'If you have to.' Elizabeth sighed. 'But don't park it too close to the others. And do remind me to have a word with your father about that later, dear.'

Lottie followed her line of sight to the array of cars parked on the verge outside the church. An eclectic mix of Rolls Royces, Mercedes and top-of-the-range BMWs, with the odd Porsche thrown in for good measure.

People were heading off towards the crematorium, to say their final goodbyes before Marcus was reduced to ashes, but Lottie, Rory, and in fact most of the residents of Tippermere had been spared the ordeal. The crem simply hadn't the capacity for that many people, so luckily, from their point of view, family and close friends took precedence and they could head straight to the wake.

The once-lush grass verges were cut through with dark slashes of freshly turned mud. Deep grooves, with churned edges that filled Lottie's mind with endless images of dark damp earth, the final resting place for most people. For her mother.

From what she knew of Alexa, today's ceremony would have amused her. The lopsided coffin making its way inside, the pall-bearers dressed in their red hunting jackets, incongruous in the dark, dismal, cold confines of the ancient church.

Marcus had been a man who knew what he wanted. Who liked the power that money gave him. Who thrived on the certainty that people would jump to his bidding. Lottie suspected he hadn't been bothered about being liked. Being important was the thing. And in death he had surpassed himself.

On one side of the aisle, the pews had been filled with a crowd alien to this country environment. Brash designer suits, large hand-bags, a flash of gold at every turn and enough make-up, perfume and pungent aftershave to make the occupants of the other pews reel in their wake. The church would never smell the same again. On that, the residents of the village and its old vicar agreed.

The Very Reverend Walterson had raised his eyebrows at the crowd at the start of the service, and raised his uncommonly heavy collection tray with disbelief (and trembling hands) at the end. No doubt he would be praising the Lord for sheep in wolves' clothing, or some such nonsense, as he sipped his sherry that evening, thought Pip, as she turned her attention back to Mick.

'You going to give me a lift? I came with Amanda, but she's off to watch her old life burn and be scattered.'

'Where are they scattering him?'

'In the indoor arena at the Equestrian Centre.' Pip had her innocent face fixed into position, which the rest of them under-stood a second later.

'He can do a running fuck.'

Rory spun around and somehow managed to keep a straight face as he looked at Billy. 'I don't think he's doing anything anymore, to be honest, Billy.' And for a horrible fleeting moment, Lottie saw a ghastly resemblance between her sometime lover and her father. They both had the curls, the grin, the 'game for a laugh' attitude, Rory was just younger, slimmer and taller. And dark-haired rather than gingery. A cloud scudded over the sun and she decided she'd imagined it. No way. 'Maybe it was a running fuck that finished him off. Wasn't exactly sprinting material was he?' The grin broke out.

'If they scatter the bugger over the rubber then I'll never get the bloody horses in there again.'

'But it was his dying wish.'

Lottie squinted at Pip, who winked back, then turned her angelic face back in Billy's direction.

'I think his dying wish was probably, fuck I wish she'd hurry up and come.'

A chorus of 'Dad' and 'Billy' rang out, and he chuckled.

'They weren't? Were they?' The angel that had briefly invaded Pip had been replaced with the normal mischief-maker.

'Ejaculation can put quite a strain on a man's heart, dear.'

Lottie waited for divine intervention, or the ground to swallow her up. Neither of which happened. None of them had heard Elizabeth creep back in their direction. People rarely did, which was why she was so successful at gathering information.

Billy shrugged his ample shoulders. 'Well they were in bed together, weren't they, Pippa?'

'That's what she said when she rang.'

'Come on, let's get to this bloody party, crack the champers open, I say a bottle of single malt to the first person who finds out if he was.' Billy smacked his hands together. 'Agreed?'

'But I don't like single malt, Dad.'

'We'll drink it for you, Lots, won't we Mick?' Rory wrapped an arm around her shoulders just as she glanced up, straight into the dark eyes of the Irishman. 'Not that you're going to be the winner. My bet is on Elizabeth.'

He winked at Elizabeth, who sniffed but looked secretly pleased.

'Will someone find Dominic for me? He seems to have strayed.'

'He's not a dog, Gran.'

'Last time I saw him, he was paying his respects and comforting the grieving widow.' Pip raised an eyebrow as she spoke, and swapped a look with Elizabeth. Not for the first time, Lottie wondered what the pair of them were up to and why they got on so well.

***

'Where have you been?' Lottie handed a rapidly warming glass of champagne to Rory and watched his Adam's apple jump as he emptied most of the contents in one gulp. He'd only supposed to be parking her car in an obscure corner of the courtyard, as per the instructions from Elizabeth, and it had taken him what felt, to her, like ages.

'Some cheeky bastard asked me to park his Roller for him, and not to scratch it.' It was debatable whether Rory was most disgruntled about being taken for the hired help, or the suggestion that he couldn't drive a car without scratching it. 'Wow, they've gone to town on this place, haven't they?' He gave a low whistle as he gazed around the high-ceilinged entrance hall of Folly Lake Manor.

'Looks like a tart's boudoir to me.'

'And you'd know, Billy?'

Billy laughed and gave Rory a none-too-affectionate slap on the back, which would have sent a lesser man straight into Lottie's lap. 'I wonder if Pip is out to win that whiskey.' He nodded across the hall to where Pip stood shoulder to shoulder with the elegant Amanda, whilst managing to grab another couple of glasses off the tray of a passing waiter. 'Anything stronger on offer, mate?' The man, who they all knew as the son of a local farmer, nodded and rushed off to raid the cellar of its best whiskey.

***

Amanda had not been looking forward to the funeral to top all funerals. Not only was she sad at losing the man who had been her closest companion for the last few years, but she hated anything ostentatious. And Marcus was ostentatious with a capital O. She hated what he'd done to the beautiful manor house, hated the over-the-top diamond he'd put on her finger the day he'd proposed, and hated the fact that she'd made no real friends since they'd moved here, apart from Philippa. Their friendship was new, still developing, but Marcus had sensed trouble and had done his best to chase her off. Luckily for her, Pip wasn't easily deterred.

'Thanks for coming. You can't begin to understand how grateful I am.' Amanda watched the froth of bubbles in the champagne glass die down to a steady fizzle. 'I just needed...'

'No problem, that's what friends are for.' Pip picked up her own glass and heaved an inward sigh of relief to be dressed up and away from horses for once. And this event promised to be a hundred times more exciting than most of the things that happened around here. Most of them involving hooves. 'Are you okay?'

'Fine. Well, to be honest, I didn't think I'd miss him this much.' Pip waited. It was common knowledge that Marcus had played away regularly and spent more time on business trips than with his wife. And it was common conjecture that Amanda had someone else, she just had to have. She was glamorous, good company and, of course, rich. She was also too bloody discreet for Pip's liking.

'I mean, I know he wasn't here much. But, I suppose, it's just knowing he's not coming back. He had other women, you know.' She traced a long nail around the rim of her glass. 'Well, of course you know, everyone knows. Oh, shit.' Tears welled up in the smoky eyes, threatening to spill onto her perfectly made- up face. Pip shoved a tissue in her direction. 'Sorry, I'm being stupid. I mean, he was a sod, and I suppose I'd stopped loving him. But I was fond of him, and he was fond of me.' She sniffed. 'Well, I hope he was.'

'I'm sure he was. I know it. Very fond.' Pip hoped it wasn't going to get to full- out tears, she didn't do sympathy very well.

Amanda took a deep breath, then a long swig of champagne and smiled brightly. 'I knew this funeral was going to be shitty.'

'It's fine, look,' Pip waved a hand, 'they're all having a great time, just like Marcus wanted.' Oh, God, she was going to have to try and console.

'No, no I don't mean in that way.'

Pip heaved an inward sigh of relief. For a moment there she thought she'd misjudged the person Amanda was. They weren't very close, but they had built up a kind of bond based on mutual admiration and a need to talk about something other than horses.

'It's just they are *all* here. I wouldn't have invited them, but it was in his will. All his family and friends. You don't know Marcus's family do you? Have you talked to any of them?'

Pip shook her head and took a good swig of bubbly.

'They are gross, I mean really. Everyone in Tippermere must hate them. If you thought Marcus could be a bit brash and throw his money about,' Pip had, but wasn't going to admit it, 'well, you should talk to the rest of them. He wanted a really big send-off, so I had to do it, but it would have been so much nicer without…' Without all the fuss, all the false emotions, she wanted to say.

Pip shrugged. 'But it's how he was, Amanda. He'd have felt a failure if he'd just sneaked off; he was making a point and that's what it was all about, wasn't it?'

Amanda nodded glumly and fought back a new rush of emotion. She wanted the old Marcus, not the one he'd become. Couldn't he have at least admitted to who he was in death, even if he wouldn't in life? God, she really did have to get a grip and pull herself together, though. She was about to make herself look such a fool in front of everybody. Talking of which… 'It's not true, you know.' She watched the froth of bubbles in the champagne glass die down to a steady fizzle as a passing waiter topped up her glass. Again. 'What they're saying.'

'About?'

'How he died. We were in bed at the time, as you know.' She gave Pip a pointed look, but she didn't flinch. Which either meant she was very thick-skinned, or hadn't been the one feeding the rumour mill. 'But we weren't…' The bubbles broke their hold on the inside of the glass, shot up to the top for air. Which is how she felt. It was noisy and hot, and she would just love to be able to escape, if only for a quick nerve-steadying fag and a glass of wine.

'Sorry?' Pip tilted her head. 'I'm sorry, it's just so bloody noisy in here.'

'We weren't…' she moved in closer, but Pip was still squinting with the effort of picking out the words, she took a deep breath, 'we weren't…'

'You what?'

'We weren't having sex.'

The words shot out, loud and crystal clear, shattering the silence, which for some strange reason had just fallen, with an immaculate sense of timing.

'Well that's going to go viral, as opposed to virile.' Rory's voice boomed out, his warm laughing eyes fixed on her, and then chatter broke out again.

Amanda closed her eyes. 'Oh. My. God. Everyone heard that, didn't they?' She drained the glass, took Pip's and emptied that one too.

'Well, maybe not everybody.' Pip's eyes had a twinkle.

'Shit. That is going to be on Twitter within the next twenty seconds isn't it?'

'Already there, I'd imagine, looking at the discreet tapping of phones. I wonder what they're using as the hashtag?'

'I suppose he'd be pleased, to be infamous.'

'It won't be news to anyone.'

'He didn't die mid-orgasm because he hadn't had one with me for months. But I guess you already knew that, everyone did, didn't they?'

Chapter 7

'Bloody heathens, get off the road.' Rory took his frustration out on the horn, banging on it, no doubt in the way he wanted to bang one of the protestors who was half-blocking the road.

Lottie wasn't even sure what sex the nearest one was, with a mass of purple and red-streaked hair, enough piercings to set a metal detector off, and a big shapeless duffel coat. 'Why do they do it?' She picked absentmindedly at a sticker that was struggling valiantly to hold its place on the dashboard.

'Because they've got frig-all else to do on a Sunday. That's why shops stay open these days, to entertain the masses.'

'But it's pointless.' She gave up on the sticker, which was fixed more firmly than it looked, and went back to staring out of the window, trying to avoid looking straight at any of the crowd. 'Did you bring my martingale, like I asked?' Silence, which meant no. She was going to die, on a beautiful, sunny April morning, in front of a crowd of hunt protestors with a multi-coloured rainbow of hair.

'God, they've all turned out this morning, must be expecting a death or something.'

Mine, thought Lottie as he pulled up in the car park of the public house and her horse stamped its approval from the back of the lorry.

There was quite a crowd, though, assembled for the hunt. The most visible member being Elizabeth, with what looked like a dead pheasant on her head and a fox's pelt draped around her neck. On closer inspection, after she'd wondered briefly if she'd forgotten to put her contact lenses in, Lottie realised that the hat was tweedy with a couple of feathers stuck into the ribbon, and the fox was just a fur collar, pulled, from the slightly moth-eaten appearance, out of the attic just for the occasion. Gran was not going to let anyone tell her what to do, the anti-hunting lobby had, she frequently lamented, taken half the fun and all the danger out of what used to be an exciting day out. First they scrapped national service, and now the do-gooders had the temerity to start meddling in matters closer to home. Surely what one did in the privacy of one's own estate was one's own business? The Barbour wellingtons and tweed skirt completed the type of outfit that made British aristocracy the institution it was. And gave protestors a handy target for eggs, which was the point.

Lottie groaned as Elizabeth squinted at the lorry then headed their way briskly. And tapped abruptly on the door with a staccato volley of diamond-hard nails. If *she'd* done that, the ends would have snapped off, thought Lottie grumpily, not that her nails had pointed ends at the moment. They were more the normal dirt-ingrained chewed-down stubs. She swung the door open reluctantly and did her best to ignore the grin that was plastered all over Rory's face.

'Charlotte, come and have a drink.'

'I need to unload the horses first, Gran.' She jumped out and her legs wobbled on impact, in sympathy with her stomach.

'You need a drink. It might make the ride a bit more fun. It just isn't the same now they've taken all the surprise away. Nowhere near the thrills and spills that we used to have.'

'It's plenty of fun with this horse.' The empty-stomach feeling had been replaced with an 'I'm going to be sick any second now' sensation. 'I'll come and chat as soon as I've got the horses ready.'

'They should be tacked-up already, shouldn't they? No time to pansy about, honestly, in my day the second we arrived we whipped off the rug and we were in the saddle.' Elizabeth shook her head in general despair of the young people today and headed determinedly off to get another drink, pheasant tail feathers waving jauntily as she went.

Lottie wobbled her way to the tailgate and leant her hot forehead against it. A sick bag should be standard issue in a horsebox, the same as on a plane.

'I can make it even more fun, and dangerous…' Rory had joined her at the back of the horsebox and was doing his best to hinder her. 'Just like back in her day.'

She slapped his hand and he tried his best to look affronted. 'Go and get a drink while I get them out.'

'I'm not going anywhere near your gran.'

'She's okay,' she peered round the lorry, 'look, she's been distracted by Tom.'

'What's he doing here? Looks like a misplaced mannequin. Or a feature for *Horse and Hound*.'

Lottie took another look and half agreed, but didn't say so out loud. He did look a bit out of place, as if no one had explained the dress code properly. Although next to Gran it was almost comic, a fancy-dress party in the middle of a pub car park was the closest description she could get to. 'He probably thought a tweed jacket was de rigueur.' Complete with leather elbow patches, hmm. 'What do you think they're talking about?'

'Dunno, but mini Tom-Tom looks bored.'

'Tab, she's called Tabatha, Tabby.' The back of the lorry dropped down and both horses shrieked a welcome and stamped their feet, sensing the excitement to come, which made Lottie feel queasy again.

Her horse had been a gift from her father, and you know what they say about not looking a gift horse in the mouth… And she hadn't been interested in this one's teeth, well, not until they had sunk into every unpadded bit of her body, repeatedly. The mare was black in colour and black in temper. She was like a spoiled toddler who had got used to being the centre of everyone's attention, recipient of cuddles because she was cute, and titbits because she was even cuter when she flicked her little toes out and scraped the ground. But the little hooves were bigger now, and she'd not taken it well when someone had suggested she might have to work for a living.

When Lottie had arrived back from Spain, her father had eyed her up and down and said 'well if you're staying here you better do some work. I've got a youngster that I picked up at a sales the other week. You can sort her out, I think you'll get on fine, two of a kind.' Which sent a little prickle of unease down Lottie's spine and when he chuckled, it didn't help one bit. Billy always had a young horse or two on the yard, bringing a promising horse on was a far cheaper route than buying one already at its peak. But the approach came with its drawbacks. Talented youngsters could be tricky customers. 'Spirited' was what they called it, Lottie thought ruefully.

The mare, Black Gold, lived up to her name. Lottie hadn't known it was what people called oil, until she'd said it was odd and Billy had completed her education with a knowing smile. And she was proving to be a slippery customer. However, she was as pretty as they came, a perfect white stripe down the middle of her face and two white socks on her hind legs. Sitting on her was like being the oil rig on top of the geyser; you tried to draw out that little bit more and didn't know if you were going to be rewarded with astonishing talent or an explosion. She was slick, slippery, mercurial. *I wished they'd called you black treacle, at least I would have had a chance of sticking on, then, and without the risk of spontaneous combustion.*

She tightened the mare's girth and checked all the leatherwork of her bridle. Then she did it again, as the horse danced around her on tiptoes, eyes on stalks and nostrils flaring until she could see the blood-red linings. The last thing she wanted to think about. Blood. Hers.

Lottie glanced down at the boots. Bugger, bending down there could get her trampled, or she might actually be sick. But if one came undone mid-jump they might never come back down to earth again. 'Stand still or I'll put you on the naughty step. Okay?' The mare rolled her eyes like a temperamental teenager, showing the whites. Then the second Lottie bent over, sharp teeth sank into her back and she just knew there'd be a perfect purple bruise. Horse hickeys were so not the in thing.

'I'd have gone for the bum, if it had been me.'

Lottie shot up so quick that the blood rush to her brain nearly overshadowed the embarrassment. The sight of Mick sitting casually on a seventeen-hand hunter built like a brick shithouse made her absurdly jealous. He held the reins by the buckle ends in one hand, his head tipped to one side, feet dangling free of his stirrups, a fan of wrinkles at the corners of his eyes and a glass in the other hand. 'You can ride with me if you need steadying.'

'How did you get here?' She frowned. Then she gave the horse another look as she tried to distract herself from the sex-in-a-saddle rider who could have given Heathcliff a run for his money.

'I rode over. Gave him a warm-up. Maybe you should have done the same?'

'Where's Rory?' She suddenly realised, as she dodged Black Gold's teeth, that Rory had done a disappearing act.

***

Rory had decided that Elizabeth had been right, Lottie needed a swift tot to settle her nerves before they set off. It did, however, also mean that he got waylaid by the old dragon herself, but the prospect of watching her torment Tom and his black-eyed daughter was entertainment worth the risk. He had half-heartedly tried to dodge past with the drinks, but Elizabeth had nearly punctured his vitals swinging the shooting stick in his direction, never spilling a drop of the drink she held rock-steady in her other hand.

'Robert, have you met Thomas and his young daughter?' The fact that she always got his name wrong should have annoyed him, except the fact that she did it every single bloody time convinced him that she was doing it on purpose, and to rise to the bait would give her a moment of glee and satisfaction she didn't deserve.

'Robert?' Tabatha's young unlined brow creased in concentration. 'But aren't you, er,' she paused, not wanting to risk embarrassment, but not wanting to miss an opportunity won out. 'Aren't you, Rory Steel?'

'I am.' He winked, and for the first time in as long as Tom could remember, he saw his daughter flush. 'Old Lizzy here gets confused sometimes.' Oh, boy, if looks could kill.

'We met briefly at the funeral, I believe.' Tom held out a hand, trying to break the awed silence.

'You're an eventer.' His daughter unfortunately was not to be distracted. But Elizabeth was obviously used to this kind of behaviour.

'Ignore him, dear. All horsemen do is swear, drink and fornicate. Believe me, I know from experience.'

Rory winked and leaned in. 'That's fuck, fornicate.' His whisper, aimed at her ear, reached all of them. A smile twitched across Elizabeth's fixed lips as the teenager turned an even closer shade to beetroot and Tom seemed to be debating whether to be rude or hold his tongue.

'And who is that gorgeous man chatting up my little Charlotte?'

Rory dragged his attention from the uncomfortable duo and over to the wagon. 'That, Elizabeth, as if you didn't know, is Mick O'Neal, my farrier.'

'Looks Irish to me.'

'He sounds it too, though I'm sure you've sneaked up on him and know that already.'

She sniffed. 'I don't sneak. Now I bet he knows a thing or two about horses. He's got a proper hunter type there, not like your flimsy creature.'

'Oh, God, I do love you, Elizabeth.' He smacked a noisy kiss on her cheek and ignored the shudder of apparent distaste.

'It looks like he knows a thing or two about women as well.'

Lottie was grinning, no sign of the earlier nerves, and Rory felt slight irritation, both at her recovery when he'd gone to get her a drink, and the hand that Mick had briefly placed proprietorially on her shoulder. It wasn't that he and Lottie were seriously involved, was it? But the last thing she needed was a man like Mick.

***

Mick rested one hand on the pommel of the saddle, and the other on his thigh, and the Irishman in him emerged as he couldn't help but think poetic thoughts at the sight of the blushing Lottie and the dancing black mare. They were a perfect picture, dark energy against the soft green and gold of the countryside. Old England as a great artist would like to depict it. If he'd have been a less principled man, he would have suggested something far more carnal than a day out following the scent of something not even remotely resembling a fox.

It was a perfect day for the chase, though. Soft sunlight danced across the ground, broken and dappled as it weaved its way through the slowly unfurling canopy of new leaves. Under the hedgerows the last of the crocus shouted out, garish and unashamed, and the daffodils towering between them glowed, small rays far brighter than the morning sun.

The whinnies of excited horses broke across the babble of voices, hooves clattering across the car park, the smell of leather lingering in the air, mixed with the familiar tang of warm horse and the odd whiff of whiskey-tinged breath.

Mick's gaze drifted over the crowd, the horses groomed to within an inch of their lives, the riders smart in hunting red or dark jackets, shirts and cravats still gleaming white, jodhpurs light, boots mud-free. For now. Around them hovered the supporters, some here for the vicarious thrill, some for the drink, some to catch up with friends, and farmers who were keen to study the damage inflicted on their fields and hedges. In return for not-so-small favours.

And then there were the others, out on the road. Lurking, waiting, ready to cause what chaos they could when the hunt set off.

'If I were an artistic man, I'd say you make a grand picture.'

'If I were a betting woman, I'd bet I'm about to make a grand fool of myself.'

Mick laughed. From what he could see, Billy had known what he was doing when he'd matched these two together. There was a certain synchronicity. The horse was a bundle of barely contained energy, with a wilful streak, just like the girl. And they both needed a calming hand. Out of the corner of his eye he saw Rory glance their way, deep in conversation with Elizabeth and Tom, a motley crew of troublemakers if ever he'd seen one.

Lottie, he'd heard from Pip, had wanted out. Wanted more than this place could offer, but instinct told him that what she really wanted was to be held long and hard until she realised that she'd found what she was looking for and should stop struggling. That home wasn't so bad after all. Which was why she'd come back.

The horse threw its head up as Lottie hiked the girth up another hole.

'Would a martingale help?'

'You haven't got one, have you? Rory forget to put mine in the lorry.' A wave of relief rushed over her face. Mick grinned, jumped off the horse and started to take his off.

'But I thought you meant a spare.' She looked downcast.

'Don't you be worrying, this old man doesn't need all the paraphernalia they've thrown on him; it's all for show.' The mare thought about taking a nip as he adjusted the tack, then changed her mind, rubbing her nose down his sleeve.

'She doesn't do that to me.'

'I'm the nice guy; you're the one who's making her work for her oats. Here.' She was legged up into the saddle before she could object.

Rory left it as late as he could before getting on Flash. Partly because it gave him time to grab another drink and partly because it gave the horse less time to wonder what was about to happen.

'Wondered when you were going to appear.' Gold was persistently pirouetting in one direction and Lottie was getting dizzy. She tried to haul her around the other way, to unwind her confused brain.

'I went to get you a tot to settle your nerves.' He grinned. 'But I drank it to try and drown out your gran.'

'What was she on about?'

Mick watched as Lottie spun in ever-decreasing circles, and Rory ignored the fact that Flash was doing mini rears. 'Can't you two just ride normal horses?'

'What? Like your boring Irish carthorse? Now where's the fun in that, man? Where did you get that thing, anyhow?' Rory took his chance, while all four of his horse's hooves were briefly on terra firma, and leapt into the saddle.

'Ed Flint.' Mick named a local farmer who was a regular hunt supporter, but on his last outing had parted company with his horse when it had decided that a ditch harboured aliens and thrown in a quick stop. Ed hadn't and had landed in the ditch, which contained no aliens, but had unfortunately contained more stones than water. He was currently the proud owner of a neck brace. His wife had put a hunt ban in place until the doctor had declared him fit. Knowing her stubborn husband was as likely to forgo a day out as he was to get a sudden urge to take up housework or knitting, she'd insisted he loan out his horse to Mick for the day.

'Still isn't up to it then?'

'Not according to Molly.'

'I think we're ready for the off.' Lottie looked nervously in the direction of the Field Master and the assorted hounds who were already in fine voice.

Rory grinned with anticipation. 'I'm going to take her to the front; she likes to see what's coming.'

'We'll settle this pair.'

Rory grinned. 'Wimps.' Then, with a wave and a clatter of hooves, he set off after the hounds, ploughing through the hunt protestors who were foolish enough to loiter in the gateway.

'I hope he doesn't go past the master again; they got so cross last time.' Lottie sighed. Rory didn't believe in rules, which didn't always go down well, and unfortunately his grin more often than not got him out of trouble. Not that this master was the type to fall for that, he'd probably ordered the whippers-in to keep an eye out and head Rory off if he looked like he was about to disrupt the order of the day.

'She's a promising mare that one. Think he'll manage to sort her?'

'I was thinking of talking to Uncle Dom, but you know Rory, he's not going to go and talk to a poncy dressage rider, is he?'

Mick laughed. 'He's lucky he's got you.'

It was on the tip of her tongue to say that he hadn't actually *got her*, but she just smiled inanely instead.

'He's a good, quiet rider is your uncle.'

They trotted out of the car park side by side and it felt strangely harmonious. As Gold settled into her stride, looking around with interest, her ears flicking one way then the other, Lottie suddenly realised she didn't feel sick any more.

By the time they entered the first field and broke into a steady loping canter, the mass of horses had thinned out, some following the direct route of the hounds, others heading down the sides looking for gates and lower hedges.

Lottie and Mick cantered on, neck to neck, Gold fighting for her head as they neared the first hurdle, the large hunter never altering his stride, and his steadiness giving Lottie a weird confidence.

As though they had an invisible bond and all she had to do was keep contact. She tightened her grips on the reins, determined to keep the rhythm, to let the jump come to them, concentrating on nothing but the sound of the horse's pounding hooves, the surge of power underneath the saddle, the rush of cold air that was making her skin smart and her eyes water.

The two horses took off together, almost in perfect stride, rising high at the first hedge, and as she gave with her hands and the horse grew beneath her, Lottie felt the grin spread across her face. Clods of earth scattered from beneath their hooves on landing, and she glanced across triumphantly at Mick, his dirty grin sending an extra whizz of adrenalin coursing through her veins. She tore her gaze from his, cool air still fanning over her burning cheeks. And all she wanted was to do it again, and again, together.

Ahead, she could make out the vivid chestnut streak of Flash, her athletic lines a sharp contrast to the heavier horses of the Field Master, his huntsman and other hunt staff. The mare was clearing the high hedges effortlessly. *Settle in the dressage and you could be a star*, Lottie thought, the star Rory needs so desperately in his yard. The reward for years of hard work and horses that were never quite good enough.

Gold, in contrast, was a careless show-jumper. She was used to poles that fell if she clipped them with lazy hooves. The outing was to teach her to respect the fences and Lottie crossed her fingers, hoping that one lackadaisical jump wouldn't wipe them both out. The horse's concentration wavered, her keen brain diverting her to sights and sounds, and Lottie gave her an abrupt kick as another hedge loomed close. The mare put in a quick stride, skewed her body as she took off, so that they nearly crashed into Mick and his solid hunter. For a moment Lottie shut her eyes and sent a silent prayer, opening them abruptly as the mare pecked on landing. With an effort, she forced her body weight backwards, knowing that otherwise she was out of the front door, and the little horse, agile from all her play-acting, sorted her feet out, like a cat on hot coals, and launched herself forward again.

Mick knew that if his horse had been stupid enough to make an error like that, the sheer weight of the animal would have been his downfall. But Lottie and her little black devil righted themselves in a way that shouldn't have been possible. Those green cat's eyes glanced his way again briefly, her cheeks now mud-spattered, her face pure mischief, and he knew the fear had gone. Give the girl a hefty dose of adrenalin and the thrill of the chase and she rose to the challenge. This wasn't the luck of the Irish that she had, but she made him think of a fiery colleen, a green-eyed, dark-haired devil of a girl who loved life and had a spirit that should never be squashed. A girl who would always run away when she sensed the trap closing in. A girl who needed a man who understood. They were galloping side by side, perfectly paced. She was near enough to touch, to kiss. Her generous mouth curved into a perfect smile.

Lottie felt, rather than saw, the change in Mick. One second he was smiling back, a toe-curling look that would have made her heart beat faster, if it hadn't already been hammering from the exhilaration that was coursing through her body. Then it changed. A drop in temperature, a more fixed look.

'Steady her down, give her time. She's running away from you.' The soft Irish brogue had a hard edge to it, and Lottie hated to be lectured, judged.

'She's fine.'

'She's a baby. Ruin her confidence now and you've lost it forever.'

She half-wanted to tell him to sod off, to stop trying to spoil the fun, she wanted to kick on and leave him behind. But that would be childish. And, she admitted reluctantly, he might have a point. The mare was pulling for her head now. Excited. And Lottie could feel the heat of her body rising through the saddle, nervous energy the only thing keeping her fired up.

She settled her weight back, matched the slower canter of Mick's horse and avoided looking at him. Christ, it was like riding out with her dad. Well, not her dad, he would have been at the front like Rory, telling them all they were riding like a bunch of pansies.

***

By the time they got back to the horsebox, Rory had already untacked and watered his horse and was sittting on the ramp having a cigarette.

'What happened to you two? They'll be calling last orders if you don't shift your arses.'

'Bollocks.' Mick took his hat off and brushed a hand through his hair. 'I've got to ride this one back, so I'll give it a miss.'

'Shove him in the box; there's room for another.'

'No, I'll leave you two on your own for once.'

'We get plenty of that. Come on! Just have one.'

'A quick one, then I'm hitting the road.' This delighted Flash no end, when the big gelding joined her in the box.

'What's up with him, then?'

Lottie shrugged as she watched Mick slip a headcollar over the horse's bridle and run the stirrups up. She hadn't got a clue what had happened out there. One minute he'd been looking at her like he wanted more than a day's hunting. Then he was lecturing her like she was a stupid teenager, which had made her feel like one; cross and frustrated. 'I think he got fed up of babysitting me.' Bossy bugger.

Rory laughed. 'Babysit you? Now it would take a brave man to do that.' He ruffled her hair affectionately. 'Come on muddy face, I need a drink.'

'Am I really?' She tried to peer into the wing mirror, which involved balancing on the step and hanging on to the bracket.

'Like you've been riding through the ditches. Not that I'm complaining.' He planted a kiss on the tip of her nose, then pulled a face. 'Eau de smelly ditch water.' Hs strong arm encircled her waist and he pulled her down so that she was pressed against his firm, hard body. And for a brief, unforgiveable moment she wondered how it would have felt if that had been Mick.

Not that he wanted to do that to her. And not that she wanted it either. She was happy with Rory. Fun, no-strings-attached Rory. She wriggled her way around so that she was facing him.

'How come you're not mud-spattered?'

He chuckled. 'There's more than one reason for keeping ahead of the field, scruff bag.'

'That's what I love about you, so romantic.'

'And this is what I love about you.' He squeezed one buttock. And she forgot Mick altogether. Well, as altogether as she could, seeing as he was stood a few feet away, his face fixed into something resembling a scowl. She pulled herself reluctantly away.

'How about just a couple, then we go home and do something more interesting?'

***

The pub was packed with riders splattered with varying amounts of mud, so she was in good company. Most were at least a drink ahead of them, given that many had abandoned the ride part way around, in the same way that a lot of football supporters left the ground before the final whistle to make sure they were first at the bar. She stood at the corner of the bar, watching as Rory pushed his way to the front to order the drinks, absentmindedly glancing at the pile of newspapers. Then he did a double-take. Staring back at her was a familiar face underneath a headline that made no sense at all.

At exactly the same time as Lottie was picking up the newspaper in the pub, Amanda was opening the large oak door of Folly Lake Manor to Pip.

Chapter 8

'I just can't believe it, who would do such a thing? I mean, it's ludicrous.' She didn't want to sound like a wailing baby, so right now she was aiming for indignation. And failing.

'Is it?' Pip eyed the bottle of premier cru Chablis and the empty glasses and wondered if it would be rude to just pour. After all, Amanda looked like she needed a stiff drink.

'Of course it is.' Amanda was still standing by the tall French windows, holding the front page of the *Mail* at arm's length as though the distance might sanitise the story.

'You could tell your side.'

'It's not my thing; I hate talking to people. Oh, shit.' She threw the newspaper on the floor and perched on the edge of one of the chairs. Pip wondered if she ever just relaxed and collapsed in a heap, like a normal person. 'Do you think everyone else has seen it?'

Pip shrugged. 'Who knows? Most of them are at the hunt today, either riding, protesting or just drinking and hoping someone will fall off. It's the highlight of the month for the St John's Ambulance brigade.' She picked up the discarded paper, just as Amanda remembered her impeccable manners and poured the Chablis. 'And for Elizabeth.'

Taking pride of place on the front page of the newspaper was the most brilliant picture of poor Marcus's coffin hoisted high on the pallbearers' shoulders. Well, high in places. Markedly lower at Billy's corner. In their hunting red jackets and topped boots, it really was the picture-perfect image of the English upper classes that Marcus had bought into.

Next to the main picture was one of Amanda, the grief-stricken widow, looking as immaculate as ever and tightly controlled. And at her shoulder was Tom.

'*Billionaire bows out to leave room for younger model?*' There then followed a very brief report on the funeral, a few details about Marcus's portfolio that left her eyes popping, and speculation about Tom's arrival in Tippermere, which included a good smattering of facts about the state of his heart since he was 'cuckolded', which wasn't a term she could remember seeing for a while, and a few more sparse facts about the state of his buoyant bank account, along with a list of his numerous high-profile conquests whilst he was at the height of his modelling career.

There was brief speculation about the state of any romance between Amanda and Tom (with a circle on the photograph to highlight the fact that he had a 'protective and consoling' hand on her shoulder), and then the article finished by saying that without Tom Strachan's intervention, the place could be sold to a footballer from nearby Kitterly Heath, or a property developer who would bring the bulldozers in. And where would that leave the picturesque jewel in Cheshire's crown? 'Bloody good pictures aren't they though?' Pip cast another assessing eye over the photographs, which were far from quick, opportunistic snaps. 'You'd have thought we'd have noticed if there'd been paparazzi in the trees, wouldn't you?'

'You'd have thought someone would have shot the bastards down. I bet Elizabeth has got a gun licence.'

Pip laughed at the vehemence in Amanda's tone. Up until now, control had been her byword, passion was for other people. Although her mum always did say it's the quiet ones you have to look out for.

'Hey, it's my colleagues you're slagging off there.' Although most of them could have done with a smattering of shotgun pellets up the arse, it would have kept their hands away from her own posterior.

And talking about arses, there was one thing you had to say about horsemen, they were toned. Buttocks didn't get any better than this.

Pip smiled to herself. There had been plenty of horsemen back in Wales, and plenty of well-muscled miners too – their skin etched deep with the daily grime they couldn't escape. Sometimes she could see a similarity between the silver-spooned men of Tippermere and the grubby pitmen of her childhood: the resolve, the determination to achieve what they set out to. The way they expected the shit that life threw at them, and ploughed their way out. And sometimes it felt like she was on a different planet. Which is how, she guessed, Amanda felt. She tried to head her off in a different, and far more interesting, direction.

'Are you going to stay?'

Amanda smiled and wished it felt more natural. Much younger than Marcus, she had married him because she loved his flamboyance, generosity and the fact that she had been sure he was a kindred spirit. She was also wise enough to realise that she was an asset.

Marcus knew how to spend his money, and he spent it on the best suits he could find, the finest leather shoes, and his wife. As a child, Amanda had decided that she wasn't going to live hand to mouth, and nor was she going to join the rat race and work in an office 9-5; she was going to marry, and marry well.

With her angelic face, mass of blonde curls and generous nature, she was as far from a normal gold-digger as could be imagined. And even further when you took into account that she also intended marrying for love. Just a very specific type of love, with a very specific type of bank balance attached. And she knew that to succeed she would have to be single-minded, determined and prepared to dedicate her life towards being the perfect wife.

In meeting Marcus, she had been, in many ways, lucky. He appreciated her sweet nature, loved her delicate beauty and respected her single-mindedness. And the fact that she was, in effect, self-made appealed to the entrepreneur in him even more. The only downside to their relationship was the age gap, that, it soon became apparent, did matter, and his need for constant reassurance of his virility from any, and every, female within a large radius. Marcus had an appetite for life, and an appetite for sex. And he knew he could control neither. And he didn't intend to try. All his wife had to do was live with it.

Some would have said Amanda had reaped her just rewards. She'd had money, and would continue to live happily on what her dead husband had left her in his will, but she hadn't had the perfect love affair that she'd dreamed of. And now, just when their marriage should have been starting on a new track, she was alone, here, in the middle of nowhere, with a guilty secret gnawing away at her as persistently as a terrier chasing a rat.

She looked at her one friend, and wished she could tell her everything. But knew she couldn't.

'I don't want to sound mean or anything, but—'

'I didn't write the piece, Amanda.' Not this particular piece. 'If you want me to put your side of the story then I will, but I didn't do this.'

'I don't know what I'm going to do, to be honest.' She kicked off her shoes and tucked her feet under her bottom, like she had done as a child, before the deportment lessons had banned it. 'But I'm not shagging Tom, I mean the funeral was the first time I'd even heard of the man, because he sent me a note, he was just being kind, he wasn't even there, for God's sake. Was he?'

Pip shrugged. 'I think I saw him briefly, loitering outside the church, but he doesn't really know anyone in the village yet, does he?'

'And, I've not said I'm selling; I don't know where they got

94

that idea from.'

Pip stared at the photo, which was undoubtedly of Tom, because she'd studied it at some length before and decided not to say anything. Not yet. If there had been something going on between Tom and Amanda, then turning up at the funeral wouldn't have been the brightest of things to do anyway. Not that she thought Tom was particularly bright. 'Everyone thinks you will sell up. They don't think you're settled here, they think it was more Marcus's thing than yours. So, there isn't some hot footballer and his blonde babe about to move in and liven things up, then?'

'Nope, sorry, don't know any. Look, I didn't think I was settled when Marcus was here.' She topped up their glasses and realised that she was beginning to feel a bit light-headed, then remembered she hadn't really eaten properly for days. 'It was his choice, but then men are like that, aren't they?' She shrugged and didn't wait for Pip to answer, as it was probably going to be something disparaging about women being able to make their own choices. Which wasn't the terms her life had worked on up until now. 'And I do miss him so much, at first I just wanted to pack a case and walk, if I'm honest. But I do like it here.' *And I can't leave, not yet. Until I've sorted things.* 'What makes you stay here? I mean, don't you miss London?'

'Sometimes. At least things work there.' They both laughed as, with perfect timing, there was a loud gurgle from somewhere deep in the central-heating system. 'And the men don't have boots caked in horse shit.'

Amanda brushed an imaginary fleck of dust from her leg. 'Marcus loved being Lord of the Manor.'

'I bet he did. Did he swish a whip at you and make you bend over to be horsewhipped?'

'I wish.' She emptied the last dregs of the wine bottle into Pip's glass. 'He had grooms for that, I was more for accompanying him out and sitting pretty.'

'Not much fun. Didn't you get lonely?'

'Randy sometimes. He *was* good to me, you know.'

'I know.'

'I didn't expect to lose him, I thought we'd grow old together living our separate lives, if you know what I mean.'

'The perfect type of security.'

'Yep. At the start I thought we were soul mates, you know, all that crap. And then for a while I wondered if I hated him, but just before he,' she paused, sighed and turned the wine glass round between thumb and forefinger, 'well, he'd decided we were actually too good together to throw it all away. He wanted us to find a way of making it work, but I... well it doesn't matter anymore, does it? Oh well, fancy getting totally pissed with me and comparing city men and this lot, it might help me make my mind up?'

Pip did wonder what Amanda had really thought about Marcus's 'making it work' strategy, the 'but' was crying out to be interrogated, and it was bloody hard to squash down the journalist in her. But while she didn't fully agree with the 'patience is a virtue' line, she did know when to bide her time. She'd interviewed enough people over the years to know the warning signs, read when it was the time to push and when it was better to back off. The trouble was, the more she talked to Amanda, the less she seemed to know about her. Which was a new experience.

'Sounds like a plan, and I've got another one, how about I introduce you to the wonders of Kitterly Heath, and the odd footballer or two?' Pip grinned. 'I got a tip-off the other day from one of the staffies on the paper that the goalkeeper David Simcock has just moved into Kitterly Heath.'

Amanda looked suitably blank, which wasn't promising.

'Footballer? You have heard of City I presume? As in the football club, not the place.' One of the factors that had played a part in Pip's escape to the country was the fact that there was not one but several Premiership football teams within commuting distance.

'Now you're being sarcastic. Is he the tall one?'

Pip laughed. 'All goalkeepers are tall. He's 6'10" of fit man, can you imagine just how much man that is?' The smile had been replaced with a dreamy look. 'Do you think if I play my cards right he'll introduce me to his manager?'

'That depends on the cards I suppose.'

'Now *he* is sexy, talk about Italian Stallion. He is one older man I wouldn't close the door on; I could get to like grey hair.'

'I thought you'd converted to the countryside?'

'I haven't decided yet.' She winked at Amanda and drained her wine glass. 'When I came here I was promised real men, but I seem to have arranged more dates for Rory's bloody stallion than I have for myself.'

'So don't you need to persuade him to talk to you, David wotsit I mean, before you move on to his manager?'

'I do, and I have.' She grinned triumphantly. 'I've snagged an interview with him tomorrow, in his new home. I bet it's all fake Tudor and fluffy bits.'

'Like this place you mean?'

Amanda didn't sound judgemental, but it still made Pip flinch. Marcus obviously wasn't a believer in restoring things to their former glory; he preferred the new-improved version.

'It's okay, I don't mind. If it had been up to me things would probably be a bit different. If I stay, there are some things that are just going to have to go. Like the bloody shagpile white rugs for a start; do you know what a hell of a pain it is trying to keep them clean when nearly everyone who comes round has been tramping in fields?'

Pip grinned. 'No, I don't know, actually. I don't do white. Anyhow, how do you feel about us having lunch with his other half next week? I'm sure if I can swing it, we can get far more juicy bits from her.'

'Is that ethical?'

'It's lunch, not a deal. And if she wants to share, well that's her decision isn't it?'

'Well, I suppose when you put it like that, why not? Now, I

want you to tell me who that guy in the yellow Jag is?'

'Yellow Jag?'

'Yeah, I meant to ask you the other day, but then I was so worried about the funeral that it went out of my mind. He was here, down at the Equestrian Centre, talking to Charlotte. You must know who it is; you know everyone.'

'You don't know?'

'No.'

'Really?' Pip reached over and picked up the newspaper that Amanda had been in anguish over. She jabbed a finger at the photograph. 'That was Tom Strachan, the guy you're supposed to be having a fling with.'

***

'Well, fuck me.'

'I thought you wanted a pint first!'

Rory poked at the other side of the local newspaper that Lottie had just grabbed from the corner of the bar. 'Old Marcus has hit the headlines again.'

She unfolded it so that she could see the whole of the front page, which displayed in full glorious technicolor the pallbearers shouldering their heavy burden.

'I thought they only did colour for state funerals?' Her gaze drifted from the photograph to the headline, '*Tippermere Tycoon Makes Way for Younger Model.*'

'I knew there was more to that Tom than he's letting on. Why would he be here otherwise? I'd say the wine bars and tarts in Kitterly Heath were more up his street.'

'He's heartbroken. That's what Pip told me, anyway.'

But Rory wasn't listening, he was already heading over to the snug, where Mick had claimed seats, carrying a full pint in each hand. Lottie followed him, tripping up over feet as she tried to read the article and walk at the same time.

'It says here,' she squeezed her way into the gap between Rory and Mick, forgetting that she was trying to avoid close contact with the Irishman, 'that the marriage was on the rocks and Marcus was the one who suggested Tom come here.'

'I thought he said he didn't know anybody here? Not that I'd trust the word of someone who ponces about with his kegs off for a living.'

Lottie ignored him. 'It says they met at some charity do in London that Marcus was a supporter of.' She peered at the indistinct picture of Tom and Amanda. 'Do you think he really is shagging her?' Then suddenly she became aware of the drop in volume.

'Hi, mind if I join you?'

Yes was the answer that came to mind first as Lottie glanced up to see the refined sexiness that was the man in question. Tom.

She scrambled to shove the newspaper under her bottom, which wasn't the easiest of tasks given the way she was squashed in between two hard male thighs.

'I can put that back if you want.' He held out an elegant long-fingered hand and for a moment she hesitated. Or there was the shove-it-out-of-the-window option and hope one of the horses or a stray hound ate it.

'Sure, thanks.'

He turned it over, eyes narrowing slightly as he spotted the blurred picture.

'Who's dug out that old picture?'

'It is you, then?' Nosiness overrode embarrassment.

'Sure.' He threw the newspaper down behind him and settled on the stool. 'Always the crap pictures that get dug out isn't it?'

'But, but…'

'Did you know you're spluttering?' Tab put her soft drink down, her tone dry as she plonked herself down next to her father with a sigh of resignation, which gained a chuckle from Mick. And made Lottie die to say, 'and did you know you're dad's got ulterior motives?' But she didn't.

'So, did that count as a good day's hunting?'

Lottie glared. 'That picture is of you and Amanda.'

'Is she in it?' He looked genuinely surprised, but totally uninterested. It seemed to amuse Mick no end, and gained him a sharp kick on the ankle.

'The hunting was grand, thank you.' Mick raised his glass. 'If a little tame at times, but at least Charlotte here didn't fall off and nobody killed themselves.'

'Disappointing for the meat wagon; they don't like going home empty-handed.' Rory put a warm hand on Lottie's thigh and did an experimental squeeze.

'Do that many people really fall off?' Tom shot a swift, concerned look in his daughter's direction. 'I mean, is it really that dangerous?'

'It's a good breaking ground.' Rory laughed at his own humour and drained the rest of his pint. 'Thirsty work.'

'I'll get them in, shall I? Same again?'

Lottie watched Tom push his way through the crowd at the bar before jabbing Rory in the ribs with her elbow. 'He's up to something.' She hissed through her teeth in his direction, trying her best to maintain a smile for Tab's benefit, but the girl just gave her a putdown, disinterested stare, then surprised them all by speaking.

'He likes it here.' Then spoiled it. 'God knows why. Everything is so old.'

Which Lottie took to include her, as well as all the other people, buildings, and well, everything. She had a point; it wasn't exactly a raver's paradise, but from what Lottie could remember, horses were as good as it got at her age. 'And even if the woman in that picture *is* Amanda, it's not a picture of her and Dad, is it?' Only a teenager could look that disparaging and disinterested at the same time. Lottie waited for enlightenment. 'They've probably cut off Mum and a whole load of other people. They do that all the time with famous people. And he was so out of his head he probably doesn't even remember it. Right,' she pushed the barely touched drink to the middle of the table, 'you can tell him I've had enough and gone home.'

'You can tell me yourself.' Tom carefully put the drinks on the table. 'Too much excitement for you, poppet?'

'Yeah, right.'

'Well that's telling us, isn't it?' Lottie reached for her drink and tried to get another peek at the picture, without being too obvious.

'Telling you, more like. Oh the innocence of youth, everything so clear and uncomplicated.' Rory raised his pint to Tom. 'Cheers mate.' Took a gulp. 'Well, come on, dish the dirt, have you been shagging old Amanda, then?'

***

As Tom weaved his way slowly back up the lane, trying to avoid the high hedges, which were jumping out at him, he'd have liked to have thought over what Rory had said. But his brain wouldn't let him. It kept taking a detour, visiting old haunts and memories, rather than working in a straight line like it normally did. Something he also wished his feet would do right now.

'God, I feel pissed.' He fumbled his way through the gate and let it clang shut behind him. Then found, when he got to the door, that he couldn't find the keyhole. The name of the house came briefly into focus if he stared hard enough, before it blurred again. Blake House – definitely the right house. 'Fuck it.' He sank down on the step, stretched his legs out and looked up the unearthly darkness of the lane. 'I could do with a fag.'

'Here, help yourself.' A packet of cigarettes landed in his lap. 'I presume that's the type of fag you mean? Not the male-model type?' And, for some reason, it didn't seem strange to find Pip hanging over the wooden gate. 'Going to invite me in?'

'I might, if you've got a lighter.'

She laughed. 'I'm always prepared: dib, dib, dib.'

He must have had a blank look on his face.

'You know, boy scouts and all that.'

'Ah, yes. But you're a girl. Don't they have something different for girls? They did in my day.'

'They did in mine too. But the scouts were more fun. I used to climb over the fence and join them round their camp fire. The girls didn't do fires, just sewing.' She closed the gate a bit more carefully than he had, and joined him on the step. 'You're pissed.'

'I am. Are you?'

'Pleasantly tipsy. I've been drinking with Amanda.'

'Ah.' For some reason, he thought the mention of Amanda should have been significant, but he couldn't remember why. 'I've been drinking with Lottie, Rory and Mick.' He tried to remember exactly how long, and what, he'd been drinking, and failed spectacularly. 'It seems to have affected my reasoning power, as well as my balance.'

'Whiskey chasers or vodka shots?'

'Fuck knows.' He grinned at her and took a long drag on the cigarette, which seemed to help. 'I know, yeah, I do. Vodka, yeah vodka. We had beer, then vodka, then both.'

'Depth charge.' Pip shook her head. 'A Rory special. All I had was Chablis.'

'Poor thing.' He put an arm around her shoulder. He took in the scent of shampoo and wasn't quite sure whether it was a wave of lust sweeping over him or a dizzy spell. He decided it was the first when other parts of his body stirred at the close proximity of a woman.

'Have you seen the papers, Tom?'

'Papers? Oh yes, papers, everybody has seen the papers.' The Amanda-link clunked back into the puzzle of life.

'Thought they might have.' She settled back on her elbows and stared up at the blue-black canopy above, watching the wisp of smoke swirl and blend its way into the nothingness as she breathed out and passed the cigarette back to Tom. 'She says it's a set-up.'

'A figment of a journalist's imagination. Smokescreen.'

'And magic mirrors?'

'Magic editing more like: the joys of Photoshop.' Tom leaned against the side of the porch, hoping it would help keep things still, the earth spinning was one thing, but not at this speed. 'I've not been this pissed for years.'

'You've not been boozing with the hunting crowd; they're good at things like drinking.'

'And risking their necks?'

'On the field and in the sack.'

'And what about you?'

'I like things slightly more civilised.'

'Have you been here long then? You seem pretty settled in.'

She smiled, a dreamy vision, all soft and hazy, which was probably more down to his pissed state, he reckoned, than actual reality. From his vague recollection of previous meetings, dreamy wasn't a tag he'd attach to Philippa.

'Not long.'

'You're not a Cheshire girl, are you?' He was talking nonsense, just to keep some semblance of a conversation going, to keep her there. And he wasn't sure why. Comfort? Adult companionship that wasn't as competitive and intense as the type these adrenalin junkies carried with them?

'From the Valley.'

'Ballet?' That left him even more confused, if that was possible. She was slim, but imagining her in a tutu was a step too far.

'Valley, you dork, not ballet. As in Wales, you know, Welsh Valleys.'

'You don't sound Welsh.'

She laughed, a light, pleasant sound that snaked its way into his addled brain then headed southwards and made him feel like he should be holding her tight. 'I worked in London for a long time.'

'Ah, yes, the journalist.'

'Then I met Lottie in Spain and she somehow persuaded me to come here.'

'It's darker here, isn't it?' He looked up at the inky sky, lit with tiny pinpricks of stars.

'Very dark.'

They both stared up silently and then he stubbed the cigarette out slowly, and Pip watched as he ground it round and round, smaller and smaller. 'Do you think you'll stay here, Tom?'

'I hope so. This has to be better for Tabatha than what she had before.'

'And what about for you?'

'It feels like I belong.' Even drunk, he instantly regretted the impulsive words. 'Will you stay?'

'Okay.' One simple word. She stood up, held out a hand, smiling as he straightened up cautiously.

And as Tom slowly stripped her in the small cottage bedroom, chintzy curtains open so that the moonlight could slip into the room and caress her slim body with its silvery hue, he stared almost mesmerised at the round, perfect breasts, at her unashamed naked stance. And as her nipples hardened under his gaze, his cock stirred in response. He reached out, rubbed one rosy bud gently with his thumb. God, he couldn't remember the last time he'd needed someone this badly. She slowly unbuttoned his shirt, slipped it from his shoulders and ran the point of her nail down over his chest until it slipped into the waistband of his trousers. Tom felt the ragged breath leave his body. It was a bloody good job he was half-cut or this would be over the second he was inside her. And he so didn't want that, for either of them.

A shiver ran over his body, a need, a want. It had been a long time since he'd been with a woman; much, much longer since he'd been with one who wanted nothing in return. Simple, straightforward pleasure, mutual need. And as he pushed Pip gently backwards so that she toppled onto the bed, he was sure that it was exactly what he was about to get.

Chapter 9

'You,' Tabatha banged the mug down with unnecessary force and Tom flinched, 'were totally wasted last night.' She sounded like her mother. Or his.

'And how would you know?'

'I heard you when you got back. You were sat outside rambling on to that woman. And,' she paused, a disgusted look of self-righteousness on her face, 'you were smoking.' She wrinkled her nose, which he translated as 'you stink'.

'Sounds like you got out of the bed the wrong side.'

'There is only one side to get out in that cell you call a bedroom.' She gave the button of the toaster an angry jab and a slice of barely toasted bread popped out, to be liberally spread with a suffocating amount of butter and honey. Tom watched as his daughter licked her sticky fingers, and gave silent thanks that she had never let her mother's nasty jibes stop her enjoying her food. Tamara had taken eating seriously. She ate just enough to live, and popped enough pills and applied enough lotions and potions to ensure that she had the healthy glow of a well-nourished human being.

He took another sip of his scalding hot coffee and regretted that he couldn't remember more of the night before. That woman, as Tabby described her, had been an unexpected but very rewarding visitor. Or so he thought from the bits he could remember. And the peck on his cheek this morning had been good-humoured enough; the cheery wave and smile suggesting that the evening hadn't been a complete disaster.

What had he been thinking? Well, he hadn't. He'd just gone ahead and done what seemed like a good idea at the time, which was something he hadn't done for years. And he wasn't quite sure if he regretted it or not yet. He'd never been cut out to be celibate, but of all the women to shag in this gossipy place, the local journalist probably wasn't the smartest of choices.

In fact, heading out to one of the nearby villages would have been a better idea. Somewhere off Pip's, and Elizabeth's, radar. At the hunt he'd been well and truly interrogated by the blunt and slightly eccentric grande dame, and he was pretty sure she had some alternative motive. And he and Pip ending up in bed wasn't it.

'Dad, Dad, are you listening? You didn't hear a word of that, did you?'

'Sorry?'

Tabby rolled her eyes and looked heavenwards for inspiration. 'I said, you've got to take me down to the yard. Merlin's arriving today, isn't he? This morning? Duh.'

'Christ, I'd forgotten.' He glanced at his watch. 'Shit, is it that time already?' It wasn't just a rhetorical, doesn't-time-fly type of question, he was having trouble focusing. Whatever happened to those digital watches with big, glaring faces?

'You aren't supposed to swear in front of me. You said if you did then I could as well.'

'Just let me drink this, then we'll go. Promise. Don't you need to get changed or something?'

'No.' She sat down opposite him. 'And why would I want to do that?'

'To, er, ride?'

'You can be so out of touch at times.' The chair scraped back with a headache-inducing screech. 'Just tell me when you're ready, then. And don't be too long, I have got stuff to do, you know.'

'Like messing about on social networks?'

'God, you sound so old and stuffy sometimes.'

'Okay, like Facebook? Poking people.'

'Like homework. And it isn't messing, and I don't poke, if you must know. It's staying in touch with my friends, you know, the friends you dragged me away from so that we could come to the sticks and stagnate.'

Tom groaned silently into his coffee. The fact that she'd strung that many words together, to him, meant she was upset. Very upset. The horse, the riding, was supposed to be a conciliatory gesture, and he was cocking that up big style. It was one thing being the firm, 'I know what's best for you' parent, but bloody hard when you knew your wilful daughter had a good point. He poured the rest of the coffee down the sink, hanging onto the counter top and staring out of the window at the picture-perfect scene. This had to work. He did know what was best for Tabatha, for both of them. It would work, just like his head would stop thumping, eventually.

***

Billy stared at the slightly podgy figure of his sometime groom and wondered, not for the first time, why she didn't brush her hair occasionally. She always looked like she'd just fallen out of bed, grabbed the first clothes she could find and headed straight for the door without even giving the mirror a glance. Not that he was exactly a picture, he didn't need anyone to tell him that, but at least he didn't look like an accumulation of a year's worth of jumble-sale visits.

Tiggy was breathless, her bosom heaving up and down, and for a moment he was distracted. Bosoms had that power over him, as did ample and nicely rounded bottoms. Not that Tigs was very good at displaying her assets in the most appealing way, but they still caught his attention at times. Like now. Not for Tiggy the skin-tight jodhpurs and clinging chaps that most of the grooms wore. No, today her ensemble consisted of red Hunter wellingtons (the only resident of Tippermere that knew they existed in that colour), a pair of baggy khaki trousers that were slung low on her hips and would have looked quite trendy coupled with the right footwear and top, and they did show off the slim waist that nestled between her ample bust and generous hips, and a smocked top more suitable for wandering around the gardens of a stately home than for mucking out horses. But at least the generous, rounded neckline did show off her wonderful pink-tinged, freckled chest to its best advantage.

'But he won't go away; he says he's got the right address.'

Billy glanced over at the big horse transporter, which was effectively blocking all access to the equestrian centre, and decided it might be a blessing in disguise. At least it meant no one else could come and hassle him.

'Who did he say he was again?' He eyed the jump pole. 'That doesn't look level to me.'

Tiggy squinted at it. 'It isn't, the ground goes up there.' She pointed to one end.

'I thought you said you'd levelled it this morning.'

'Did I?' She looked vaguely at him, then back at the jump. 'I think I said I meant to do it, but then someone rang and asked if I'd groom their dog for them and I might have forgotten.'

'Might have? Tiggy you're fucking hopeless.'

'I know.' She grinned. 'But you love me anyway.'

Victoria Stafford (not that many people in Tippermere knew her actual name was Victoria) was like one of the spaniels that occasionally frequented her grooming salon. Shaggy, lovable, eternally optimistic, and totally unreliable. She could show complete devotion, but was totally uncontrollable due to a scatty brain and a total inability to concentrate on anything for longer than it took for a new distraction to appear on the horizon. Which was never very long, due to her interest in more or less anything that moved, and quite a few things that didn't.

'So, who is it again?' Nice though the thought of being blocked off from civilisation was, if he didn't get the huge vehicle shifted back out of the gate, the feed merchant wouldn't be able to deliver, and that would be serious.

'He said he's here for tea.'

'Tea?' The woman had lost it this time. 'Since when did I do tea? Send him up to Stanthorpe, I'm sure he'll oblige, might even provide cucumber sandwiches.'

'Let me finish, oh and don't be nasty, he's a nice man.' Billy was emanating an air of tetchiness, which usually meant he was worried.

'I thought you had.'

'I'd paused. I was trying to remember. Yes!' A triumphant smile lit up her features, transforming her face. 'T. Straw, Mr T. Straw, that's what he said.'

'Tea and straw? You're excelling yourself today, Tigs.' Billy kicked at the school floor in the hope of knocking some of the rubber out from under the jump stand and getting something that looked vaguely level. 'Ah, you mean Strachan.'

'Do I?'

'Tom bloody Strachan, that gay ponce that just moved in the village.'

'Gay ponce?'

'You know, the model, with the stroppy goth daughter. The one,' he inclined his head in the general direction of Folly Lake Manor, 'that is screwing her ladyship, according to our local rag.'

'He's gorgeous; he's not gay. Is he? And how can he be if he's, er, screwing Amanda?'

'Who knows? And I was talking about screwing financially not physically. Now be a love, go and find Lottie, it's her bloody problem. And tell her to hurry up, will you? The horse will think it's on the bloody Titanic with this surface.' He scuffed at the ground again with his boot, then headed back over to the horse, which was standing, reins dangling, patiently waiting.

Tiggy, realising she'd been summarily dismissed, watched as he sprung lightly into the saddle. He was all man, was Billy. She didn't care what people said about him, or what they used to say. He had a heart of gold and was so demanding and authoritative it made her go weak at the knees. Literally.

It made her heart ache that Billy wasn't happy. And she knew he wasn't. Everyone on the circuit in Tippermere thought of him as a happy-go-lucky type of guy, who liked to play the field, who always had a good joke to tell. He was no different in that way to most of the other riders. They worked hard, in a physically and mentally demanding sport, and at the end of each day they played hard. They were like actors on the stage, all bravado and confidence, but a man like Billy needed more.

He was devoted to Lottie, his free spirit of a daughter, in the same way he'd been totally addicted and devoted to her beautiful but wild mother. Alexa had been elusive, impossible to pin down, and Billy had fallen, as many had, head over heels in love with that side of her. But he had also loved her vulnerability, had wanted to care for her. Tiggy remembered when Charlotte had been a toddler. The proud Billy, when he had been home, had put her in the saddle before she could walk, had laughed at her chuckles and demands for more. But he hadn't been home enough; he'd been on tour all summer, every summer. He'd played away in every sense possible. And slowly he'd destroyed the one thing that meant the most to him.

Tiggy sighed. She could never compete with the beautiful and whimsical Alexa. Nobody could. But Billy wanted, needed, someone to love him the way Alexa had. Not because he was cuddly and a laugh, not because he shagged with the abandon of a man intent on being the best, despite his ever-spreading girth. He wanted a grand passion. A woman who took him seriously.

'Stop mooning and pop that pole back before you go will you, love?'

She looked at him as he cantered around the edge of the arena.

'You should have a riding hat on, William.'

He chuckled. 'And you should be finding my daughter. Then get your arse back here and give me a hand.'

'Oh, you do have such a way with words.' But at least, Tiggy thought as she watched him kick the horse on towards the fence, he seemed to have recovered some of his normal bonhomie. But she doubted that his way with words would extend to telling her what was on his mind. Though it didn't take a genius to guess that the answer probably lay up at the house, and in the hands of Amanda James. And in the notional 'For Sale' board that everyone was convinced had materialised on the day Marcus James breathed his last breath.

**

The horse, when it finally came down the ramp of the massive horse transporter, wasn't what Lottie expected at all.

'That's it?'

She looked past the driver into the cavernous exterior, as though she expected there to be a string of horses in there. Or at least one more, because this one was a mistake.

'Yup. Here you go, love.' The driver handed her the end of the rope, had the ramp back up with the type of indecent haste that said he was expecting trouble and passed her a docket to sign, along with a horse passport.

'Merlin, bay gelding, Mr T. Strachan. Sign here, love, and then I can get back on the road.'

'What's wrong with it?' Tiggy looked from the horse, to Lottie, then back to the horse again, as the driver expertly turned the transporter and edged it out of the yard. She looked again, as though she half-expected there to be a leg missing, or something equally obvious. Tiggy's devotion to the yard went only as far as Billy; it didn't extend to any kind of equine knowledge, which for some strange, unexplained reason (given the highly strung horses

111

Billy worked with) hadn't yet caused any catastrophes.

'Well, I don't know. It's just I expected something a bit more, well…'

'More flashy, less carthorse?'

'He's a cob, a Welsh cob, not a carthorse. Really, Tigs, I would have thought you'd know something about horses by now. All the time you hang around Dad.'

'I don't hang around.' Tiggy kept her tone mild, refusing to rise to the bait. 'I help him out, when I'm not too busy.' She flapped the bottom of her smocked top to let some air in and wished she was one of those people who kept their cool whatever the weather. She only had to sense the sun and her skin went a horrible pink that clashed with her auburn hair, and her internal temperature rocketed. She loved the British summertime; it just didn't love her.

'Tom's into dogs, you know, maybe he'll bring you some business.' Lottie had never been quite sure what Tiggy did with her time. She had lived in Tippermere for all of her life, and after her author husband had run off with his editor, she'd set up the grooming business. But there wasn't much call for dog grooming in Tippermere. Most of the dogs, as far as Lottie could see, were short-haired terriers, or Labradors, or working spaniels and border collies that enjoyed life in the mud and didn't want, or need, a bath or a haircut. Which was why, Charlotte guessed, Tiggy had become a more or less (when it suited her) permanent fixture around Billy. The meagre pay he gave her kept her fed, and she liked the company. Why Billy put up with her was more of a mystery. She knew zilch about horses and was totally unreliable, prone to wandering off talking to herself just at a crucial moment. 'And I wouldn't flap your top around like that, he thinks you're about to take off.' Lottie felt instantly guilty as Tiggy coloured up even more, if that was possible, and shot Merlin a worried look. She was nice, very nice, and the one permanent fixture around Billy's yard.

'Well, I think he's quite pretty.'

You would, thought Lottie. He looked slightly wild, like Tiggy's own dogs, which didn't say much for her grooming skills.

'Handsome.'

'Butch.' Tiggy grinned and gave him a tentative pat, then rapidly retreated, like the tide on its way out, when the horse flicked his ears back at the sound of a car turning into the centre. 'I'd better get back.' She waved a hand in the vague direction of the indoor school as Billy's gruff tones filtered across the yard to them, 'I'm supposed to be putting poles back up, or something.'

'You shouldn't let Dad boss you around, you know.'

'I don't.' Tiggy's voice was soft as she met Lottie's look. 'I like helping him out.' She shrugged her shoulders. 'He's sweet.'

'Sweet? But he never even says thanks, and you don't even really work for him.'

'He does in his own way.' Tiggy stepped back in alarm as Merlin circled Lottie at the end of the lead rope.

'He could get one of the grooms to pick up dropped poles for him.'

'But I like doing it.' There was a gentle smile on Tiggy's face that Lottie couldn't quite work out. Like she was, well, fond of him. 'And he needs someone.'

'Needs?' She furrowed her brow. 'He's got lots of people, and,' now she was feeling slightly peeved, 'he's got me.'

'You're grown up Lottie, you've got your own life. Have you never thought that he might be lonely?'

Which was the strangest idea she'd ever heard, and she would have dwelled on it had it not been for the ear-splitting shriek. 'Merlin.' The car had barely scrunched to a halt on the gravel before the door was flung open and a gangly mess of stick-thin legs encased in stretch denim, long black hair and a t-shirt that looked like it belonged at a punk rockers' convention practically fell out, but somehow hit the ground running – straight over to the gelding, who nickered a soft welcome of affection as the previously unemotional Tabby draped herself around him.

Good Lord, Lottie thought in shock, was the girl kissing her horse? Could that actually be a smile of pure happiness on her face? But Lottie knew exactly how it felt. When she had been Tabby's age, her horses were her everything.

Tom slowly edged into view, running fingers through his floppy Hugh Grant fringe and looking similarly abashed. And as if he'd been run over by a juggernaut.

Lottie grinned and forgot all about the weird Tiggy who had taken the opportunity to run back to Billy. 'Pip said you'd be a lightweight.'

Tom stared back, horrified that details of the mad coupling had already spread through the village like wildfire, including a detailed description of any sexual deviancies and shortcomings he was presumed to have.

'She said that?' What had she meant, lightweight? Small, totally inadequate? Hung like a horse suddenly took on a whole new connotation of expectation and disappointment.

'You'd never stand the pace, she said when she texted.'

Texting? She'd been texting in the middle of that? Was he really so pissed that he'd missed her waving her mobile phone around in between thrusts? And he'd got there, and so had she, unless all those animal-like noises had been because her mobile had got stuck somewhere it shouldn't. Or were they to disguise the fact that she was actually reporting the whole thing while he'd been buried deep between those evenly tanned and toned legs?

'And she was right, I mean all-nighters are the norm around here, you know.' She was obviously amused at his aghast expression.

'It was *practically* all night.' Tab had temporarily untangled herself from her long-lost horse and added her normal touch of sarcasm to the proceedings.

Shit, she hadn't heard, had she? Tom had assumed that from her attic bedroom, which she'd insisted on having, the noise wouldn't have reached. Or he would never have let things go the way they had. But he was half tempted to add that it was pretty much all night, which coupled with copious amounts of the local brew and the vodka bombs, or whatever Pip had called them, had left him feeling like he'd been turned inside out. Depth charge; that was what she'd called them. And it figured. How the hell he'd even got it up was a bit of a mystery, let alone had the energy to do what they had done. That type of lust was something that he'd thought had disappeared along with his youth and acne. And she'd said he was a lightweight?

'No it wasn't,' Lottie was laughing at Tab, 'it was only ten thirty. Eleven tops when he left.'

'Dad had his own party.' She gave them a look of disgust and turned her attention back to all things equine.

Lottie stared, and Tom stared back, as the truth of the situation dawned on him. No one was accusing him of under-performing. The comments were about the dazed look in his eyes, not the diffused feel in his pants.

She was just talking about his early departure from the pub, followed by his hung-over state this morning. 'You had a party and didn't invite us?' Lottie looked crestfallen, and he felt a sudden stab of guilt at mentally accusing her of discussing his sexual prowess behind his back, and at making her feel left out.

'It was a private party.' Tab glanced from one to the other. 'You know? Party for two? Look, do you two mind if we put Merlin in a stable? I mean he has got to be tired; he's just stood for hours in that box.'

Lottie glanced from the horse to Tom, and back again. Torn between obvious duty to horse-kind, and a more pressing duty to find out just who he'd been with. After all, he wasn't supposed to know anyone here, was he?

Tab cleared her throat noisily.

'Sure, of course, I mean, come on I'll show you.'

'Great, thanks.' The words came out of Tom's mouth in a 'grateful for the distraction, and now let's move on' kind of way.

She'd have to ask Pip. Pip would know; she knew everything. Or, if she didn't, Elizabeth would. Not that it was a good idea to ask her, unless she really had to. Maybe it was Amanda. Maybe the papers had been right all along. He had been very insistent about coming to the equestrian centre, hadn't he? He could have quite easily found some penny-pinching farmer who was more than happy to rent out a field and a stable. But he'd wanted to come here, so his darling, precocious daughter could have riding lessons with her; someone he knew absolutely nothing about at all. But did that mean he was actually *after* Amanda? It was almost believable. They'd look quite good together. She tried not to stare too obviously as she imagined them arm in arm, or snogging. Or in bed, being very polite and making the proper oo and ah noises at the right times, which was something she'd never managed to do. It would all be very proper and perfect. Oh my God, what was she doing, imagining them in bed? What if he guessed? Lottie cleared her throat in an attempt to clear her dirty mind. 'Er, great that you're settling in so quickly.' But he wasn't really listening, he was staring over the fields with a glazed look.

***

Tom only half heard. None of this was turning out quite how he'd planned. Not that there had been any big master plan, but it definitely hadn't involved hitting the national headlines, landing a two-page spread in the local rag and getting the best shag of the decade followed swiftly by the hangover from hell. Nope, it had involved obscurity in the countryside. Yeah, great to be settling in, who the hell had coined the phrase 'rural idyll'? Except, for some strange reason, he actually couldn't feel upset about it. Although the primary aim had been to settle Tabatha, and right now she didn't look that settled, even with her precious four-legged and furry friend in tow.

'Are you going to come or not, Dad?' She was glaring at him.

'Sure I am, poppet.'

'I told you not to call me poppet.'

So much for the happy phase – that had lasted about five minutes, at a push. Maybe once she got the animal bedded and boarded she'd admit to being slightly satisfied.

'Oh yeah, I forgot to tell you. Mom rang this morning.' And with a satisfied smirk on her face, mission accomplished, she turned and strode off after Lottie.

His own happy phase exploded into the ether as he stared after her, his mouth open, with a new churning in his stomach that had nothing to do with vodka.

Chapter 10

If Tippermere was the epitome of English countryside, then Kitterly Heath was the Lady of the Manor. Elegant, refined and yet, in its subtle way, shouting out a message of money and glamour. Lady Bountiful.

The single main street curved graciously from one end to the other; a prize necklace adorned with a carefully crafted range of jewels, some flash and sparkly, some more refined and quietly glamorous. All were designed to part the wealthy residents from their stash of cash. Designer shops, wine importers and estate agents vied for attention with the type of village shop that has all but disappeared from the villages of England, and there was, of course, an upmarket nail salon, flanked by the kind of shoe shop that displayed only designer labels with killer heels and heart-stopping price tags, and a sweet shop that sold candy canes and flying saucers at sky-high prices. But the point was, if you needed to look at the price, Kitterly Heath really wasn't the place for you.

At one end of the village stood a proud and solid-looking church, dating back (so the plaque proclaimed) to the 14th century. But whilst the building looked relatively understated and traditional, the churchyard told a different story. Within the surrounding walls, its occupants competed even in death. It was crammed full of local dignitaries, with the type of imposing headstones that would have cost an arm and a leg and anywhere else would have been laid flat for health and safety reasons.

The village was flanked at its other end by a private school, with its origins in a deep and respectable past, but with so many additions and modifications proudly paid for by competing benefactors it could have dignified any surroundings.

In between the two sentinels nestled a quintessential village that was as small as it was perfect.

Here, you could find a small deli selling a wide range of local cheeses, sitting alongside more glamorous foreign delights that Harrods would have been proud to display. A few short strides on along the wide pavement was a local butcher, proudly displaying game, hanging still in its furred and feathered splendour, with the best steaks and pork for those with less adventurous tastes. And scattered with glorious abandon between the upmarket purveyors of all things culinary was a range of tea shops, wine bars and restaurants that could cater for any taste, provided that money was no object. And if you could afford to live in Kitterly Heath, then it was a given that money was indeed no object.

There were three broad categories of resident in the village. The type who had lived here for generations, and inhabited the grand but slightly dilapidated mansions just up the hill. Then there were those who had made their money in the City, following perfectly respectable (to some) careers that usually involved money. And then there were the others. The ones who ensured recession didn't exist in this cosy corner of Cheshire. The ones who had made it here on the back of a skill set that could cause tutting and censure. The pop stars, the footballers – after all, two major rival teams were based within a short Ferrari drive away – and the actors who hankered after a country-estate address to add to their Hollywood and City portfolio.

Pip squeezed her moped in between an eclectic selection of BMWs, Mercedes and the odd Rolls Royce, wishing money was no object for her, and headed into the bakery to pick up a few of her favourites. She'd need something to eat before heading off to the interview. Footballers' wives weren't in the habit of stocking carbs in the cupboard and an evening of drink followed by a night of surprisingly athletic shagging had left her absolutely ravenous.

Tom had been something of a revelation; even half-cut, well, more than half, he'd looked like he was completely wasted. But he'd been an amazingly good lover, with the type of stamina that had left her mildly shocked. And, for his age, he had a very well-maintained body, which she supposed went with the territory – not something City bankers often took that seriously. They thought that if they had the barely discernible start of a six-pack, then they'd got it made. And if they could keep it up for more than the requisite three minutes, they were a lothario in the making. She'd always done her best to avoid getting involved with other journalists; not that they weren't good for a laugh and a drink, or ten, but muddying her own patch wasn't her style. Nor was sleeping with someone who made their living out of extracting secrets. But her social life and job in London had meant it was surprisingly easy to get laid, if and when she desired. This part of Cheshire, with its close-knit community and out-of-control grapevine, was an altogether different kettle of fish, as her mother would have said. Tom was different.

As she ate the freshly baked pie, she stared at the photographs that were tastefully displayed in the estate agent's window, and tried to imagine what she would buy if she were, by some highly unlikely stroke of fate, able to snag herself a millionaire, as Amanda had done. Obviously Tom, for all his attractions, was too old, and came with a stroppy teenager attached and, she guessed, enough emotional baggage to last a lifetime. He was sweet, rich, from what she'd heard, and good in bed. But hey ho, even in a highly optimistic frame of mind she knew they'd be a disaster together, even if they could find a single thing in common, which she sincerely doubted. From the rumours she'd heard, his wife had become totally bored when he'd hit his mid-life crisis and decided to become a slippers-and-sweater type of guy. What a total waste. Maybe he'd grow out of it.

She flicked a crumb of pastry from her hair and studied the artfully posed photographs. You could buy anything your heart desired here, providing you were minted and not skinted, as she was: a Georgian mansion, a fake Georgian mansion, original or fake Tudor splendour, or the type of mansion that had obviously, and misguidedly, been inspired by Hollywood glamour and erected by owners who were confident it was buried so deep in a generous acreage of land that no council official, however petty, would be able to deny the appropriate planning permission.

As she took another distracted bite, which was far too big, a flake of pastry tickled at the back of her throat and she fought the urge to cough and shower the immaculate pane of glass with melted cheese and ham. Just as her eyes flooded with tears, she caught the eye of the woman behind the desk inside, who glared at her with the type of knowing stare that came from hours of practice assessing a person's wealth. Estate agents here could identify old money, new money and no money within seconds. The disdainful look told Pip that she'd been labelled pretty accurately and dumped in the final category, which annoyed her and sent her straight in through the fingerprint-free glass door. Plonking the remains of her slightly greasy and very flaky-pastried lunch on the neat pile of business cards, she very slowly and deliberately sucked the remnants of the pie from her thumb and forefinger and tried to ignore the woman's look of distaste and the fingers that were just twitching to move the offending object from her pristine desk, well, from her view more probably.

Pip paused and let the silence widen into an uncomfortable gulf that just had to be filled. She was good at her job for many reasons; one being that she knew just how to sow that seed of uncertainty. Then, shooting the woman her best 'I dare you' stare, she launched into a list of requirements that had the kind of price list attached that was impossible to ignore, just in case.

121

A very satisfying half hour later, after convincing the harried estate agent that it wasn't worth the risk of ignoring her, and insisting on seeing anything and everything that might or might not suit her and her imaginary billionaire Arab sheik husband, Pip pushed the intercom button on the very imposing, but slightly tacky, entrance gate and waited to be let in.

'It's Philippa Keelan, from the—'

'Oh, hi babe. Come in.' The soft voice was a long way from landed gentry, but was refreshingly down-to-earth and sounded genuinely welcoming to Pip's jaded journalistic ears.

There was a metallic click and then the gates slowly, but majestically, swung open to reveal a long, curved driveway that disappeared behind a mass of rhododendron bushes. A few seconds later, Pip drove around the curve to reveal an amazingly perfect house. Whatever she had expected, it wasn't this. Most of the celebrities that purchased properties in the area seemed to delight in knocking down the imposing houses and replacing them with something which they considered more in keeping with their own image than that of the surroundings. But this property looked like it had been lovingly restored to something probably even better than its original glory.

It was even more impressive inside, and so was the girl who opened the door: incredibly tall, slim, with the blemish-free complexion of a model, clothes that were the kind of deceptive casual that comes straight off the catwalk, and a genuine, if apologetic, smile.

'David won't be long; he's just finishing a game. I'm Sam, by the way.'

'A game?' How could he have arranged an interview on a match day? Pip fought the bubble of annoyance. There was a time and place for sweaty, just-off-the-pitch footballers and this wasn't it. 'But there isn't a fixture today, is there?' She wasn't particularly genned up on the game, just the players, but…

'Naw, not football.' She giggled. 'He's on the Xbox, babe. Come on, come through. We can sit in the kitchen and have a glass of wine. Or is it too early?' She looked worried, as though she might have just committed some indescribable faux pas.

'Wine sounds good, except I have to drive.'

'Davey will take you back, honest, it's no probs. You only live in Tippermere, don't you?'

'Er, yes.'

'Great, that's sorted. Have you lived here long? I mean, I don't mean to be nosey, if you don't want to say…'

Pip laughed at the open, honest face. 'No, I don't mind, and yes, I've not been here long.'

'It's just the girl who rang from the paper said it was just so lucky you're here now. A coincidence; we only moved in a few days ago. Do you like it here? I mean, the village is very quaint and all that, but…'

'It's quiet?'

'Yeah, I mean, I'm not complaining.'

'It's nice enough, when you get to know it. But it's not big city. I haven't really decided if I like it or not yet. What about you? Apart from the quiet bit?'

Sam shrugged. 'The house is gorgeous, but to be honest I think I need a dog or something, or I'm going to end up talking to myself.'

'A dog?' Pip scanned the immaculate kitchen.

'We always had one at home when I was a kid.' For a second the smile slipped but was back almost before she'd noticed.

'I know someone, just the guy who can help you out with a dog, if you're serious.'

'Sure, I'm serious, but don't mention it to Dave yet.' She winked a perfectly kohled baby blue.

'He's into dog rescue or something, I'm sure he'll get you sorted. How about I sort something out for next week? And, while I'm at it, I'll introduce you to this great girl I know, we can start you up a dog-free social life as well.'

'Really?'

Sam looked as though she might be eternally grateful, and Pip couldn't believe her luck. 'Really, you can bring David along too.' She raised the goblet – there was no other way to describe it – of wine. 'To the dog thing that is, not the girlie get-together. Once you've told him.'

'He might be training, is it okay if it's just me? I mean, I understand if—'

'Just you is fine.' Pip grinned. This was too easy. Within five minutes of stepping into the house she'd sorted a meet with Amanda, which would cheer up the three of them no end. And she had the ideal excuse to rope Tom in, and then she could work out if Amanda and him actually did know each other or not, seeing as neither of them would spill the beans. Face to face it would be obvious. And she'd have a nice story to please the ed. Footballing star, stay-at-home glam-but-lonely girlfriend with her adorable new pooch (everyone loved a puppy pic), maybe more, maybe even an intro to the rest of their team. And his manager. Oh, yeah, now that was a thought worth hanging on to.

If Amanda liked Sam, and she was pretty sure she would, she might even persuade her to throw one of her parties, and then they could invite David's sexy manager, who she knew only lived a few miles away. It was the manager who'd persuaded his new signing to move here. Under his watchful eye.

Or was it too soon for Amanda to be throwing parties? Tippermere was always up for a party, but maybe Amanda wasn't. It was hard to judge; one minute she swore she wanted independence and hinted that her marriage had been on the rocks, the next she looked like she'd just lost her soul mate.

'Aw, thank you. That's brill, isn't it Dave?'

The entrance of David, in jeans, sloppy t-shirt and a smile, cut short her musings. Dave was tall, much taller than he looked on the TV, in fact he positively dwarfed the tall but willowy Sam. And he was ripped. Seriously, in the way only a sportsman could be. And not in the way every horse hero in Tippermere was. This was seriously pampered, physio'd, and suited-and-booted type of fit. The type that involved a proper diet, facials, serious haircuts, training and designer gear. Pip would have swooned at his feet, if it hadn't been for the fact that she felt shagged out, too old, and zero competition for the dazzling smile of adoration that Sam was directing his way. Instead she settled for admiring the physique and drinking his no doubt very expensive wine.

'Nice place you've got here.'

'Cool, isn't it? Nice to meet you, I'm David Simcock. Has Sam been looking after you?' He held out a hand as his other squeezed Sam's waist affectionately.

'She certainly has.' They were perfect. Beautiful, glamorous, in love.

'The place is all down to my pa; he's a property developer. Got some ace people in to do it up for us. Done a good job hasn't he?'

'Amazing.' The word 'property developer' hit Pip square in the middle of the most devious part of her brain and did a loop-the-loop. Elizabeth would love this.

'He loves it round here. Looking for other places he can sort. In fact, I think him and mom would quite like to move into the area, keep an eye on us.' He winked at Sam and settled onto a bar stool next to her. 'So, fire away. What do you want to know?'

Pip took a long swig of wine. The day had just got even better. A property developer who was looking for other places would really get the ears waggling. Elizabeth would love to hear about this, and if Tom was trying to sneak under the radar, well she knew just how to flush him out.

And David and his girlfriend were about to discover just how wonderful their new home village could be.

***

'I need a dog.'

'Sorry?' Tom stood in the doorway of the cottage and stared

at Pip as she waved off what appeared to be the driver of a very new Ferrari with blacked-out windows. 'I thought you said you didn't believe in keeping pets in small houses?'

'Not for me, silly. Can I come in?'

'Well, I—'

'Tom.' She gave him a look. 'I promise not to jump you, if that's what you're worried about.'

'Shh. Tab is upstairs, and she's already been complaining about last night.'

Pip shrugged.

'Complaining to Lottie.' He liked Lottie, but he wasn't sure he wanted her to know what he'd been up to, well, more specifically, who he'd been up to it with. The grin that spread across Pip's face wasn't what he'd expected.

'If you don't want to be talked about then you have to live the life of a nun in this place, well, monk in your case. I mean, what did you expect? It's a village, for God's sake.'

'But—'

'And if you do keep your cassock buttoned, they'll make something up.'

'I wasn't aware I had a cassock.' He raised an amused eyebrow, wondering where she was going with this.

'Come on, let me in, this is important. You're going to have a party.'

'I am?' He stepped back. 'I'm not. Seriously, Pippa.'

Pip had decided that it was definitely too early for Amanda to be throwing parties. But Tom was a different matter altogether. And he had contacts.

'Hang on, didn't this conversation start with a dog?' He let her walk past him, into the spacious kitchen, and sit herself down at the breakfast bar.

'Yeah, what did Lottie say?'

Ah, so she was bothered. 'Coffee? She's not said anything yet. Names weren't exactly named, but she looked like she wasn't going to give up. She wants to know who I was up late playing with.'

He looked a mix of frustrated, knackered and bemused, which was pretty adorable. Very Hugh Grant, to her mind. 'You're right, she won't give up.' Pip giggled. 'I think part of the reason Rory loves her is because she reminds him of his flaming terriers. She's already texted me twice asking when I'm going to be down at Rory's yard. So, what exactly does she know?'

'Well, it is my fault I suppose.' Guilt flickered across his features as he watched the coffee maker do a final splutter. 'I looked wasted when we went down there this morning, and Tab ended up saying I'd been up practically all night partying.' Tom plonked two mugs of coffee down; he needed a coffee even if she didn't. Well, the thing he actually needed most was an afternoon nap. How could living in the country be so bloody exhausting? 'And, for your information, I am not having a party.'

'You're not?' Pip ignored the coffee. 'But it's the best way to meet people.'

'I've met lots of people, and I came here for peace and quiet. I don't think I'm up to meeting people anymore.'

'These are interesting people, real proper people. They don't talk horses all the time, and,' she leant forwards conspiratorially, 'you can meet Amanda.'

'And why would—'

'Squash the rumours. You know, about you and her. Unless,' she twirled a spoon round in her cup, despite not having added any sugar, 'you do already know her.'

'No party. And no Amanda. If people want to gossip, then fine.'

'You don't mean that, I know you don't.' Frustratingly he'd ignored the actual issue of whether they had already met, and the way he looked, she felt more like hugging him than inter-rogating him.

'You do, do you?' He took a sip of coffee and decided Pip would wear him out, even without sex.

'You'll find reporters under the bed.'

He shrugged.

'And following Tab around.' Children always clinched it, even if it was playing dirty. 'And you've got to; I've arranged it. Well, I've not actually arranged the party.' She paused. 'Maybe we should just go to Amanda's place.'

This did catch his interest. For some reason, every time he went anywhere near Folly Lake Equestrian Centre, he found himself staring up in the direction of the Manor House and wondering what it was like. Pip, honed to every muscle twitch, spotted his lapse and leapt on it. He was hooked.

'You'll love it, and so will David and Sam. Maybe you could bring the dog with you?'

'Pip, who are David and Sam, and how have we got back on to a dog? What dog?'

'Sam wants a dog; she wants to rehome a poor abandoned mutt.' She'd made that bit up herself, after realising what a brilliant byline it would make for the article. 'And you've got lots.' An abandoned dog was probably better than a puppy, providing it was cute. An abandoned puppy would really clinch it. And it would make a brilliant photo opportunity; all she had to do was sneak Tom into the picture as well and she had a winner. After all, who could resist a gorgeous guy, lovable dog and a footballer's wife, well, girlfriend. If she could work in fiancée that would be even better. She was a genius.

'I don't just keep a stock under the bed, you know.'

'Really?' She feigned astonishment. 'Well, actually, I suppose I would have heard the odd whimper and wail the other night when you ravished me.' He seemed to have gone a lighter shade of pale, if that was possible. 'But I thought you said you'd set up some dogs' home with that what's-her-face, politician's wife?'

'It's his mother, not his wife. Yes, I have, but we don't just let anyone do a pick-and-mix.'

'This is not just anyone, this is David Simcock and his girlfriend. And you, Tom, are going to give them the perfect housewarming

128

present to help her settle in. She's lovely, really, well you can see for yourself. I'll sort something for one day next week, you, me, David, Sam and Amanda and lunch. Oh, and the dog. Better go, got to put Lots out of her misery.' For a moment she thought about mentioning David's father, a hint that he might be interested in Folly Lake Manor, but she bit it back. No need yet; she'd use it as a clincher if she needed to. But for now it looked like he was going to play anyway. Well, from the state of him, not exactly play, more just roll over on his back and play dead.

It wasn't that she wanted to cause him grief; she genuinely liked him. But she did want to know why he was here, and she was going to find out. And for the sake of Lottie and her rumbustious father, it was about time someone put the pressure on and tried to find out exactly what was going to happen to the Equestrian Centre and the village they were so fond of. Elizabeth had her own sneaky and time-proven methods, but Pip was always in favour of the direct approach. 'Right, I'm off. Don't forget the puppy. I'll text you when I've spoken to Amanda. Now, I wonder what I can get away with telling Lottie?'

For a moment Tom forgot about the dog, and the lunch. 'You aren't going to tell her are you?'

He sounded shattered and Pip couldn't help but throw a wink his way. 'Oh, I never tell anyone anything I don't have to. Don't worry, lover boy.' She planted a smacker of a kiss straight on his lips, which somehow managed to make his head throb as if he'd been hit with a sledgehammer. He really did need to lie down. 'I might tell someone else, though.'

He tried to ask who, but by the time the words were out, they hit empty air. She'd gone.

***

'I thought you would at least come for a drink after the drag hunt.' Lottie was slightly peeved, firstly that her friend seemed to

129

have abandoned her for somebody possibly more interesting (and less obsessed with horses and Rory), and secondly because she obviously knew things and wasn't in any hurry to share. She had become more and more suspicious of Pip's responses to her texts and the fact that she seemed to have disappeared down a black hole (no mean feat in Tippermere), only now to pop out like a white rabbit from a magician's hat when it suited her.

'I was busy.' She grinned, not put out by Lottie's accusing tone. 'And you know, I don't like the whole hunting scene, all that unharnessed testosterone, male bravado and bloodlust floating in the air.'

'I'd always thought you liked an overdose of testosterone, and there isn't any bloodlust. Even Tom was there.' Lottie shot her a look to see if there was a response, but Pip was frustratingly deadpan.

'So I heard.' She put a foot on the bottom rail of the outside school and joined Lottie in watching Rory do his best to persuade Flash to at least perform some of the steps he wanted her to.

'And he disappeared early for a romantic encounter.'

'How do you know? I wouldn't have thought after a session with you lot he'd be up to it.' She grinned, and Lottie decided to try another tack.

'Do you think he does know Amanda? I mean, they were together in that picture in the paper, although Tabatha said it was a set-up.'

'And teenagers know everything.' Pip flinched as the horse kicked her heels within inches of the rail, sending a clod of compacted sand and rubber her way. 'I honestly don't know, it's strange.'

'And I think it was her that he met up with after.'

'Do you?' Pip kept her gaze fixed firmly on the horse and forced the grin back where it belonged. Out of sight.

'Well, apparently he spent most of the night with a woman, and he doesn't know anyone round here, does he? So I thought it figured that it must be her.'

'He doesn't know her either, according to him.'

'Okay, maybe it was someone he met in London and brought here, but it seems odd, doesn't it? I mean, he was tipsy when he left us. Do you think the papers were right? They do say there's no smoke without fire. Maybe he really has come here to chat up Amanda. He'd make quite a sexy Lord of the Manor. And they would look good together, wouldn't they?'

'Hmm.' Pip pondered the thought; Lottie had actually got a point. 'But,' she paused, 'he did get here just *before* old Marcus kicked the bucket, didn't he? Nope, I'm not sure. He doesn't seem to be after her, but Elizabeth seems to think he's up to something.'

'Gran? What's she been up to now?' Lottie sounded resigned. Elizabeth didn't need a fire to create a smokescreen; she was more than capable of summoning one out of thin air. 'She doesn't even know Tom; she's only met him once.' But thinking about it, she'd gone out of her way to talk to him at the hunt, which, at the time, Lottie had just put down to general nosiness. 'And she hardly knows Amanda really – she never did approve of her and Marcus being in Folly Lake Manor. She said Marcus had got less taste than she had in her little fingernail, and how he got Amanda was a complete mystery. But I can see Amanda and Tom together, though, can't you?' Lottie had a dreamy look on her face as she watched Rory battle on with dignity. 'They're both so glam, but so sad.'

'Tom isn't sad.'

'He is. He always looks like he needs a good hug.'

'You'd need a hug if you had to go home to Tabby kitten every night.'

Lottie laughed. 'I thought you were the one who said she was okay? Just a teenager, you said, when you were trying to persuade me to give her riding lessons. Maybe she needs rubber or nylon?'

An image of Tabatha in a rubber onesie was the last thing Pip wanted in her head right now. 'I'd keep your fetishes to yourself, Lottie. Tom already thinks you're a bit strange.'

'Does he?'

'Well I don't know why you've got that innocent, hurt look on your face. You swig his champagne, promise him attention, then forget you said you'd meet him, and I daren't imagine what else you've said to him.'

'I did not promise him anything.' Genuine indignation filled Lottie. 'Like what? And what do you mean, fetishes? I haven't got any fetishes.' Lottie had now caught up on everything Pip had said, and was hit by a familiar feeling of confusion. 'Have I?' She couldn't think for the life of her what Pip was on about. Okay, she did like it when Rory wanted to slap her on the bum, but that wasn't a fetish, was it? And how did Pip know, if it was? 'Who's been saying things?' She bit the inside of her cheek. 'And what did they say?'

'You just said it. How can you suggest Tab is wrapped in rubber or nylon and think that's normal conversation?'

'Did I?' She pulled a face. 'I didn't. Rubber. Why would I wrap Tab in rubber?' Now she was totally perplexed, enough to ignore the fact that Flash was heading for them at a hundred miles an hour with a grim-looking Rory seriously considering a bail-out before he did indeed lose his balls, along with other parts of his anatomy.

'You just said,' Pip took a hasty step back, 'she needs rubber or nylon.'

Lottie giggled, then put a hand over her mouth, and giggled a bit louder, just as Flash reached them and put a smart 180-degree turn in that showered them with rubber and made Pip go pale. 'I was talking about Flash, her bit, you know? I think she's fighting her bit, and if it's softer she might stop, but Rory's too much of a wuss to try a bitless bridle, aren't you?' Despite the horse's antics, Rory managed to flash the V's and Lottie gave a broad grin. 'I think black leather is more Tabatha's style really, don't you? Does he really think I'm weird?'

'I think he fancies you, actually.'

'Bollocks.'

'He lusts after your fit body.'

'And who can blame a man for that?' Mick, with his broad forearms, was disturbingly close, which made the already shocked Lottie even more flustered about which way to turn.

'Pip!'

'And you confuse him.' Pip shot Mick the type of look that was designed to silence him, and got a wink in return, which she ignored. 'He thinks he wants a life in the country, but it scares him. All those rough men and tough women and scary, dirty horses.'

'And who would want to settle for a man running scared eh, Pip?' The pointed remark in her direction caught Pip off guard, just for a second.

'Can't we have a private conversation just for once, without a man butting in?'

'Maybe,' he leant in closer to the two of them, humour lacing his voice, 'if you weren't standing in the middle of the yard it would help.' The warmth of his hand in the small of her back sent an unfamiliar sensation through Lottie's body; one that wasn't particularly unwelcome. He made her feel on edge, and from the look on Pip's face it wasn't just her.

'Maybe if you were shoeing horses it wouldn't be a problem.' Now that was an interesting one, thought Lottie, Pip rattled. She didn't often get sarcastic and irritated, but she was now.

'Oh you've got a sharp tongue in that head of yours, treasure.' Mick gave an easy laugh and put a finger under her chin. 'It will get you into trouble one day, I'd say. But it was the fit body of Lottie I was after. When that horse has finished her job and dumped him, will you tell the man I need a word, darling?'

He chuckled and, with a broad grin, left them to it.

'That man is so fucking annoying.' Pip was bristling like a cross cat; his comment about Tom had annoyed her. What damned business was it of his if she'd spent time with Tom? And how did he know anyway, or was it just a good guess?

'Hmm, I suppose he is, but he's sexy isn't he? You really reckon I confuse him, Tom, that is?' Lottie frowned. 'And he's scared? How

133

can anyone be scared in Tippermere? You've come over very philosophical.' She didn't think she was capable of confusing anyone but herself, but Pip in her current frame of mind was interesting.

Pip dragged herself back from thoughts of Mick to concentrate on Lottie and the conversation they were supposed to be having. 'You don't think it's scary because you belong here. You came back, because you couldn't not. It's a part of you.'

'Rubbish. I just ran out of money and Todd pissed me off. I never said I was coming back for good.'

'True, you didn't.' Pip's tone was dry. 'But Tom's the same. He's here for a reason, and I want to know why. And so does he.'

'You're being weird.'

'I know. But, trust me, there's more to that pretty boy than meets the eye.'

'You're beginning to sound like Gran.'

Pip just smiled.

'So, do you think it was Amanda he was with last night?'

'No, I was.' Which wasn't a lie, and Lottie could take it how she wanted. She was with Amanda, she was with Tom. It was a good job Mick had taken the hint and gone.

'And she didn't admit she knew him? I mean, how can they expect us to believe them when that photo has been in the paper. Even if goth girl does say it's a set-up. Oops.' Lottie's attention was back on Rory, as he did a spectacularly gymnastic, and decidedly unplanned, dismount.

I told you it wouldn't work, was on the tip of Lottie's tongue, but she very wisely bit it back because the look on his face suggested he wouldn't take it well. His latest strategy was to try and take the edge off Flash by a good long lunging session, before climbing on board to practise his dressage moves. It wasn't working. If anything, she was using it as a limbering-up session so that she could be more athletic once he got in the saddle.

'Maybe she's agoraphobic.'

'Maybe she's taking the piss.' Rory was staring at the horse, who was looking back unconcerned.

Pip sighed. Bloody horses, even she knew the comment had to be about the horse, not Amanda or Tab. Lottie could be such a catch if she spent more time on manicures and less time on mucking out. And Rory, well Rory had a body that she reckoned a good ninety per cent of the female population who were above the age of consent would be quite happy to use and abuse, and he was fun. And he was mad about Lottie. Even if she didn't realise it yet. They were in denial, Pip decided.

'I think she needs Dom.'

'Who, Tab? You're probably right, a firm hand would sort her.'

Lottie gave a dirty laugh, which made Rory, even in his mad state, perk up and grin. 'No, I mean Flash, silly. And I meant Uncle Dom, not a dom.'

'I think.' Rory reached them in two easy strides and leant on the rail, brushing fragments of the arena off his breeches. 'You can do whatever you want with her.' He leaned forward to kiss Lottie on the cheek. 'And that goes for the charming Tabatha and the lethal Flash. Then you can rub arnica into my bruised bits, darling Lots. Do you want to help, Pip?'

'No, I don't. It's my day off.'

'But this is pleasure not business.'

'For you, maybe. I'm sure Lottie will rub whatever you want, though. I've mucked out the stables, so is that it?'

'If you're going to be a prude, I suppose it is.'

'I am. Right, I'm off to do some research.' She winked.

This left Lottie with more questions than answers, and Rory trying to decide whether throwing his girlfriend over his shoulder and marching to his bedroom was acceptable in this day and age.

'Don't look at me like that?' Lottie was grinning, even as she was warning him off. 'Mick wants to see you.'

'I don't care,' Rory vaulted over the rails, 'what Mick wants. Come here, and give me what I want, wench.'

Lottie squealed and made a run for it, Rory in hot pursuit,

forgetting the niggle of annoyance that had filled him when he'd seen his farrier friend with a hand on Lottie's waist moments earlier. If he'd not lost his concentration he wouldn't have been thrown off. But every cloud, as they said. He made a lunge, caught her leg with one hand as he fell, taking her with him. 'Now, let's see what a firm hand does for you, shall we?'

Chapter 11

'*England's safe hands to scupper model's best shot?*'

Elizabeth read the headlines then folded the newspaper neatly. 'Clever girl, another gin?' If there was one thing she liked it was a clever brain, another she liked even more was a mischief-maker. And the picture was a classic: Amanda flanked by the imposing figure of the England goalkeeper on one side and the immaculate Armani underwear model, Tom, on the other. 'And how did you do that, dear?'

Pip smiled; she was actually quite pleased with herself for orchestrating the photo shoot.

'How about you tell me what you know about Tom first?' She poured them both a generous slug of gin, added a splash of tonic, just to be polite, and sat down.

Elizabeth gave her the gimlet stare, and then her wrinkled face suddenly broke into a grin that threatened to crack it open. 'You are a wicked girl.'

'You're worse.'

'Thomas, ah, the gorgeous Thomas.' Elizabeth took a sip of the drink, found it exactly how she liked it and took a proper mouthful before tipping her head and holding the picture at arm's length so that she could see it better. 'What do you know about him?'

Pip shrugged. 'Only the normal. Successful model, grasping

wife, broken heart.' Sexy body, pretty good stamina and a hangdog look and floppy fringe that could break a softer heart, she could have added, but wisely didn't.

'But before that?'

'Well.' She sat back and filtered the few facts she did know through her brain again, just in case sifting through uncovered something new and more interesting. The devil is in the detail, didn't they say? But in this case, she was obviously missing something, or hadn't joined all the dots together in the right way. 'I do know he's from a rich family, his father was a banker, but it's hard to find out more, and believe me I've tried. Tom never tells anyone anything, and I mean anything.' Even when his legs are tangled around yours.

'The more money you have, the deeper you can bury the facts. You're right though, his father was a banker.'

Pip waited. She'd suspected for a long time that Elizabeth knew more than she'd volunteered.

'He was rich, seriously rich. A very nice, well-educated man with an impeccable background.' She gave a heavy, resigned sigh. 'But unfortunately he got greedy. There was a scandal and some kind of boring crash.' She waved a hand dismissively, but Pip wasn't falling for it. Elizabeth might play the female fool, but she wasn't. Being bored with the facts was an act. Pip was pretty sure she knew every single one and had interrogated each within an inch of its life, and knew to the nearest pound how much the Strachan's had lost and how closely they'd judged escape. 'He had to sell the family estate and move, to Australia I think.' The corner of her mouth quirked into the semblance of a smile, and she took another sip of her drink. 'Appropriate. Took his wife and family and disappeared down-under until the feathers stopped flying. Not a very original escape, but then the man was a mathematician, so I suppose it's what you would expect.'

'And?'

'And?' Elizabeth looked innocent as she drained her glass. 'Olives would have been nice.'

'The point?' Pip went over to the cabinet and rescued a bowl that looked like it had been served more than once. It could have been herbs or dust that decorated the dull green surface, she wasn't sure.

'Some people might call you rude, dear.'

'Oh come on, spill.'

'The family home that they had to sell, when Thomas was still in nappies—'

'Was Folly Lake Manor?' Pip uttered the words just to fill the gap. She didn't mean it; a preposterous idea.

'I knew you'd work it out in the end, dear.'

Pip blindly reached for the gin bottle and sloshed another generous measure into both their glasses while it sunk in. Wow, this was better than she could have imagined. 'Christ, he's got the hots for the place not the grieving widow. Hasn't he?' She glanced at Elizabeth. 'So he does want it, he wants it back doesn't he? And you knew all along.'

'I'm not sure. He was born here, but I'm not sure he knows.'

'Don't be daft, he must.'

'He was a baby when it happened. And they hid everything well; some people can be discreet, my dear. My guess is that he knows it was this area, but not this house.'

'Some coincidence.'

Elizabeth reached for the tonic bottle, which was unheard of. 'I'm not sure. His father kept things close to his chest, so I do think it could be coincidence. Although I'm sure his mother would have loved to see him here.' She paused to ponder, then her normal decisive tone returned. 'But if young Thomas doesn't know, he will do when this news filters through to his parents, and that could be interesting. Ever been on the wrong end of a gagging order, dear?'

'You've done this on purpose!' Pip tried to digest the news, and failed. Tom had never given a single indication that he was seriously after this place. The article had been a bit of fun, encouraged by Elizabeth, to stir things up. But thinking back, he was interested in the bloody place, and it was more than casual. One mention and he'd perked up, and she'd been daft enough to think it was Amanda who was the lure. In fact, any mention of Folly Lake Manor made his metaphorical ears prick up. Which was how she'd persuaded him to go to Amanda's and meet David and Sam. But she'd never for a moment thought his main interest was the house, she'd just assumed it was the glamorous and restrained Amanda. Model fodder. Just the type of woman that appealed to a man like him. But this changed things.

'Oh, Philippa,' Elizabeth smiled, '*I* have not done anything.'

Pip grimaced and tried to work out if she was being manipulated by the old dragon or not. And why? The first article to hit the headlines, with Amanda and Tom, had been spontaneous, and irresistible. And she hadn't actually been responsible for it. But the latest one, with David and Tom in the frame, had been carefully judged and was all her own work, it was a lead-in to the double-page spread, complete with puppy picture, which her editor had been gagging for. Once she got Tom to give up a frigging precious puppy. 'So, you reckon he wants to buy the place?'

'I think he's drawn to it, but he doesn't know why yet.' She patted a dog, which Pip took to be Holmes given the way he rolled over and showed his ample belly absentmindedly. Bertie was above that kind of thing. Or was it the other way round? 'I'm sure he's getting there, though.'

'You're up to something, aren't you Elizabeth?'

'Nonsense. What on earth could I be up to?'

But she was, Pip knew. There was more to this than met the eye. She was stirring for a reason, she never did anything without a reason, but Pip just had to find out what.

'Hmm, I'm not sure, but you are, you terrible woman. Why would you want him back?'

The older woman laughed. 'Now, who said I wanted him back, Philippa?' It wasn't often anyone dared to call her terrible. Most of her family were boring, sadly. Apart from the irascible Lottie and her beautiful, and totally unsuitable, suitor Rory. It took Elizabeth back, when she watched them, to the days when William had dated Alexa. Two comets on a collision course. A repeat performance would be too sad for her to bear. But although she interfered at a superficial level, she was too wise to try and alter the course of destiny. They'd find out, they'd learn, with or without her. Tippermere, Tipping House, was her life. But without Charles and the children it meant little. Apart from a legacy. To pass on when the time was right. When things had been sorted.

'Well, if you don't want him back, you want someone else to think he is. Don't think I'm not going to find out.'

'I don't doubt it for one minute.'

Pip had spoken the words without really thinking about it, but Elizabeth's response pulled her up short.

'And now you, dear girl, have made Thomas the filling in rather an interesting sandwich.' Which hadn't been Pip's intention, she didn't know there was another layer to this particular story. 'So, your premiership footballer is interested in building a property portfolio, is he? Because he certainly isn't interested in that woman.'

'Nope, he's not after Amanda.' Pip grinned. The message that the nation might have taken could, given the headline of the previous week, have been that the prize was the grieving widow. But headlines were known to mislead. 'He's madly in love with a stunning Essex girl, but, you will like this bit, his father is a property developer.'

'Poor boy.'

Pip presumed the reference was to Tom, but who knew with Elizabeth? 'Poor girl don't you mean? Look at her.' She picked up the discarded newspaper. 'She's loaded, glamorous and lovely, that shot should be every woman's dream, except the truth of it is that one of them is obsessed with another woman, and the other is… well Lottie reckons he's sad and lonely. Well, she reckons they both are.'

'She might have a point. What do you think?'

'I think he's desperately trying to find the meaning of life.'

'But aren't we all, dear? That's a given, but it's what he thinks he's after in the meantime that is the interesting part.'

'I don't think either of them is after a relationship, to be honest.'

'Really?' Elizabeth raised an enquiring eyebrow, which Pip missed altogether, so intent was she on trying to work out in her head what Tom really did want.

'Oh well, I better get off and see a man about a dog. Again.' Pip grimaced. 'I'm going to sort this bloody photo opportunity if it kills me.' She grabbed an olive and counted her blessings that Elizabeth worshipped the blue bottle and forsook anything that required more than a quick chew before digestion. Then wondered if it was wise when the herbs tasted more potpourri than anything remotely related to an edible plant. Spitting them out would have been rude; she tried to push the bits to one side and hoped she didn't accidentally swallow any more. 'And then, when I've let this particular pussy out amongst the pigeons, we'll see who breaks cover.'

'You're mixing metaphors, my dear. Be a darling and top my drink up on the way out, and Pippa?'

'Yes?' Pip shot her a look of suspicion.

Elizabeth winked. 'Don't forget to send me an update on your cats and dogs, and feel free to spit the olive out. We don't want you choking, do we dear?'

As Pip had so accurately guessed, Elizabeth did have an ulterior motive behind her meddling. And it involved protecting her future. Her children's future. But with Philippa's help it was developing into a much more interesting situation than she could have envisaged. With the property-developing Simcocks on one side, and an immovable object on the other, who knew what direction poor, uncomprehending Tom would decide to head in? Her primary concern, though, had to lie with her own interests, and interfering with the future of Folly Lake Manor was something she would only do if it proved necessary.

'We don't, do we? Who would help you with your schemes if I did?' There was no rancour behind the comment, though, Pip loved Elizabeth almost as much as she'd ever loved anyone. They had a bond, a shared inquisitive side to their nature, a yearning for facts, coupled with a desire for mischief and a way to lighten a boring life. Her mother had never understood her need to disrupt, but Elizabeth did. Never unkindly, the aim was not to hurt, just to make life more interesting.

Pip's idea had been to force Tom into showing his hand. To settle the future of Tippermere once and for all. But she was sure that Elizabeth had some ulterior motive. Why on earth would the Stanthorpes have any interest in what happened at Folly Lake? True, they wouldn't want any riff raff and unsightly developments scarring the landscape of their ancestors. But it was more than that, Pip was sure. And Pip's instincts very rarely let her down.

***

It wasn't a puppy. It was a leggy mutt of a dog with a black patch over one eye, one ear that stuck up and one that flopped down, and an alarming tendency to start scratching at odd intervals, and at such odd angles that it occasionally led to a confusion of legs and a collapse, which to Pip spelled out a bad case of fleas or ringworm, and an IQ that wouldn't challenge a hamster. But Sam was entranced.

'Oh. My. God. He's adorable.'

Pip smiled encouragingly. He was a rag tag bag of bones from where she was sitting.

'Look at those cutesy ears, and he's smiling at me.'

About to be sick, I'd say. 'He loves you already.'

'Can I really have him?'

Tricky one. From what Pip could remember, the brief spiel from Tom involved words to the effect of 'you can take photos but that's it, nobody is taking a dog home until background checks

143

have been done'. It sounded to her like they were lining up the Spanish Inquisition, not trying to find a waif and stray a new home with as many Bonios to eat and trees to wee on as its little heart could desire.

'See how you get on. I mean Tom has lots of dogs to choose from.'

'But he's gorge.'

Pip smiled what she hoped was the winning smile and nodded at the photographer. The little soirée with Tom, Amanda and the Simcocks had been awkward. Even if she had managed to get a photo that made them look like they were heading for a lifelong membership of admiration club capital. Who said the camera didn't lie? But Tom had been more than insistent that nobody, and he meant nobody, could just walk off with one of his rescue cases.

Maybe asking David about his father and just what he'd do with Folly Lake Manor if he got his hands on it wasn't exactly diplomatic. But, at the time, how was she supposed to know that Tom had his own eye firmly fixed on the prize? She'd thought the Strachan prize involved Mandy, not her mansion. The only good thing was that the man himself was involved in another photo shoot today, which meant he was a few hundred miles away and couldn't ruin things.

'He is, erm gorge. If we take some pics, though, is it okay if we just say you were here looking for the right one to adopt, you know, not exactly say this is the one, or,' think fast Pip, 'everyone will want him. His old owners might even suddenly come back when they realise just how lovely he is.'

'Oh, I see what you mean, babe.' Sam's face had dropped.

'Just between us, of course.'

'Sure.' It lifted again, the golden smile breaking out as she gave Pip a hug. The 'gorge' pooch, sandwiched between two female forms, did what dogs do when they're trapped in a desperate situation.

'Oh, shit.' Except it wasn't. Pip pulled back as the warm glow of satisfaction turned to a warm patch of damp.

'Ah, the poor little thing's piddled.'

The dog wriggled, sensing freedom, a fresh spray arcing out as Pip jumped back, desperate to get out of range. Sam hung on, behind the line of fire, her mouth open in astonishment as the fountain slowly lost its force and spluttered down to a dribble.

The girl, who Tom had said was in charge, looked on in disapproving silence, finally cracking under Pip's stare. 'Shall I take him off you?'

'Bit late now, unless he's got a reserve tank.'

Sam giggled. 'He can hold his drink just like Davey, by the looks of him.'

This made Pip blanch. No, she wasn't going to ask if squeezing him had the same effect. He was a footballing hero, he went out onto the green pitch and fought for his country. Imagining him peeing his way between the goalposts wasn't part of the equation.

'I'll make a point of not hugging him too hard, then.'

Sam laughed properly then, and juggled the dog into a firmer hold. 'Do you think we could smuggle him out? Tom would never know, would he?' She looked at the kennel maid with wide eyes, then back to Pip with a secret smile. 'We could make a very generous donation, you know, just to help feed all the others.'

'Photo first.' Pip waved firmly in the photographer's direction. 'Do your stuff, Jon, and stay out of his range of fire, just in case.'

The dog's tank was obviously empty, because the rest of the afternoon was dry in every sense. And looking through the photos, Pip had to agree with Sam that the dog looked adorable. Even better from the other side of the room. In fact, Sam and her canine friend looked like they were in love; two shaggy-haired cohorts who'd finally met their perfect partner. It was just a shame that David had ruled himself out of the session by claiming his physio was more important.

'No.' The kennel maid was adamant. She might have been slightly star-struck, but was still pretty disapproving and determined.

'Nobody need know. I can smuggle him out in my bag.'

Pip shot a glance at the large handbag at exactly the same time the kennel maid did. 'It's not big enough.' Almost in unison.

'But they don't need to know that; you can just say that's what happened. He disappeared.'

'I'd get the sack if I started losing dogs.'

'Can't you ring Tom, Pip? You can persuade him, I'm sure you can. The way he looks at you I bet you could get him to do anything.' Pip wasn't too sure about that. Anything might have been on the agenda when he was pissed and stripped of his faculties and his pants, but stone-cold sober Tom could be surprisingly resolute when it came to his pet project. But... she smiled. His partner, the politician's mother, she suspected, might be a different kettle of fish altogether if it came with a promise to give her son some much-needed local election support.

'Give me five minutes. And whatever you do, don't let that animal near a bowl of water.'

***

'Do you think you'll ever get married?'

They were sitting in the front of Sam's four-by-four, with the dog, named with outstanding originality 'Scruffy', sitting between them as they swung onto the motorway. 'Swing' being exactly the wrong motion as the dog slid along the leather seat towards Pip and heaved alarmingly.

'Shit, stop the car, he's going to be sick.'

'I can't babe, I'm on the motorway. Can't you give him a sick bag or something, there's one in the glove compartment.'

'You keep sick bags in the car? You never said your driving was that bad.'

'Carrier bags.' Sam laughed as the dog retched again and slid slowly back the other way.

'Bugger, he's coming my way.' Pip made a dive of her own

towards the glove compartment. The only bag she could see was decidedly green all right, and not in an eco-friendly sense, more in a Harrods sense. 'I can't, I just can't.' But then she discovered she could, as the dog gave a more serious heave, its back arching as it wobbled between them. There was a lot to be said, Pip thought, for crates on the back seat rather than pampered pooches loose on the front. There was also a lot to be said for decent air-conditioning, which after she'd opened the window briefly and nearly blasted her and the dog out into the slipstream, Sam had switched on and shut the fresh air out.

'He's so sweet. You're so clever finding him.'

Pip was pretty sure she'd be more convinced once she was out of range. 'I'll get to know him better when you've found out how to stop him recycling so efficiently.'

'Dave will love him.'

Which reminded her. 'I think it's you he loves, not a dog. So, have you thought about getting hitched?' Fiancée would look so much better in the article, and besides she was curious. Sam didn't even wear an engagement ring, yet the pair were obviously besotted with each other, even to Pip's cynical eye.

'Me?'

'Yes, you and David. You've been going out a while now, haven't you?' Pip hung onto the door as Sam peeled off the motorway and hit the roundabout at a speed that left her and the dog colliding. He looked at her with doleful eyes, as though deeply apologetic but seriously seasick. She could sympathise.

'Yeah, years. We knew each other before anyone had even heard of Davey. Well, his club had, but you know he hadn't been signed big or anything.'

'So, come on, you must want to? Don't you? It is serious, I mean I can tell that just looking at the two of you.'

Sam stroked the dog's woolly head, pulled at his ears thoughtfully. Perfectly manicured fingernails teasing at the silky coat. Scruffy shifted and tried to scratch her away with one hind leg and promptly fell off the seat and into the foot well. Maybe they were made for each other.

Pip hauled him out and hoped it was just a nervous twitch.

'This is off the record, right? I mean, I'm sure you wouldn't say anything to anyone, you're just so lovely.' Sam pulled off the main road, drove in silence down the long lane until finally coming to a halt outside the large gates. The engine ticked over as the gates slowly opened.

'If you want, I'm fine with off the record.' Pip shrugged. She liked Sam, and she liked David. And she wanted the real interview, the one with his manager, even more than she wanted to be friends with them. And she felt decidedly safer now they were driving slowly up the driveway and had stopped by her moped.

'Well, we are.'

Sam was out of the car, dog deposited on the gravel before Pip had even opened her door. 'You?' She let the words do a few laps of her brain, just to make sure. 'You are? As in, you're married? To each other?'

Sam laughed 'Of course to each other, who else would we be married to? We got hitched ages ago, when we were on holiday, but you know how it is.'

Pip wasn't sure she did know how it was. 'Do I?'

'We got paid not to be married, you know, until we could have a big exclusive wedding; it's going to be filmed and everything. The full works, and they're sending us to this private island that's owned by what's his face, you know, that Virgin bloke. Don't say a word will you, babe? Please? Dave will be so cross if he finds out I told someone. This is just so exciting, I can't wait to show him.'

Show him? For a moment Pip was confused, then realised. It was the dog that was exciting. After all, who would be excited by a fairy-tale wedding and being whizzed off to a private island?

'That moped is seriously cool. Maybe I should get one.'

Pip offered up a silent prayer. Sam let loose on anything two-wheeled didn't bear thinking about. 'You'd have trouble getting

Scruffy on it.'

'Lunch tomorrow, then? At the wine bar. And you can tell me all about Amanda. She's sweet. I think she needs cheering up and I've got just the thing.'

Chapter 12

'Gross, isn't it?'

'Sorry?' Lottie felt herself go red and regretted the way she'd been staring at the car. The fact that Tab had noticed was bad; the fact that she'd voiced the exact words that had been in her head was worse. 'Well I—'

'Yellow is so naff. I mean, there is a reason you can't normally buy them in that colour. It isn't standard.'

'He had it ordered specially?' And she'd just kind of assumed a man like Tom would at least have some taste.

'No, stupid. He bought it for Mum as a surprise. He ordered it in black, but no one can keep a surprise from her. She opened the order and rang them up and told them they'd made a mistake, and that if they couldn't do it in the colour she wanted she'd cancel the order. She likes to be noticed.'

'Red gets noticed.'

'Red is even more naff.' Ah well, that told her. 'I think he's only driving it to piss her off.'

'No he's not.' Tom appeared from wherever he'd been, which Lottie suspected was just having a nosey around the grounds, just in time to catch his daughter out. This seemed to amuse him, considering he was quite good at it, but didn't seem to bother her at all. 'He's driving it because the other car is in for repair.

Or had you forgotten?'

'It's been in for ages.'

'That's what happens when your teenage daughter tries to teach herself to drive and exits through the wall, not the open doorway.'

'Funny.'

'Not really. Go ahead, don't mind me.'

Lottie studied Tab, who was sitting astride her horse, and thought how unfair it was that riding came as naturally to some people as walking. Even though, with a dad like Billy, it should have been in her genes, she'd had to work bloody hard to turn herself into any kind of decent rider.

Not that many people who knew her would agree with her self-assessment; as Dom and many others had observed, the only thing that was holding Lottie back was Lottie herself. She was harder on herself than anyone else ever was, took every criticism to heart, and yet her natural empathy with a horse was an asset that many riders would have killed for. She might not be the most skilled, but her instinct to read her ride would never let her down, as long as she listened to it and believed in it. But right now it was her empathy with another rider that was at the fore.

'Can't you go away, Dad? Please? You upset Merlin. You know he doesn't like you.' The normal acerbic tone that Tab adopted as second nature was laced with uncertainty. Lottie widened her eyes and tilted her head in a way that was supposed to suggest 'bugger off', but Tom just smiled in his lazy way and winked. She flicked a hand in a 'go away' gesture and he sat down. She'd more or less exhausted her repertoire of discreet hints. Short of the direct 'piss off', she wasn't sure what came next.

Unfortunately, Tom hadn't seen Lottie for days, and now he had the opportunity, he just wanted to sit and lust over her body and imagine what life would be like if he was ten years younger. And at least he was safe here; Lottie seemed straightforward, uncomplicated and fun – unlike most of the residents in Tippermere. He had a horrible feeling that he was the main source of entertainment, well, secondary to the horses, of course.

It wasn't that he regretted his tangle in the sheets with Pip; she was clever, funny and sexy, with a guaranteed no-strings-attached label, and she'd been as skilful in bed as he suspected she was in everything. But she seemed determined to stir him up and turn his planned semi-retirement in the country into something completely different.

He sat back on the bench, ankles crossed, as the riding lesson started and, for a moment, forgot all about ogling Lottie. It wasn't just Lottie, it was this place, here, that had a pull on him. And he wasn't just safe from Pip here, he felt safe from everything.

'Hi, mind if I sit down?'

Okay, he was deluded. Amanda was looking at him pensively, and he hadn't the heart to tell her to go away. She was sweet, pretty and easy company. She was also prime gossip fodder. He shifted nervously then decided he was being stupid. He was a grown man; he could talk to who the hell he wanted.

'Sure. But my daughter will blow us away if we make a noise.'

'I just want to watch.' It was a whisper and she sat down a polite distance away on the bench. 'They scare me a bit, to be honest.' It had taken the best part of an hour for Amanda to talk herself into coming down here. She'd used the excuse that it was to chat to the easy-going Tom, but it wasn't that. She could do that anytime. No, the real reason for being here was far more intimidating, and right now she was starting to feel jittery. She could kill a stiff drink.

Tom smiled. She didn't need to be honest – it was written all over her face, and the way she flinched every time the horse got within ten yards. 'Is it the horses that scare you, or Lottie and Tabatha?'

She smiled and relaxed a tiny bit. He was nice, much nicer than Pip had suggested. But then again, Pip was a complex person and the way she'd talked about Tom had suggested she knew him in a far more intimate way than she was admitting to. But Amanda had instantly warmed to him when Pip had invited him along with her new footballer friend. His whispered asides had made her feel included, and he'd been genuinely interested in her and Folly Lake Manor. He'd even been asking about the changes that Marcus had made and, on impulse, she'd asked him back to look through the photographs she'd taken when they'd first bought the place. She didn't, Amanda thought with a slight pang of regret, fancy him. She just wanted him there, like a comforting old jumper. It was a long time since she'd had anything that remotely resembled a jumper, or old. Apart from Marcus. 'Both scare me. Do you like horses?'

'Not really. I'm just the one who pays.' Lottie had brought Merlin to a stand and was messing about with his tack, her wonderfully toned bottom, covered in a skin-tight layer of material, only a few feet away. It was making it hard for Tom to concentrate when all he could imagine was nakedness.

'She's nice, isn't she?' Amanda was just trying to sound interested, when in fact she felt more like being sick and doing a runner. And, on closer inspection, the massive horse seemed to be more of a he than a she, but Tom didn't seem concerned.

'Very.'

Maybe he was confused as well. Although you would think he'd know the sex of his own horse, unless he was just too polite to correct her. But, right now, the horse seemed intent on displaying more and more evidence of his manliness. She was just mulling over whether to point it out and possibly display her ignorance (or highlight his), or look away, when she was almost catapulted off the bench.

'Not bad for a kid.' Amanda gripped the wood, and Tom bounced a couple of inches in the air as Billy plonked his substantial form on the other end of the narrow seat, which was a complete killer for Tom in the fantasising-about-Lottie stakes, and for Amanda in wondering about how to sex a horse. Billy's ginger curls were directed towards Tab. 'Could be a half-decent rider if she stuck with it.'

Tom stared at him. 'Really?'

'Not that kids stick with anything these days. Bloody lazy, the

153

lot of them.' He raised his voice from loud to bellowing. 'Relax your bloody knees, girl, you're not trying to squeeze him to death, then maybe you'll stop bouncing like you're on a trampoline.' Tab deepened to a darker shade of crimson beneath her hat, if that was possible. Her face had already been a good colour from her exertions, as the over-fresh Merlin, excited to be in new surroundings, was doing his best to prove he was in charge. Tom bit his tongue or his daughter would disown him, and Amanda stared down at her clasped hands in embarrassment.

'Stop interfering, Dad.' Lottie knew that whatever she said it wouldn't make the slightest bit of difference. What Billy thought, Billy said.

'I'm only trying to help, love.'

Lottie had one hand planted firmly on her hip, the other grasped around the handle of a lunge whip, which it looked like she was planning on putting to a new use. Merlin took the opportunity to throw in a sly buck, followed by a scrape along the school wall.

He was, Lottie decided, acting like an escaped convict raiding a retirement home, taking every chance he could, with no thought of the consequences. It would have been nice to join him. She'd had a pony like him, once, years ago. He'd use every low branch, every gable, every fence and hedge as an implement to try and dislodge her, and then he'd use his superior strength to either tank off in a direction he chose, or more likely he'd yank the reins out of her hands and put his head down to graze. And no amount of kicking or tugging would make the slightest difference.

Tab was actually doing a good job, and right now her father, Billy, was being the proverbial pain in the arse. 'Haven't you all got something else to do?'

'Well actually…'

She felt instantly guilty as Amanda stood up awkwardly. Amanda was the least of her worries, though what the hell she was doing there, looking like she was visiting an alien planet, she wasn't sure.

'I just wanted to ask you something, Charlotte, but it doesn't matter if you're too busy…'

'No probs.' Lottie was intrigued; it looked like it did matter to Amanda. This was a strange one. what on earth would the woman want to ask her, Lottie?

'Well, if you don't mind, it's just.' It had taken her over an hour to build up the confidence; she couldn't bottle now. The problem was, everything she'd ever faced up to in the past, she'd wanted to. It had been part of her master plan. But this was more important. This was because she wanted to, for someone else. This wasn't just about her, and her bloody life plan. It mattered.

She took a tentative step towards the barrier, then stepped back as Merlin headed with the determination of a tank in her direction. Lottie, acting like he wasn't doing anything untoward at all, set off up the school, away from the horse, and the eaves-dropping Billy and Tom. 'It's just,' Amanda's normally reserved tone dropped lower, which was tricky considering she'd had to scurry to keep up with the long athletic stride of Lottie and was now finding it hard to breathe normally, 'I mean, it's probably too much trouble, you're busy.'

'Go on.' Lottie leant in closer, intrigued, and Amanda whispered her request haltingly.

'Well, er, sure.' It wasn't what Lottie had been expecting at all. 'I'll have a thi—' But she never did get to think about it, let alone finish the sentence.

'Mer-lin.' Tabatha's cry was half anger and half frustration as Merlin flew past at a speed that belied his size, then threw in an emergency stop and ducked his head between his knees with perfect timing, depositing Tab in a neat ball on the floor in front of him and pretty much slap-bang in front of Lottie and the shocked Amanda. He lifted his head and actually, Amanda thought, looked quite pleased with himself.

Lottie tried not to grin; Tabby kitten fitted her perfectly, a spit-ting ball that the men would soon be queuing up to cuddle and try and cajole a purr out of. 'You are just so out of order, you great oaf.' The great oaf looked around, planning his escape to pastures new and green with grass.

As Lottie turned to help, Amanda scurried off, leaving the men staring speculatively after her. 'I'll lunge you.' She gave Tab a leg up into the saddle.

'Aren't you supposed to check she's okay?' Tom looked worried and wondered, not for the first time, if this really was a good idea. 'Tab, are you?'

'Shut up, Dad' and 'Shut up, Tom' were shouted in perfect unison.

The problem was that when Lottie clipped the lunge rein and went to pick up the whip, the clever Merlin knew exactly what was coming. He also knew she was concentrating more on what Amanda had just said to her than she was on him. He took off, at a headlong gallop, straining against the lunge rope with Lottie hanging on at one end in the centre and swearing. Tab hung on for dear life during her wall-of-death ride, trying desperately to gather back the reins that he'd yanked out of her hands. Tom would have liked to have been able to shut his eyes, but he couldn't.

'I'm getting dizzy.' The wail drifted behind Tab, and Tom could sympathise with his daughter wholeheartedly for once. He was getting bloody dizzy too. Merlin kept his head down, arched his back and put in a buck as he debated whether to charge Lottie or change direction.

'Bloody amateurs. Come on, let's leave them to it.' Billy shook his head sadly as he motioned to Tom to follow him, totally unfazed by the goings-on, and Tom was torn. Was he better staying and supporting his daughter, or was it wiser to be ignorant of the whole situation? Given that he was the only one that seemed shocked, ignorance might well be bliss.

'She's a bit of alright that Amanda, isn't she? Her husband was a tosser.' Billy kept to himself the thought that Amanda had made her way down to the yard to eye up Tom. After all, why else would she be here? In the past, she'd only ever set foot down here when she'd been looking for Marcus. She had, in a roundabout way, asked him about riding lessons after the funeral, and at first he'd not been sure if she was being coy and it was some kind of obtuse chat-up line. And then he'd realised she meant it. But if she wanted someone to act as chaperone while she wheedled her way into Tom's life, then she was asking the wrong man.

Billy watched the rapidly retreating figure. She was fanciable in a posh, perfect kind of way, but he preferred his women more down-to-earth. Which, he suspected, Marcus had as well, given the rumours that had been flying about. And the giggling from the tack room. The good thing about grooms, as opposed to women like Amanda, as far as he was concerned, was that they were like cushions. Comfy, plump and forgiving. All you had to do after a pummelling was cuddle them back into shape. And they usually did have a shape, and a heart. Alexa had been different to the rest of them. She'd had it all. The breeding and the manners, but also the body, the brain and the warmth and wickedness of a real woman. Unlike, he suspected, Amanda. That girl seemed as brittle and likely to break as one of the antiques that had been artistically arranged around her home. Look but don't touch. He shot a glance at the immaculate Tom. Now a woman like Amanda would appeal to him, he reckoned.

Tom just shrugged and didn't comment.

'So you're not saying you don't fancy her?'

'She seems lovely, but I'm really not here to get involved with anyone.'

'Ha. That's what my Lottie said when she came back, but she can't keep away from Rory. Met him, have you?' He watched with interest as the other man shifted uncomfortably. 'Can't keep their hands off each other, not that I'm one to talk, but I've got my eye on him. I look after my own, and if he hurts her... well, I'm sure that's how you feel about your own daughter, isn't it? Right, enough standing about yakking,' Tom wasn't sure he had been yakking, 'some of us have got work to do. You could do worse than her,' he nodded in the direction Amanda had gone, 'and this place, you know.'

Elizabeth had been right when she'd cornered Billy unexpectedly in the pub, Folly Lake Manor could do a lot worse than get landed with a man like Tom, and if they could encourage him in his pursuit of the lovely widow, then why not? It was a damned sight better than getting some premiership footballer and his wife in the place. They'd be installing Jacuzzis and football pitches before he'd had a chance to move the bloody horses. That photograph in the local rag had been the last straw. Safe pair of hands my arse. 'Dread to think what your goalie friend would do if he got in there first. Seeing him again is she?' Matchmaking really wasn't his thing; in his world, if you wanted something or someone, you just got on with it. But right now, if he could stop Amanda James selling up and bolting, then it was worth a try.

Tom had paled. 'I haven't got a clue, I really don't know what she's arranged.'

'Course you don't.' He tapped the side of his nose. 'Say no more. She seems interested in you, though.' Tom was now looking confused and deciding that he could well be doing more harm than good. He would have the full wrath of darling Elizabeth bearing down on him if he wasn't careful. Billy settled for a knowing wink, tapped the ever-present whip against his boot and headed off to the safety of horses and willing women.

Lottie and Tab had, in the meantime, decided that enough was enough for one day. Tab was surprisingly efficient in the saddle, despite the scathing comments from Billy, although Lottie knew he meant well. It was just his way. Blunt.

Giving her lessons could actually be fun, and it might mean she had someone to help with her own horse. As long as they could persuade Tom to stay away.

She leaned on the stable door, watching Tab untack her horse, and sighed, if Tom and Amanda wanted to have a fling, then fine. But why not just get on with it? Why the hell did they have to rope her into the equation? And why, when the woman had obviously come down to the yard to ogle the model, did she say she wanted riding lessons? She was obviously scared shitless of horses. And, come to that, what the fuck was she going to teach her on?

'Tab? You wouldn't mind lending me Merlin would you?'

'Is that a good idea?' The girl was giving her headstrong horse a loving cuddle, all forgiven.

'What do you mean?'

'Isn't it obvious?' Oh dear, she was back to being her normal scathing self. 'The papers are already giving Dad hell over that picture of him and Amanda, if she's seen on my horse...'

'Who's been seen on your horse?'

They both turned at the sound of Pip's voice and Tab rolled her eyes. 'See.' She turned her attention back to her horse. For some reason she didn't like that woman, and it wasn't just because she'd been intent on shagging her dad's brains out. God, why did grown women have to make those stupid noises? It was just so demeaning. And stupid. And yuk. When she got a bit older and got herself a man like Rory, she wouldn't act like that.

'You're getting more and more like Elizabeth, creeping up on me, Pip. You made me jump.'

Tab glanced under her eyelashes from Lottie to Pip. It was weird that they were friends, because Lottie seemed okay. Apart from the fact that she had Rory, which just wasn't fair. He was the type of guy just made for her. Rory had everything.

'You're paranoid.' Pip grinned. 'Oh my God,' she looked from Lottie to Tab and back again, 'you're talking about Amanda, aren't you?'

'What's this about Amanda?' Tom had wandered back towards the stables unnoticed, keen to get his daughter to pack up so that they could go home.

Lottie went bright red and stared at Pip, who didn't seem to

159

give a monkey's either way. 'Great, now everyone knows, and it was supposed to be a secret.'

'But she hates horses.' Pip was frowning, then glanced at Tom and a small, and he thought sneaky, smile spread across the perfect features, which immediately put him on edge. She might be sexy, but she was damned good at making him feel like she was up to something. And he was part of it. Her 'ahh' just consolidated the fear into a hard lump in his chest.

'What are you all talking about?' They ignored him, which wasn't something he liked.

'One condition.' Tab teased an imaginary knot out of her horse's mane. 'You get me a job helping out at Rory's yard, it's boring here.'

'Will someone tell me what the fuck you are going on about? And just for the record, madam, don't even think you can go and work for Rory.' Tab gave him a killer look, and Lottie and Pip just stared. They'd not heard Tom raise his voice before. But Billy's comments had wound him up. The comments about Amanda, which meant that the whole village obviously thought he had the hots for her, and the comments about Rory. If Billy was worried about the indestructible Lottie, then Tom was going to make damned sure that the man didn't get within touching distance of Tab.

'That is just so unfair.' Tab was definitely spitting. She'd folded her arms and was practically stamping her foot as she stomped out, catching the stable door he was holding open for her with one steel-toed boot.

'It isn't.'

'You are so busy shagging everything that moves.' There was stunned silence as Tab gave Pip her most condescending look then turned her concentration back on Tom. 'And even when I say your latest tart can ride my horse, you won't even let me go and work on a decent yard.' She did stamp her foot then, clanking the stable door shut behind her. 'With a real man. And,' Tom just knew from the look on her face that it was about to get worse, 'I'm going to ask Mum what she thinks.'

'Come here, young lady, you just listen…' But Tabby wasn't listening, she was striding across the yard, breaking into a run as Tom went after her.

'Ouch. It'll end in tears.' Pip shook her head. 'And where does she learn language like that?'

'And what,' Lottie tipped her head on one side and studied Pip more closely, 'did she mean by shagging everything that moves, eh?'

Chapter 13

Lottie had that strange empty feeling in the pit of her stomach as she stood holding Flash just outside the entrance to the yard. Coming to see Uncle Dom was a bit like visiting her gran: it made her feel like an awkward kid again. The pair of them had something that nobody else in Tippermere had got: that natural authority, that aura about them that said 'old money.' It gave them confidence, even if most of the money had long since gone and left them with the type of debts that would have sent most people into a spiral of despair. But people like the Stanthorpes didn't do despair, they preferred the Dunkirk spirit and determination. And the only way out was death.

They'd been born into a certain type of life, and it was never going to leave them. Elizabeth and Dominic Stanthorpe had the breeding and background that money just couldn't buy, and with it came a kind of arrogance that couldn't be eradicated or ignored. They could trace their ancestors back through more generations than a kennel-club-registered best of breed. The term 'landed gentry' could have been coined for them, but much as Lottie loved them both, she sometimes felt like the runt of the litter. Or worse. She had a feeling that the Stanthorpes liked Billy, although even if they hadn't they would have been polite, as society dictated, but she sometimes felt that she and her dad just weren't quite good enough. They were a disappointment that had to be endured. Dom could make her feel small, insignificant and stupid without even trying. And now she was bringing Rory's horse here. And his opinion of Rory was probably much the same as his opinion of Billy. Hoi polloi.

But however stupid and unworthy she felt, she always felt a kind of proud awe when she stood here. She *was* part of this place, whatever lapse in the breeding plan had been responsible, and it was the most amazing, magnificent place she could imagine. And it was a part of her. Just like her dark hair and long legs. And nobody could take that away.

Lottie paused for a moment and took a deep breath. However many times she came here, whatever mood she was in, no matter who had been bugging her, Tipping House Estate could brush it all away, with one single sweep of its history and majesty.

She could remember coming here as a little girl, and even then it had seemed magical. She would tiptoe through the archway, leaving behind the generous spread of parkland, the old oak trees and the avenue of elms, take a step away from the timeless space, the blue of the sky and green of the grass that was in perfect harmony whatever the time of year, or decade, and step into a perfectly preserved slice of history.

Now, she did what she'd always done then: stopped and looked behind her before taking that step into another world.

Her shabby horsebox was the only jarring part of the view, the reminder of who she was and how she didn't fit. But Lottie could ignore it at times like this. To her left was the house, as reserved and elegant as the people that inhabited it, to her right the estate. Acre upon acre of land that had served for generations, immaculate lawns that merged into gradual undulations of green that had been home to the local point-to-point event for more years than the family could remember, and beyond that the copses of trees and undergrowth that sheltered the pheasants until shooting season was upon them once more.

Folly Lake Equestrian Centre was the brusque workman; Tipping House Estate was the Lord.

A small smile played over Lottie's lips and she took a deep sigh of appreciation before turning round again. And then there was the stable yard, the place that always drew her back. That felt like home; the heart of the place. It was cobbled, with small worn stones that spoke of thousands of footfalls, of hundreds of horses. In the centre was a fountain, tinkling its song of harmony, and to each side original old oak stalls that had housed the hunters and hacks of yesteryear. This wasn't the yard of the working horse, this was the yard of gentry, of hushed tones and mounting blocks. Of lords and ladies, of side saddles and equitation.

Perfect planters were positioned with pinpoint accuracy at either side of the fountain, and at the far side, directly opposite the entrance, was the old indoor school. In the round. Small and dark by modern standards, but perfect for precision and the kind of hushed awe that Dominic liked to work in. Respect and restraint came naturally in a place like Tipping House.

The whole yard whispered, hushed and sedate, but Elizabeth had always been the spark in the place. She might be a stickler for tradition, but she was also a closet moderniser. And Lottie had a feeling that was why she missed Alexa so much, why she'd clung to the child her daughter had left behind, Lottie, and wrapped her arms around her (though obviously only in a metaphorical sense, as Elizabeth didn't do grand, maternal gestures like hugs); why she forgave the unfortunate sullying of the genetic pool. Elizabeth wanted life, not just grandeur.

Lottie stroked Flash's nose absentmindedly and tried to pull her attention back to why she was here, which she didn't really want to do. Dom would give her that look and not have to say a single word; she'd just know she was useless and doing it all wrong. But she wanted to help Rory, she just knew that this horse could be the winner he needed. And if that meant swallowing her pride, she'd do it. She clicked encouragingly at the horse, more for her

164

own benefit than the mare's, if she was honest, and took a step forward. Just at this moment a figure stepped from the shadows on the other side and gave a startled, but quite restrained, squeak of alarm that made Flash toss her head in mock horror and take a step back.

'What the f—' She had been about to let off an unbalanced amount of steam, which would have reflected her wound-up nerves. But instead she felt her jaw drop. She stared. It was Amanda, looking as shocked as she was, and they obviously both had the same thought in their heads: *What the hell are you doing here?*

'I just popped...' Guilt made Amanda's words come out first.

'...came to see Uncle Dom.'

'Elizabeth had asked...'

'.., help me sort this horse.'

'...better be off.'

Lottie knew she shouldn't stare, but she couldn't help it. For at least two minutes. Well, the time it took Amanda to scurry past (if you could call the still-elegant steps and the way she held herself a scurry). She was still staring as Amanda settled into her neat little sports car, pulled the door shut with a clunk of finality and drove out of the yard as fast as she politely could, no doubt to avoid any more questions. Flash pawed the ground and gave her a wake-up nudge. She should have told Amanda that she'd sorted a horse for her to learn on, but her brain hadn't regained that amount of function yet.

It was strange. Very strange. Amanda had gone weird since the funeral. Maybe it was grief. It could have a strange effect, couldn't it, just like pregnancy? Lottie gave an involuntary shiver and hoped she could avoid both as long as possible. I mean, the woman had always kept as far away as she could from horses and in the space of a few days had been asking for riding lessons (which Rory in a flash of generosity had offered to help with when he'd heard), and now she was loitering around Uncle Dom's yard, where there was nothing apart from Dom and horses. And no one just 'popped in' to see Elizabeth or Dom.

It was, though, she thought, as she led the horse through the impressive archway, more Amanda's type of place than the equestrian centre was. Tipping House Estate was the type of place people would kill for. In fact, people had died for it, if Elizabeth was to be believed.

Dom was looking pointedly at his watch by the time she'd finally persuaded Flash that the plants weren't edible and that the fountain wasn't a mysterious spaceship and got her as far as the entrance to the school, at which point the mare decided that the end of the world must be about to dawn and no way was she going to walk willingly into the dark cavern of gloom to certain death.

'Sorry.' She tugged on the reins.

He raised an eyebrow, which got her back up.

'I got waylaid.' Flash decided to go into reverse, and the cobbles didn't help with stability – for either of them. 'By Amanda.' There was a definite reaction, which she all but missed as her horse nearly ended up sitting on her haunches, panicked, shooting forwards and tried a new tactic of circling her at speed. 'Said she'd come to see Elizabeth.' The words came out in tremolo as she was whizzed around on her heels. Getting a grip had never been more appropriate.

Dom ignored the antics, his face as straight as ever. 'Yes, well, we'd better get on.'

Oh yeah, once we get in there. Like a spinning top losing its impetus, Lottie slowed down.

'Here.' Frustration got the better of him, despite his normal steely self-control and determination to make people solve the problem themselves. He had the reins firmly in hand and Flash was escorted into the centre of the school before her brain had a chance to object. Lottie slunk in behind, a mixture of embarrassment and unwillingness competing for first place in the 'why I shouldn't be here' stakes. 'You must love him very much.'

'Sorry?' Lottie, keen not to be seen to be delaying things further, was hopping on one foot, the other in the stirrup as Flash circled her with determination.

Dom watched silently as his niece fought for control. He was fond of her in a way he couldn't understand. She was totally disorganised, totally ungroomed and totally determined. The latter being the only attribute that he could recognise as being inherited from his family. The fact that she was related to him, and as a niece not some distant connection, had never ceased to surprise him. But the fact that she was mad about someone as unreliable as Rory did not surprise him at all. It just reminded him of Alexa's obsession with Billy. And, more painfully, of how it had all ended so harshly and so suddenly. To have Charlotte disappear in the same way from his life as his sister had done would be a pain he couldn't ignore, and would, despite her outer appearance, destroy his mother. It could have all been so different. So different if she hadn't been so wild, if that man hadn't been so damned unreliable.

'Get a grip, Charlotte.'

She landed with a thump in the saddle and grinned triumphantly, in that irresistible way that reminded him of her mother, made it impossible to be grumpy. But he was. Dominic was frustrated in a way he seldom let himself be, with people.

'What did you mean? Love *him*? She's a she.'

'Not the horse. The man. To bring that damned horse here and submit to my tender care.' He shook his head and let himself smile. A genuine smile, even if it was a little thin. A smile which said he understood.

Lottie felt her cheeks heat up. 'She's a nice horse.' And Rory is a nice man, she wanted to say, but didn't. Dom wouldn't understand. In all the years she'd been aware of him, which was pretty much all her life, she'd never known him have a girlfriend, or boyfriend come to that. 'What was Amanda doing here?' She couldn't help herself, it just spilled out.

'And what makes you think I'd know? Right, shall we make a start?'

After thirty minutes of bouncing around, well it was probably closer to twenty but Lottie had got to the stage where breathing was a task in itself and monitoring time belonged to a different dimension, Dom let them stop.

She thought she was pretty fit, but the way he made her ride, using muscles that she was sure couldn't actually exist in real life, she usually forgot to breath and it was just an accident of nature that the bouncing horse forced air in and out of her lungs.

'You really need better control of your core.'

Right now any kind of control over her wheezing would have been good, let alone her bloody core. And she had a stitch. When you watched Dom ride he made it look so bloody easy, like all you had to do was sit up and sit still. It was the still part that was difficult. But she had to admit that she had been starting to enjoy herself, apart from the breathing bit. Flash had settled and had fallen into an outline as if she was made for dressage, she'd stopped fighting and started to respond to Dominic's persist but quiet demands.

'I thought you said it was open spaces she didn't like?'

'Yeah, well, I guess I didn't know about the dark small spaces.'

'But she has settled.'

'Mm.' Lottie bit the inside of her cheek and looked straight at her uncle, who was obviously waiting for more. 'So you're saying Rory just needs to keep at it.'

'No. I didn't say that.'

'But she…'

'Charlotte.' He shook his head at her, as if she was still ten years old. 'Ask yourself how you felt when you brought her in here, and how you feel now. Then ask yourself how Rory feels when he enters that dressage arena with her.' She was looking at him blankly, and he really couldn't be bothered waiting for her to work it out. Not today. 'He hates it. He's scared of being made to look a fool. When he hits the cross-country course he's got enough confidence for a whole herd of horses, but drop him in a dressage arena on a horse that—'

'But he rides all kind of green horses, he's not stupid.'

'I didn't say he was, Charlotte. But he's not interested, is he? It's a pouf's game.' He raised a knowing eyebrow and Lottie felt herself go the kind of colour that a day on the beach with no sunscreen usually sent her. 'He can get away with that attitude with a lot of horses if he's done the groundwork, but this one wants his full undivided attention. Like you gave her today. She wants to be nurtured, encouraged and believed in. She's not one of the lads. I've seen him work her over jumps and they're a good team, so he's the one who can do it. Tell him if he wants the main prize then he's got to stop pissing about.'

Lottie stared at him, wide-eyed and open-mouthed. She'd never heard Dom say anything remotely like 'pissing about' before. In fact, if she'd have said it, he would have given her a 'wash your mouth out' type of look. Come to think of it, he'd been acting strangely since she'd got here.

'So you're not going to help—'

'Charlotte, you don't need my help. You can help each other. She can do the job, you've just proved that. Now go and prove it to that boyfriend of yours. If you're sure it's worth it?' His tone was soft, almost gentle, and Lottie stared at him. She wanted to say 'you're not talking about the horse, are you?', but she daren't. Because she didn't want to hear the answer.

'Right.' Dom shifted awkwardly, back onto firmer ground. 'And how is that horse of yours coming on?'

Lottie dismounted and patted the, by now, completely laid-back Flash. 'Fine, since Mick helped me she's been better.'

'Mick?' He'd raised an eyebrow and made her feel like that stupid teenager again.

'Rory's friend, the farrier, you know.' She was getting flustered, which was stupid, and going red, which was even more stupid.

'Ah, yes.'

'Well, he wasn't exactly helping me, we rode out together. At the drag hunt. Rory didn't mind.' Now, why the hell did she add that? Maybe she did fancy him a bit, well who wouldn't? But she didn't have the real hots for him, it wasn't like there was ever anything going to happen between them. 'He's nice.' Okay, she was making it worse. 'And he's so experienced, with the horses I mean.' Dig a hole, Lottie, keep digging. 'And strong, a strong rider.'

'I'm sure he is.' Dom was ignoring her embarrassment and was edging her back towards the archway, out of his hair, so he could get back to his work. 'I cannot believe your father still has that wreck of a horsebox.' Which was a better topic of conversation than Mick.

'He doesn't trust me in his other one. Uncle Dom.' Lottie wavered. Mentally hopping from foot to foot, she'd tried to raise it with Rory, but he never took her concerns that seriously, and she didn't want to talk to Elizabeth. But she was worried. She had even, briefly, nearly raised it with Mick. Just because he was a good listener, but it didn't seem fair. He didn't understand anything about her, or her family.

'Lottie.' Dom didn't often call her Lottie, he usually called her Charlotte, and when he felt affectionate, Charlie, which made up her mind.

'What do you think will happen with Folly Lake?' His face clouded over, which wasn't what she'd expected, but she bashed on. She'd started; she had to spit it all out. 'Do you think Dad will be okay? I'm worried about him, it's his home, it's important to him.'

'I know.' He put a hand on her shoulder. Of all the people here, he knew better than most just how important that place was to Billy. And he knew that in some strange way he could probably influence what happened, could take back the control that he'd never had over Alexa's destiny. Without Folly Lake, Billy would flounder – that was the one certainty in all of this. And if Billy drowned, then maybe his daughter would be dragged down too. A daughter who didn't know why she was here, what was important to her. 'He'll be fine.' What else could he say?

'But there must be something we can do. I mean can't you and gran do anything? Has Amanda told her what she's going to do?' Lottie jumped from one thought to another. She just knew deep down that the yard meant more to Billy than just bricks and mortar. No one had ever said much to her, but something told her it was his anchor, the thing that kept him sane. And she was pretty sure that Uncle Dom knew it, and probably knew why. On the outside Billy might be bluster and fun, but on the inside she suspected it meant very little.

'I'll ask your gran.' Dom squeezed her shoulder, which was pretty demonstrative for him.

'He'll go to pieces if he loses that place, won't he?'

'Maybe.'

It wasn't really the confirmation she wanted.

***

Dom got on his own horse the moment Lottie left the yard, and did the one thing guaranteed to steady his nerves. Ride. He shouldn't have had a go at her, or Rory, but he was sick to the back teeth of watching people who seemed intent on wrecking their lives. He was sick of standing back and watching the people he loved career about as though it didn't matter. But it did. Everything you did mattered, every decision. And Billy was proof of that.

'Have I missed Charlotte?' Right on cue, his mother arrived; he tried his best not to let the irritation show. But Elizabeth would gloss over it anyway. Onwards and upwards.

'You have. Mother,' he nudged his horse across the arena in a perfect half pass, pausing until they reached the other side, 'don't you think it's time we explained it to her? She should know.'

'Nonsense. There's a right time for everything, and this isn't it. And you shouldn't blame yourself, Dominic.'

'I don't.'

She made a pfft noise that was far more descriptive than words.

'There are some things best left in the past, and others that will be explained when they need to be.'

'But she needs to know, if Billy loses that place…' He turned the horse around on its quarters so that he was facing her.

'And is he going to?' Elizabeth gave her son a look that was more knowing than he liked. 'Maybe we should wait and see what happens before we get hasty. Come and see me when you've stopped cavorting, I need your advice.'

Dominic sighed. His mother never needed anyone's advice. She just liked an audience, approval. But at least she hadn't outstayed her welcome and had left him in peace; not that he was finding that easy at the moment.

Life had seemed remarkably straightforward at one time, the nice, ordered way it was supposed to be, until Amanda had crashed into his life begging for help. He should never have interfered; he should have made her go and find someone else to help. But then, Alexa should have never have married Billy, and Billy should never have led the irresponsible life he had.

He circled slowly, collecting the horse tighter and tighter until the stallion was like a coiled spring and then let go so that the extended trot carried him effortlessly across the small space, floating on air. Dom loved the sensation of riding, the strength wound up, controlled, and then that heady feel of elegance, perfection, as they went, in perfect harmony, to the next level. Amanda had just, with one simple sentence, set them all off in a new direction, a new freedom. Except, for a man like him, there was no freedom – something she'd never understand.

He'd looked at her face, cleared of the doubts and the worries. 'Don't try and talk me out of it, Dominic. I've got to do it, for myself, not for anyone else.' And he couldn't, daren't, say anything. The decision had been taken, taken straight out of his hands.

He closed his eyes briefly to hold the image; Elizabeth would be furious. And he didn't want her to be. She'd suffered too much over Alexa. He had always hated Billy for what had happened, had harboured a grudge, even though he swore to himself he wasn't that type of man. But now it would look like he was getting his own back; payback for that incident that they'd never discussed again. Never let pass between them from the time the ambulance had arrived and he'd left them together. Man and wife. For the last time.

Dominic nudged the stallion, asked him to drift across the arena. So easy, if you knew how to ask a horse properly. So difficult to explain, to put into words. Which was exactly the problem he had in his life. Words. How the hell was he going to explain to his mother? To Billy? Did he have the guts?

He'd never let himself get close to anyone, always known that his duty was more important than his heart, his hopes. Until now. Until he'd let his feelings for Amanda seep out from the box he'd locked them in, spread into every part of his life.

Chapter 14

'Uncle Dom is acting weird.' Lottie slipped the halter from Flash's head and watched her canter off into the field.

'Nothing new there, then.' Rory draped an arm over her shoulder and blew a raspberry on her neck, which didn't help with her thought processes at all.

'He said you were capable of sorting Flash on your own.'

'So he doesn't always talk crap then.'

She pushed him away, laughing, and tried to concentrate. 'You've got to give her your undivided attention and—' she paused, 'stop pissing about.' Undivided attention from Rory – now that did sound appealing.

'Now I know you're making it up, Dom doesn't say things like that.'

'Well he did, I told you, he was acting weird, and Amanda's been up to see Elizabeth, now why would she do that?' She wrinkled her brow. It was weird and it bothered her. Elizabeth and Amanda were chalk and cheese. In fact, as far as she could think, her gran had not paid the slightest bit of attention to Amanda James until her husband had died and the threat of a sale had loomed large. Elizabeth was not going to sit back and let her tranquil surroundings be trampled on by anything remotely nouveau and loud. 'Do you think Elizabeth is up to something?' It was fine if it was in Billy's favour, but who knew? Lottie was pretty sure her grandmother would never intentionally leave Billy homeless, but with the way things were between her dad and Dom, who knew?

'Haven't the foggiest. This field looks like it needs topping already.'

'Rory?' That undivided attention bit had been niggling at her ever since Dom had said it. When was the last time, well any time, when it had just been her and Rory? Alone. No interruptions, nothing. Before she'd gone away it had been one big party and she'd been loathed to be the spoilsport and break it up, until one night too many when they'd been drunk and they'd somehow lost each other and it hadn't seemed to matter to him. He'd just gone home, crashed. And she'd been left feeling like they were just friends with benefits.

It had hurt. It had brought home to her just how hopeless the whole thing was. She'd never been that important in her father's life. He'd been the flame, the centre of the limelight, playing to the crowds and loving every minute of it. A girl in every port, or in his case, every stable and horsebox. She'd never felt that the house was her home, there were no loving touches, just a constant stream of grooms, riders, horses and nannys, the nearest thing to a constant was Tiggy, and of course her gran. And she'd suddenly realised, with that one action, that she'd wanted more from Rory. She'd expected more. Which wasn't fair because, as her gran had said often enough, you make your own bed and you can't blame other people if it's lumpy. Which was a strange thing, as she could have sworn her gran would have never made a bed in her life. It was probably something she'd eavesdropped on.

But sitting feeling sorry for herself wasn't really Lottie's bag. Even if she had thought she'd fallen in love with Rory when she was about fourteen, been over the moon when he'd kissed her at a hunt ball, devastated when he'd danced with someone else, then stupidly grateful when it was her he'd had the last drunken dance with.

True, they'd had lots of fun, but they never actually talked about anything. Well, they did talk about horses, and field topping. And he did take sex as seriously as he took all his physical exploits. He seemed to take it as a challenge to discover a new erogenous zone every time he touched her. So on the Cosmo scale of 'does your man make you come?' he was a resounding ten and a half (doing magazine quizzes was a hobby of hers, and she took them nearly as seriously as her horoscopes). But on the 'does he understand you?' scale, Lottie had to reluctantly admit he probably hadn't got a clue, and on the 'will you spend the rest of your lives together?' quiz, then the answer was probably 'only if you want to turn into a spinster with a cat (well substitute horse) and a pot of tea (well bottle of champagne)'.

'Do you think we should rest this paddock? Looking a bit rough.'

'Rory? Do you think we should talk more?'

'Talk? We do talk. What are we doing now?'

'I know we talk. But I mean about us.' When she'd returned, after a very brief, slightly awkward spell, he'd leapt on her with such undisguised enthusiasm that she'd almost forgotten every good intention to be cool. On reflection, maybe he'd just been feeling very randy and wanted to admire her tan.

'Why do we need to talk about us? Oh good, Mick's back, I need him to look at one of the horses.'

'Rory, do you lo—'

'Shit.' Rory was staring at the screen of his smartphone. 'I knew I shouldn't have sold that bloody horse to him.'

'Oh for God's sake.' Lottie spluttered in frustration, she'd been on the brink of asking him that question she'd always steered clear of. The big, four-letter word, love question, and he was more interested in his bloody phone.

'Sorry, were you saying something? You know that youngster I sold on to Frenchie? He's only gone and qualified him for the—'

'Forget it.' But, she realised, Rory didn't have anything to forget. Nothing had really changed, even if he had jumped on her with undisguised, and very unexpected, glee when she'd arrived back in Tippermere. Maybe he just didn't actually love her. Maybe that was the point, even though she couldn't push him completely out of her life even when she was lying on a beach with another man.

'I knew I should have asked him for more, gave him away. Jammy bugger.'

'It's no wonder I went to Barcelona.'

'Hmm, sure.' Rory juggled his phone expertly in one hand and squeezed her shoulder absentmindedly with the other.

'What have I missed?' Mick glanced from Lottie's frustrated expression to Rory as he jabbed out a reply to the text he'd just received.

Lottie glared, deciding whether she should grab the phone and drop it in the water trough, or try another tactic. 'Nothing yet. I was considering stripping to my knickers and bra and doing a cartwheel to see if Rory would actually notice me.'

'Were you now? Now there's something I wouldn't want to miss.' Those Irish eyes were doing the creased-at-the-corners twinkly thing that made Lottie go funny inside, and almost made her forget that she was supposed to be cross.

'You've not got that red stringy lace thing on have you?' Rory, it seemed, did hear some things. She reckoned they called that selective hearing.

'It's called a thong. And no, I haven't you can see it through these jodhpurs.'

'And that's not necessarily a bad thing, treasure.' The deep throaty chuckle had an even worse effect on her than the gleaming eyes. And now she was less annoyed, it was beginning to have a serious effect. Talking knickers with Rory was one thing; maybe not such a good idea with Mick.

'It's not a bad thing at all, believe me, mate. And the pushy-up bra that goes with it has its bonuses.'

'Rory, shush.' She didn't know whether to laugh, cry or just die of embarrassment.

'I thought you said you wanted to talk?' He acted the innocent, a trait he shared with Billy, which could win her over on most days.

'About us.'

'This is definitely about us.'

'No, it's about my knickers, which is totally different. And I want to talk with just us.' Lottie was starting to splutter. 'You are impossible.'

'Maybe that's why you love me.' He grabbed her hard and planted a soppy kiss on her cheek.

And that was probably the trouble. She did love him, but the only time he really paid any attention to her was when she was riding one of his horses, or they were in bed and he had an altogether different type of riding on his mind.

'Are you coming to the pub with me and Mick?'

'Or are you coming somewhere much more exciting with me?' Pip had sneaked up and managed to pop between them like a genie out of a bottle. 'We have been invited out by the lovely Samantha.'

Rory and Mick had both decided to pay attention. Rory undraping himself from around Lottie, which had got tricky with Pip sandwiched between them, and Mick shoving his hands deeper in his pockets.

'Samantha? Is that Miss Made in Essex herself?'

'She's not from Essex.' Lottie shoved Rory in the ribs. 'And she's very nice actually.'

'Not much horse talk going on there, then, but plenty about love and sex.' Mick gave her a knowing look and, annoyingly, Lottie just knew she had gone an even brighter shade of pink than all her earlier exertions at Dom's had turned her.

'We do have other things to talk about than men, you know.'

'I could listen to that kind of talk.' Rory chuckled and Pip let out an exaggerated sigh. There were times, rare she had to admit, but there were times, when she longed for a less macho set of men surrounding her. 'Not that it would matter what she was going on about.'

'Can you two just shut up for a bit? I'm trying to talk to Lottie here.' She gave them her stern look, which had zero effect. 'It's part of her cheer up Amanda campaign, a pamper party.'

'As in pamper the new pooch?'

'Rory, what is it with you?'

'Well why would Lottie want to go off swigging bubbly with a group of posh girlies when she can come for a drinking session with me and Mick? I ask you.'

'Let me count the ways.' Pip grinned and held up a finger to start counting them off.

'You don't want to, do you, Lots? Anyhow I thought I was going to help you cheer poor little Amanda up, give her riding lessons. Much better than pampering crap.'

'That is supposed to be a secret.' Lottie resisted the urge to stamp her feet, and tried to ignore Mick, who she could see out of the corner of her eye as he winked in Pip's general direction. 'Is there anybody left who doesn't know about the lessons? And you're supposed to be helping Tabatha, not Amanda. You said she could help out here, remember?'

Rory all but took a backward step, a look of slight horror spreading across his features. 'Oh no, you are not saddling me with spitting Tabby kitten. I never said she could come here. Amanda maybe, Tabby no.'

Lottie folded her arms and pulled away. 'Stop going on about Amanda, anyone would think you fancied her. You're very keen all of a sudden to give a complete novice lessons. I thought you didn't do that?'

'Always room for exceptions.' Mick and Pip could both see the warning signs, but Rory trampled on regardless, all over Lottie's crumbling feelings. 'And I did say I'd fall on my sword to help out the community, and of course your dad.'

'That's big of you.'

'Never heard it called that before.' Pip raised an eyebrow and cast in her two pennyworth, trying to break the tension. But for once Lottie didn't see the funny side, which was strange. The good thing about Lottie and Rory was they didn't take each other too seriously. Nothing too lovey-dovey, and never a hint of jealousy. Which, as far as Pip could see, was a massive bonus, well, a necessity given the number of groupies Rory had, and the swathe of male riders whose eyes were constantly fixed on Lottie's bum whenever she was competing in her tightest jodhpurs.

Mick didn't offer any help when she glanced his way, just a shrug of amusement. Come to think of it, he seemed remarkably attached to Lottie, considering he hardly knew her. That Irish charm wouldn't wash with her, but maybe he was thinking about aiming it full force in Lottie's direction. 'What's it to be then, Lots? The boring pubs with this pair of comedians, or are you up for a pamper party?'

'Party night.' Thinking about it, Lottie wasn't completely sure. 'Definitely party night.' She said it again to convince herself. She did actually like just going out to the local pub, but Rory was annoying her and reminding her just why she'd hightailed it off to Australia to escape the endless horses and the fact that he didn't really listen to a word she said. And Mick was winding her up in his very discreet way, and making her feel a lot hotter than she should.

'Really? You'd rather go to wagland than The Bull's Head?'

'She would.' Pip grinned triumphantly. 'You wouldn't understand, you're men.'

'Well you know where to find us when you get bored of being girlie.'

'Don't worry, I won't. Not that you'd notice anyway.' What was the point? For a brief moment Lottie wondered why she'd ever bothered coming back. And then she remembered. Todd the tosser. Yeah, well, maybe she did need a girl's night out more than she'd realised.

Four hours, two bottles of champagne and a lot of girlie talk later, Lottie was far from bored. She had also just discovered what 'pamper' really meant. Up until now, after being brought up by a single dad and an assortment of grooms, then having moved on to a work-obsessed Rory, with a side serving of the resolute and restrained Elizabeth (who probably thought pampering was for lily-livered fools), her girlie side had never been revealed, let alone released. For her, pamper meant treating herself to new knickers, or more sensibly a seat saver for her saddle (which was more about increasing stickability than comfort, if she was honest), and even the trip to foreign climes had been fairly basic and consisted of flip flops, backpacks, cheap hotels (or tents) and drinking beer on the beach. But she had never, as in never ever, even imagined herself sitting in a hot tub with champagne on ice, following a massage that had tickled parts of her she didn't know she had. Parts that not even Rory had found. Yet.

She had also, sadly, discovered that Rory had been right. Well nearly right. It was a 'pamper the pooch' party. Scruffy the mutt, who she'd only seen in the tabloids up until now, had greeted them at the door, blue ribbon in his hair and a sloppy wet grin that suggested he was out to have as much fun as everybody else. Luckily that didn't extend to the hot tub, though if it had, Lottie was sure he would have had his own swimming costume. For a terrible moment she had been seriously tempted to ask if such a thing as a 'dogkini' existed, but had decided that if one didn't, Sam would have one designed, so she kept the thought to herself.

'Isn't bathing in champagne supposed to be good for your skin?'

'That's ass's milk.' Amanda giggled, even she had let her hair down and was more at ease than Lottie had ever seen her.

'What's ass's milk?' Lottie was pretty sure her brainpower had deserted her – maybe when her muscles had got unknotted so had her mind.

'It's ass's milk that is good to bathe in.' Pip kicked her feet up out of the tub so that she could admire her newly painted multi-coloured toenails.

'I bet champagne is too.' Sam grabbed the nearest bottle of

Bollinger, held it above her head with a flourish and then sent a cascade into the tub.

Lottie gawped open-mouthed and then her feet floated up of their own accord as she leant back and stared at the ceiling. Maybe that was what had happened to her mind; it had just floated off. Tippermere and the village of Kitterly Heath might only be separated by a distance that was practically non-existent, in tangible terms, but as far as the mindset and habits went, they might as well, Lottie decided with glum finality, be on different planets.

'Should you have…?'

'It's okay, babe, it isn't the vintage stuff.'

Oh, so that was alright then. She really hoped that Scruffy didn't decide to drink the water when they got out. Not that it could make him any loopier than he already was.

'Right, time to stop loafing about; the real party is about to start.' Samantha had sensed, like the perfect host she was, that the mood was about to slip. She was bouncing about in a way that mildly resembled her recently rescued mutt and, as far as Lottie could see, it was just as genuine.

'What do you mean, start?' Lottie had thought this was as good as it got.

'Grubs up.' Sam was already out of the hot tub, totally naked and totally unperturbed by the three pairs of eyes that were locked firmly in her direction. Lottie glanced down with a guilty start. Hadn't she always been taught it was rude to stare?

But it did look like Sam was used to it. Maybe, Lottie thought, it was a result of too many Brazilian waxes, and frequent pool parties where everybody inspected everybody else's boob jobs.

'Come on, everyone out, chop chop, it's fun time.' She grinned, a wide unaffected grin that would have smitten a premiership football player, if she hadn't claimed one all of her own years ago. 'If you don't, I will let Scruffy dog in.'

'Hell, don't you dare.' Pip was out of the tub, chastely covered with a borrowed bikini. 'You wouldn't.'

182

'Oh he loves the hot tub, him and Davey play for hours in it.'

Pip stared, as though expecting hairs and dog debris to appear from out of the bubbles.

'Don't worry, babe, I've had it cleaned. Someone does it every day, I mean, you know what men are like.' She pulled a face. 'All that hot air comes from both ends.'

Lottie caught Amanda's eye and they both started to giggle, and in that moment Lottie decided she did actually like Amanda quite a lot, even if the woman did have the power to ruin Billy's life. Maybe she should talk to her about that. Soon. When her head felt a bit clearer.

Lottie's head didn't get a chance to clear. The 'grub', it turned out, was good old fish and chips, eaten with fingers and served with a side of several more bottles of champagne. And presented by topless waiters.

'Don't tell Davey, will you?' Sam licked her fingers then wiped them on a pristine white napkin and accepted a top-up.

'Doesn't he approve of semi-naked men in the house?' Pip grinned and resisted the urge to manhandle the nearest man, who had the type of tan and six pack that made her literally drool. She hadn't seen a man like this since she'd moved to Tippermere. Men in riding gear with a whip in hand had a certain appeal (well that was partly down to the whip, she had to admit), but man grooming like this stirred memories in neglected parts of her body. She propped her head on her hand and stared. Longingly. 'I could offer to take them home for you?'

'Oh no, I don't mean that.' The guffaw was unexpectedly loud from the petite Sam, but from the way the dog just cocked an ear slightly, Pip guessed a full-bodied laugh was normal around here. 'I meant,' she leant forward conspiratorially, and Lottie, trying to do the same, nearly tipped forward into what was left of her chips. She flicked a piece of batter out of her fringe and tried to concentrate. 'Don't tell him about the chips.'

'Won't he smell them?' Amanda, who up until this point had

hardly said a word, which was her normal way, finally spoke up. She had no objection to fish and chips, in fact they'd been a nice change and had actually sobered her up a bit, but they did stink, didn't they? Chips were like smoke, the smell just lingered.

'Never thought about that, babe. Although he's not that good at noticing stuff, so he might not, and he's away for a couple of days on some training thingy.'

'Training thingy?' Pip had been hoping she might bump into Sam's other half for two reasons. One, Elizabeth had asked her to find out more about Mr Simcock senior, and two, she still wanted to wangle an interview with his manager, who was newsworthy as well as swoonworthy. In fact, just thinking about him had put her off the semi-naked man hovering at her elbow. Well, not entirely put her off, but certainly distracted her.

'When the season finishes they all go off.' Sam waved a hand in the general direction of what could have been France, except the way the dog sat up, he obviously just took it to mean the cupboard. 'But when they come back.' She leant forward over the breakfast bar and lowered her voice. Even the dog stilled, one big ear bent over, the other pointing to the sky. 'Hang on.' She jumped up and the other three girls shot upright as Scruffy went into a spin chasing his tail and growling at his own back end. Sam ignored him and dug into a kitchen drawer, finally finding what she was after. Three envelopes. Gold. Naturally.

'Here, this is what I'm celebrating. I nearly forgot, aren't I an airhead? I bet you all thought I was mad having a party just for Scruffy.' She giggled and Lottie squirmed self-consciously and hoped she hadn't noticed.

The three girls stared, then Lottie picked hers up and turned it over as though it might bite.

Pip caught on first, grinning. 'You aren't?'

'Open, open.' Sam clapped her hands and the dog gave a large echoing bark of encouragement.

Amanda was the first to open hers, carefully prising the flap

184

open, as though she was planning on reusing it. Which naturally she wasn't – recycling had never been high on her agenda.

As the stiff, heavily embossed card slipped out of the envelope, she felt herself sober up. Instantly. If she'd thought Marcus's funeral had been ostentatious, then this was obviously going to take it to a whole new level. This was going to be the wedding of the year. It said so on the invite. 'Wow, congratulations.' It sounded a bit lame to her own ears, but Sam was smiling.

'Thanks, hun. We're just so excited. And I want you to be our star guests.'

'Star?' Pip was looking sceptical. 'What about all the A-listers?'

'Well, you're going to be *my* star guests.' Sam's enthusiasm was not to be muted, not even by Pip. 'I mean Davey's mates will come, obviously, and then the magazine has insisted on some other people.'

'Exactly how many?' Pip was laughing.

'I think there's a couple of hundred, or it could be more, I mean, I can't exactly remember, I wasn't paying that much attention, to be honest. You will come? It will be fab.'

'Of course we will, won't we?' Pip nudged Lottie in the ribs.

Lottie, who had finally decided it was safe to open the envelope, had done so with a characteristic abandon that had been known in the past to tear the contents apart and lead to judicious use of sticky tape. This card was made of sterner stuff and emerged from the attack unscathed. 'But what am I going to wear?' A wedding was one thing, but a wedding with footballers and film stars? Lottie suddenly realised that champagne in a hot tub was just the start. 'I mean, thank you, its brilliant, you're brilliant, it's great and er, congratulations.' Maybe she could just wear her normal stuff and blend into the background.

'Well, whatever you wear, it's not going to be riding breeches.' Pip had a raised eyebrow.

Maybe not, then.

'Hey, we can have a girlie shopping trip.' Sam was clapping her hands again. It reminded Lottie of a seal, which was unkind. It was just her brain still wasn't working properly; she'd got overload.

'Max has made us cocktails to celebrate. Even Scruffy has got one.'

'Don't tell me he's going to be best man?' Pip rolled her eyes as the buff body of Max loomed large, carrying bright-blue cocktails. She tried to decide if he was the man she'd just been on the verge of propositioning, or a different one. They all looked remarkably similar.

'Don't be daft.' Sam giggled. 'He's ring-bearer.'

Lottie had a sudden vision of him sitting, tongue lolling and two gold rings balanced on the tip, until he closed his mouth and swallowed, just as the vicar put his hand out for them. 'He hasn't got hands.'

Sam looked back at her blankly.

'He's got paws. So how can he hold the rings?' She patted the slobbering, excited dog on his head.

'Oh I see what you mean, babe. We're putting them on a ribbon, you know, tied to his collar. He's such a handsome boy, aren't you?'

The blue cocktails were surprisingly nice, in fact very moreish, and seemed to knock the bubbles right out of Lottie's head. And the music, when the ever-helpful Max put it on, knocked everything else out. It was only when Lottie was stood centre stage, with a very tipsy Amanda, on the large lounge coffee table, rocking to 'I Love Rock and Roll' that she remembered about her earlier urge to quiz her new best buddy. I mean, it was important, this was about her Dad and the one place she'd called home.

Admittedly, she had wanted to get away (but that was more to escape Billy's fame and reputation rather than the man himself and Folly Lake), and it hadn't been particularly, well 'homely', but it was theirs. And she wasn't ever going to go back, so it didn't really matter to her, not really. But it did to Billy. Tiggy said so. Repeatedly. And without Folly Lake, would Billy still be Billy? And would Tippermere be torn apart? The thought of Tippermere changing forever made her feel a bit queasy. Although how much of that was down to the champagne swilling about on top of chips she wasn't sure.

'Have you met Tiggy?'

Amanda, mid rock, gave her a startled look and dropped her air guitar. 'Tiggy?'

'She works for dad, you know the mad dog groomer.'

'I've met her.' Amanda giggled. 'She looks like a spaniel.'

'Exactly.' Lottie was glad they were on the same wavelength.

'One that hasn't been groomed.'

'I know. I think,' she stopped dancing for a moment and looked earnestly at the other girl, 'that she fancies dad.'

'Really? Is that okay?'

'Well he is old enough to make his own decisions, you know.'

For some reason Amanda found that statement funny, so Lottie did as well, even if she was being serious. It also gave her the courage to tackle this head-on. 'Why did you go and see Uncle Dom the other day? Was it about the equestrian centre?'

Lottie was too drunk to notice the hesitation.

'Maybe. They offered to help me sort it out.'

'Oh.' This was nice, Lottie decided. Everybody was nice. 'Do you need help? I could help.' She looked at Amanda hopefully, realising this could be the perfect way to make sure nothing bad happened.

'You're so sweet.' Amanda hugged her, which was a bit unexpected. 'Everybody is.'

'Including Tom, he's sweet isn't he?' She thought she'd throw that one in, just for good measure.

'Is he?' Amanda giggled and Lottie wasn't sure if that meant she knew him and was pretending she didn't, or she didn't and was pretending she did. Either way, it was too complicated.

None of which exactly answered any of Lottie's pressing questions, but did leave her thinking that maybe she should stop worrying. About everything.

But it was during the second rendition of 'It's got to be perfect' that she had a sudden urge to talk to Rory and ask him if it ever would be. Perfect that was. Except he didn't answer. Not even on the sixth ring.

She glared at the phone, which was actually flashing several text messages from Rory that she'd not heard. It was typical, though, that when she did actually really need to talk to him, he was too busy. And not listening.

'*Milly, Molly, Mandy doesn't need you to jump in and save her, Uncle D is her hero!!!*' Sending the text was probably a mistake, and not just because it was bloody hard to press the right buttons when she couldn't quite see straight. It took about ten attempts, and even then some of the words didn't look quite right. But she was cross. And he had made that comment about falling on his sword, which was uncalled for. But as soon as she pressed 'send' she felt churlish. She'd already told Rory that her uncle could sort his horse better than he could; she was now telling him that the man he swore was gay was also better with women. Not that she'd actually said that, but he might take it like that. And she didn't mean it; she was just cross. So she immediately followed it up with '*Love you bucketloads*' and sixty (or so) kisses in the shape of a squiffy heart, not that she was sending him a wonky heart, she was sending him the real deal, and blamed Pip for that distortion. Pip was playing air guitar and nudging her elbow at a critical point and she just couldn't start all over again.

'You aren't texting lover boy again are you?' Pip rolled her eyes and made a lunge for the phone, which Lottie managed to drop down her own cleavage just in time.

'No.' The air of innocence didn't wash.

Except she hadn't texted Rory. In her drunken state she'd actually sent the texts to Billy. It might have been Rory who had been texting all night, but she'd missed the fact that the very last one had come from her father, requesting that she return his horsebox, unscathed, in the morning because he had told someone they could borrow it. It had occurred to her that it was a very strange

188

text for Rory to send, but she decided there was obviously some hidden message in there that she'd been too drunk to understand. So she just hit reply.

***

Billy might have been shocked by the second text from his inebriated daughter, if he'd got round to reading it. But the incoming first one had woken him up from his doze, sending the cat that had been snoozing on his ample stomach spitting off into a corner. It was soon snarling from the safety of a wardrobe top as the fuming Billy crashed around the room for clothes, and he was on his way out before he even realised that he had another message. Six pints later, after being forcibly ejected from the pub by a tired landlord who thought that closing times were there for a purpose, he headed home for the comfort of a whiskey bottle.

The last thing Billy saw, before passing out, was his daughter's heart. He'd wanted to reread her text, try and make sense of just how Dominic intended to ruin his life once and for all. But all he could see was X after X after X, that became sex and eggs. And nothing made any sense at all. Not even the fact that his simple request for Lottie to return the horsebox had triggered a response that was as confusing as it was unexpected.

Elizabeth had asked him to push Tom in Amanda's direction, hadn't she? Not to jump in and chat up Amanda himself. And why did Lottie know about that anyway?

He closed his eyes and wished the world would stop moving. He'd thought Dom had called a truce, but now he was showing his true colours. Determined to finish off Billy once and for all.

The sex and eggs swirled around in his brain and turned into an image of Alexa. Laughing, waving, falling. And Dom was shouting, throwing eggs.

189

Chapter 15

Whilst Lottie was experiencing a day of total contrasts and a fair bit of unprecedented, for her, hedonism, Tom Strachan was having an altogether different kind of day in his supposedly tranquil country escape.

'Believe me, I have not come here because I want to.' Tamara Strachan glanced around the cottage and sniffed. She had never, ever, in her whole life been in such a poky hole. Tom must have completely lost his mind. 'What on earth were you thinking of, bringing Tabatha here?'

'What on earth were you thinking of, raiding my fucking bank account and buggering off to Spain with that—' He couldn't think of a polite word to describe his ex-manager, or his nearly ex-wife.

'It wasn't Spain, it was Italy.' Tamara picked up a brass jug and stared at it. 'Weird.' Then she put it back down and brushed her hands together to remove the imaginary dust.

'I thought it was Madrid?' For a moment curiosity overrode his disinterest.

'Milan, much classier.'

Tom reserved passing judgement. 'So, why the hell are you here? Worried you hadn't ruined my life effectively enough?'

Tamara gave a short laugh and folded her arms. 'You don't need any help with that, darling.'

'Well, I know you aren't interested in having your daughter, and I haven't got any money left, so what is it now?'

'I'm here to help you, actually.'

Tom gave a short laugh. 'Well that would be a first. Excuse me if I'm sceptical.'

'We were good together once.'

'Once being the operative word. What are you after, Tam?'

'Nothing. I'm here to deliver a message, actually, from your father. And I do wish you'd call me Tamara.'

'You, a messenger? Pull the other one; what's in it for you?'

'Why not let's just say I felt a tiny bit guilty.'

'Let's not. You need a conscience to feel guilt.'

'It doesn't have to be like this between us, can't you forgive and forget, Thomas?'

Tom looked at his glamorous soon-to-be ex-wife and wondered how they had ever thought it would work. He'd not seen false eyelashes like that on anyone since he'd been here, in fact he was on the verge of laughing at the whole ludicrous sight. In the city it worked, but here the hideously high platform shoes, skinny jeans and trendy, shocking-green leather biker jacket just looked ludicrous, even on her. As did the red lipstick that used to turn him on, and the dark pencilled-on eyebrows.

And the pert breasts that looked like they were loaded and ready to annihilate him.

'You've had a boob job.'

She shrugged. 'Everyone has their tits done, Thomas. Don't sound so stuffy.'

'New nose as well?'

'Stop trying to change the subject.'

'I see you've made good use of my money, then.'

He had a strange urge to ask if the aforementioned breasts were rigid, or if they bounced when she ran. Then quelled it. That would be stupid. Tamara didn't run. Not for anyone.

'Don't you want to know what your father wanted?'

'Nope. He doesn't feature in my life any more than you do, sorry did.'

'You can't just write people off.'

'Can't I? You did.'

'Now you're being petty and stupid.'

'No, Tamara. You're being stupid coming here. I can't think of a single good reason for us meeting face to face, unless there's something urgent with Tab.' His stomach suddenly dipped, like he'd hit the bottom of a bungee rope. Not that he knew how that felt.

Tamara had told Tab she was heading over, they talked, they must, and if he was honest, he didn't like it. But, whatever her faults, Tam was Tabatha's mother. She'd given birth to her, if nothing else. And he wasn't going to inflict the same rift on his daughter that had been shoved on the adolescent boy he'd once been. But what had Tab told her mother? Had she said she hated it here? If he'd had an iota of sense, if he'd not been busy ogling Lottie and playing with horses, he'd have found out what it was all about the second Tab had mentioned it. Instead of hoping it would go away. He should have headed her off – perhaps even have got in his bloody car and driven down to London.

'Well, is it Tab?' He hated having to ask.

'No.' The single syllable was voiced with reluctance.

Tom felt relief rush through him. If it wasn't anything to do with Tabatha, then they were good. She was happy. She was here to stay.

'I told you, it's your father.'

'So why not just tell me the rest, Tam. Then you can do us both a favour and go.'

'Tamara.' She glared, and forgot for a moment that she was supposed to be being nice, on a mercy mission. 'He wanted to know why you're here, so I offered to come and find out. I mean, it is weird, even for you. Why not Oxfordshire, or somewhere remotely civilised?'

'It is civilised.' He tried to keep the weary note out of his voice, and failed.

'But it's in the middle of nowhere. It's miles away from every-where.' The way she said miles suggested another planet. Tom had forgotten how small Tamara's world was. It consisted of London and a few key cities scattered around the world. Tam simply got in a taxi to the nearest airport and identikit boutique hotels and catwalks magically, after a couple of drinks and a nap, appeared. Nothing else counted.

'And why are you in touch with my father?' It was years since Tom had seen his parents. Years since they had upped sticks and moved to Australia. And then they'd sent him back, alone, to boarding school because his father said that was best.

He'd not gone back. He'd not seen them. They'd not attended his wedding, the birth of his daughter or any other major, or indeed minor, event. And, come to think of it, they had never met Tamara. 'Since when have you been talking to my family? Thought they might add some coins to your coffer, did you?' Tom gave a rueful laugh. If she'd thought she could extract anything from Mr Strachan senior she'd been barking up the wrong tree.

'I haven't. He called me, because he couldn't get hold of you. He contacted my agent, in fact. You haven't been answering your emails, apparently. Do they even have broadband here?' She gazed around as though expecting to see some evidence of the Dark Ages.

'I don't look at my emails anymore. I set up a new account.' To avoid you, he could have added.

'Why here, Tom?'

'Why not? And what's it to do with you, or him?'

She shrugged. 'He asked me to give you this.' She delved into the depths of what seemed to him a ridiculously large, and fairly empty, bag.

Tom looked at the envelope with suspicion. 'So, what does it say?'

She gave a slightly edgy laugh. Tom knew from the past that she had no compunction at all about opening other people's mail. Back in the last few limping weeks of their marriage she'd been scrupulous in searching through his emails, letters, text messages, in the hope of something damning she could use as grounds for divorce and a massive settlement. 'How should I know?'

'You're talking to me, remember?'

'He said that you shouldn't rake the past up, or something like that. He said they'd moved on and so should you. What did he mean?'

Tom was damned if he knew, but hoped it didn't show on his face.

'And he said if you get his name in the papers he will sue your ass off even if you are his son. Those were his words, not mine, by the way.'

'That's it?'

'Do I get a drink before I go?'

'No.'

'I'll have to give your father your phone number if you won't talk to me.'

'Do what the fuck you want, Tamara. You always bloody did.'

Tom had never felt particularly bitter about anyone or anything before. He'd never thought he could hate anyone. Until Tamara. Tamara had shown him emotions he didn't want to own. And that was what he hated most about her. Hate and envy were ugly time-wasters, and now he'd been dragged into acknowledging they existed.

'You've changed.'

'No. Tam. I remembered who I was supposed to be. This is the real me.'

'You'll regret it. You can't just do what you want, you know. Not anymore; nobody even remembers who you are now. You'll never get a decent job again.'

'Finished?'

'You never used to be this mean, Tommy.'

He opened the door without a word. He never used to have anything to feel mean about.

'She's not coming back, is she?'

Tom had stared out of the window for a good ten minutes after his soon-to-be ex-wife had disappeared in a cloud of exhaust fumes. 'Nope.'

Tab took the word at face value. 'You promised to take me down to see Lottie and Rory.'

He frowned. Was it his memory that was getting worse these days, or was his daughter's capacity to manipulate getting better?

'Why?'

'To see about a job there. You promised. If you bought me a car you wouldn't have to.'

'You're not old enough for a car, and I can't remember agreeing to that.'

'That woman you fancy will probably be there.'

'What woman?'

Tabby rolled her eyes in teenage despair. 'The one you had a private party with, remember?' She gave a very brief, and fairly accurate, imitation of some of Pip's repertoire of oohs and aahs. Tom glared as she hit the 'oh yes, more' and Tab stopped, aware she was stepping into the danger zone.

'Just watch it, young lady, or you'll be grounded and not going anywhere.'

'Anyway, what did she want?'

'I'm not sure.' Tom frowned. Whatever his father wanted, he wasn't interested. 'So, is Lottie expecting you?'

Tab shrugged. 'She promised. We did a deal. It'll be cool, come on. You can stare at her bum.'

Tom grimaced. Did teenagers hear and see everything? And why did she all of a sudden sound so like her mother? The cloud of doom that he had hoped he'd escaped edged its way over the horizon again. This time he wasn't going to let it take over, to hell with Tamara and to hell with his father.

But the cloud didn't lift, it intruded that little bit more as he drove Tabatha to the yard. And it was a big black cloud in the

195

shape of his father. As he got closer an idea started to form. Pip. The girl who followed stories like a bloodhound followed a scent was his only chance. He knew he had a choice. Wait until his father inevitably 'sued his ass off' for something he didn't know he'd done. Or ask Pip to help him find out exactly why his long-estranged family were suddenly interested in him. He just had to work out how to accomplish it without becoming the main headline himself.

Chapter 16

'OH-MY-GOD he's dead.'

Tiggy stared at the wailing girl who had literally run headlong into her and was jabbering out words like a machine gun spitting out bullets.

'Sorry?' It was easier to say something than try and pick out individual words, although she was pretty sure the last one had been 'dead'. Which was a bit worrying.

'Dead, he's dead, come on.'

Ah well, she had been right about that bit, then.

Tabatha was now tugging at Tiggy's arm, an expression of alarm on her normally pale, unemotional features.

'Who's dead?'

'Billy.'

That single word was enough to send Tiggy running towards the open door of the house like a greyhound that had spotted the rabbit, or more realistically like a Golden Retriever that had spotted an unaccompanied morsel of food.

Billy wasn't dead. But he was sprawled across the living room floor as if he'd been hit by a meteor. And he was muttering.

Tiggy put her hands on her hips and waited for her lungs to catch up with her need for oxygen. Running was something she normally did her best to avoid. 'Dead men don't talk, Tabatha.' She nudged Billy's ample stomach with the toe of her boot and the volume of his muttering went up a notch. 'William Brinkley, you should be ashamed of yourself, you big oaf.' But she was worried. She'd not seen him this drunk since, well, since they'd threatened to take Lottie off him.

'Bastard.'

'Hey.' She sat down on the floor next to him. 'Who's a bastard?'

'They're all fucking bastards.' Even muttering, it was pretty clear what he was saying.

'They haven't sold Folly Lake, have they? Come on, get up Billy, you need to go to bed.' Billy staggered up, with help, then flopped on to the nearest chair. There was no way, Tiggy decided, that she could get him up to bed in this state. She glanced over at Tab, who she'd briefly forgotten existed. That slip of a girl would definitely not be any use.

The open-mouthed Tabatha, who seemed to be fighting a battle between the horror of stepping back into the house of a man she thought had been a goner and the urge to listen in, was shifting from foot to foot uneasily.

'Cunt.' Tiggy flinched. She had never, ever, heard Billy say that word. Plenty more, but not that particular one. Which meant he was either more upset than even she had realised, or still so drunk he didn't know what he was saying. And considering the amount of alcohol she'd seen him happily put away over the years, she opted for upset.

And the less people that heard Billy's hangover words the better. She waved a hand. 'He's fine, love. You go and do whatever you're supposed to do with the horses.'

Tab hesitated.

Billy groaned and put a hand to his head, 'Christ, I feel sick.' And Tab decided the safer option was to leave. At speed.

***

198

Billy groaned, and put his head in his hands, as the first whiff of coffee reached his nostrils and turned his stomach. It was the brandy that had done the damage. He never had been able to drink brandy. But once the last dregs of whiskey had disappeared he hadn't really seen that he had much choice.

'Drink it. It might help clear your head.'

He pushed the cup further away. 'Clear my stomach more bloody like. I feel shit.'

'You look it. What's up? What's happened, Billy?'

'Nothing, I had a drink too many. Go and help Tab for me, Tigs? There's a good girl.'

'Don't you try and "good girl" me, William. You should know me better than that by now. Is it Dominic and Elizabeth again?'

He stared blankly at her for a moment. 'He's out to get me, Tiggy. That bastard never did forgive me or accept the truth, did he? It's always been my bloody fault; never anything to do with him. Oh no, he's too bloody perfect. He couldn't have my girl, so now he's out to screw me once and for all.'

'Are you sure? I mean, why?' Tiggy never had heard the full story about that fateful night. No one knew except Billy and Dom, and they weren't telling. But the bad feelings had never gone away, and as Billy had struggled to rebuild his life, the Stanthorpes had moved in and tried to take the one remaining thing he had away from him. Charlotte.

Tiggy was sure that deep down they'd done it because they wanted the best for her. It couldn't have just been to pay him back, make him suffer. For God's sake, the man had suffered enough having to bury the girl he was devoted to.

Despite his reputation and desire to live life to the full, any fool could see that the soft spot Billy had held for Alexa outweighed everything else in his world. Even his horses. And even Elizabeth and her son must have known that, and to punish him more would have taken people far more heartless than them.

But Billy believed otherwise. Billy was sure it was Dom trying to pay him back. A man on a mission. And even though the two men were outwardly civil, there was something that ran deep; some animosity between them that made Tiggy uneasy.

'I'm going to go and sort the bastard out.'

'Don't Billy. Please. You'll make it worse.' She wasn't sure what 'it' was, but Billy was in a state, a bull at a gate with a sore head. Yeah, she was mixing her metaphors but right now a bear would have been a godsend, and he wouldn't be out to mend bridges. He'd be burning them with a vengeance.

'What do you think he's doing, Billy? It can't be that bad.'

'Really? Taking this place from me isn't bad?'

'But he can't! It isn't his.'

'So why is he in cahoots with Amanda James then?' Billy shook his head. 'I knew when I saw him at the funeral snooping round that woman that he was up to something. I should have sorted him out there and then.'

Tiggy cringed. A punch-up at a funeral would have been a step too far even for Tippermere.

'But you don't know that he's planning anything, do you?'

'He'll probably persuade her to sell it to some fucking wanker who will turn the whole bloody estate into a theme park and bury me while they're at it.'

'But you don't know, do you? Do you, Billy?'

'I'm going to bloody well find out.'

'Billy, promise me you won't go and start a row.' He stared back bleary-eyed. 'Promise! I'm not going anywhere until you do.'

'Maybe not today. Not sure I'd have the strength to flatten even a wimp like him.' He sighed. 'Actually I can't be arsed, he's a complete wanker.' His weak attempt at a smile held none of its normal love for life and devil-may-care attitude, it didn't come close to masking the pain on his face and the blank despair in his normally warm eyes.

Tiggy swallowed hard to try and shift the lump in her throat, and wished she could just hold him close and make it better.

200

'Be a love and go and keep an eye on that girl, will you?'

'You'll be okay, and you won't go off anywhere?'

'Tiggy I don't need mothering. If you want to help me just go and stop that kid doing anything stupid with my horses. Christ, I feel ill.'

***

'He's not going to die is he?'

Lottie, who was still recovering from the emergency stop she'd had to execute to prevent her rust bucket of a car colliding with one of her father's favourite horses (currently towing a wild-eyed Tabatha across the driveway), persuaded her fingers to loosen their grip on the steering wheel and she peered up from her position of forehead on top of said fingers.

'Sorry, dye what?' For a brief out-of-this-world moment she had an image of her father dip-dyeing his best show shirt and breeches.

'He looked awful, I thought he was dead, and then he kind of groaned and she told me to go away.'

'He? She?'

'Your dad. I was so sure he was dead, you know. I've never seen a dead body, but he was just lying there.'

'Tabatha,' Tiggy's melodious tones broke into the surrealistic imaginings that had briefly replaced Lottie's normally prosaic world, 'isn't this horse supposed to be in a field somewhere? I'm sure we don't normally have him just wandering around, do we?' There was a note of doubt in Tiggy's voice, as though she really wasn't quite sure what was normal, but it did spur Tabatha (who was actually far more clued up) into taking charge of the two hundred and fifty thousand pounds-worth of horse at the end of the lead rope and taking him off to a place of relative safety.

'I'm not sure your father likes cars just being left in the middle of the driveway, does he?' She smiled warmly at the bemused Lottie, who had concluded that her father couldn't be dead. Tiggy just wouldn't have stood for the demise of her hero.

'He's not even nearly dead then?' The only worrying bit was that it looked like he'd left Tiggy in charge, which was totally unprecedented. Even she wouldn't do that.

'Oh no, heavens no. Whatever gave you that idea, love? Dead drunk more like.'

'But you said it was really urgent, that I come over straight away,' Lottie frowned, trying to remember exactly what the text had said that had sent her grabbing her boots and heading out before she'd even finished her coffee. And coffee was important to Lottie – a vital ingredient of her day. 'You said one of the horses was ill.'

Tiggy blushed at the accusing tone. She'd not quite known how to get Lottie over here. Saying her father was ill would have been a lie and would have worried her. And Tiggy didn't want any more upset. The only thing she could think of was to say it was a problem with one of the horses; they didn't matter that much, did they? It was only a little white lie, and there could actually be something wrong with them soon if Tabby was left to her own devices for too long. And she knew that Lottie was just like her father and would come scurrying at the mention of anything being wrong with one of the horses.

'Sorry.' She took a deep breath, then decided to go for the full truth. 'I thought he was going to head over and do your uncle Dom a serious injury. He is just so upset.'

Lottie stared blankly and wondered who was going mad, her or Tiggy? She needed a rewind button so she could start the day again. 'Upset, why?'

'He showed me your text.'

'Text?'

'You know, the one about Dom and Amanda.'

'What text? I never...'

'The one you sent last night telling him to leave Amanda alone because...'

Lottie didn't hear the rest, the words just drifted by. It had suddenly dawned on her what Tiggy meant. There was only one text she could possibly mean.

Bugger. The one she'd sent to Rory, or rather tried to send to Rory whilst dancing on a table. She grabbed her mobile and scrolled through the texts. Crap.

And that explained why Rory hadn't understood her drunken mumblings last night when she'd finally managed to get her key in the keyhole, and eventually worked out how best to get up the stairs and into bed.

Well, there was a fair chance he wouldn't have understood anyway, but she had thought he would have at least laughed about the heart. It had taken a lot of effort that had, even if it hadn't been perfect. The thought had been there, and he hadn't even had the decency to mention it. Which she'd sulked about until she fell asleep, turning her back on him and ignoring the fact that he'd snuggled up and pushed his erection none-too-subtly against her. She'd even managed to hold her breath and pretend she was asleep when he'd cupped her breast in one warm hand and kissed her neck. That bit had taken a considerable effort, and more willpower than she normally exerted. Kissing her neck was guaranteed (well almost) to send goosebumps down her arms and lead to her displaying varying degrees of wanton behaviour. But she hadn't, because she was cross.

She studied her feet. 'Did he get two texts from me?'

'Er, yes. Were you drunk, Lottie? That second one was a bit unexpected.'

Lottie felt herself go bright red. 'It wasn't meant for him.'

'Sorry?'

She knew she was mumbling. 'I meant to send it to someone else.'

'Oh.' Tiggy stared then grinned as the penny dropped. 'Don't tell him, will you, love? I think he was rather chuffed about that one.'

'And he's okay?' Better to change the subject.

'Oh yes, yes, nothing that a good sleep won't sort.'

'And the horses are okay?'

'Yes, yes, all fine at the moment, although…'

'So I can go home?' Billy would forget the soppy text pretty quickly. He forgot everything after a couple of days, but right now it would be more than embarrassing for both of them.

'Oh no, I mean, please don't. I'm worried about Billy and what he might do.'

Which reminded Lottie of the earlier strange comment. She knew that her Dad and Uncle Dom didn't exactly get on, but they didn't hate each other. Did they? And why would her text cause a problem in the first place? All of which she said to Tiggy, and was even more flummoxed by the 'it's all a bit complicated, love' response.

'Oh, leave your car here, I don't think he'll be coming out. Let's go and have a cup of tea in the tack room, dear, it's about time somebody told you what was going on; not that it's really my place to…'

***

'So, Dad is upset exactly why?' Lottie peered into the biscuit tin in the vague hope that there would at least be crumbs left. Since coming home from Spain she'd been determined to do something about what Rory had coined her 'Spanish tummy' (she was pretty sure that phrase was supposed to refer to something even more unsavoury, but Rory had insisted on using the term), and the 'something' involved trying not to eat two rounds of toast for breakfast and to skip the mid-morning bacon sandwich. But the effort had left her feeling permanently hungry and just as podgy. So her new plan had been to have a regime of riding more horses and entering more energetically into sex with Rory. This had been fine until last night, when she'd been sulking. To make up for the lack of sexual gymnastics, she'd skipped both rounds of toast and her stomach now felt like an empty barrel and was making alarming noises – a bit like the pipes did at Tipping House.

'He thinks Dom has a plan to sell this place from under him.'

Tiggy forgot about the biscuits. 'Dom? But why would Uncle Dom want to do that? I mean, it's our home, well Dad's home, and I thought everybody wanted to make sure Folly Lake wasn't sold to someone who might bulldoze it. And anyway, it isn't Uncle Dom's to sell, is it?'

'But you said he was helping Amanda.'

'Did I?' Lottie racked her brain and tried to remember exactly what she had said. 'But that was a bit of a joke more than anything. That one was for Rory as well, it wasn't for Dad.'

'Oh.' Tiggy digested the news while she sipped her tea. 'So Dom isn't friends with Amanda?'

'Well, I don't really know. She was there when I went the other day, which seemed strange, and I think she went to see Elizabeth not Uncle Dom. But I don't get why Dad is upset. And Amanda's nice; I don't think she wants to see the village ruined.'

'He thinks Dom wants to wreck his life.'

Lottie reluctantly registered the fact that Tiggy had now said the same thing more than once, and it still didn't make sense. 'Uncle Dom? But, he's Uncle Dom, I—'

Tiggy put down her mug and gave her a weak smile. Lottie guessed it was supposed to be reassuring, but it looked a bit sickly and made her stomach dip alarmingly, in the way she guessed it would if a policeman came to the door and said he had bad news. Not that she knew how that would feel.

'Years ago, Lottie, before you were born, Dom and Billy were mates. They were so close,' Tiggy crossed one finger over the other, 'like this. Like brothers, even though they were so different. People used to call them the three musketeers, your mum, dad and Uncle Dom. And they caused all kinds of mayhem, from what I've heard. I mean, I wasn't actually close to Billy then, I know, I was married and had other friends, but it's what I've heard.'

Lottie wondered how long this would take, and what Pip would make of it, and whether she would get back in time to help her muck out.

'But when your mother died, Dom blamed Billy.'

She stopped thinking about mucking out.

'Dad killed Mum?' It was such an alarming thought, it tumbled out before she could stop it.

Tiggy looked shocked. 'No, no. Don't be silly.'

'But you said—'

'Billy loved Alexa; he was mad about her. Totally.' Tiggy paused. 'Look, I don't know exactly why, or what happened, but something serious did. They've never got on the same ever since. Billy won't talk about it, but then it got worse,' she paused and Lottie had the impression that whatever she was about to say mattered, really mattered. 'Your gran and Uncle Dom decided that you shouldn't stay here with your dad. They thought you'd be better off going back to Tipping House with them. You were the most important thing in the world to him, Lottie. Don't ever let anyone tell you otherwise. He had a terrible time fighting them to keep you with him.'

'What do you mean, going back? I never lived there, I've always been here with Dad.' Lottie realised that the coffee was crashing about in her mug like a tidal wave and put it down on the floor at her feet.

'No, you haven't. Not always.' Tiggy shrugged apologetically. 'Didn't you know? You were born there, Lottie, at Tipping House.'

'No.' Lottie felt curiously light-headed. 'No, you're wrong.'

'Maybe I should shut up. I just wanted, well I'm worried…'

'Shut up?' Lottie folded her arms, to keep in the feeling that she was going to explode imminently. 'You can't just say stuff like that and then shut up.' She leant forward and studied the undecided Tiggy more closely. 'If you don't, I'll go and ask Dad.' That did the trick, instantly.

'Well, I don't know much.' She cringed at the speculative look. 'No, I don't. But I do know that when you were born you all lived

206

up at Tipping House. You, your mum and Billy. After you were born, Billy wanted to move out. He told me he couldn't stay and he wanted to bring you back here to the place he'd lived when they first got married.'

'Why, Tiggy? Why would Uncle Dom hate him?'

'I don't know.'

'You must! You know everything else.'

'I only know the tiny bit that your dad told me. He doesn't talk about it much.'

'Don't I know it.' Lottie muttered the words as she stood up, but was pretty sure by the alarm that was spreading over Tiggy's features that she'd heard.

'I don't think he's in a fit state to talk at the moment.'

'It isn't him I'm going to ask.' Lottie pushed open the tack room door, and nearly tripped over a crimson-faced Tabatha.

'What should I do next? Sorry, I just came to see… it's just I turned the horses out and I didn't know who to ask.'

'Ask Tiggy. She knows most things.' Which might have been a bit unfair, especially when it came to horses.

'Where are you going, Lottie?' Tiggy gave Tab a reassuring smile then jogged after the striding Lottie breathlessly, wondering why on earth she worked with these fit people, who were constantly either in crisis or just behaving in a super-fit way, when all she wanted to do was sit down with a nice cup of tea and a biscuit. She got to the car just as Lottie started up the engine.

'If Uncle Dom and Gran really are up to something then I want to know why, seeing as Dad isn't ever going to bloody tell me.'

'Don't do anything silly, I mean, maybe you should talk to him first?' She clung on to the half-open window, hoping Lottie didn't press a button and make mincemeat of the end of her fingers. 'When he feels a bit better, that is. I'm only trying to help him. I'm sure he wants to tell you.'

Lottie revved the engine and Tiggy fought the urge to jump back out of harm's way. She was a pacifist; an easy-going, low-adrenalin wimp in an adrenalin junkie's world. But she loved Billy, and his daughter, far too much to watch them destroy what they had. 'Lottie, just wait. He only kept it quiet because he loves you and he was so frightened.'

'Dad doesn't do scared.' Billy had never backed off from anything in his whole life, well definitely not in the life Lottie knew about. And he'd always taught her not to. No was never an option as she'd grown up. It was man up and get on with everything, a trait, strangely enough, that he shared with Elizabeth.

'He was scared you'd hate him.'

She stopped revving the engine, stopped staring fixedly at the stuffed Bagpuss on the dashboard and looked at the wild-haired (and wild-eyed) Tiggy, who was floundering about like a beached whale.

'Why would I hate him? He's my Dad.'

Tiggy, who had been brought up in a household where a man thought it was his right to use his wife as a punching bag when the fancy took him, decided not to voice the first response that had come to mind. 'He thought,' she took a deep breath – did confidences matter at a time like this? Billy had told her all kinds of things at the end of a long day, when they'd shared a drink, but he was the type of man who thought opening his heart was a weakness, and he'd be mortified to know she was spouting off. And to his daughter of all people. But all of a sudden she couldn't stop the splurge of verbal diarrhoea. He deserved better than he'd got. It wasn't right that he stood to lose everything. And if anyone could help, his headstrong daughter could. 'He thought you'd think he was silly and possessive, that you would think you'd have been better off with them, up there, rather than here.'

'That's stupid.'

'Stupid is relative, Lottie. Everything was taken from him when your mother died, and it would have finished him off to lose you too. Billy was never stupid, just scared.' She loosened her grip on the window and flexed her fingers. 'He fought to keep you, Lottie, and now he's fighting to keep this place. You and Folly Lake kept him sane, and now he's sure that Dom is involved in taking it away. But I just can't believe Dom would hold a grudge like that, whatever happened. It just doesn't seem right, somehow. I mean, whatever happened, it can't be that bad, can it?'

'I'll let you know.' Lottie pressed the button for the electric windows.

'Don't do anything silly, will you, please?' Tiggy had her head sideways, as though it would help the words get through, and grabbed hold of the window again. 'All Billy wants is someone to look after, someone who admires him and a place to call home, with a regular supply of food and sex, that's all.'

Lottie cringed at the last bit. Sex? Who talked about sex at his age? It had been bad enough hearing about it when she was younger, but even the thought of it now was too yuk for words. 'He's just like all men, really, even if he is your dad.' It would have been nice if she could have shut the window completely, but there was a small gap, created by Tiggy's fingers. Any minute now she'd be pressing her face to it. 'He just needs to be someone's hero, and all those girls who scream at him from the stands don't count. You were the only one who counted, Lottie, and this was your home. Even if you never come back to stay, it's your home in his eyes. It's all the happy bits.'

Chapter 17

Normally Lottie considered herself a pretty safe driver, but the highway code wasn't uppermost in her mind as she sped along the narrow lanes, the green hedgerows a dizzying blur as she took a corner slightly too quickly for comfort. Dizzy was the last thing she felt, though, as the broad, black rear of a horse came towards her at alarming speed.

'Shit.' It would be so undignified to be killed with her nose buried up a horse's back end. She could imagine the headlines, 'Promising eventer, Charlotte Brinkley, died today of suffocation after embedding herself in a horse's arse. The horse's rider was unharmed.'

She wrenched the steering wheel to one side, clipping the grass verge with a satisfying clump and embedding a good clod of Cheshire mud under her front wheel arches, and ground to a halt inches from a ditch (she knew there was a ditch because she nearly fell in it as she clambered out), mortified that she had nearly added to the road kill statistics.

'I am so sorry.'

The horse, which had half reared as it felt a brush with destiny up its back end, was now doing a fair imitation of a cat on hot coals, but the rider seemed remarkably unfazed.

He grinned as only he could.

'Oh, it's you, Mick.'

'Whoa there, where's the fire?' Warm Irish tones snaked around Lottie's ruffled feathers and her adrenalin levels did a dive, then peaked again as he winked.

Lottie felt something crumple inside, and it must have shown on her face. He leapt off the still-dancing horse and landed just inches away from her. 'Everything okay, treasure?' She could handle this, until he put a reassuring hand on her shoulder, which made her face do funny contortions in a bid to stop the tears springing out from her as though she was a leaky watering can. There would be that many, she was sure, if she let go. She bit her lip instead, which hurt. Which had been the point, but she hadn't expected quite that much of a sting.

'Uncle Dom hates dad, and I sent him this stupid text.' She sank back against the car bonnet, which was surprisingly warm, well hot, and had to edge her way along to a cooler spot.

'You sent Dom a stupid text? What, like the kind old Rory would?'

Lottie felt marginally less close to tears, but then more hot and bothered as Mick joined her in the leaning-against-the-car exercise as his horse decided to pack in the histrionics and put its head down to eat grass.

'Oh, hell, I think maybe I'd better just let the fire go out on its own.' She kicked at a tuft of grass and tried to ignore the heat that was radiating from his body, or maybe it was her that was hot and he was just normal. 'No, I sent Dad a stupid text, one that was meant for Rory, but I was drunk and it is just so hard to make things out of x's you know.'

'I think you lost me, somewhere right near the beginning.'

He really was, Lottie thought, incredibly sexy. It was everything, the complete package. And, unlike Rory, he was actually trying to talk to her, properly. Like he had at the hunt, when he'd been more than happy to tag along with her at the back. He made her feel safe and wanted. She swallowed hard. 'I just.' It came out as a squeak, because he'd put a hand on her leg, well, thigh. In a tingly kind of spot near the top. To move would look rude and she'd burn her bum on the bonnet of the car.

'Do you think Rory loves me?' Lottie was pretty sure her brain hadn't instructed that to come out of her mouth, and it came out a bit abruptly.

'By the way, he went on about you while you were in Spain, I'd say so.' He didn't move away. 'I was fed up of hearing about you to be honest, until,' he was giving her the full-on sexy look, studying every inch of her face until she felt like squirming, 'you came back and I realised why.'

'Oo.' She fought to lower her tone a couple of octaves. 'Oh, I mean, he talked about me, like, a lot?'

'He did. And I can see why.'

'Oh.' She tried to avoid looking straight into those all-knowing eyes. 'So, he did miss me. A little bit?'

'Oh, he missed you, treasure. I think you mean more to him than he realises.'

'I missed him.' She looked everywhere but straight at him, and missed the pained look that briefly crossed his dark features. Mick didn't really want to talk about Rory and Lottie missing each other, but if that was what she wanted, he knew he had to. 'I didn't think he was that bothered, though, really.' She risked a glance and he was studying her intently. 'Have you ever loved anyone?' She had to stop looking at him, it wasn't good for her. Definitely not.

'I thought I loved Niamh, but I guess I couldn't have.'

'Why?' Oo, he was too close.

'I wouldn't be here now, would I? Love needs space, my darling, and if you're too scared to let it breathe, then I guess you don't believe in it.'

'Oh.'

'Niamh had to grasp and hold tight, she didn't believe. But Rory let you go.'

'Well, we weren't really dating properly then, and he didn't care.'

'Oh, I'd say he did.'

'Oh.' She really must stop this 'oh' business. 'But he doesn't even notice I'm there half the time. He doesn't hear half of what I say.'

'But does he hear the half that matters?'

'Well...'

His eyes were twinkling. 'Maybe you should say less?' The rich, deep laugh stopped any thoughts of irritation dead. 'So, did you find what you were looking for on your world travels?'

The only thing that came to mind now, when she thought about Spain, was that flaming beach and its army of police.

'Or was it here all along?' He patted her thigh, but this time it was more friendly than lustful, which was slightly disappointing. 'I'd take you away from all this, my gorgeous Lottie, if I thought you'd want to go.'

Was begging on the menu? But he was kidding, just being nice.

'Tempted by the Black Stuff and the leprechauns, chicken?'

Or maybe not. It would be handy to know if this was harmless flirting, or something else. Somebody should write a book, an idiot's guide to understanding come-ons.

'So, where were you off to in such a hurry that you nearly sent me into the hedge? Or is it a secret?'

Lottie wasn't sure if he'd changed the subject because she was turning a funny shade and he didn't want her to keel over, or he was bored.

'I was going to see Uncle Dom and Gran, Dad's upset at them, and Tiggy says they had a fight years ago, and I don't understand any of it.' She paused and dared look at him again. 'Why does nobody ever tell me anything around here? I don't feel like I know anything. Even Tiggy knows more about Dad than I do.'

'Have you wanted to know?' Mick had been quite pleased to see Lottie, even if he'd rather it had been in different circumstances. She was sexy, fun and he hadn't adjusted his initial impression that Rory just didn't deserve her. He'd be more than happy to give her freedom as well as someone to come home to, but something told him that her choice had been made a long time ago. And the choice wasn't favourable to Irish farriers with wild fancies. 'Have you ever asked about why old Billy clings on to that place of his like it owns his heart? And why your uncle looks at the man like he wouldn't throw him a lifebelt if he was drowning?'

'It's his home.' Lottie kicked some more at the clod of earth. 'And where else would he go? And they're just so different him and Uncle Dom, I mean Elizabeth is,' she didn't want to voice her concerns, that they just weren't good enough, 'well I think she wanted Mum to marry someone like she had, someone posh, not just a showjumper. And,' she paused, 'she doesn't like Rory either, it's the same.'

'True.'

Lottie watched the horse, quietly munching away, and wondered how Mick did that. They just chilled when he was about. If she'd been on the end of the reins, the horse would have got fed up and wandered off by now.

'So you were on your way to get some answers?'

'Well, yes.' It sounded a bit daft when he said it out loud like that. Exactly what she planned on saying when she got there she wasn't quite sure.

'Anyhow, darling, if it's Dom you're after talking to, then he's away today competing.'

'Oh shit, yeah. I'd forgotten about that.' She slumped back, the last of her urge to run into battle ebbing away. She didn't want a fight with Uncle Dom, and definitely not with her gran, who she adored in a very roundabout way. But she needed facts, and she needed to stop Billy pushing the self-destruct button. But however much she thought about it, and now she had had time to think, she couldn't see that her only living relatives would actually be involved in a plot to take the only home she'd ever known away from her and her father. And, there was, of course, the issue of living at Tipping House. Had that really ever happened?

'Why don't you come back to the yard? I think old Rory needs you. He's expecting a visitor this morning.'

Lottie raised an enquiring eyebrow.

'Teenage Tabatha, which I do believe you arranged.'

'Oh hell, he won't be happy about that.'

'Isn't that the truth? Teenage groupies at an event is one thing; on his own doorstep is altogether more frightening.'

'Maybe I should come back and go and see Uncle Dom later. Oh God, Mick. Why did I ever come back to Tippermere?' It was a pathetic wail, even to her own ears.

'There's a saying my mam used to tell me. "Your feet will bring you back to where your heart is",' he patted her knee and pushed away from the car so that he was stood facing her, 'and with those words of wisdom I'm off to let my horse take me to where the food is.'

'I'll race you.'

'Ha, now is that a good idea, darling?' But he had gathered his reins and jumped on to the horse before she'd even had a chance to stir herself. Then, with a wicked grin and a wink, he circled the horse and clicking encouragingly swung in front of her car and straight over the hedge.

'Hey, that's cheating.'

***

The yard was slightly overcrowded when Lottie eventually turned in and found that there was nowhere to park her car. So she abandoned it in the middle, blocking in the big yellow Jaguar (that car really was a travesty).

'What took you, treas?' Mick led his horse past; a horse that he'd had time to untack and hose down by the look of its steaming bay coat.

Lottie went for the mature and sophisticated response and stuck her tongue out.

In front of the block of stables stood the rest of the welcoming committee: a jovial Rory, who she could tell from his stance was actually not jovial at all, but as close to cross as he came; Tabatha, tongue practically hanging out as she looked at him with a mix of awe and teenage lust; Tom, who looked slightly bored but when he spotted her looked relieved and Pip, who was watching it all with a bemused but slightly detached air.

'Doesn't anybody do any work around here anymore?'

'Says the girl who ran off in the middle of mucking out a stable and wasn't seen for hours.' Rory had sidled up and put a possessive arm around her shoulders, and Tom's smile became a bit more fixed. Jealousy wasn't a normal part of his nature, but for some reason he couldn't stop lusting after Lottie, along, it seemed, with half the population of Tippermere.

'We came yesterday.' Tom gave his best apologetic smile, and hated himself for it. 'But there was nobody about. We aren't in the way are we? It's just Tab seemed to think she had some kind of arrangement with you.'

'And your dad is still out of it, and Tiggy was flapping about, so I thought I might as well leave them to it and come here.' Tabby, Lottie noticed, had changed her top since she'd seen her an hour ago at Folly Lake. In fact she'd changed her boots and jodhpurs too. The whole outfit was decidedly more clingy, but she seemed to be swinging between putting it all out there with a thrust of her hips and a pout, and being self-conscious and awkward, twiddling her hair and shuffling her feet.

'What's up with Billy?' Pip perked up, her ears tuned to anything remotely newsworthy.

'I thought he was dead, I did; he was just laid there, like dead.'

Lottie glared at Tabby, trying to send her a subtle 'be quiet' message, but it was too late.

'Seems to be a bad habit around here, dropping dead unexpectedly.' Pip could just see her day improving in leaps and bounds. She could feel a headline coming on.

'He's not dead. He's,' Lottie didn't really want to announce the fact that he had stunk like a whiskey distillery and was as green as new-mown grass. A few drinks was par for the course around here, but normally in the company of others, but everybody knew that Billy hadn't done out-of-his-mind drunk for a long time. Not since that last binge a week after burying the woman he loved, the day her mother had calmly told him that maybe his daughter was better off somewhere else. 'He'd just got a hangover; he was asleep when you barged in.'

'I didn't barge.' Teenage indignation made Tab thrust everything out. In a few years' time she'd be having people's eyes out, Lottie thought. 'I just went to find out what he wanted doing and he was there, on the floor. It's cursed that place.'

'It isn't cursed. He's just worried and he thinks Uncle Dom and Gran are up to something.' There, it was out, and they were all staring at her.

'Elizabeth is *always* up to something. But I don't know about Dom. He's only interested in the horses.'

Lottie decided it was time to own up. 'It's my fault, I sent him a text last night saying Uncle Dom was helping Amanda out.' It was her fault. She'd stirred things up without meaning to.

The simultaneous 'Is he?' from Pip and 'With the sale?' from Tom went ignored. All she heard was Rory's soft, 'Oh dear.'

'It was meant for you. I was texting you, but I sent it to him by mistake. It was just a joke because you'd been going on about helping her.' Now she felt even worse. 'But I sent you another, nice text too.' Much, much worse.

'I'm sure he'll be fine.'

'What do you mean?'

'It's just with their history.' Rory shrugged. 'He'll be fine, it'll blow over.'

'I'm not sure, he was really upset.' Lottie bit her lip. 'He thinks Uncle Dom is plotting to get him thrown out.'

'I didn't think it was that bad.'

'What? What bad. How come you know and I don't? iI isn't fair.

Even Tiggy knows. Why would Uncle Dom hate him?'

'I don't know exactly, but there was a big fall-out. So, what was my other text, then?'

Lottie felt herself go red. Describing her wonky heart in front of everybody was a step too far. Even telling Rory himself was a bit embarrassing; she wasn't often over the top with her affections. Out of the corner of her eye she could see Mick watching her, a glimmer of laughter in his dark eyes.

'I'll show you later.'

'I was hoping you'd show me more than that.'

'And what makes you think Dom is helping Amanda, if you don't mind me butting in?' Pip was on the scent.

'She said so.' Lottie was trying to ignore the way Rory was squeezing her buttock affectionately.

'Did she?' This was news to Pip, who was slightly miffed that she'd missed out on that nugget of information. As far as she knew, Elizabeth had been encouraging everybody *but* her son to get involved with the grieving widow. She knew all too well that the woman had been needling Tom, and had even egged Billy on. But this didn't make any sense at all. Unless it was just another of Elizabeth's attempts to draw Tom out, in which case it seemed to be working. He'd gone an interesting shade of grey and looked remarkably agitated.

'Did she?' Tom sounded slightly shocked. All his attempts to discuss the sale of Folly Lake Manor with Amanda had fallen on stony ground. It was as though she hadn't any interest in a sale at all. As though she had other things on her mind, which he'd thought was completely reasonable, given her recent bereavement.

'Ignore Dad, he's in a mood 'cos Mum came round and said Gramps is going to sue his ass off if he rakes up the past.'

'Tabatha.' It came out more sharply than Tom intended, but he had the start of a migraine and had reached the end of his normally good humour.

'Oh, really?'

And even though it shouldn't, Pip's casual tone sparked even more suspicion in his already tired brain. She knew something. He narrowed his eyes and tried to figure out why Philippa Keelan would know something about him and his father that he didn't, even before he'd asked her.

But she was a journalist. She dug into everything. She couldn't help it. Digging further into his past would be a piece of cake for her; that was if she hadn't already done it and was waiting for him to fall into the hole. It really was time their relationship was put on a more even footing and he got something back in return, other than eye-watering sex. 'You're not busy for lunch are you?'

'I think I might be now.'

Tabatha rolled her eyes. 'So, can I work here or not?'

'Yes.' Pip grinned. 'Tell you what, I'll give you a list of jobs, then I'm going to bugger off and take your dad out for lunch.'

'You can't just subcontract your job.'

'Watch me, Rory. And don't expect any pay from him, Tab, we all do it for love around here.'

Tab went red and Rory scowled. If anything was going to make him dig in his pocket, a comment like that was. 'Lottie will give you a riding lesson in return. Okay?'

Tab gave him the adoring spaniel look, which Lottie decided was a younger, less-sophisticated version of the look that Tiggy gave Billy on a regular basis. And it didn't even fade when Pip abruptly pushed a fork in front of her.

'Six stables to skip out before we exercise the horses, Tab. You up for it?'

Tabatha was up for it. If it meant she could stalk Rory, even at a distance, she was up for anything. And from the way she alternated between shovelling shit and texting, Lottie and Pip reckoned most of the teenagedom from her previous school knew about every single detail. With added photos.

The worst part, Lottie decided, was that the weather had heated up, which meant that Rory was riding in a t-shirt and Mick was stripped to the waist, shoeing horses, which left the hormone-ridden Tab with eyes on stalks, and even made her feel surprisingly randy. And it was obviously affecting Rory, whose eyes had a message all of their own every time he looked at her.

Once she'd satisfied herself that all of her morning's tasks had satisfactorily been passed on to her new apprentice, including straightening out the towering muck heap (which looked about to topple), Pip knew she could move on to the interesting bit of the day, who was stood next to his car looking completely out of his depth, and more than a little bit grumpy.

'I think you'd be happier with less clothes on.' She grinned at the hapless Tom, who had a slight sheen of sweat on his immaculate brow. 'Or maybe we should have a long, cool shower before the main course.'

'Has anyone ever told you you're scary?' He didn't look that scared.

'Of course.' She laughed easily. 'Well now it's just you and me, Tommy boy. And I think I might have just what you're looking for.' Pip hooked her arm through his, which left him wondering just what it was he was letting himself in for and looking around furtively to check his daughter hadn't noticed. 'So are we going on my scooter or in your sex-mobile?'

'If you honestly think I'm going to get on that pink Vespa, you've got another thing coming. Tabatha already has mixed feelings about my sexuality.'

'Well, I don't.' Pip planted a kiss on his cheek, which had him diving towards his car and wondering whether it would be rude to just bundle her in. 'You worry too much.' She laughed at him.

'You'd worry if you lived with Tab and had her mother come calling.'

'Ah, so that's what is at the bottom of your sudden interest in wining and dining me.'

'Not Tamara; it's what she said.'

'And you want me to use my superior investigative skills to

your benefit?'

'A lot of long words for this time of day.'

'I know, I'm showing off. Horse, shit, and competition entry form are the only words that are used to express oneself around here.'

'You've already used your investigative skills, though, haven't you? I'm surprised you've not published anything.'

'I may have, but I don't use everything. I store it up.' She winked. 'And I like you. I wouldn't drop you in the shit without letting you know first.'

'Gee, thanks.'

'Welcome.' Pip settled herself in the car. 'Where are you taking me, then?'

'Not the wine bar, smelling like that.'

'Ah, yes. Forgot about the stink.' She opened the window. 'The local pub it is, then.'

'Suppose I better move my car, hadn't I?' Lottie said to nobody in particular, then discovered that she wasn't the only one who'd been watching Pip. Mick, showing a serious set of abs and swinging a file, was at her shoulder, ready to fetch the next horse up for trimming.

'They won't be going anywhere if you don't.'

'Do you think there's something going on between that pair?'

She glanced up, straight into the dark eyes, which happened to look darker and deeper than she'd ever seen them, with not a hint of twinkle. 'She should be careful with a man who's been through what he has.'

Lottie wasn't sure if the comment meant that it was Pip or Tom he was concerned about.

'She's not daft.'

'Oh, I know that. Sharp as a tack, that one, and she needs a man who knows what he wants, instead of wasting time and talent. She's just going for the easy option.'

'Have you told her that?'

'I have.'

There was something about Mick, Lottie decided, as she watched him head for the stables, that was a bit too deep for her ever to understand. She preferred his light and flirty side; she could cope with that. But she would love to be a fly on the wall when Mick and Pip got together. Something told her neither of them would pull their punches.

***

A pint and a shared platter of mini pork pie, sausages, game terrine, prawns and chips later, Pip leant back and surveyed the bemused Tom.

'What's tickled you?'

'You've got a healthy appetite.'

'All this fresh air. If I ever go back to a desk job, I'm going to balloon.'

'I doubt it.' Despite the faint whiff of eau de horse, Pip still managed to look like she'd just stepped out of a high-powered meeting. Perfectly groomed, sleek hair, understated make-up. More racehorse than workhorse. The type of girl that once he'd have been happy to have gone home to every night, and he could still like her, fancy her, in fact lust after her. She was intelligent, strong, funny. And so much like the women he'd left behind.

'So, Tom, tell me what you're after. 'Cos I know it isn't my body.'

'Well I do like your body, quite a lot, actually.'

'I was told,' she cocked her head on one side, the hint of a grin at the corners of her generous mouth, 'that you were lusting after a place, not a woman.'

'And who said that?'

'Elizabeth.'

'Now there is a dangerous combination, you and Her Ladyship.'

'She's a clever lady.'

'You both are, that's what's frightening. So where is this place

I lust after? Tippermere?'

'Oh no,' she leant forwards, put her elbows on the table and her chin in her hands so she could study him better. 'She was much more specific than that.'

'Really?' Tom was intrigued, and slightly confused about the turn of conversation, but he doubted either Pip or Elizabeth were the type to speculate unnecessarily.

'Really.'

'And does this have anything to do with the visit from my ex-wife bearing threatening messages from my father?'

'I think so. Just humour me first, what was the message?'

'He told me not to rake the past up, or get his name in the papers or he'd sue me. Does that mean anything to you, seeing as you represent the press in these parts?'

Pip grinned. 'It does. It means lots actually. It means that when Elizabeth told me you were infatuated with Folly Lake Manor she was right.'

'I'm not—'

'And she said you probably didn't even realise yet. Clever old trout, isn't she?' Trout wasn't the word that immediately sprung to Tom's mind, but slippery fish about fitted.

'And what has this got to do with my father, even if it does miraculously turn out to be true?'

'Do you know why your parents went to Australia?'

'How do you know they went to Australia?' The hairs on the back of Tom's neck were prickling in an alarming manner.

'Elizabeth told me. Well?'

'Not really, I think he went over there because of a business opportunity. I don't know, I was a baby. Then, as soon as I was old enough, he shipped me back over here to boarding school.' The start of the end of what had always been a tricky relationship.

'They went because the business here had gone tits-up.'

'An elegant turn of phrase for a wordsmith.'

'He was involved in something dodgy here, which is why he

doesn't want you getting his name in the papers again.'

'And what exactly has this got to do with my unrecognised infatuation with Folly Lake?' Which he had to admit, he was strangely drawn to.

'You were born there, Tom.' There was the type of silence Pip had only heard in church before. 'Your father has connections, he saw the picture of you and Amanda, at a guess, and he panicked.'

'You obviously don't know my father. He was never the type to panic.' The words came out automatically, but Tom wasn't really thinking about his father. He was thinking about Folly Lake Manor.

'Maybe you should chat Amanda up?' Pip was nudging for a response.

She got one, a short humourless laugh. 'Lovely as she is, I'm not in the market for a relationship again.'

'But she is lovely. And, from what I've heard, there are other people making a move.'

'Stop trying to needle me, Pip.' But he was needled, at the thought of someone new moving in, of the house that felt like home being taken over by strangers. Turning it into a place he might never get the chance to visit again.

'Lottie reckons that even Dom is offering advice.'

'I thought Rory said he was gay?'

'He probably has; he's probably said you are too.' She grinned.

'I'm not going to chat someone up just because I like their home. Money and love are like petrol and water, they coexist not mix.'

'Bit deep for you.' She was still studying him, like a cat studied a mouse. Maybe he should just freeze, play dead until she got bored and left him alone.

'And I've heard that David's dad has arranged to come over and see it.'

'How do I even know you're right?' But she was. He knew it. Folly Lake Manor, a place he'd instinctively felt comfortable in. His destiny. He didn't need to know any more, but he was going to find out anyway. 'I need to talk to Elizabeth.'

Chapter 18

Elizabeth narrowed her eyes to a squint. Despite the fact that the sun was glinting off the metalwork of the car that was speeding up the long driveway, she was fairly sure that it was her one and only granddaughter who was hell-bent on disturbing the peace and quiet of Tipping House Estate on this sunny Monday morning.

It wasn't just that the car was belching out black smoke at regular intervals, but more the fact that very few people dared to use the refined surroundings as a race track, and partly because she'd been disturbed from her early-morning cup of earl grey by a phone call from Pip. Charlotte, it appeared, was upset. And Thomas, Pip had declared, was also on a fact-finding mission.

Elizabeth sincerely hoped that she didn't have to talk to both of them on the same day. Unveiling the past was hard work

'Bertie, Holmes, come on boys. Charlotte has come to see us.' Bertie wagged his tail with a slow force that swung his whole body from side to side, and the more sedate Holmes shoved a wet nose into Elizabeth's hand as the trio made their way to the grand front entrance.

'How about a nice gin and tonic?'

'Gran,' Lottie accepted the brief kiss on each cheek from Elizabeth and the slightly more sloppy kisses from the dogs. 'Isn't it a bit early?'

'Never too early. I've been up for hours, now pour me a proper one like Philippa does, not one of those watered-down affairs.'

Lottie sighed. 'Maybe you should do it yourself.' And got a mock shudder from Elizabeth.

'Don't be ridiculous, dear. I have never made my own drinks, and I'm far too old to start now. And do put your shoulders back; you'd have a figure worth looking at if you did.'

'I don't want people staring at my boobs,' Lottie muttered as she poured the drinks, but the sharp ears picked it up.

'Gentlemen admire, not stare, Charlotte.'

But Elizabeth was wrong. They would be staring, because after a brief scramble about in Rory's bedroom that morning she'd been unable to locate her bra, which meant it could be anywhere. Well, almost. When they'd finally got rid of the adoring Tabby, Rory had done a good job of parting Lottie from most of her clothing at various spots around the yard.

She could, of course, have gone home for more undies, but she'd needed to visit Tipping House before she chickened out and modified the ever-growing list of questions down to a lame 'don't you love me?' Which Gran would have thought weird, and wouldn't have solved any of Billy's problems, including his impending homelessness.

'Now come and sit down next to me.' She patted the seat, which Lottie took as a sign that if she wasn't careful it was her that was going to be interrogated, rather than the other way around. Elizabeth had a way of taking control, which was intimidating for the unaware, and bloody annoying for those who knew her.

'Why does Uncle Dom hate Dad?' Better to get in there before the diversionary tactics took hold, or she got cold feet.

'Hate isn't a very nice word, dear. Do sit down, you'll give me a crick in my neck looming over me like that.'

With a sigh, Lottie gave in and sat down, clutching the cut-crystal glass full of gin with an obligatory splash of tonic. 'You don't really want to get rid of us, do you?' Despite Rory's cheering-her-up tactics, which had been pretty impressive, even by his standards, Tiggy's words had come back to haunt her in the early hours. Well, not actually that early; she had been too exhausted and loved up. But they had come back as soon as Rory had thrown back the sheet, opened the bedroom curtains and threatened to drop her in the water trough.

She really did have to find that bra later; it was one of her better ones. In fact, she did have a vague recollection of watching it fly across the tack room shortly before Rory had promised to shag her senseless half way up the ladder to the hay loft, which she was pretty sure was impossible, but had been game to try.

Oh, God, why was she thinking about that when her gran was just about to announce, for all she knew, that her and her father were worthless and their home was just about to be turned into a theme park, or a low-cost, out-of-town, concrete shopping centre? It had to be her old habit of burying her head in the sand and hoping it would all go away. She'd done that as a child when anything nasty happened, run away and hidden in a ditch at the end of the field and concentrated on winning Badminton and Olympic gold for her country. In fact, she could distinctly remember doing that the day her GCSE results had been published. Things would work out; that had always been her philosophy. Things happened for a reason. But this time she wasn't sure. This wasn't just a quirk of fate.

'Of course we don't want to get rid of you. Whatever gave you that idea?'

'Well, Tiggy said…'

'Ah.' Elizabeth put her glass down on the table, out of range of Bertie's whipping tail. 'But have you spoken to your father, Charlotte?'

'Not yet.' Watching ice melt had never been more fascinating, but eventually she looked up and met her gran's look. 'Tiggy said you wanted me to come back here, but I never did live here, did I?'

'Tiggy was correct. You were born in this house, Lottie. And like the selfish old lady I am, I wanted you to stay here. But it was for your own good too; I did think it best.' The thump, thump, thump of two Labrador tails broke the silence. It was the first time that Lottie could ever remember feeling awkward in her grandmother's presence. Intimidated before, yes, but this was different.

'So you did try and take me away from dad; what she said was true.' Her heart seemed to have curled up into a hard lump in her chest. It hurt.

'It isn't quite that straightforward. Come on,' Elizabeth stood up, the dog-tail drumming increased in tempo, 'it's easier to walk and talk. And you need some fresh air.' Which was another first, thought Lottie, Gran abandoning a half-finished gin and tonic. 'It isn't that I don't like your father, that's untrue. William is a fine man and I can understand why Alexandra fell in love with him. And she was, you know, in love.' Lottie knew she was under scrutiny, but she concentrated on not tripping down the stone steps. 'She loved your father with her whole heart. He made her happy.' She gave what sounded like a wistful sigh, if Lottie didn't know better. 'And what more could anyone ask for their child?' Lottie shrugged. Elizabeth, old and wise enough to realise when the need for facts was stronger than the pain that might come from knowing them, decided to carry on talking.

'You were indeed born here at Tipping House, Charlotte. When your mother found out she was pregnant, we were of course delighted, and it made sense for her and William to move into the east wing of the house. It was where her old room was when she was growing up. There was more than enough room for both of them, and you when you were born. We had staff there to help, space for a nanny,' Lottie realised her mouth had dropped open, and shut it quickly, 'and it was much more suitable than their house at Folly Lake. Horses can be so time-consuming, and William had a good head groom who could ensure things ran smoothly when he wasn't there.' There was a brief lull whilst Elizabeth bent down to pick up the stick that one of the dogs had retrieved. 'And there were, of course, the late night parties after a successful event, which weren't always appropriate with a baby. But when you were about six months old they insisted on moving back to Folly Lake. It was their choice, I think,' she looked shrewdly at her granddaughter, 'William found it a little suffocating here.' She indicated the gate with her stick, and Lottie opened it, Bertie and Holmes forging ahead through the gap, tongues lolling. 'After the accident, your father went to pieces. You won't remember, you were too young, but he was no longer drinking for fun, there was a serious edge. I urged him to bring you back here, where you belonged, but he refused, and I have to admit that Dominic was not happy. Something happened between them that night.' She shook her head, her voice drifting uncharacteristically for a moment, then pressed on at a pace that even Lottie was finding hard to keep up with.

'And so I asked him to let you come back here on your own, let us take care of you, and he refused. Maybe it was misguided, but that yard of his was no place for a young girl, especially with a cavorting father, however much he loved you. I do not dislike your father, Charlotte. I greatly admire him, but if you have heard rumours that I fought to keep you here, then unfortunately you've heard the truth. The man was heartbroken and in no fit state to look after a child, he was drinking and,' she paused as though the coming word was unsavoury, 'womanising. But he did come to his senses and cleaned up his act. He has been a good father to you, Charlotte, I couldn't have asked for more, and despite our differences he has been fair, and made sure that you and I have always seen as much of each other as I wanted. Maybe we should have told you all this before, but I always think that when the time was right we would know.' She paused for breath and glanced at her granddaughter again to see if there was any response.

'Remember, Charlotte. There is no greater love than that which a parent has for their child. That is something that your father and I share; I know he has always done his best for you and would die for you. Don't roll your eyes, child,' Lottie hadn't been called a 'child' for a long time and she wasn't sure she wanted to be now, 'he would do anything for you in the same way I would for my own children. We share that, and I do admire him. But I also love you, and my deepest wish was always to see you happy and secure. Everything that was done by all of us was always with your best interests at heart, however misguided it may seem to you. Now,' she paused at the entrance to the cobbled yard, the place Lottie loved so much but had somehow not realised they'd reached. 'Let us go and see if your uncle will talk to us, because I have a feeling that what you really want to know only he can tell you.'

'Dad thinks he hates him.'

'So you said.' She paused and gave Lottie the full-on assessing look. 'I doubt for one moment that's true, dear. I do wish they'd sort out their problems, though, but men are never very good at that type of conversation, are they? Bertie, do stop that. What has he got?'

Lottie, who thought it looked remarkably like a slice of leftover pizza, declined to comment, on either issue.

***

Dominic was surprised to see Lottie at the yard, and even more surprised to see the rest of the entourage, which consisted of his mother and both her Labradors, one of which seemed to be eating what he could have sworn was the remains of yesterday's supper.

He'd had an uninterrupted morning, schooling one of his favourite horses, and was still bathed in the glow of success from the previous day's dressage competition, where his stallion had excelled himself. He had been looking forward to a discreet after-noon meeting with the lady who appeared to still be the centre spindle of the gossip mill that was Tippermere.

'Charlotte and I have been having a little chat.' Oh, why did those words leave him with a feeling of dread? Whilst he could remember suggesting that it was time Lottie found out about the past, the fact that they'd now both turned up in the yard was not what he'd intended at all.

'There are rumours abounding, apparently,' and why did it look like his mother was amused? 'That you are in collusion with Amanda James, and are on a mission to evict William and Charlotte and turn Folly Lake into a, what is the term – amusement Park? And no doubt completely destroy the village in the process.'

Dom glanced over at Lottie, who was doing her best to wrest what was definitely the contents of the horsebox bin from the jaws of the fatter of his mother's two dogs.

'Nonsense.'

'Exactly what I thought. There you are, Charlotte.'

Lottie gave up on trying to prise the dog's jaw apart.

'What do you mean, there you are? There you are doesn't exactly work, does it?'

Dominic shifted uneasily, not quite sure what was coming next. He and Amanda had been discreet up to the point where, actually, even he was unsure what was going on. But, he was quite happy to leave things as they were until he had worked out a way of discussing it with his mother that wouldn't cause upset, or a battle. He really didn't want a battle. And he didn't want to get on to what 'collusion' might mean.

'Why on earth would I want to evict you and Billy? You're my niece, for heaven's sake.'

'Everyone says you fell out. Tiggy said it, and Rory kind of said it.' She hadn't got as far as checking with her dad yet, but whilst Tiggy loved to listen to the gossip, she rarely added anything original.

'Whatever disagreements I have with your father, do you honestly believe that I want to see the countryside flooded with tourists, and seeing either of you homeless?' His voice softened from its imperious, defensive tone. 'I do know what that place means to you both.'

'You really can be a sanctimonious twat.' The broad tones that could only belong to Billy Brinkley made everyone, including the dogs, stop what they were doing. Lottie took the opportunity to grab the food that was falling from Bertie's gaping jaws.

'Maybe your father should be the one to explain.' Dom looked at him, feeling strangely relieved at the interruption. The rift between them was the least of his problems right now, not that he would have ever imagined that his presence could have been quite that welcome.

'He's right.'

'Dad.' Billy was the last person Lottie expected to see here. But he was, his curly hair looking more askew than ever, the balding spot in the middle seldom on view and making him look, to his daughter, surprisingly vulnerable. Suddenly Lottie felt an indescribable urge to hug him. So she did.

He wrapped his arm firmly around her shoulders. 'I need to talk to you, Stanthorpe.' His normal gruff tone rougher than ever, but with an edge that made her want to cry. 'But first I'm going to talk to my daughter. And then I'm coming back for you, and you can explain what you've been plotting with Amanda bloody James. I'd come up with something bloody good, because if you think I'm taking it lying down, you've got another bloody thing coming.'

This left Dom looking slightly shocked, Elizabeth fighting a grin and Lottie unable to block the vision of a particularly striking picture of her father lying down, a well-known ex-model turned dressage-rider astride him, which had hit the headlines several years previously.

Chapter 19

'I'll come with you.'

Lottie dropped the stirrup iron that she was scrubbing with the type of dedication which suggested she expected a genie to materialise, and got an undeserved eyeful of soapsuds. 'Shit, bugger.' Rubbing it was obviously a mistake. 'Damn.' Not only was her eye now stinging like hell from the soap, she also seemed to have dislodged her contact lens, which meant that even if she could open her eye, she wouldn't be able to see beyond the end of her nose. 'Bugger.' She rubbed a bit more tentatively and was pretty sure the lens was back in place, even if she was as red-eyed as Rory when he'd been out partying until 4a.m.

'Having fun over there?'

'Not really.' She tried a squint, which didn't hurt too much. 'What did you just say?'

'Having fun?'

'Ha, very funny, the bit before that.'

'Do you want me to come with you?'

'Sorry, where?' For one daft moment she'd been under the illusion that Rory was offering to go to see her dad with her to hear the big explanation.

After leaving Tipping House, Billy had realised he had a potential buyer due to arrive within the half hour to look at one of his young horses, and Lottie had realised that a gin and tonic with her gran had gone to her head and any excuse to put off something that could change her life forever was a good one. Agreeing to go and see him after evening stables had seemed like a goodish idea, until she'd driven home and decided she felt sick.

So she'd moped around the stables feeling that she had a vague idea, obviously it was not exactly the same, of how a prisoner on death row felt. At the same time she felt wrung out and pathetic in a way that she couldn't remember since clambering out of a particularly stinky lake that a horse has unceremoniously dumped her in during a three-day event from hell on her twenty-first birthday.

'I can come with you to see Billy.' He nuzzled her neck. 'Thought you might like some company.' Then nipped with sharp teeth so that she almost emptied the bucket of water in her own lap. 'I don't like it when you're a mardy bum.'

'He might not—'

'He won't mind.'

'How do you know?' She gnawed at the inside of her cheek, torn between the need to have Rory with her and the idea of a cosy and confidential father-and-daughter chat.

'He said so.'

'Oh.' So much for father-and-daughter confidences. Maybe it was something so bad that he just couldn't face her on his own.

'I rang him up after you'd put Rio back in the wrong stable and left the gate of the field open twice.' Rory pulled her with him over to a chair, omitting to say that after remarking on it to Mick, the other man had said if he didn't find out what the hell was up with Lottie then he'd do it for him. Along with a few other things.

'Ah.'

'He said it was up to you, but he didn't mind.' The strong thumb running up and down her inner thigh, well particularly the up bit, was beginning to distract her from thoughts of doom and gloom. And if Billy didn't mind an audience then maybe it wasn't that bad after all.

'You probably shouldn't be squeezing those bits, I am practically a lady, you know.'

'But you like your bit of rough, don't you?' He kissed his way along her collarbone. 'Fancy being a Lady Chatterley and I'll explore all your passages?'

'You're being rude now, aren't you?'

'Trying. But you'll always be a lady to me, darling.'

'Even when I'm throwing stuff onto your muck heap?'

'Even when you're tipped over my knee with your knickers down.'

'You're doing it again.'

'This weather makes me randy. Shall we have a quick poke before we head out? We could call it stress-relief.'

'What do you think happened?'

'I haven't got a clue, darling.'

'It can't be that bad, can it?'

'I just don't know, let's wait and see shall we? But no,' he kissed the tip of her nose, 'it can't be that bad. It is old Billy we're talking about here.'

***

Lottie was slightly surprised to find Tiggy in the big farmhouse kitchen, and no sign of Billy. For a horrible moment she thought that either something terrible had happened, or Billy had just forgotten she was going, until he appeared, beer bottle in hand, looking liked he'd spent the past hour pacing around the house. Which he had.

He motioned for them to collect beers if they wanted, then headed through to the snug and, the second they were in, launched into what had to be a prepared speech.

'Dom was there when it happened. When Alex died, and we both knew it was my fault.'

'It wasn't—'

'You don't know, Vicky.' It took a moment even for Tiggy to realise Billy was talking to her. Nobody called her Victoria these days. Except the Inland Revenue. 'You weren't there, it was just me, Dom and Alex. And I killed her.'

Lottie had never heard her mother called Alex; it was always Alexa or Alexandra, but then her father had never spoken much about her anyway. And when he did, it was always 'your mum', she supposed.

'Do you want us to go?' Rory was looking from Tiggy to Billy and back.

'No, it's time people knew, lad. Keeping secrets is a mistake.' Billy sat down heavily. 'A big mistake. And if Lottie hates me,' he was studying her intently, like he was studying the final round of the competitor that stood between him and the trophy, 'at least you're here to look after her.'

It was a bit, Lottie thought, like a family crisis meeting. Except they weren't really family. And she wasn't entirely sure why Billy assumed that Rory would want to look after her, or why he was so convinced she'd hate him. Except the bit that worried her was that Tiggy had said much the same.

'I did love her, you know.' He stared at Lottie, and for the first time she noticed that his clenched hands were trembling. Until Tiggy put one hand on top, steadying, hiding.

Lottie just nodded.

'We'd been at the hunt ball, it was up at Tipping House in the grounds and so we were there right to the very end. It was a beautiful night, too good to end the party, so we headed down to the stables to check out the horses. There was a full moon, or as near as damn it, lighting the whole bloody yard up and there was Dom's newest buy sticking its red head over the door and kicking away like he wanted to join the party.' For a moment Billy covered his face with his hands, then he took a breath, ran his fingers through the thinning curls of hair. 'He'd bought it for a song because it was bloody brilliant, but it was mad as a hatter. Totally fucking beautiful and unpredictable, just like Alex. She loved that horse, had been begging for the ride and Dom kept saying no. He didn't know, but she'd been on it before and wanted to compete it; it wasn't even getting to the top that she was interested it, she just said it was meant for her. She sneaked in when he was away competing.' A small smile played over Billy's drawn features, even now just the thought of her impish grin as she did what she shouldn't brought back the best bits of the short time they'd had together. 'That night I dared her. We were mucking about and it was as much about shocking Dom as anything. She wanted to stick two fingers up at his serious attitude, show him she could master the animal. But I dared her.' Billy looked across the room, but he wasn't seeing the faces of Lottie, Rory or Tiggy. All he could see was Alex, dancing around the fountain in the centre of the cobbled yard.

The moonlight bounced off her dark hair, shimmying over the ball dress. She kicked off her high heels, danced her way along the top of the stone surround of the fountain basin, laughing with a vivacity that should never be dampened. And then she'd leaped, knowing he'd catch her, wrapped her long legs around his waist as he swung her round until they were both dizzy. Alexa should have lived forever.

'It wasn't your fault, Billy.' Tiggy gently nudged him back to the present. 'It was how she was, nobody will say it, but it was just how she was.' Tiggy knew, like everybody else did, that Alexa always had her own way, always wanted to be centre-stage, but no one dared say it now she was dead.

He sighed, didn't look up. 'Tig, she shouldn't have been on the frigging horse, half-pissed, in a cobbled yard in the early hours of the morning. I let her, worse than that, I bloody dared her. It was fine at first, then it slipped, panicked as it lost its footing.' He looked up then, straight at his daughter, but what he saw was the panic in the horse's face, knew that Alex never saw the danger until it was too late. 'It kicked out as she fell. We waited on that yard for hours for the ambulance, but it was too fucking late by the time they got there. She never even said goodbye. I held her and never even said goodbye properly. I thought it would just be concussion. And that,' he stood up abruptly, went to stare out of the window, 'is why Dom hates my guts. He said that night, as we waited, he couldn't forgive me, that I was a stupid useless bastard who didn't deserve her. He said I was supposed to look after her not make her worse. We never spoke about it again. And then,' a bitter note she'd not heard in his voice before crept over the flat tone, 'he decided to take you away from me, and when that didn't work he bided his time, pretended to call a truce. Until now. Now he's decided to take the one other thing that means something to me. This place is all I've got left of your mother. We were happy here, and he didn't understand that either.'

'It was a freak accident, Billy.' Tiggy's voice was soft, her fingers warm against his clenched cold fist.

'It was my fault. She wouldn't have done it if I hadn't egged her on.'

'Maybe he blames himself.' For the first time, Rory spoke, filled the awkward silence as Lottie felt the words spin round in her head.

'Bollocks. Now what the fuck are they doing here?'

***

They, it turned out, were David Simcock and his entourage, which consisted of the smiling Sam (resplendent in low-cut top and strikingly high red shoes), a grey-haired, slightly shorter and slimmer version of David, and the dog, who was wagging his tail like he was hoping he could detach it from the rest of his body. And they were standing by the gate trying to decide if the 'danger keep out' sign was for real or not.

Sam caught sight of them staring through the window and waved frantically, her ample bosom moving in time and successfully obliterating the rumours of a boob job, which caused the dog to start a hyperactive pogo.

'What the fuck do they want? I'm going to blow the smiles off their faces.' Billy started to open drawers in the bureau as the happy bunch headed up the path, oblivious to the threat inside. 'Waltzing in here thinking they can buy the bloody place. I bet that twat has set this up.' The first press of the doorbell increased his agitated drawer-opening.

'What are you doing?' Tiggy had switched from supportive to worried.

'Getting the key to the gun cabinet. I told Dom I wasn't going to let him do this. Screw him.'

'Not literally, I hope.' Rory looked bemused.

'Gun cabinet? Gun? You haven't got a shotgun, have you?' Tiggy, who was taking the threat much more seriously, looked alarmed and was bouncing about like a demented Tigger between him and the door.

'Of course I have, woman, what else would I shoot the bloody rabbits with?'

Sam, who had got fed up with pressing the doorbell, was now peering through the window and alternating between waving wildly at Lottie and making exaggerated gestures towards the front door. Lottie did her best to smile back. She was glad that her father had been stirred from his depressed reverie but slightly worried about the effect it might have had on his mental state. She had never, in her whole life, seen him this agitated and animated.

'It wasn't your fault, Dad.'

He stopped rifling through the drawers for the key, as though someone had pressed an off-switch, and turned to look at her.

'It's like when I went to Australia.'

There was silence.

'Rory couldn't have stopped me, and you couldn't have stopped Mum. She did it because being bored and safe wasn't how she wanted to live, and that's why she loved you. You let her be herself,

Dad. And,' Lottie didn't really like the way everyone was hanging on every word, because she was well aware that she often rambled on, talking nonsense, but now she'd started it seemed daft to stop, 'she probably wanted you to notice her too.'

'You left me and went to Barcelona because you didn't want to be bored?' Rory was staring at her.

'I left you because you don't even notice if I'm there, or what I'm saying. And I didn't go to Barcelona, I went to Australia. See, you don't even know where I went.'

'I do listen to you.'

'Well you do now, but you didn't yesterday.'

'That's not—'

'Dad, why did you fall in love with Mum?'

'She took a part of me and I didn't want it back.' Billy sat down in the swivel chair by the desk. 'I wasn't whole if she wasn't there; Alex made me into something I couldn't be on my own. When we had you she was so happy, she said it was her way of capturing all the bits of me she wanted to hang on to forever but was frightened she might lose. She was wild and impulsive, but she still needed me, she relied on me. Dom was right, I could have stopped her.'

'No, Dad. Uncle Dom could have, but you couldn't. You wouldn't have been the man she loved if you had. She relied on you not to stop her. It was an accident. Tiggy is right.'

'I'm not so sure a judge and jury would agree, love.'

'But it isn't a trial, is it?'

'If I'd loved her, I'd have—'

'You did love her, and that's why you let her do it.'

'I love you too, Lottie. Your mum would be proud.' He went suddenly gruff and embarrassed. 'Be a good girl and tell those twats to stop banging on the door will you, or I will get that bloody shotgun out.'

But Tiggy had already gone to do the deed and returned, minutes later, looking relieved that there was still no sign of any firearms. 'They're on the way to see Amanda and just wanted to say hi, that dog is a cutie isn't he? I told them we were a bit busy and they were fine about it. And that man with them is David's father; he was so charming, lovely chap. He did a great job on doing up their house, apparently. Some kind of developer.' She beamed, completely unaware of the effect her words had had on the rest of the room's occupants. 'Anyone fancy a nice cup of tea?'

Chapter 20

Amanda James had given herself a severe talking to, but even she wasn't convinced that she wanted to be here with a horse and a pregnant Lottie for a riding lesson.

Arranging it in the first place had been a bit impulsive. It was a bit, she decided, like cutting your flowing locks off when you split up with a boyfriend. To signal a new start, shed the old, prove you could do whatever you wanted.

Except she hadn't split; she hadn't had the chance to do that. Plus she actually liked her hair just like it was. And she was concentrating on nonsense to stop herself thinking about the fact that she had to clamber up onto a dangerous animal that could cart her off at high speed, then send her flying through the air at a velocity that was guaranteed to result in broken bones or, at the best, the type of bruises you saw on medical dramas.

She'd spent an exorbitant amount of money on the full ensemble, hoping it would a) make her feel like she had no choice but to get on a horse, because she'd look incredibly stupid if she didn't, and b) give her the confidence that she could do it, after all, looking the part was half the battle, wasn't it?

Unfortunately, standing in front of Lottie, she now felt a little bit overdressed. Her new friend, who, judging from the account from Pip, who didn't offer faint praise, and the array of rosettes in the tack room, knew exactly what she was doing around horses, was dressed in moss green breeches that barely covered her calves, short boots, with some alarming purple socks bridging the gap, and a polo shirt with a generous slurp of green horse slobber down the front. She was also looking what could only be termed incredulous.

'You really have never, ever been on a horse before?'

Amanda shook her head with a force that made her new, marginally too-large riding hat tip forward slightly until she had to peer under the peak to see Lottie and the enormous horse. Which had returned to its role of rubbing its great hairy head up and down Lottie's bust.

She pushed him away and grinned. 'Oh well, never mind. It's easy. I mean, if Rory can do it then anyone can. Loving the gear, by the way, where did you get it?'

Which Amanda translated as, you definitely didn't get anything like that from around here.

'Online, I just went off pictures, really. I think I went overboard a bit, didn't I?'

'A bit. You look ready to go and pick the gold medal up from the podium.'

The joke wasn't helping distract her, even though she guessed that was Lottie's purpose.

'It really isn't any big deal, you know. Here, hold the reins on his neck. Are you sure you want to do this? You don't have to, you know.' Lottie was now looking concerned, as she realised just how pale Amanda was (which was evident when she pushed the riding hat back where it should be), and noticed that her hands were trembling.

'I do.' Which was 'I do have to', not 'I'm sure I want to do this'. 'Why?'

Now there was a question she wasn't sure she was ready to answer. 'I'll tell you later, if I survive.'

Lottie's easy laughter echoed around the indoor school. 'I have

243

never killed a client yet and believe me, I'll be very cross if you ruin my perfect record. Right, keep your hand on the pommel and hold the stirrup like this.' She twisted it round. 'Foot in. No the other one.'

God, this was embarrassing. Amanda swapped feet and hopped around, hoping the horse didn't move.

'Now all you do is put the other hand here on the saddle, no, keep your foot in the stirrup and spring up. I've got him, he won't go anywhere, will you Merlin?'

Merlin shifted and whisked his tail, then stamped a foot. Amanda decided he hated her. Already.

'Just imagine it's like getting on,' Lottie paused looking for inspiration, 'a bus.'

'A bus?' Buses weren't hairy, didn't bite or kick, and had seats that it was bloody hard to fall off. She hopped a bit more, and thought springy thoughts. Merlin shifted to the side and a squeak of alarm escaped as she realised she was in danger of doing the splits for the first time in her life, unless she hopped very quickly. Shit, she just had to get a grip and do this. With a momentous effort, mentally as well as physically, Amanda gripped the saddle with both hands and attempted to 'spring'.

The whole saddle shifted round towards her, the foot that had left the ground missing its return spot and immaculate cream jodhpurs met terra firma with an ungainly clump, as her other foot, still in the stirrup, disappeared underneath Merlin's ample stomach.

'Oh bugger, the girth's loose.' Lottie, who didn't seem to have noticed that Amanda was now at her feet in an ungainly heap and on the verge of hysterical tears, was staring at the saddle, which had slid round Merlin's generous barrel.

'He doesn't like it too tight until you get on.' Tabatha, who Amanda had been too stressed to spot lurking in the shadows, had joined them and was hauling the saddle straight. 'And he doesn't like his coat ruffling up.'

I don't like my bloody coat ruffling up, thought Amanda, as she watched the girl undo the saddle completely and reposition it. She clambered back on to her feet as Lottie unceremoniously hiked the girth as tight as it would go. 'There you go, I'll hang onto the other side this time.'

How could it take two assistants to get her into the saddle? Amanda had never been so embarrassed or so out of her comfort zone in her life. They made it look so easy, these horsey people, leaping on and off like it was the easiest thing in the world and she was dying to just ask for a ladder, or a crane. And how the hell was she supposed to get down once she was up there?

'Shall I give you a shove?' Tab, ignoring the request to hold onto the other side, had crept up behind her and made her jump. 'No.' The noise sneaked out like she was a hamster being squeezed and she made a heroic attempt to clamber on board. No way was she going through the indignity of having a goth girl boosting her backside.

Somehow, by some miracle, she had overcome gravity and was up, wondering how anyone could look elegant in this position. And how one stayed on once the animal moved.

'Here hold on to the pommel.'

'What?'

'Front of the saddle.'

Fuck, fuck, fuck.

'Are you okay?'

'Fine.' She forced the word through gritted teeth and dug her fingernails into the hard leather of the sticking-up bit of the saddle in front of her. 'Can I get off now?' was the one and only thought in her semi-frozen brain.

'I'll just lead him round until you get used to it.'

Get used to it? Never in a thousand years, thought Amanda as the horse lurched forward and she very nearly tipped off. Was she ever going to get used to this? She felt like a marble that had been dropped on a table that wasn't quite level.

'Put one hand on your stomach.'

'Sorry?' Was the girl mad? That meant letting go. As Merlin tripped, which she was sure he'd done on purpose, if she was capable of stringing a thought together, her fingers tightened.

'Sit up straight, woman, you look like an old crony.' The bark came out of nowhere, and Amanda, who had been incapable of seeing anything beyond the horse's ears and Lottie instinctively shot up straight, a habit borne out of years of being instructed by a mother, who despite not having the money to buy a hat thought all ladies should act like they had one on their head.

Astonishingly enough she didn't fall off and the feeling that any second now she was going to hit the deck dissipated slightly.

Billy strode into her field of vision. 'Okay?' He was looking at Lottie in a slightly awkward way, which was something Amanda couldn't remember seeing in the ultra-confident, tubby figure before.

'We're fine, thanks.' Lottie scuffed a boot in the rubber-flecked surface and for a second Amanda forgot she was on top of a horse.

'I'll leave you to it then, shall I?'

'Sure.'

'Stop gripping that poor bugger with your knees like you're trying to squeeze the last breath out of him, love.'

Amanda felt her jaw drop down in sympathy as her knees dropped open.

'Fresh air between your thighs might be good if you're looking for a good seeing to, darling, but not if you're riding a horse. I know just how he bloody feels.' And with that muttered parting comment, he strode out of the school, tapping his crop against his boot.

Amanda gulped and wondered how floppy knees and wrap-around thighs were supposed to work.

'Do you want to go any faster?'

'What? No, no.'

'You're doing fine.' Lottie smiled up at her and continued the

246

slow plod around the school. 'Just let go a bit.'

It suddenly dawned on Amanda that she actually was doing fine. Billy's terse instruction to sit up and stop crouching over the horse like a big cat about to sink its teeth into dinner, had unstiffened her shoulders and had her looking at where she was going, rather than where she didn't want to. The floor. She wasn't quite sure what her legs were supposed to do if she wasn't allowed to hold Merlin in a death grip, though.

'Just imagine you're a puppet, let your legs just hang loose, all the weight in your heels. You need a haircut, don't you Merlin?'

'No he doesn't, he likes being like that.' Tab was still lurking in the shadows, which Amanda presumed was to make sure her precious horse wasn't being maltreated.

'He's handsome.' It was the first thing she'd said without a quake in her voice, not a particularly clever thing. But progress. It proved that her brain hadn't permanently been disconnected from the rest of her, although the fact that she was sitting on a horse rather disputed that.

But Tabby's 'he's mega' seemed to signal approval.

'Where your hand is, under your tummy button, that's where your balance is. If you think about that you'll go with him.'

Sitting up straight, hand on tummy and feeling like a puppet wasn't quite how she'd imagined this riding lark, and it didn't look as if she'd be heading over any jumps (well not voluntarily) any time soon.

'Is your dad,' she clutched at the saddle as Merlin missed a step, 'okay?'

'He's fine. I don't know about you, but I'm getting dizzy, we're going to turn round and go the other way.'

Merlin lurched, Amanda grabbed, and every thought of hand on tummy disappeared. She needed to hang on.

'He's just, well he's a bit worried about if…' Lottie let go for a moment to swap to the other side of the horse. 'About you.'

'Me?' It was a mistake to screech because the horse's head was tossed in the air and her ungripped knees decided that hanging free was a bad survival policy. Lottie didn't seem to notice the minor crisis, though.

'Okay? Shall we try without stirrups for a bit?'

'Yes, no. Fine, I'm sorry I'm so pathetic.' Sit up straight, relax, if she repeated the mantra often enough maybe it would stick. 'What about me?'

'Yes, you without stirrups.'

'No, I meant your dad. Why is he worried about me? Does he think I'll harm his horse?'

'Merlin isn't Dad's, he's Tab's. He's frightened,' Lottie stopped, which meant Merlin stopped, which meant Amanda nearly fell off and had to clutch a handful of mane and shove herself back into the saddle. 'Dad that is, not Merlin. He knows that you're dealing with Uncle Dom, and Dom hates him, so he'll tell you to sell up to some other developer who'll bulldoze the place,' she took a breath, 'and he'll lose everything. Come on Merlin.' She clicked at the horse, who took a step forward and jolted Amanda out of her astonished silence.

'But I—'

'What on earth are you two up to, meandering around like you're riding Blackpool donkeys?'

***

Lottie didn't know whether it was good that Rory had arrived just when he had, at the point when Amanda was going to fall out with her for good and never speak to her again, or bad.

Amanda, though, had ignored Rory. 'But why would I do that? I'd never just tell you to go, you must believe that, I thought we were friends.' She sounded slightly put out. 'And Dominic wouldn't try and do that, why would he?'

'He hates Dad. They had this massive row.'

'Really?' Amanda had stopped clutching the saddle. 'Are you

sure? I wouldn't have thought he hated anybody, does he?'

Lottie was now totally confused.

'And I thought he was your uncle, did I get that wrong?'

'Yes.'

'He's not your uncle? But I—'

'I mean yes, he's my uncle, and no, you didn't get it wrong.' But what had her and Billy got wrong? And she had seen Amanda over at Tipping House, hadn't she? Lottie was thinking so hard about what she did and didn't know that she'd unconsciously speeded up and the shout of alarm, as Merlin briefly broke into a trot for two strides, brought her back to the present. Lottie could quite honestly say that she had never seen anyone quite as scared as Amanda, which was another confusing thing. Why exactly did she want riding lessons?

'Why do you want lessons, Amanda? You hate horses.'

'I don't hate them. They're just so big, and fast, that's all. But I thought if I was going to stay, I needed to fit in a bit.' Lottie looked at her sceptically. 'Well, there is a bit more to it than that, but…'

'So you're not selling up?'

'Well, I don't know for definite what I'm going to do. I mean this place is massive, and I don't know anything about anything. You don't mind if we stop now, do you? It's just I'm sure I've got a big bruise on the inside of my knee, and my fingers hurt.'

'Your fingers hurt?'

'I think I've been hanging on too tight. And I'm not sure Pilates works quite the same as this, I mean I'm not convinced my inner thighs will ever meet up again.'

'Sure, if you want. But you've only been on him about half an hour. And isn't a gap between your inner thighs supposed to be a bonus?'

'Not when it extends down to your ankles. Half an hour, God, it feels like hours, how do you sit on one for ages? You are sure it's only been half an hour?'

'Positive.'

'Gosh, your father must hate me. I mean, I didn't know he thought I was going to do that, and he still let me come here and he's being nice.'

'Well, what else can he do?'

'How do I get down?'

Lottie stared blankly at her. She couldn't remember the last time anyone had asked how to get off a horse. Or on, come to that.

'Take both your feet out of the stirrups and then just put your leg over.'

'I'm not convinced my leg will go over like that. I think I've seized up.'

'Not over the front, over the back.' Since the funeral, Lottie has discovered that she rather liked Amanda. And even with the thought in the back of her mind that if Billy was right then two seemingly nice people were plotting together to destroy her childhood home, it was still quite hard to dislike her. Being sat on a horse, scared stiff, had also seemed to loosen Amanda's tongue; Lottie had never heard her say so much. Even after several bottles of champagne and a dance on the coffee table.

'Oops sorry. But how do I?' Amanda had seen hundreds of people jumping off horses, but now she couldn't, for the life, of her work out how they did.

'I could always help.' Rory grinned good-naturedly at them and got a chorus of 'no's'.

Lottie aimed a slap in his direction as he stepped up, keen to assist. 'Just tip forward a bit, hold his mane.'

Amanda was pretty sure that her skin-tight breeches, purchased more for appearance than practicality, were going to split straight down the centre of her bottom and show off the blue knickers she'd worn for luck and to give her confidence. And if the breeches didn't, she might. It also seemed a bloody long way down to the ground, and gymnastics had never been her forte. She'd been the girl at the top of the rope in the school gym, not sure whether it would be more embarrassing to ask for help or to slide down and get severe rope burns all the way down her inner thighs. 'Just let go' had never been an instruction that had worked for her.

She closed her eyes, said a silent prayer and did as instructed. For a brief, horrifying moment, her knee got stuck on the cantle of the saddle and a vision of the horse galloping off with her hanging limpet-like onto his side, like a Russian Cossack, flashed through her mind. Then her body weight took over (no doubt leaving a massive bruise on her inner thigh – how did one explain that whilst having a bikini wax?) and she slithered ungracefully to the ground, still clinging onto mane and saddle.

She took a deep breath and asked the question she still wasn't sure she wanted to, 'Can we do it again next week?'

'Really?' Lottie looked surprised.

Amanda laughed, probably she thought bordering on hysterics now she was back on the ground. 'I know I was terrible, it's okay if it's just too much of an ordeal.' She patted the horse tentatively, in the middle, between the biting and kicking ends, feeling slightly braver now she was out of the saddle and rapidly increasing the space between herself and horse.

'No, it's fine, no problem. I just wasn't sure you exactly, well, enjoyed it.'

'Nor am I.' Amanda laughed 'But it's something I need to do. And, if you've got a minute, you couldn't come back up to the house could you? I'd like to show you something, explain why David's dad was here.'

'I'll do the horse for you.' Rory had taken the reins from Lottie's hands, knowing that in her state any information would help. He was worried about her. Lottie always just got on with everything as though she hadn't a care in the world, but since Billy's revelations, she'd had some of the stuffing knocked out of her. The prospect of Tippermere being turned into a giant theme park had bothered them all, but not seemed quite real. Talk of death, disaster, passion and feuds had somehow made it all more real. And made them realise that, for Billy, this was a much bigger deal than just losing bricks and mortar. It was a symbol. If he lost Folly Lake Equestrian Centre, he lost everything.

Rory liked Billy, even if their relationship was more combat than camaraderie at times, and he had realised (quite unexpectedly) that he loved his daughter. It had hit him when Billy had been talking about Alexa just what losing Lottie for good would be like. He'd seen her trip to sunnier climes for what it was, a brief escape, and would have been shocked if she hadn't returned. But, as Mick had told him, letting her go had been the right thing to do, but not giving her a reason to stay now she was back might be the wrong thing. One drunken session after they'd all been to the drag hunt, the intoxicated Mick has suddenly become a talker and told Rory he was an idiot, that if he couldn't be bothered to make an effort then he didn't deserve her.

The words hadn't hit home until they'd been listening to Billy. The man Dom had accused of much the same.

Being in love wasn't something that had ever really been on his horizon, not even in the distance, but as Mick said, it's a gift not a bloody right. God, that man must have kissed the blarney stone last time he was home and turned into a sentimental git to boot. Or, it could just be, Rory had reasoned, that the man fancied Lottie rotten and was hoping Rory would cock up.

Merlin was tugging on the reins, eager to head for his hay net. 'Are you sure?'

'Go.' He gave her a kick up the backside. It was hard to believe the relieved, but still pale and shaking, Amanda could be part of an evil plan, and disdainful Dom might not like Billy, but getting involved with a woman to undermine anyone just didn't fit the picture of Mr Perfect. 'Don't forget to come back, though, I need a lift back to the yard.'

***

'He's sweet, isn't he?' Amanda gave Lottie a sideways glance. 'He

252

must really love you.'

'Love me?' Lottie looked slightly alarmed.

'But you're so close.' Her voice had a wistful edge that completely mystified Lottie. 'It must be lovely to share everything, to like all the same things. You know, share interests.'

Which wasn't how it seemed to Lottie at five o'clock on cold winter mornings, when sharing meant forking muck into the same wheelbarrow.

'Did you love Marcus?' It was easier to redirect the conversation than ponder about whether Rory did actually love her.

'Yes, I suppose I did. It seems like another life, though, now, I mean, I didn't even know you then, did I?'

'No, but I was away quite a bit of the time.' Lottie tried to be generous.

'It was easier to just stay in the house and let him look after me. I can't believe I spent all day just tidying up, cooking food and trying to look my best for him.' She hadn't forgone the manicures, gym and facials, but it was hard now to remember just how she did spend all her time. Without Marcus, life had shifted on its axis. Man time had been replaced with Sam and the Kitterly Heath girls, Lottie and the Tippermere horses, and Pip who was careful to straddle both camps. And many men, from what she could gather. Tom had been practically blushing when she'd asked him about Pip, who had been much less coy.

She liked Tom – he was easy company. As much out of his depth here as she often felt, and yet this place seemed to have a hold over both of them. They were ducks out of water, and yet both were reluctant to leave, to let go. And Pip, with the nose of a bloodhound and less sensitivity, seemed determined to capitalise on it. She wasn't yet quite sure if the girl was a wonderful friend, or whether they were all just walk-on parts in some big play she'd put on.

Pip knew everyone, and Pip organised everyone. Except Tom had an edge that said he wasn't going to be bossed around unless it suited him. He'd been unbothered about the photograph of them together but strangely sensitive when she'd mentioned David's visit. Which reminded her…

'Sam and David's house is beautiful isn't it? I hadn't been until we had that girlie night. That's why I asked if she'd put me in touch with David's father.' She linked her arm through Lottie's and led her into the house and across the vast hallway into what Marcus had called 'the snug', although it was about as snug as a ballroom. It was just too big, dwarfing even the antique green Chesterfield sofas and the table with its enormous brass-clawed feet. But Marcus had had the money to fill it, even if he hadn't had the taste to make the finished room look either classy or refined. Amanda longed to make it cosy but elegant; a room with a roaring fire and winged chairs that she could curl up in.

Tom had looked comfortable in here when he'd stopped by. With his easy elegance, he could fit in anywhere, she reckoned. But it had been seeing him sitting there, the epitome of real English elegance, that had spurred her into action. Tom had gifted her an image of a future she couldn't ignore.

'Was your father really going to shoot them?' She grinned, relief now that her ordeal was over, making her feel positively giddy.

'I'm not sure.' Lottie sat down. 'I don't think he would shoot to kill, though.'

'Ah.'

'He knows he can't kill all the enemy one shot at a time, and bullets are expensive, you know. It was more a statement of intent, I think.'

'I think David was shocked, but Sam just thought he was kidding. He said, just imagine the headlines if the wedding of the year was cancelled because an Olympic medal-winning showjumper had gone on the rampage with a double-barrelled shotgun. Did he win an Olympic medal?'

'He did. He wanted to put it in the coffin with Mum, get her to look after it for him.'

'Gosh.' There was silence.

'He said he'd only lose it. He always pretended it wasn't that important to him, but it was. Tiggy said he fell asleep with it in his hand the day he won it.'

Amanda wondered if it was wrong that she'd never had a single thought like that about Marcus since he died. She missed him, but he was gone. He didn't fill her waking hours; she didn't want to share the disaster or triumphs with him. The satisfaction in finally conquering her fears and sitting on a horse was something she wanted to share with someone else. Even if it was so trivial in the grand scheme of things.

'These came this morning, I wanted to show you and try to explain. I'm so sorry your dad has been so worried, I just never thought to explain. But to be honest, I haven't sorted it out in my own head what I want to do. I just know I've got to do something, and for once in my life it's got to be the right thing for me.' She pulled a roll of papers from the inside of a cardboard tube, slightly worried that now she had started to talk, she didn't seem to be able to stop. Maybe horse-riding had been like therapy, which was why some people actually enjoyed it. Or maybe, which was more likely, for her it had been like shock treatment. 'Tom gave me the idea. I was showing him some photos of this place when we bought it, and he said he'd seen photographs of what it used to look like in some magazine or other, and he was very diplomatic, but he was only thinking what I was, that it would be so lovely to restore it, you know, like Sam's house has been.'

'So, you see a lot of Tom?' Lottie didn't like to say it, but she'd been under the impression that Tom was more interested in Pip than anyone. But he had, whilst denying he wanted a woman, been spending a lot of time studying her own arse (even if he thought she hadn't noticed). Maybe there was more to Tom than met the eye, though he was bloody discreet about it.

Amanda blushed. 'Not loads, I think he likes to come here to hide. It's a bolthole, and he's fun, in a kind of droll, laid-back way.

I like him. He's got Tabatha harassing him at home, and I think he likes Pip, but he's a bit scared of her. And he says Elizabeth is like a mafia mama.' She giggled.

'So you've not?'

'Shagged?'

The word sounded slightly shocking from Amanda's lips, thought Lottie.

'No, he's not really my type and I don't think I'm his, but he is lovely isn't he?'

'Lovely.' Lottie agreed, secretly wondering if it was Amanda in cahoots with Tom, not Dom. Maybe somebody had mixed the words up somewhere along the line and her poor uncle had been implicated unfairly.

Except he had been in a very funny mood when Elizabeth had taken her down to the stables.

'Anyway,' Amanda smoothed out the papers, 'Anthony, David's father, came and had a look round and did these for me. They're like architectural impressions of what we could do. He said they're only rough, to give me an idea.'

'So you're staying?' Lottie suddenly saw a bright light at the end of the muddied tunnel.

'Well, to be totally honest, I don't really know yet.'

Back to doom and gloom.

'But I want to do it up, and if I do end up selling, then maybe we can find a buyer who will want to keep it as it is.'

'We?'

'I. I meant to say I. Anthony has clients who are interested in places like this, and it is in good nick. But I do like it here; it's just, well, it's just complicated.'

Lottie wanted to ask what exactly was complicated, but Amanda was busying herself putting the drawings away and she got the message. No-go area.

'Dad thinks Dom is trying to persuade you to sell.'

'Dom isn't trying to persuade me to do anything. Honest.'

Amanda looked Lottie straight in the eye and could answer with complete honesty. Sometimes she wished he was; sometimes she wished that all the answers were easy. 'This time I'm making my own decisions, Lottie. This time it's got to be perfect.'

Chapter 21

'Mrs Stanthorpe.'

'Lady.'

Tom gave her a blank look, not sure whether the eccentric old lady had completely lost her marbles and was unable to even identify his sex, or whether this was some kind of strange test.

The corner of her mouth twitched. 'It's Lady Stanthorpe, actually. But I am joking, young man, come in. Call me Elizabeth, I did tell you that before, let's not stand on ceremony.'

Tom stepped into the large hall and for the first time had some appreciation about what stepping into the past meant. And what inheritance was all about.

He'd thought the place had been imposing enough from the outside, but now, with the inner, slightly shabby, grandeur of the mansion, and the indomitable Elizabeth, who he had not met on her own turf before, he felt a bit out of his depth and began to wonder if it was a mistake coming here.

Elizabeth seemed to sense it, and leaving him to close the door, she set off across the cavernous entrance hall, leaving him to gallop in her wake like one of the Labradors that always accompanied her. He couldn't remember seeing her without the dogs, two happy consorts who knew their place and relished it.

Tom guessed, in the time he had for a brief glance around,

that every stick of furniture in the vast space was original. No reproduction failures here. Even the oak-clad walls, solid doors and incredible staircase spoke of a wealth of times gone by; he floor worn and polished from the footfalls of thousands, pitted from the nails of dogs; the wood mellowed and aged from the corrosive bath of daylight, the light and shade of nature.

He stopped briefly to gaze at the paintings that hung in regimented fashion on the walls, the features of Elizabeth staring out from each in an unnerving fashion.

'A motley crew, aren't they?' A ghost of a smile flitted across her features.

'I haven't got a past, a history, like that.'

'Now is that a problem or a benefit?' She didn't wait for a response, and didn't give him the opportunity to ponder about her meaning. 'Come.' The imperious tone was a final summons before Elizabeth disappeared through a doorway in the far corner and for a fleeting moment Tom felt like he was being called to his execution or to meet a modern-day Miss Havisham, who would drain his life of all joy. Well, the bit that Tamara had deigned to leave behind.

'I was wondering when you'd turn up. You will join me for a drink, won't you?'

Oh Lord, not musty sherry, please not sticky, sweet sherry that had been standing for a year and a day.

But it wasn't sherry. When Tom finally pulled himself together and followed Elizabeth, he was surprised to find himself in a uncharacteristically bright and airy room, with modern touches blending perfectly with the old. And she was waving a hand at the drinks tray, which had already thoughtfully been prepared with a good stock of gin, tonic, ice and lemon. 'Be a darling and pour. I don't like to admit to it, but it is so nice to watch a man do these things. It is funny, isn't it, how you miss the little things? When dear Charles was alive he could be such a buffoon at times, but he did his best to look after me in his own way. And he poured a bloody good gin and tonic. Sign of a good man, that is.'

Which didn't help Tom relax at all.

'Don't drown it, will you? I really can't see the point of a good gin if you can't taste the stuff. And help yourself to an olive. Can't stand the things myself, taste of potpourri.'

Tom, who had until now actually thought he did like olives, took one look at the bowl and adjusted his opinion. It seemed that the alcohol was more important than the food in this place.

'So how are you settling in, dear? Philippa tells me your daughter is getting stuck into things. Good for her, I say. A girl needs to get her hands dirty these days, then she can handle whatever, and whoever,' she winked, 'comes her way. Although these men can be a bit down-to-earth, if you get my drift.'

Tom got her drift, and he didn't really need it pointing out to him. And he was now beginning to suspect that Elizabeth was having a bit of a joke at his expense.

'So, Thomas, to what do I owe this visit? Not that it isn't very pleasant of you to pop by, of course. But I don't for one minute flatter myself that you like to visit old ladies and their country piles.'

She'd obviously sensed the fact that he was getting dangerously close to reaching his limit. Pip had been right when she'd said the woman was smart. She was smart, she was matriarchal and she was domineering. And, he was convinced, she was up to something, a something that unfortunately he seemed to be playing a minor role in.

He put down his untouched drink. 'I think I need your help.'

'Go on.'

'If my father is upset enough to issue threats via my ex-wife, then it means that what you told Pip is right, and I really would like to understand the full story. I don't like being threatened, and I don't like him. If I understood a bit more, if I understood him, then I wouldn't feel like he's about to drop a bloody big boulder on my head and bury me.'

Tom ran his fingers through his flop of a fringe and reminded

Elizabeth of a little boy lost; a little boy who just wanted to please everybody and ended up losing himself. And losing his grip on reality.

He was so totally unlike his father in every single way, except one. He thought somebody else could put the world to rights for him. Fix the problem. And, when she came to think about it, they also both seemed to like making a mountain out of a molehill. Which had meant that when Strachan senior tried to tell people he was heading for a serious meltdown, nobody knew whether to take him seriously, until it was too late.

'You aren't close to your father, I take it?'

'We'd be a world apart even if he was on this side of the hemisphere. He was a bully who ran away, but sent me back.'

'Misguided, yes. But a bully? Not really. Your father is an educated man, Thomas, who made mistakes and didn't want to stand up and be counted. He did run away, but he wanted his son to be brought up and educated in the same way as he was. Through the very best old-fashioned English education system. But as you became established in your own right, if he'd maintained contact with you then somebody would have made the link, and he didn't want them to.' Elizabeth held her glass out for a refill and watched Tom closely. There were certain mannerisms that he'd inherited: the way he held himself, but how much was from the public-school upbringing and how much was genetic, unavoidable?

She could say that his father had been a lovely well-meaning man who was a complete coward, who had run away from reality in just the same way his son was trying to. Strachan senior had run off to hide in Australia; Strachan junior had tried to bury himself in the countryside. It was just slightly ironic that it was the same rural hideaway that his father had fled. Very ironic. Too much of a coincidence.

'When your parents bought Folly Lake Manor he wasn't quite so publicity-shy, which is why I instantly recognised you. There's something of him in those photographs of you; I'm surprised the press didn't recognise it. Although maybe they weren't looking, maybe he is yesterday's news and they aren't as old as I am. It's a beautiful place, isn't it?'

Tom nodded dumbly, wondering if this was part of the interrogation.

'You're drawn to it, just like he was. A fool and his money.'

'Are easily parted.' He raised an eyebrow. 'And Tamara already has most of mine.'

'Your father invested his in the property and in the lifestyle he thought should accompany it. Strange how that place has drawn the flamboyant in, isn't it? What makes it a status symbol, I wonder?' She paused, but Tom waited, not having any answers, although he was fairly sure the question was rhetorical. 'From what I gather, he was a victim of bad timing and carelessness. He'd speculated, invested money he hadn't got and then was unlucky enough to have the banks call in loans at an inopportune time. He was, as I said, a clever man. But he wasn't a realist; he played with theoretical numbers, speculated, played games. Which is fine,' she stared at him, 'with monopoly.' She resisted the temptation to add, but not for a grown man with a family to support. 'You were young when it happened. He fled, taking you with him, and the property was repossessed and put up for auction. It changed hands a few times before an old friend of Alexandra's and William's took it on and offered them a lease on the equestrian centre in return for help in managing the estate and land. When he had a stroke it was sold on to Marcus James, who honoured the arrangement with William. And now it seems it is time for change again. It would be such a shame if it were bulldozed, don't you think?'

Tom blanched. 'But I could never afford it.'

'Oh I know that, dear boy, but you could influence the future. If you wanted.'

'Why is my father threatening me? I mean, I can understand he doesn't want his past being dragged up, but I've already been in the papers.'

'Exactly. As a model – a man in his own right. Have you never wondered why, as your profile rose, your parents drew back?'

Tom thought about it and knew it was the truth. The missed wedding, Tab's christening, all those important events in his life, the milestones they'd ignored, had been when he and Tamara were riding the crest of fame. In every newspaper, magazine, on TV, their every move followed and recorded.

'And if you make yourself too interesting now, he's afraid they might dig.'

'Dig?'

'I think it's more of a friendly warning, than a threat.'

'Friendly? I thought you said you knew him.' There was a hard edge to Tom's voice that Elizabeth hadn't heard before.

Elizabeth sighed. How often one misunderstanding could make for a lifetime of hurt, of estrangement.

'I'd assume,' she passed over his comment, 'that he thinks you came back here because you knew the history, and he wants to make it clear that if you're going to court the papers then he doesn't want any reference to himself, or your childhood. He's a sensitive man, like you.'

'I didn't court the papers.'

'No, but you courted young Philippa.' She winked at his discomfort.

'I think she courted me, if we're totally honest.'

The guffaw took him by surprise. 'She isn't for you, is she?'

'Far too clever and conniving. A bit like you, actually.'

'And you just want to fade from the limelight and have a quiet life, Thomas?' She put her glass down and stood up abruptly, so he followed suit. 'You'll get it, my boy, but first let's have a little stroll. I quite like the idea of a walk with an underwear model. Boys.' The boys fell in, like the seasoned troopers they were. 'Here.' She picked up a photograph as they passed the hall table at a rate of knots.

Even though the picture was black and white, faded and dog-eared, the house was instantly recognisable, the couple stood in front, holding a baby swathed in an old-fashioned christening gown, smiling out at him like long-lost family. They *were* long-lost family. His.

'Where did you get this?'

'Do you recognise it? It was taken at your christening, and I do believe your parents also have a copy. I think that's why Folly Lake Manor seemed familiar to you.'

She steamed ahead and Tom hurried to keep up.

'I kept in touch with your mother for a brief time after they moved, and I know that despite your father's intention to leave everything behind she held on to a few mementoes. That photograph is one of the few she kept, and I'm sure you would have seen it when you were tiny.'

'It did seem familiar when I saw it, when I arrived here.'

'What brought you to Tippermere, Thomas? Why here?'

Now that was the million-dollar question. What the hell was he doing here? It was something that had niggled at him more and more lately. 'I honestly don't know. I thought I just picked it at random; a nice country village away from London but with motorway links, you know, the standard commuter-belt bollocks.'

'But?'

'But I'm beginning to wonder. Ever since I got here I've felt like a target for manipulation. Have you and Pip thought about hiring out your services to the mafia?'

Elizabeth laughed and actually, Tom decided, looked quite pleased with herself.

'That picture of you and Amanda was taken not too far from here.'

'Was it?' Tom racked his brain and couldn't uncover anything that gave him a hint. 'It was some charity do, I think.'

'It was, held at the local golf and country club.'

'It was just an engagement I was booked for. You get shoved in a car and then deposited at the other end. For a long time I hadn't a clue where I was or where I'd been. And that,' he looked rueful, 'was on the days when I was relatively sober and clean.'

'Your mother wanted you to see this place, to know your history, but of course your father was dead against it. So she made sure your name made its way onto the guest list.'

'I vaguely remember that we were supposed to stay over, but Tamara was ill.' He tried to remember more, but nothing came. It had been unimportant at the time, there was no reason to remember. 'But that wasn't why this place stood out. In fact, I think a lot of the reason was because of Rory Steel. Tab even had his picture on her phone and I think spotted him in Country Life or some magazine like that…' When he thought about it, it had been Tab who had spotted the village as she flicked through her horsey magazines. Tab who had known that these few square miles were crammed with equestrian expertise.

'And why do you think your daughter is so fixated on that particular rider?'

'Sexy? Young and dashing?' Tom shrugged. He couldn't for the life of him see why teenage girls went soppy over horse-riders.

'When those complimentary tickets came your way for Olympia, Rory and Lottie were sitting just yards away from you and your impressionable daughter. They were there to support Billy, but if you were a teenage girl and one of your long list of heart throbs was sitting within touching distance, probably smiled at you, I'd imagine he'd go to the top of the list, wouldn't you?' She patted his arm. 'Now I wonder who sent those tickets to your agent?'

'Hell. You're saying it was Mother, aren't you?'

'I think she just wanted you to see the place, to find some of the pieces of the jigsaw. She didn't want to just bury the past, hide it from you.' She chuckled. 'But of course she could have never imagined that Marcus would drop dead and you'd get drawn into all this. You really are the cat amongst the pigeons.'

'Wonderful.' Tom struggled to understand the ramifications of his desire to bury himself in the countryside, to align that with the position he now found himself in. 'Feline is better than feral

265

I suppose. So, what did you mean, earlier, when you said I can influence the future?'

'Well, you don't want to see it destroyed, lost forever, do you?'

'I don't.'

'Do you think it's your destiny, Folly Lake Manor? Do you think you've come back here because you want it, if you could afford it, that is?'

'Hell, no, I really didn't know. Well, I hadn't realised...'

'Good, that's what I thought. It isn't your destiny, but it is someone else's.' Elizabeth linked her arm through Tom's and thought how wonderful it was when a plan came together. 'Let me tell you a little story.'

**

'You are kidding?'

Tom just raised an eyebrow. He constantly swung between thinking that Pip was actually quite nice and a feeling that ranged from mild dislike to fear. 'Kidding about what?'

'You haven't actually read that letter?' Pip was in the house, had gone through to the kitchen and was messing around with coffee cups. 'Sorry, I am absolutely dying for a drink, you have no idea the rush I had on to get all those stables skipped out so that I could come down here.'

'How do you know I haven't read it?' Tom had wandered after her and wondered if maybe a girl like her needed a much firmer hand.

'Elizabeth told me.'

'What is this, the Tippermere terrorist organisation?'

She grinned and raided the biscuit tin. 'I am absolutely famished. Honestly, Tom, you are such an idiot.'

'He's a dork.' Tabatha had wandered in unnoticed and had the fridge door open.

'Shouldn't you two be working?' Maybe he should just give in and let them walk over him, it would make life easier.

'Lunch break.' Pip spoke through a digestive biscuit.

'I wouldn't have thought dork was an in-word these days.'

'It isn't.' Tab, armed with a can of cola and a handful of biscuits, was already heading for the lounge. 'But nor are you. I thought it suited you.' And then she actually grinned, which confused him for a moment.

'You're spending too much time together.' He looked from one to the other. It was good and bad, but which carried the most weight he wasn't quite sure yet.

'So where is it?' Pip, who had given up on the biscuit barrel and moved on to a chunk of cheddar she had found in the fridge, sat down expectantly at the breakfast bar.

'Sorry?'

'The letter?'

'I haven't got a—'

'It's on the table in the hall, Dad.' The voice carried through from the lounge and Tom wondered if it was an idea to shut the door, but there again, what harm could it do? Tab seemed to be growing up fast, and if she had a fraction of her mother's genetic make-up (which she had), then what he didn't tell her she'd find out by other means if she was interested. He was still musing over this when Pip returned with the letter.

'How could you not read it?'

'I got the gist from Tamara, and what difference does it make?'

'I don't believe you, how could you not? Can I?'

'Help yourself.' He took the mug of coffee, which had been unceremoniously dumped in front of him.

'I think Elizabeth's right. He's not actually threatening you, I think he's almost apologetic. In fact,' she scanned the page again, 'it's almost like he's embarrassed but too macho to admit it.'

'You've managed to get a hell of a lot out of a one-page letter, a bit like when you have to analyse a poem at school.' She glared at him, but he decided now was the time to stop the various women that surrounded him from taking his good nature as a green light for bossiness. 'They come out with all this crap and deep meaning, and how the hell do they know? Maybe the poet just liked the words, or was pissed, or just rambling. Like I appear to be.'

Pip raised an eyebrow at the outburst, then turned her attention back to the letter. 'I think he was shocked that you turned up in the papers and were standing outside Folly Lake Manor. Elizabeth said it was his pride and joy; he was obsessed by the place, and so it must have been a shock, mustn't it?'

He stirred the coffee slowly.

'Mustn't it?' Pip was not to be put off. Something he should have known by now. 'Seeing you just standing there.'

'So what was he doing reading the local rag, eh? In Australia?'

'Well the story did get beyond the local rag, I mean, even if you're not big news these days, Marcus was, and David is. And Elizabeth reckons that he keeps an eye on what you're up to.'

'Does she now? Have you women really nothing better to do than speculate about my father?' He helped himself to a cookie, which just proved he was wound up as he'd had a lifetime ban on sugary snacks since starting up his modelling career and been warned they would ruin his skin and send him into middle-aged spread before he was thirty.

'Elizabeth said your mother rang her.'

'Really?' He stopped the stirring abruptly. His father he had never really missed, but his mother had been different. She had tried to keep in touch, even though she hadn't approved of his marriage, but it was difficult. An intermittent contact made difficult by time differences and work, and the fact that she wouldn't call if she thought Tamara would answer. And as time went on, their relationship seemed to become more strained by the distance between them, by his refusal to talk to his father and, he guessed, by his father's refusal to talk to him. Working as a go-between could never have been easy. And he realised now that the more successful he'd become, the harder it had probably been.

But he'd not spoken to her for months, and something had stopped him telling her that they'd moved. After all, there was never any chance that she would pop in. It wasn't an issue, and it would have meant admitting that he'd ditched the life he'd created, that he'd run away to bury himself in the peace of the countryside.

It surprised him that she knew where he was. It surprised him more that she had kept in contact with Elizabeth. How on earth his parent's marriage survived he had no idea. They seemed to have no clue about what the other was doing.

'You don't talk to your father at all, do you?'

'Not for years. Apparently he hadn't spent all that money on my education for me to just fritter it away on a silly notion. He said he'd disown me if I didn't get my act together and concentrate on a proper career, so I saved him the trouble.'

'Ouch. Maybe he didn't mean it?'

'Like he didn't mean to ban home visits if I didn't get good grades? Like he didn't mean to stop my allowance the day I signed my first modelling contract and joined a load of "ponces" one step away from being a call boy? He said I needed a wake-up call, said he didn't owe me a living.'

'You're tougher than you look, aren't you?'

'I'm not tough, Pip. But I do know how to look after myself. I never finished my degree because of him, but it did mean I had to make a success of what I'd chosen to do, so I guess I owe something to him.'

'But what about your mother?'

'They have a very traditional marriage, and although he didn't ban her from seeing me or anything ridiculous like that, just the distance made it difficult. And when I was younger, I guess I just thought she should have tried harder.'

'I don't think I ever want children. It must be hell – all those expectations.'

'On both sides.' Tom's tone was dry, but Pip reckoned he'd lightened up. And he really was quite adorable, like a lost puppy

269

who'd got tired of digging a hole and was wondering whether or not to flop.

'I heard that.' Tab's voice echoed through from the lounge, her mouth full of biscuits, from the muffled edge to it.

Pip grinned, dropped the letter and then straddled his thighs, tugged gently at his full bottom lip.

'I don't thi—'

'Shh, she'll hear.' She rocked her hips, felt his cock harden in response. 'Fancy a bit of no-strings-attached wild sex?'

'You are a hussy.' He was laughing at her, not quite sure if she meant it. But she did. Pip was done with talking and solving problems. And Tom was cute. Which was just what she wanted at the end of a frustrating morning. She slipped her hand between them, unzipped his flies. 'You can't...'

'Watch me. That's half the fun of it, risking getting caught.' He was in her hand, getting harder with every stroke of her fingertips. 'Or rather feel me.'

'Oh shit.' Tom looked into her eyes, which stared straight back at him, and shook his head. 'You'll be the death of me, woman.'

'What a brilliant way to go.' Short skirts and no knickers had seemed a good plan to Pip when she'd popped to the loo earlier, and she was right. One wriggle of her hips and he was inside her, his face tightening as he slipped into her wet channel.

'Christ.'

Pip grinned, one hand on her clit as she eased herself up and down. 'Come.' She'd been on the verge the moment he was inside and she could see he was fighting it, a gentleman to the end. But that one word tipped him over the edge. He bucked his hips, surged deeper inside her, his fingers curling round, digging into her waist. And as her body tightened around him, her clit throbbing against her fingers, Pip closed her eyes. And she would have loved to have just seen Tom, but it was Mick that filled her head. Stripped to the waist, dark eyes burning into hers as he told her to leave Tom alone.

Chapter 22

'Where's your passport?'

Lottie looked up from the smelly foot she was putting a poultice on.

'Sorry?' She looked up at the mare, then back at Rory. 'She doesn't need her passport, she's not going anywhere.' Paperwork was a nightmare with Rory around. Knowing every one of his horses needed a passport was one thing; being able to locate them was another. To Lottie it would have made sense to keep them in one place, but however hard she tried to keep to the plan, late nights and long days weren't conducive to organisation and paperwork. Getting back from an event at midnight, with a tired horse and an elated or depressed Rory, usually meant that sorting the lorry was the last thing on their minds. Until they were packing it to go to the next competition.

'Not the horse, you silly moo, you, your passport.'

Lottie dropped the horse's foot down slightly more abruptly than she'd intended and wondered if it was her that was going mad, or Rory. Not that he looked mad; he actually looked quite sexy with his open-necked checked shirt and clean jeans. And he was grinning, slightly self-consciously.

'Any idea where it is? We can't find it. And why are you doing that, I thought I asked Pip to?'

'She doesn't like it; the stink makes her feel like throwing up. And before you even think about saying it, no, you can't ask Tabby.'

'But we've got to go. I did tell you, and she bloody knew.'

Rory, Lottie decided, was acting very strangely. It was probably because he hadn't got any competitions lined up for the weekend. And he was dressed like he was off out.

'What are you up to?' She eyed him suspiciously. According to a recent quiz she'd completed in Cosmo, he was either about to dump her (unexpected), having an affair (unlikely) or about to propose (impossible).

'Trust me.'

'Those are the words that are most likely to convince me you're up to something. What are you after? And why—' She'd picked up the yard brush, and was about to ask why he was all dressed up with nowhere to go (well, nowhere as far as she knew).

'Don't start brushing the yard, woman. Give it here.' Which shocked her into silence. She could never, ever remember Rory stopping her working, well, apart from the time he'd thrown her over his shoulder, dumped her in an empty stable and pretended to ride her to victory after she'd teased him about falling off. It was quite a long time ago, but it still made her feel hot. All he had to do since that day was gather her hair up in one hand so that the cold air touched the back of her neck and a shiver of expectation ran through her. Shameless hussy were the words that sprung to mind, but she didn't care. 'Go and get changed, we're going out.'

'Oh, I love it when you're firm.'

'I suppose I could put you over my knee and spank you, but,' he glanced at his watch. Which was odd, as he hardly ever wore one. Apart from when he was competing and needed a timer. 'But we haven't got time, please Lots, shift your arse.'

'Okay.' She pushed the stable door shut and gave him a quick kiss, because he looked gorgeous and hassled. 'Get changed into what?'

'Just normal clothes.'

'But for what? For the pub, shopping, you know it does matter.'

'We're having a couple of days away.'

'There's an event you forgot to tell me about?' She racked her brain for some entry on the eventing calendar that she'd somehow forgotten. It came up blank.

'No. Look, if you must know, your friends ganged up on me and said if I didn't understand you I should take you—'

'Are you two gassing all day, or will we be getting off? And shouldn't you be getting changed, treas? Not that you don't look gorgeous as you are, but you're cutting it a bit fine.'

'Are you coming too, Mick?'

Now she was confused. And even more when the car horn blasted across the yard and made her jump. Pip grinned and gave it another blast.

'Will you lot stop pissing about, we're going to be late.' In denim shorts that showed her slim legs off to perfection, and a halter-neck top that showcased tanned shoulders, Pip looked more festival than three-day event type of weekend away.

'Okay, who is going to tell me what's going on?' One of the terriers, alerted to the possibility of a fun outing, was already in Mick's pickup, front feet on the steering wheel, and seeing Lottie put her hands on her hips, it yapped out for reinforcements. The other two came hurtling across the yard, a stick between them, which very nearly sent the passing Tab into the air. With the timing of a true showjumper, she jumped just as the convoy came through, unfortunately forgetting that she had a running hosepipe in her hand, which shot a stream of cold water straight in Mick's direction.

Lottie tried not to laugh, but one look at the horror on Tabatha's face and she couldn't hold it back any longer.

Mick shook his head, drips of water spraying over his shirt. 'The Jack Terror trio aren't bloody coming.'

'Will someone tell me where we're going, please? Why am I always the last to know everything?'

'Because you're always the last to get ready. Go, now, quick.' Rory gave her a shove towards the house. 'Jeans, t-shirt and denim jacket. Now.'

'But Pip's got shorts on.'

'Pip isn't coming with us, she's just along for the ride.'

'Boots?'

'Shoes.' Came from Mick along with a simultaneous 'sandals' from Pip and a 'for fuck's sake hurry up,' from Rory. Lottie hurried up.

'I thought we were going for a romantic vibe on this trip?' Mick shook his head, which scattered a fine shower of water over the dashboard, as Lottie squeezed into the back of his vehicle along with the three dogs, and Rory.

'Are we?' Rory sounded mildly surprised as he took the opportunity to let his fingertips stray over the soft, exposed skin of Lottie's shoulders, down to where her breasts swelled out from the skimpy t-shirt. He'd known exactly what was going through her head earlier, and he really would have liked to have pushed her onto all fours and tried to show her who was boss. Even if she was usually in giggles, until she hit that point of no return. He shifted, trying to accommodate his growing erection without being too obvious. Lottie put her hand over it, which didn't help.

'Well so Pip and Amanda told me.' Mick started up the engine, shaking his head again. 'Romantic, not rude. You two better not do anything on my back seat.'

Rory grinned and put his hands behind his head. 'Nothing to do with me, mate. Anyway what's Amanda got to do with this?'

'Amanda helped me pack.' Pip giggled and put her feet up on the dashboard, Rory gave a dirty laugh, Lottie frowned and Mick crunched the gears. Everybody, it seemed, had the holiday vibe. He gave in, wound all the windows down and turned the radio up.

Half an hour later, with a particularly bad rendition of 'Good Vibrations' blasting out from the back seat, Mick pulled in to the drop-off point at the airport. 'Don't do anything I wouldn't.' He

274

winked at Lottie, handed Rory the case and watched Pip join in the dogs' farewell bounce. Surprisingly she carried on bouncing all the way back over to him and almost gave him a hug, then realised what was happening and backed off. Mick grinned, and waited.

Pip gave as close to a blush as he'd ever seen. 'I hope they have a great time.'

They watched the crowd in the departure hall swallow up Lottie and Rory.

'They will.' Mick slammed shut the rear door and felt strangely like a decision had been made for him. The lift inside him couldn't even be quashed by the site of the three terriers doing a wall of death run round the inside of the car.

'Now we've got rid of that pair, how about playing hooky?' Mick's fingers brushed hers as he opened the door for her, too slow not to be deliberate. With Lottie and Rory messing about in the back of the car, and Pip's tanned slim legs on full display in the front, he'd finally decided he needed to give in to the urges that had been bothering him for a while. When he'd first seen Pip he'd thought her attractive, but he'd veered towards the much simpler, gentler vibe that Lottie gave out. Lottie was like a wild bird, beautiful, but needing her freedom. Pip was dangerous, sharp and with an insatiable urge to get to the bottom of things. And he hadn't wanted anyone to get to the bottom of him. But the more time he spent with her, the more the need to challenge her came out, the desire to show her what she could have if she really wanted it.

Pip needed a firm hand, not the easy wishy-washy delights of an insecure man like Tom. And, if he was honest with himself, he needed a woman who wasn't afraid to answer back, to know her mind, even if it did make him feel like he was teetering on the edge of something like a very deep snake-filled pit.

'What type of hooky?'

'Your call. But no horses' feet or muck heaps involved.'

'You fancy Lottie, don't you?' Pip tried to ignore the goosebumps, and the fact that being stuck in close proximity to Mick, hemmed in by leather seats, glass and metalwork, was an altogether trickier prospect than having a go at him on a stable yard. Verbal sparring was fun, but this looked like it could be something more serious. And dodging serious was a favourite habit of hers.

She could always, she supposed, open the car door and make her escape, except they were now moving, and she wasn't that desperate.

'I'm not going to be lying, darling. She's quite a meal to feast my eyes on, but she's not mine to touch.' His hand briefly made contact with her exposed thigh as he took the handbrake off, and Pip gave an involuntary squeak.

'No, she's not.' Even to her own ears Pip sounded a bit uptight, not her usual relaxed and easy-come, easy-go self.

'Do you never go back to Wales?' His hand was back on the steering wheel, which was a bit annoying.

'Not often. Do you ever go back to Ireland?'

'I was planning on doing it soon. Must have given me itchy feet watching the two lovebirds go off.'

'Do you think they are?'

'Lovebirds? Oh yes, bound for life. Flighty, sociable, but inseparable.'

'And pretty.'

'Indeed.'

Pip wasn't quite sure why she was pushing him, except she had seen the looks he gave Lottie, seen how easily they got along, with none of the friction that seemed to exist between herself and the dark Irishman. Insecure and jealous weren't two of her traits, so obviously it couldn't be because of that.

'Fancy coming along? To Ireland when I go. I'm sure you could find something to write about, even if it's only to moan about the fine tradition of hunting.'

'It's archaic and cruel. You need to move with the times.'

He laughed. 'Just because an idea is new, doesn't mean it's better. Besides,' he paused as he swung onto the motorway, 'it's a basic instinct for a man to hunt down his quarry.' He glanced at her briefly, then turned his gaze back to the road. 'And there's nothing wrong with basic instincts.'

'Where are we going?' Even unsettled, Pip couldn't miss the fact that they'd come off the motorway a junction early.

'I'm taking you up to the Edge. Fancy it?'

'Sure.' There was a tingle between her thighs and a strange feeling at the pit of her stomach that Pip hadn't felt for a long time.

'They say there's witches and the likes up there. We can do a bit of hunting of our own, I thought.'

'Planning on stripping me back to my basic instincts are you?'

'Planning on stripping you bare, darling.' The deep, throaty chuckle left Pip squirming in the leather seat with absolutely no doubt at all about what playing hooky was going to involve.

***

'Did you pack this case yourself?'

'Yes. Well, no.'

The girl behind the check-in desk, who had been smiling nicely, stopped abruptly. There was a deadly pause. 'Yes, or no?'

'No.'

'Bet they don't hear that often.' Rory groaned.

'But I didn't. You did.'

'Well, actually I didn't.' He shrugged apologetically.

The girl now looked like she was about to call someone a bit more senior, and the queue of people behind started feet-shuffling.

'You didn't?'

'How would I know what to put in? Pip and Amanda did it.'

'Pip. Oh, God.' Lottie put her head in her hands and rolled her eyes at the girl, who was still looking undecided on the next course of action.

'You didn't pack the case?'

'I didn't. But it'll be fine.'

'I'm sorry, but you do need to know what's in it. You have to pack it yourself.' The girl looked pointedly at the prominently displayed sign, which Lottie thought was a bit excessive.

'I do? Sorry, I do. Well, I do. Would you trust a friend like her to pack your case? Shall I open it?'

'Excuse me, love, but some of us are waiting to catch a plane here.' The man who had been waiting impatiently behind them, shuffling feet and coughing, had obviously listened in, and was now getting worried about the prospect of Lottie emptying the entire contents of her suitcase onto the desk for inspection.

'Sorry, I am honestly, truly sorry. But I queued too, you know, and it's not my fault it's a surprise trip, is it?'

'Ahh.' His wife grinned at her, then more broadly at Rory. 'Bless, isn't that romantic, Bob. I wish you'd do something like that for me. There isn't a hidden ring in there is there?' She nudged Bob in the ribs and threw Rory a wink that was more leery than loving.

Bob didn't look impressed. 'Bloody soft if you ask me.'

'But I'm not, Bob. Am I, love?'

'Er, no.' Getting hot and bothered was something Lottie had been expecting to get once the plane had landed at the other end, not before they'd even boarded.

Lottie finally got to grips with the lock on the case, and wished she hadn't as it burst open. It wasn't just the sheer quantity of knickers spilling forth that bothered her, it was the colours. This was not going to be a discreet nude-undies trip, this was multi-colour mayhem.

'On second thoughts.' Bob had lost his grumpiness and seemed to be showing a particular interest in her favourite red undies, which she hastily pushed underneath one of the few t-shirts that had been packed.

'I've not got anything sharp or inflammable or anything, have I? You can see. Look,' Lottie delved through the contents, then pushed them back down. 'I've packed it myself now.' She hastily crammed the overflowing lingerie back, grabbing the leopard-skin bra as it made a bid for freedom. 'My God, those aren't my shorts, where did those come from?' She held what looked to be skin-tight (well, definitely skin-tight given the size of her thighs) white shorts up, then seeing the look on Bob's face hastily dropped them back into the case and fought a losing battle to keep the top pinned down as she tried to coax the zip round, trapping pink lace and satin in the process.

'I'm not sure, I might have to ask—' The check-in girl was looking seriously confused. She obviously hadn't been faced with a knicker selection this large before.

'No, please don't.' Asking would only prolong the agony. 'Look, it's all fine.'

A look of sudden relief flooded her features and got rid of the frown lines. 'You do know that case is small enough to take on as hand luggage; you've no need to check it into the hold, you know. And you have already checked in.'

'Is it?' Rory stared at the offending case. 'And we've checked in? Well, why didn't Pip say so?'

'You probably weren't listening.'

'Would you like to carry it on, Sir, Madam?'

'Do I want to?'

'It hasn't been paid for, so you will have to pay if I put it in the hold. Although there is always the possibility that they will offer to take it off you at the gate.'

'Will they? Shall I? So why not just give it to you now, if they're going to take it anyway.'

'You'll have to pay if I take it now.' The check-in girl was getting bored.

'We'll keep it.' Rory decided that Lottie and her knickers had entertained the crowd for long enough, and he was getting quite keen on the idea of a private viewing, having spotted a red thong that he was pretty sure he'd never seen displayed between her buttocks before. In fact, if he stood here much longer, his hard-on might start to cause a visible problem. 'Come on.'

'Can I see your passports and booking confirmations, please sir?'

'Passport. Where's my passport?' Lottie suddenly remembered that whilst she'd been holding a horse's foot, Rory had been asking where her passport was and she couldn't remember saying. They'd been distracted, by Mick, and dogs.

As the check-in girl looked like she was going to spontaneously combust, Rory decided to take charge. Grabbing Lottie's hand in his, and the, by now, firmly fastened case in his other, he shot his best winning smile in the crowd's direction.

Cries of 'give us an update on the knickers on the trip back' and 'why don't you have knickers like that?' echoed behind them as they headed towards the departures gate.

***

'This is worse than qualifying a horse for the Olympic team.' Rory, who was perfectly used to all the paperwork that had to accompany his horses when they went abroad, didn't think it should apply to him, a mere mortal. The sight of a snaking queue of people, packed three-deep, disappearing into the distance, seemed to have flicked a switch in him. He had no control and he didn't like it.

The fact that he'd been organised enough to have boarding cards and passports packed somewhere (even if it took him a while to remember exactly where) had impressed Lottie. So he'd been pleased with himself. But as the realities of travelling cattle class from Manchester Airport sank in, he increasingly began to wonder why the hell he'd allowed Pip, Amanda and Mick to talk him into this. Surely a weekend away at a cross-country event would have worked just as well? And they'd have had horses to distract them too. He texted all three of them to say as much. Amanda was the only one that responded, and it seemed a bit curt. 'Exactly. No distractions. Concentrate on Lottie not the horses for once.' He didn't share the update, but turned his attention back to the queue, which had diminished to quite an extent. They were now feet away from the finishing line. And the stripping-off routine.

'Why didn't you tell me we were coming to an airport?' Lottie tugged off her wedge-heeled sandals and dropped them into a plastic tray, followed by her belt, mobile and jacket. Then she risked the scanner, just knowing it would go off.

It wasn't even as though she'd have the fun of being frisked by an even mildly attractive man, just a middle-aged woman who looked like she'd had a very bad day. After sticking her arms up, down, turning around, sticking her legs out, having fingers inside her waistband and having a security wand perilously close to parts she'd rather keep private, Lottie was finally allowed to put everything back on in double-quick time while people queued behind her to grab their own trays back.

'You must look suspicious.' Rory planted a kiss at the base of her neck as she tried to balance on one leg to put her shoes back on. He'd perked up now that the hell was over and a drink-filled bar would soon be within his grasp. 'Cheer up, I thought girls were supposed to like surprises.'

'Maybe I'm not a normal girl.'

'That's probably why I love you.'

Lottie stopped dead, and nearly caused a pile-up of a family of four with matching luggage, who were close behind. 'You love me?' He'd never said that before.

Rory looked confused. Then decided he was obviously scoring bonus points without even trying. 'Let me show you the ways.' He winked. 'I'll start off by buying you a drink.'

'And telling me why we're catching a plane to Barcelona?'

Two glasses of champagne later, Lottie wasn't that bothered about exactly why or where they were going. It just seemed a nice idea. And it seemed remarkably and wonderfully romantic of Rory to take a couple of days off just as the eventing season was starting to heat up. Maybe he did listen after all.

Chapter 23

'It says there's a two-hour delay on the departure board.'

Lottie looked uncomprehendingly at Rory. She'd been expecting him to announce a departure gate, not a delay.

'Some muttering about air traffic control strikes, from old Bob.'

'Oh, no. You've not seen him, have you?' Lottie wasn't sure she wanted a conversation with a man who'd spent ten minutes studying her entire lingerie collection, plus some extras she had never seen before either.

'Well, he is on our flight. He was near the departure board moaning about the state of the country and how the great should be taken out of Great Britain 'cos of the trade descriptions act. I did point out that this might not be team GB's fault.'

'Bet that went down well.'

'And I said they make bloody good knickers. His wife tried to kiss me, then she said she was sure she'd seen me before somewhere, so I scarpered.' Rory had been told, in no uncertain terms, that this was about Lottie, that horses shouldn't be mentioned, and autographs shouldn't be signed. He had sneaked a quick look at *Horse and Hound* in WH Smiths, on the way back from the departure board, and he had checked the British Eventing website on his phone while he was in the gents, but that was it. 'Look, would you be really upset if we didn't actually go to Barcelona?'

Lottie's face fell. That just had to be the shortest-lived display of listening and caring in the history of modern man. So much for some time together, although the time they'd spent together so far in the airport probably topped any other record. But surely 'togetherness' meant more than a departures lounge?

Rory saw the look and felt a moment of panic. He had wanted this to work, he really had. The lecture from Mick had struck a chord after listening to Billy's outpourings. Dominic might be a bit of a stuck-up, pompous prick sometimes, but the words he'd thrown at Billy about not being responsible and looking after his wife were not a million miles from Mick's. And yet he knew Billy had loved Alexa with a passion; everyone in the village did and everyone involved in the horse world did.

'Show her she's important before someone else does. If you don't want to look after her then there's a queue waiting behind you,' had been Mick's parting words. It was supposed to be a discussion about Mick and Niamh, but somehow Mick, with his clever tongue, had twisted it round to be all about Rory, and how it was all his fault Lottie had gone abroad, and it would be all his fault if she headed off again.

'I don't mean not have a break, just not Barcelona.'

'Well no, you booked it, not me.'

'Instead of spending all day in airports, why don't I book us into a nice hotel – we could explore your underwear collection.'

Lottie grinned, and Rory was shocked at how pleased he felt. 'Well, to be honest I'm not all that keen on going.' She hadn't been; it was just the fact that Rory was taking her that had been exciting. 'It wasn't quite the same after they arrested Todd.'

Rory felt a twinge of something that resembled jealousy, mingled with relief that he hadn't completely cocked up. 'Give me two minutes, then we're getting out of here.'

***

A luxury hotel was a definite improvement on an airport departure lounge. Once the manager had realised that the caller did actually want the junior suite immediately, that it wasn't a joke, and that he'd be able to add 'daughter of a gold-medal winner' and 'up-and-coming eventer' into his autobiography as padding (he was convinced that he had a potential gold mine on his hands, maybe a film adaptation, or at least a mini-series once he neared retirement age and could spill the beans on all the celebrity guests and their strange and compelling habits), he sprung into action. By the time Lottie and Rory had made their way out of the airport (which was easier said than done), there was a uniformed chauffeur, complete with printed card, waiting to escort them to a limo and on to the hotel.

A bottle of champagne, complementary chocolates and a slightly pompous and very ingratiating member of staff were awaiting them, prepared to ignore the casual attire, which was not normally seen on their guests.

Lottie launched herself on to the bed. 'Thank God he's gone, I thought he was going to offer to undress me.'

'Shag you more like. Why do people like that assume we don't understand TVs or wifi.' Rory grabbed the ice bucket and headed for the bathroom. 'Bring the glasses, woman, I'm going to fill this enormous Jacuzzi and then give you the kind of sorting you won't forget in a hurry.' He was somehow managing to kick off clothes as he went.

Lottie giggled. 'I've got an excellent memory, so I remember all of them.'

Two minutes later, glass in hand, and having her feet massaged, Lottie sank deeper into the water so that the bubbles came up to her chin. 'Will Rio be okay while you're here? I mean, who's riding him?'

Rory, who hadn't forgotten that 'horse' was supposed to be a banned word, guessed the rules could be bent if Lottie was the one who started the conversation. And anyway, Mick, Pip and

Amanda weren't there to hear.

'I sent him to Dom's for a couple of days.'

'You what?' She briefly popped up out of the bubbles so that he could admire her full breasts and tightening nipples. 'Really?'

'Really.' He traced a finger lazily along her instep and wondered if doing it with his mouth would have been an arrestable offence on a Spanish beach; there were definite advantages to being where they were. It actually surprised even him that he had sent the horse up to Tipping House, but Amanda and Pip had suggested it (when the break in the horse's training schedule at a critical point in the season had been his first objection to their mad plan), and then the man himself had rung to arrange transportation. He was amazed that either of the women had managed to persuade Dom but presumed that the name of his niece, who he was clearly baffled by but had a huge soft spot for, had swung it. 'I hope he doesn't give the horse ideas of grandeur so that he tries to piaffe his way over the cross-country course and make me look a twat.'

Lottie laughed and blew him a kiss. 'You can do that yourself.'

'Did you really go to Australia because I don't listen to you?'

'Nobody listens.' She stared into her glass, watching the bubbles lose their grip on the side of the glass and spring up to the surface. And shatter. 'I don't want to be like Mum was with Dad, trying to get your attention. Either you notice me, or you're not that bothered.'

'I am bothered, you silly cow. And everyone knows Billy was mad about your mum.'

'Except her.'

'Maybe she just liked him to show it, prove it. She must have known.'

'I think she did like to be the centre of things a bit, but how would she know if he didn't say so? And I wanted to do something just for me. And not just be Billy's daughter.'

'He's a big shadow to grow up under, Lots, but I'm not. I missed you when you were away.' It had been a revelation to Rory just how much he had missed Lottie when she was away, at first it had just been annoying that things cropped up that he wanted to share and she wasn't there. But then it had got worse; he'd wanted her back, wanted to know what she was doing.

'I've never been anywhere but Tippermere, you know. I just wanted my own life, to do what I wanted, rather than what you all thought I should do, just for a bit.' She missed out the 'and you didn't care anyway' bit, because she was beginning to realise she'd been wrong on that count, and maybe he was right. With Rory she wasn't in a shadow; she could do, and be, what she wanted. 'What if,' she shifted her gaze and studied his dark, familiar face, 'I'm missing out on something better?' There was always that, even if so far she hadn't found it. In fact, her world trip had proved a bit of a flop, in more ways than one.

'Thanks.'

'I don't mean you. I mean, you know, all we do is horses.'

'So, is that the dream? Barcelona, beaches, was Todd what you were looking for?'

Lottie didn't need to even think about the truth. It had always been there like a shining beacon in front of her. The dream since hormones had kicked in had been Rory. Rory who she'd idolised, Rory who had let her help him out with the horses, Rory who was a best buddy, Rory who had casually slipped into the role of protector and occasional date. Rory who would have run a mile if he'd realised just how stupidly infatuated she was. So she'd done the running instead.

She did her best not to look embarrassed. 'No, I wasn't looking for Todd. We just bumped into each other and he was a bit of a laugh, that's all.' Well it had been more or less all. 'But do you know why they arrested him?' She didn't wait for an answer. 'He had three wives already. Three! Can you believe it?'

'I'd say one was enough for anyone.' Rory shifted his emphasis from her feet, further up her calf. He was not really interested in Todd, but determined to at least look like he was paying attention.

'Do you think he was after my money?'

'Have you got any?' Rory grinned, forgetting the serious soul-searching stuff he'd been instructed on. ''Cos I might have jumped in quicker if I'd known.'

'Cheeky bastard. You know I haven't.'

'Shame. And I was going to take you all that way, and now I've splashed out on this place...'

'Nasty. You know I'm broke, but maybe he thought 'cos of dad and everything. See, I go all the way to bloody Australia and I still can't escape my flaming dad.' She sank back and stared up at the ceiling, which she hadn't realised until now was mirrored. 'Why would you have a mirrored ceiling in a bathroom?'

'I'm going to show you in a bit. So you weren't in love with him?' Rory tried to look like the response didn't matter as much as it did. After all, he'd asked, and he needn't have.

'Love? With Todd?' She giggled, and for the first time didn't feel like gritting her teeth when she said his name. 'You're kidding me.'

'Good. Would I have got arrested if I kissed your boobs on the beach?'

'Yes.'

'Thank God for that air traffic control strike then.' He lunged forward, sending a wash of water over the side of the bath and kissed the parts in question.

Lottie was suddenly glad they'd not made it onto a plane too. He might be super-fit, and his torso might have a reasonable tan, but she just couldn't picture him spending all day spread out on the sand.

And much as she liked him naked, she loved to see him in his figure-hugging clothes; they just suited him. And he looked ten times sexier than any of the men that had surrounded her on the beach, even Todd, and particularly those dressed only in budgie smugglers. Men's bits were wonderful when they were attached to the man you fancied; not quite so much when they were part of a beer-bellied, nut-brown wrinkly.

'When I was in Barca, I kept thinking about all the things I could be doing, but I forced myself not to move and to chill.' She sank a bit deeper into the water and realised that for the first time in ages she was actually following Todd's instruction. Chilling. Which brought his four S's to mind, but she was only interested in the fourth one. Sex. Right now. With Rory.

'You're funny. So, it wasn't your idea of heaven?'

'Nope. But I did try. Very hard.'

He laughed, a rich carefree sound. 'You're not supposed to make yourself enjoy it.'

'I make myself enjoy you.' She grinned.

'Cheeky madam.' He pulled abruptly on the leg he was holding and Lottie disappeared under the bubbles, still holding her champagne glass aloft. 'You're going to pay for that, young lady.' And when she'd surfaced, still laughing, he deposited the glass on the side of the bath, and deposited her very firmly astride his lap. 'And I'm going to show you why there are mirrors on the ceiling.'

Chapter 24

Tiggy clutched the flowered quilt under her chin and wondered how on earth she'd ended up in bed with Billy Brinkley.

The why wasn't a problem. Good Lord she'd been lusting after him for enough years, but the fact that it had actually happened was a bit of a shocker. And the fact that she didn't quite know what to do next, in the broad light of day, was another problem.

Whilst Tiggy was trying to work out how to get out of bed without showing any of her wobbly bits, Billy was pondering the fact that he couldn't remember feeling quite so randy since he'd won his gold medal. And he was trying to work out whether to tease Tiggy out of the duvet as though she was a teetering newborn foal, or whether the direct alpha male route would get her over the hurdle, and out of the sheets, quicker.

With years of experience successfully coaxing young horses and riders to face their worst fears, Billy was fairly confident he'd find a way that worked. It just had to be before the horses started to kick their feed buckets and wonder where the hell breakfast had got to.

Ten minutes later, with a softly whimpering, fully uncovered Tiggy begging him to finish what he'd started, Billy realised he'd not lost his touch.

'You need to talk to Dominic.'

Maybe he had lost his touch. That really wasn't something he should be hearing just as he worked up to a climax.

'Oo don't stop.'

Which sounded better. 'I hadn't been planning to.'

'Pleeeeeease.'

Billy wasn't sure if the 'please' was connected to the Dom issues, or the not stopping one, until the silky softness of her inner thighs closed in tighter around his waist. But it wasn't her skin, gorgeous as it was, it was the look of need in her large hazel eyes as she gazed directly at him that made William Brinkley feel, for the first time in nearly twenty years, that making a woman truly happy was what he wanted to do.

'Oh Billy, Billy, Billyyyyyyy.'

It took considerable willpower to stop his trembling arms from giving way beneath him, and for a fleeting moment Billy felt like maybe his passion days were numbered, and then she smiled. He collapsed on to the bed beside her, and ran his fingers through his hair.

'I know. I will do.'

Tiggy didn't say a word, she just leaned over, kissed him and wrapped an arm around the broad chest. She'd known he'd go eventually. It was just when that was the issue, and Tiggy believed that the sooner you faced your demons the sooner they dissipated into the mist of memories. 'That was nice.'

'Aye. But I could kill a cup of tea, though the horses might not appreciate it.'

'Stay there, I'll get one and how about a fry-up?'

'It's not a Sunday is it?'

'No, but it would be nice, wouldn't it?'

Tiggy was suddenly worried that she'd overstepped the boundaries, but Billy leant over and gave her the type of resounding smacker on the lips that made the world wobble. 'It would. What on earth would I do without you, Victoria Stafford?'

***

'Pistols at dawn is it?' Dominic raised an eyebrow and completed the almost-perfect half-pass across the school, spoiled only by a slight break in stride as Billy plonked himself on the bench that ran along the side and put his feet up on the rail with a heavy clunk.

'I always did say you were crap at keeping track of time.' He flicked dirt out from his short fingernails with an old nail that he invariably had in his pocket and watched the man with whom he'd once done just about everything two heterosexual men could do together. They were chalk and cheese, as Tiggy would say, but Alexa had bound them together. Made it work. Without her, they hadn't stood a chance, they'd fallen on different banks of the stream and the deep rift between them had been unbreachable. Not that either of them had tried to build bridges. 'So, do you still deny it?'

'Deny what?' He circled the horse around its haunches, each bounce so slow the world seemed to be holding its breath.

'I don't mind spelling it out, if that's what you want. It's no skin off my nose. I'm not the one who's got anything to hide. Do you still say that you and Elizabeth haven't been meddling and advising Amanda James on what she should do?'

'I do.'

'You lying bastard.'

Dom pulled the horse up, with perfect precision, inches from Billy's feet, and his eyes were as hard as the nail Billy held in his hand. 'You'll apologise for that.'

'Like hell I will.'

'What Amanda does with that Estate is her business, and what would I have to gain anyway? Mother likes to meddle, but I don't.'

'You'd get rid of me, once and for all, wouldn't you?' Billy's voice was soft, but it carried across the still air of the school like a ripple across water. 'The perfect solution.'

'You fool.' Dom shook his head slowly, the cool anger melting as he looked at the man who'd once been like a brother. 'I don't want to get rid of you. And mother would die if Charlotte ever left. I couldn't do that to her, not even if I wanted to. Not again.'

'But she was here. Lottie saw her, other people have seen her.' Through narrowed eyes, Billy tried to work out if he was hearing the truth or not. Neither man nor horse moved a muscle. 'She told Lottie you were helping. And why else would she be here, eh? What the hell do you have in common? And then that developer was over.'

'I didn't advise her to do that.'

'I don't believe you.'

'That's because you don't want to. Just like I didn't want to believe that I was partly to blame for what happened.'

'Blame, you?' Billy gave a short, unbelieving laugh.

Dom slid from the horse, slowly pulled the stirrups up and ran the leathers through them. 'It was my horse.'

'It was my dare.'

'This isn't a competition, Billy.' He loosened the girth, then rested his forearms on the saddle and looked straight at Billy, for the first time in years. 'I do blame you, I admit that, but I know part of it was down to me. And,' he paused, let the sigh reverberate through his long frame, 'part of it was just her. I do know that. I could have tried to stop her, but Alexa was pretty hard to stop when she put her mind to something. I gave her the means, you gave her the reason.'

'What do you mean?'

'She was jealous, jealous of your flings and your partying, she was used to being the centre of attention and I think she suddenly didn't feel like she was any more. I do blame you for that. I will always blame you for that bit, Billy.' He took his riding hat off and studied the other man. 'I hated you for a long time, because it was easier than taking the responsibility myself. And I did try and tell you, but you wouldn't listen. You were too busy playing the martyr, too busy drowning your sorrows.'

'You tried to take my daughter, the only thing I had left.'

'How else were we supposed to bring you to your senses? You were losing it, permanently pissed, it's a wonder all your owners didn't pull out, man. That house was a hovel and you were a self-pitying idiot who couldn't even look after a bloody dog.'

'Say it like it is, don't pull the punches, will you?'

'It was true. And it was no way to bring up Alexa's daughter.'

'My daughter.'

'Your daughter. Alexandra loved you, Billy. I loved you for God's sake, but you'd pressed the self-destruct button.' He pulled the reins over the horse's head. 'I haven't told Amanda James to do anything; if she sells up it isn't because I told her to. It's up to you whether you believe me or not.'

'I believe him, Dad.' Billy half-turned, to see Lottie silhouetted in the entrance of the school, looking an eerie replica of her mother.

'So do I.' Rory slipped his hand into hers. 'He's not lying, Bill.'

**

Lottie had been more than a little alarmed to get back to Folly Lake, still on a sexual high, to find it deserted, well, apart from Tiggy, who didn't really count and was behaving in a very strange manner. She was mopping the kitchen floor, which was weird. One, because she didn't do cleaning (as far as Lottie had ever been aware), and two, because it wasn't her floor. It was Billy's. And she was humming. Tuneless, but happy.

'Where's Dad?'

'Oh, you're back. Did you have a lovely time?' She all but pinched Lottie's cheek, which was a step too far.

Lottie retreated to the safety of Rory's side. 'Great thanks. Dad?'

'He's gone to see your Uncle Dom, dear. They needed to chat.'

'Oh, God.' Lottie all but shoved Rory back out of the door. 'He didn't take his shotgun did he?'

'Don't be silly. It'll be fine. You aren't staying for a drink, then?'

Lottie wasn't so convinced it would be fine. And she definitely didn't want a cup of tea. She was seriously worried that somebody had sneaked ketamine or some hallucinogenic drug into

Tiggy's mug when she wasn't looking. She really must check – she wouldn't put it past Tab if she was being egged on by one of the other grooms.

'What do you think he's gone for?' Lottie struggled with the seatbelt that had got trapped in the car door and was now doing its best to strangle her.

'To bury the hatchet.' Rory leaned across, released the belt and pulled the door shut.

'Oh no, don't say that, I mean, where is he going to bury it?'

Rory laughed. 'It's about time they manned up and sorted this whole thing out. Do you think he's really got the hots for Amanda?'

'Don't be silly.' Lottie looked mortified, so shocked that she forgot the car was in gear, so it bunny-hopped then stalled. 'She's far too young, I'm sure he wouldn't still do that. Would he?'

'Well he is single.'

'But, he wouldn't. She'd have told me.'

'Well if he's going to go for a woman, it's more likely to be her type than someone like Tigs, isn't it?'

'But he likes Tiggy, and she's far more his type. And she looks after him. He can't, he just can't, that would be so, so embarrassing. It would be so gross if my dad fancied my friend.'

'I was talking about Dom, not Billy, you silly pillock.'

'Oh.' Lottie restarted the car and giggled with relief. 'Who said Dom has the hots for her? I mean, I thought Tom did, but I think that's just Gran and Pip stirring things, she said he was just a friend. Amanda, that is, when she was showing me the plans. Gosh, the plans, I should have told Dad. Shouldn't I? Christ, we better get a move on, where are the car keys?' She groped in her jeans pocket, panicked when they weren't there. Rory put a hand over hers. Stopped her dead.

'They're in the ignition, Lots. Calm down, it'll be fine. But yeah, I think you should tell Billy about the plans, I can't believe you didn't.'

'I was going to, and then you packed me up and I forgot all

about it.'

'Can we stop yakking and go and rescue your relatives? I've got a bill to settle with Dom, and I need to collect my horse, and then I really do need to get the horses back on their toes. We'd better swap your bone-shaker for my wagon and go in that. Kill two birds with one stone.'

'Don't keep saying words like "kill" and "rescue".' Lottie groaned. 'You aren't taking this seriously, are you?'

'Lottie, Billy isn't exactly the killer type, is he?'

'But if someone's desperate….'

'He's not desperate anymore.' He dropped a kiss on top of her head. 'But, if we ever get married, remind me we need to emigrate.'

Married. He'd said the M word, and he'd said the L word the other day. And taken her for a weekend away. With a trembling hand, Lottie put the car into gear and wondered how she'd ever thought life in Tippermere was predictable.

***

'You go and load your horse and I'll find Dad.'

'I'm coming with you. You don't think I'm going to miss Dom trying to out-manoeuvre bronco Billy do you? In fact, where's my iPhone? I need to video this, it could go viral on YouTube.'

'I can hear them, in the school. Come on.' Lottie grabbed Rory's hand and headed towards the place she loved so much, with more confidence than she felt.

It was odd to see her father and uncle squaring up to each other. She'd not seen them do more than pass the polite time of day for years. But they weren't squared up it was more like they were both reaching out, but neither would take the hand that was offered.

They both wanted to sort things out and she didn't miss the look that was almost relief on her father's face when she spoke, said she believed Uncle Dom. It was almost like she'd given him permission to relax, trust.

'Amanda's doing the place up, not selling it. She told me, showed me these plans that David's dad has done for her. Well, she's not selling yet, I mean. She might one day, she said she couldn't make promises, but she wants to restore it, get rid of all the crap. So that means it won't get bulldozed, doesn't it?'

'Sorry, what did you say?' But it wasn't Billy that looked surprised, or sounded like he'd just found out it was Christmas. It was Dom.

Chapter 25

'You've done what, Elizabeth?' Pip stared at Elizabeth, raised an eyebrow and wondered if age just gave you the right to do whatever you liked. Or whether, which was more likely, the woman had always done exactly what she wanted.

'I have got young Thomas's car resprayed. It looked quite appalling, I'm sure you'll agree. So little Tabatha drove it over. The gentleman I spoke to at the dealership was very helpful, in fact I think he was relieved. They sorted it in super-quick time.'

'But she's not old enough to drive; she's not passed a test.'

'Oh, the roads are quiet. It wasn't far and she promised to be careful.'

'And you want me to take it back?'

'I do, dear. Well I can't, with my arthritis and dodgy hip, can I?'

'And he doesn't know?'

'Well, no, but he did agree to do me a little favour and give Amanda a lift to the wedding. So I decided I'd pay him back with a nice surprise.'

Pip wasn't sure. Elizabeth, as with many who had a similar upbringing, believed in looking after her money. This was obviously an investment, but she wasn't sure why.

'You're up to something, aren't you?'

'Tut, tut, dear. Such a suspicious mind. And you've been up to something too by the look on your face.'

Pip, who didn't think she had got a look, did her best to match Elizabeth's gimlet stare. 'He won't let you push him into Amanda's arms, even if Folly Lake Manor is at stake.'

'I wouldn't dream of trying, Philippa. But he does like her, they have a lot in common. A nice boy, though he can be a bit ineffective.'

'Do you mean affected?'

'I know exactly what I mean. He's not one to swim against the tide; his father liked to avoid the waves as well. But he was more than happy to agree to accompany the poor girl to the wedding.'

Pip, who thought Amanda was far from a poor girl, was beginning to wonder where this was heading. The fact that Elizabeth's extravagant matchmaking efforts, which had involved her having to practically bribe the press to run the story and photographs, had spectacularly backfired didn't seem to have dented her enthusiasm at all.

'But you do know he doesn't even want to get married?'

'I'm sure you know far more about that than me, dear.'

Pip ignored the comment, and the accompanying look. 'And you know that she's thinking of staying? She's asking David's dad to look at restoring the place.'

'Oh yes, I do know all about that. I think he'll do a wonderful job, from what I've heard. Poor Marcus was rather uninformed in these matters. So sad, but at least he didn't live long enough to do any lasting damage.'

'Elizabeth!'

'I do think they have a lot in common, that couple, and they do look a good match, don't you agree? Right, now dear you wanted to talk about the music didn't you?'

Pip wasn't sure now whether Elizabeth had completely discounted everything she'd said, had a shockingly bad memory, or was plotting something new. She decided it would probably be easier to interrogate Tom, who had none of the wiles or ability to mislead that Elizabeth had.

'And then you can drop the car off for me.'

'Won't he be missing it?'

'Oh no, he's been busy up at Folly Lake Manor. I don't even think he's peeped into the garage.'

'And how do I get back for my scooter?'

'I'm sure you'll persuade someone to give you a lift. How about that nice Irish chap?'

Pip sighed. Was there absolutely nothing that Elizabeth didn't know about?

***

'She's up to something.'

'No news there, then.' Tom grinned and gave his car the once-over. It definitely looked better, in fact any colour was better than the bright yellow that Tamara had insisted on. She'd wanted to be noticed. Tom on the other hand liked understated elegance and to blend into the background.

'I think even I might stand a chance with Lottie now. What do you reckon?'

Pip rolled her eyes. 'Can you give me a lift back there for my scooter? I mean, why couldn't she have just called you and asked you to go and pick the damned thing up?'

'I hadn't got a car.'

'Very droll. Well you've managed without for the last few days.'

'Walking up to Folly Lake is one thing, but the hike up to Tipping House is pushing it a bit too far. Even for a man with my physique.' He grinned, and Pip couldn't help but join in.

'So, she persuaded you to go with Amanda to the wedding? What about me? I might have presumed.'

'You never presume anything, Pip. Besides, you and Lottie are helping out, so you'll be going early. But, no, she didn't exactly persuade me. I do have a mind of my own, you know.' He quirked an eyebrow, waiting for her to dispute it.

'Carry on, I'm not saying anything.'

'I happened to mention to Elizabeth that I'd sort of arranged to keep Amanda company, keep the wolves at bay so to speak, and she had a double gin in celebration.'

'She doesn't need to be celebrating to have a double gin.'

'And said she had a nice little surprise in store for us. Not everyone has an ulterior motive, Pip.'

'Elizabeth normally does, though.'

'I think she promised my mother she'd keep an eye on me.'

'Ah.'

'The plans that Amanda's had drawn up for the place are amazing. It will be beautiful if the finished article lives up to the promise.'

'Good for selling, I suppose.'

'I'm not convinced she will; she does like it here. So, are the rumours true about you and the Irish chap?'

'Can't a girl even breathe around here without the rumours starting?'

'Breathe maybe, shag in the woods, no chance.'

'We spent one afternoon together, that's all.' And then a very uncomfortable sleepless night wondering whether it was best to avoid him, pretend nothing had happened or go for a full-frontal attack. Pip had always favoured a direct approach, but this time she'd been knocked off kilter. The whole episode had caught her unawares and afterwards she hadn't known quite how to react, or how she felt. Mick confused her.

She might have come to Tippermere to seek out fit horsemen, but since arriving she'd actually spent more time with fellow interlopers, like Tom or the guys in Kitterly Heath. Now that the real deal (even if he wasn't exactly Cheshire born and bred) had swept her off her feet, she had the alarming desire to do a runner to the safety of the city, which wasn't like Pip at all. The fact that Tom and Amanda had gravitated together was something she could well relate to.

Chapter 26

'You won't breathe a word to anyone that this isn't, you know, the first... I mean, they all think it's the real thing.'

'Of course I won't, Sam. I promised.'

Sam was pale underneath her fake tan, and her blue eyes shone out bigger than ever from her slim face. Not for the first time, she was panicking that her false eyelashes were about to get dislodged, and she'd fall flat on her face halfway across the lawn. Which, given the height of her heels and the amount of moss in the grass, was a distinct possibility. When she'd actually said 'yes' to David on a sunny beach, it had been perfect. This repeat performance for the papers was something altogether different. 'Oh no, where's Scruffy?'

'Stop panicking. He's with David.' Which wasn't entirely accurate, but given Sam's state, probably the safest answer.

Scruffy, the ring-bearer, had disgraced himself. Having suffered Tiggy's tender care and ministrations (she was the only dog-groomer in the area) for two hours, he had been fit to burst. Luckily, the diamond and platinum rings had not yet been attached to his collar when he'd spotted the old tabby cat, who considered herself queen of the castle. She'd bolted, taking Scruffy perilously close to the wedding cake several times as they weaved in and out of table legs, through the herb garden until he was adorned with parsley and mint, and then on towards the ornate fountain, which had been turned on in honour of the occasion. The cat, having a strong aversion to water and an even stronger self-preservation instinct, bounced on and off the wall with surprising agility, given her age, but Scruffy did not. By the time the dog had clambered out of the water, the cat had taken refuge in a nearby tree and was watching the proceedings with disdain.

Having dodged David and his father, Scruffy had had an irresistible urge to shake himself dry, which led to the waiting staff and the immaculate white table cloths having an impromptu shower. Weaving himself through the opposition, like a premiership footballer heading towards the goal, he went for a final sprint towards the newly dressed rose beds, where, with a bark of pure joy, he gave a victory roll. Tongue lolling, the manure- and herb-streaked dog finally surrendered himself to a giggling Tiggy, who offered a refund on the grooming bill. David said no. But when she offered to shut him in an unoccupied stable with a bowl of water and a bone, the answer was a resounding yes. The ring-bearer had been officially relieved of his duties.

***

'Oh yes, sorry, I'm having palpitations here. It's so nice of Lady Stanthorpe to let us get hitched here, isn't it? After that mix-up at the other place. I mean, who'd have thought that horrible little man would have tried to make money out of us and sell tickets? Well, I know we're not getting hitched exactly, but, well…'

'Sam, slow down and breathe for heaven's sake. You're wearing me out. I know what you mean, and I promise not to breathe a word about you know what, and you can call her Elizabeth, you know.' Pip paused. 'But not Liz.'

'Oh no, she told us all to call her Lady Stanthorpe. It's wonderful isn't it? She's so posh. A real lady.' Sam sounded wistful. 'Do you think she's met the actual, real Queen?'

Pip sighed. 'Probably.'

'Can you see my knickers through this, babe?'

'I can't see anything through it, Sam. It's satin.'

'I mean, the line of them, I did wonder if I should ditch them? But then I thought, with the slit up the side, well if anything happened, and I wouldn't put it past these photographers to hide under the rhodies and shoot up my skirt.'

There were plenty of rhododendrons, the girl had a point, and it was rather a large slit, without which the dress was remarkably restrained and sophisticated.

'I'd keep them on unless you want "bush" type headlines.'

Sam giggled. 'No bushes round here, babe. Where's Lottie? She is here, isn't she?'

'Of course she is. Last time I saw here she was trying to stop an impromptu football match that Rory, Mick, David and Billy were trying to organise. They looked a right load of arses, except David of course.'

Sam's face fell. 'Oh gosh, Davey's not getting green streaks on his new white jacket is he? Those grass stains are hell to get out, you know. His agent will kill him if he comes out green.'

'They can Photoshop the pics.'

'Yeah, but they won't, will they babe?'

***

Amanda had been quietly dreading the wedding for more reasons than she could bear to list. The main reason, if she was honest, was that much as she loved Sam, and knew that her heart was very much in the right place, she just had a horrible feeling that the whole affair was going to be even more overblown than Marcus's funeral. Which would bring back memories she'd rather leave buried. She was also very worried that Sam, in full matchmaking mode (which seemed to have built to a crescendo as the wedding day approached), might well lock her in a room with one of the football players and refuse to let them out until baby-making practice was in progress, or at the very least a date had been arranged.

Samantha seemed to have seen her as a challenge, sending her regular links to Facebook pages and Twitter feeds of just about every single (and some about to be single) premiership football player in the country, along with the odd golfer and one very memorable rugby player, who she really wished had taken selfies with more clothes on. It was very off-putting when you felt you just had to look again and enlarge the picture, just to make sure that what you thought you were looking at wasn't something entirely different. Like a curledup mammal.

And then there was the other, unavoidable situation. Where she just *had* to stop putting it off and explain what she had decided to do, where she had to admit once and for all how she felt... and then wait for the walls to crumble. It was strange, she'd always felt completely in control before, whatever the situation, always felt that she could handle things. But, for the first time, she was petrified, it was a risk. A bit like jumping off a cliff. Or getting on a horse...

She'd told Lottie that this time it had to be perfect, and she knew perfect didn't exist. But it had to be right for her; it had to be what she truly wanted. But that didn't mean it was right for anyone else. For him.

'We can go for a swift drink on the way, if you want?' Tom was looking at her in that gentle way he had. He understood, he cared and that made such a difference. Elizabeth was a clever woman.

'Wouldn't it be a bit rude?'

'We've got plenty of time, we won't be late. We could sit in the beer garden at The Bull's Head, drink Pimm's and pretend we're off to some posh do.'

'We are.' She grinned. 'Does my bum look big in this?'

'Nope, but I'm sure with a few more riding lessons it will flatten out a bit, then you'll fit in fine.'

'You're so rude.'

'I know, it's part of my charm.'

**

The Bull's Head was packed to the gills with journalists discussing the best way to stake out the wedding, though most of them seemed to think that it was still being held in Kitterly Heath, which Tom and Amanda agreed was probably Elizabeth's doing.

Terrified of being spotted, identified and grilled, Tom drove round to one of the houses that bordered onto the pub's beer garden, gave the landlord a quick call and soon took charge of two glasses of Pimm's over the fence, which he delivered triumphantly to Amanda, who was sitting in the car.

'Don't worry. I know the people who live here, and I do know they're away at present. Cheers!'

'Cheers to you too. The car looks nice.'

'It does, doesn't it? Much better, and the bonus is that everyone is still looking out for a yellow car, so they don't spot me. Elizabeth had it done as a gift.'

'That's nice.'

Tom did sometimes wish Amanda wasn't quite as polite. Any normal woman would have been asking why, not just sipping their drink. And just as politeness was part of Amanda, deception was not an integral part of Tom. He needed to tell her what he'd agreed to do.

'Stop worrying about the wedding and ask me why she did it. Besides, if Sam thinks we're an item she might back off.'

'But she knows we're not.'

'I could persuade her otherwise.'

'Don't you dare.'

'This is more fruit cocktail than alcohol. Amanda, I—'

'Oh damn, it's Pip texting, they're wondering where we are. Oops and another one. She's worried we'll get locked out because they've got all this security on the gate, to check the press don't get in.'

'I thought that was the whole point, the press.'

'Only the *right* press.' She typed a quick answer out. 'We really should go. Sorry.'

Tom was sorry too. There were things he wanted to say to her, things he wanted to explain. Things that he couldn't cover in a two-minute drive with paparazzi lining the route.

'Amanda?' He turned off the lane that led from the pub and onto the narrow winding road that took them over to Tipping House.

'Mm.' She was distracted, gazing out of the window, which didn't help. Though he did know that the whole wedding thing bothered her, in fact it seemed to be some kind of massive ordeal that he couldn't quite fathom. Sure, he appreciated that it might bring back memories. But she'd seemed fine in their recent chats. This was more of a twitchiness than sadness.

'Amanda, there's a reason I'm comfortable at Folly Lake Manor, a reason I keep coming back.' He swerved to avoid a photographer, who appeared to have fallen off the high wall that bordered the estate.

'Not just to see little old me, then?'

'Sorry, that sounded awful. I didn't mean it like that. Of course I come to see you, but there was a reason I was drawn to the place from the beginning. I,' he slowed to turn into the driveway, wound down the window to show the invitations, 'I was born there.'

'Sorry?'

'I was born at Folly Lake Manor. Then my parents had to sell up and leave when I was still a baby. I didn't remember the place really, but in some strange way I felt like I'd come home.'

'Oh.' She stared ahead, a small frown creasing her brow, sharp lines between her eyebrows. 'Are you trying to say *you* want to buy it?'

'No, no, good heaven's I could never afford it. But I think that's why I'd love to see it restored to its former glory, it means a lot to me, I—'

'Oh, Tom, you're so sweet.' She kissed him lightly on the lips.

'Come on, we better go in, Pip is texting me again. We can talk more inside.' And as she got out of the car, then took his hand, he wondered when the hell he was going to have the opportunity to tell her the part he really wanted to. To ask her if what Elizabeth had told him was true.

***

The wedding service was as uneventful as one can be when the guests are a mix of B-list celebrities who want to hit the A-list, A-listers who can't remember anyone's name and aren't quite sure why they're there, magazine journalists and photographers who just have to have the perfect shot because they've paid a bloody lot of money to be there, footballers and their very glamorous wives and girlfriends who are comparing heel heights, frock labels, tan lines and wondering when the bubbly corks are going to start popping, and a number of Tippermere and Kitterly Heath residents in various states of bemusement, shock, awe and last-minute panics that they hadn't turned the horses out.

It was the bit that followed, the posed shots for the glossies (well, one particular glossy) that caused the problems.

The whole thing was closely orchestrated by a very bossy girl called Jasmine, who had been sent by the glossy magazine that was sponsoring the event, and the photographer's assistant, Xander, whose sole purpose in life seemed to be to spot celebrities (which he was excellent at) and make sure they took centre stage.

'This is like herding cats,' he raised his voice from a mutter to a shriek, 'look, darling, will you just take the heels off so we can see the guy behind.'

'I certainly won't.' The 'darling' in question, who had credits in Doctor Who and had been considered for a role alongside Sean Bean no less (or so she told everyone), glared at Xander. 'It isn't my fault he's small.' She turned to see the manager of the groom's football team (known by Pip, and many others, as Yummy Jose), who was not used to having his lack of stature pointed out.

Jasmine, sensing a riot was about to break out, rushed in to usher Jose into a more prestigious spot, and gave the 'darling' an assessing look in an attempt to work out just how important she really was as far as readership figures went.

'She shagged Sean, Jazz.' Was Xander's whispered message.

'Bean or Penn?'

'Bean.'

In a quandary, Jasmine weighed the importance of a tenuous link to Game of Thrones against an established link to the World Cup team, which normally would be a no-brainer, except this one was a worthy pin-up with a massive female following and speculation was rife (particularly in their magazine) about an imminent divorce.

Snub Jose and she might be saying goodbye to the promotion she had been working on for the last five weeks. And she had made more sacrifices than normal this time, given that the man she'd had to woo was overweight, had halitosis and a nasty line in the need to spank. Hard. With a brush, which she was sure had left bruises that would never go. 'We'll go with Jose, Xander, unless she takes her shoes off.' Which, she had to admit, was also partly because she had her own ideas on what Jose could be doing after the wedding, and partly because aspiring actresses with big boobs and even bigger egos got on her tits. They needed bringing down a peg or two sometimes, and she had the power.

Pip, who had immediately assessed the situation and taken a seat in the wings with a bottle of bubbly, was working out an angle for an exclusive of her own and wondering just how much she could piss off the overbearing Jasmine by getting to Jose first.

'What are you plotting?' Mick, who had recognised that a mere farrier and part-time eventer wasn't going to cut the mustard with the glossy mag brigade, had spotted Pip and decided to corner her. Since their little encounter on the trip back from the airport, she'd been surprisingly elusive, which just made him more determined.

'Apart from taking over the world?' Pip, looking surprisingly relaxed, winked and passed over the bubbly so he could have a swig. 'I so need to corner yummy Jose.'

Mick laughed. 'Before Jasmine eats him up, you mean?'

'An exclusive would be such a scoop.' They watched Jasmine stick out her chest as she coaxed the manager into a more prominent position. 'I hope he doesn't trip up, he'll suffocate in those.'

'Oh, the claws are out today, aren't they? I'm sure he'd be more than happy to handle both of you.'

'Yeah, sure he would. Want to know a secret?'

'Not if it's football-related.'

'They're married.'

'Well I know that darling, we're at the wedding.'

'No, I mean they already were. This is just a publicity thing; they got hitched on holiday. Sam told me, but don't mention it or David will kill her.'

'Can't say it surprises me, with them lot. Anything goes.'

'What do you think Elizabeth's up to with that pair?' Pip nodded in the direction of Tom and Amanda, who she had just spotted walking shoulder to shoulder, the picture of elegance, towards the marquee that was housing the reception. They were in deep conversation, Tom's floppy fringe mingling with Amanda's blonde waves as he concentrated on her every word.

'I'm not sure, darling. But we're not the only ones that are wondering.'

Off to the right, champagne glass in hand, Dominic Stanthorpe's gaze was fixed on their every step, his mouth a tight, thin line.

***

It was hard to know who was more excited about the plans for the house, thought Amanda. Her, or the enthusiastic Tom who had inspired her to actually invite Anthony Simcock into Folly Lake Manor and suggest what could be done.

Tom, however, was finding it a struggle to keep up his level of interest. He loved Folly Lake, was drawn to it as though by some magnetic force of nature that was impossible to resist, but talking about blueprints wasn't really his bag. But he had promised Elizabeth to stay by Amanda's side, to hang on her every word. And he had wanted to explain, if her damned phone hadn't gone off mid-Pimm's.

'I was thinking of contacting Mother, I'm sure she'd love to hear about the house and your plans.'

'You could ask her over.'

'That's probably a step too far, but who knows. Amanda, it was Elizabeth who told me about my parents.'

'I think she's probably quite nice underneath that forbidding exterior.'

'And she asked me to look after you today.'

'That's so lovely of her, and I wasn't sure she really liked me, I mean I've not lived here forever, and I'm not horsey—'

'I think she likes you a lot.' He took a breath. 'Amanda, she knows what's been going on.'

'No.' Amanda stopped dead, her hand over her mouth, and instinctively knew he was telling the truth. 'She can't, we've been so careful.'

'You need to be more than careful with her around.' He gave a short but good-humoured laugh. 'Is that why you had the riding lessons, for him?'

'Yes, I, well I was trying to… It's complicated, but Tom, I never thought I fitted in here, but now….'

'You're fitting in fine.' He grinned. 'I'm not sure you'll be competing at The Horse of the Year show any day soon, but…' He took her hand, raised it to his lips. 'He's a lucky man, but he really needs to stop pussyfooting about.'

'I need to talk to him.'

'You do, it would make life a hell of a lot more peaceful for the rest of us if Elizabeth could step down from her battle station.'

Dom was startled when Amanda stood on tiptoes to kiss Tom, and even more startled when she spun around and started to head in his direction.

Brought up by a mother who believed in standing one's ground, he did so.

'Dominic, we have *got* to talk.'

'Should this wait a few minutes? The photo shoot seems to have finished and everyone's going past into the marquee.'

'I don't care any longer. I really don't. I've tried to be restrained and sensible about this, but if I don't actually tell you how I feel I'm going to explode. And I've waited for you to do something, because you did promise. And I am patient, and I wish I'd rehearsed this, because I haven't a clue where it's going now.' Amanda ran out of steam and stood rocking slightly. Then added the punchline. 'And I think she knows.' And held her breath.

Dom pursed his lips and took what seemed to be an age before he finally spoke. 'I did wonder. When mother gets an idea she's worse than those dogs of hers once they've got wind of the Sunday roast. No stopping them.'

'I think she encouraged Tom to be nice to me just to see if she could get a reaction from you. Does that sound horrid? I mean, I'm probably completely wrong, and she wouldn't dream of doing anything like that, but…'

'Oh yes she would. Mother knows a hundred ways to smoke a fox out of a hole. It's been a bit chaotic around here since old Marcus died. She must have been in her element kicking Tippermere out of its normal slumber. And she probably thought poor Pip would get all the flak for getting us in the press. Wicked woman.'

Amanda stared open-mouthed. Not only because Dominic was taking it all so calmly, but because it had never occurred to her that Elizabeth may have been instrumental in all the headlines and gossip.

'What are we going to do?'

'Well, for one, I need a proper drink, and then I think it's time to turn the tables.' Amanda decided it was probably best not to say that she had a good idea that was exactly what Elizabeth had expected, and wanted, her son to do. 'Can I ask you one question, though, Amanda?'

'Of course, ask me anything, you know you can.'

'What exactly made your mind up about staying on at Folly Lake?'

'Isn't it obvious?'

Dom shook his head. He'd worked out possible reasons, but he wasn't that keen on voicing them. 'It was a bit unexpected.'

'Let's get that drink, then I'll explain.'

***

'Oh I do love it when a plan comes together. Isn't that what they say, dear?'

Lottie looked at her gran and raised an eyebrow. 'Well it depends who you're talking about. What have you been planning now?' After an extensive buffet, which seemed to consist of excessively fancy but exceedingly small morsels of food, and more wine than she'd had in a week, interspersed with some hilarious and very impromptu speeches, Lottie had let her guard down and allowed herself to be cornered by Elizabeth. And Rory, who supposedly had just popped to the gents (for the third time, once he started he couldn't stop), had conveniently, for him, not reappeared to save her.

'You'll find out, all in good time. Did you and young Richard have a nice weekend in that Spanish place?'

'You know he's not called Richard.' Elizabeth shrugged. 'We didn't go, we just booked into a luxury hotel and spent two days in the bath tub. It had bubbles, and champagne.'

'In my day, a lady didn't discuss those things, too much

313

information, dear.'

'I bet you did what you liked, and discussed what you liked.'

'And did you decide whether you want to stay, or go off galli-vanting again?' The question was a touch sharp, and Elizabeth's eyes were boring into her as though she was an eagle about to pounce on a mouse. Lottie didn't like being easy prey.

'I don't think I ever said I was going again.'

'I don't recall you saying you were staying either, child.'

'I've got to stay for Dad.'

'This is not about your father, dear. He'll survive whatever happens, and he's got that Tiggy person as well.'

'He hasn't "got her", she works for him.'

'Oh, I think you'll find it's more than that.'

Lottie decided she didn't really want to linger on that possibility. 'Well I don't know yet what's going to happen, do I?'

'The fate of Folly Lake Manor doesn't matter. Stop digressing and say what you really feel.'

Lottie didn't think she'd ever heard her gran refer to how someone felt before. Things were done out of a sense of duty, a need, and things like that. She sighed. It was hard really to work out why she'd left, on days like this. Even if Rory did seem to have buggered off again. When she'd been away all she really thought about, if she was honest, was coming back. Of what she was missing. Of Rory.

'I don't think I ever had a choice really, did I?' She'd been scared of staying, of him finding out just how crazy about him she was. Scared of being rebuffed and living forever in her father's shadow. Just doing the same old stuff and not knowing if she wanted to or not.

But it had been daft. Tippermere was in her blood; Rory was the boy she loved. Her dad, annoying as he could be, was her dad. Why couldn't she just have faced up to it?

'Mick said,' she wrinkled her brow, trying to remember exactly what he'd said, repeat it word for word, which wasn't easy after a few glasses of wine on a relatively empty stomach, 'it's the people, not the place, treasure. You can be anywhere, or nowhere.'

'He seems quite fond of you, and what do you think, dear?'

'He also said that they had a saying when he was at home, about your feet taking you to where your heart is, I think I get it now.'

'Charlotte, you do digress almost as much as poor Dominic does. Beating around the bush and being whimsical never got anything done.'

'You're funny.' Lottie grinned, and knew that she was one of the few people who dared talk to Elizabeth that way. 'Uncle Dom doesn't digress or dither, he's just careful. And he doesn't want you to run his life.'

'As if I would.' She sounded faintly huffy, but pleased.

'Mick was right, I came back for Rory. I love him, Gran, and I think he loves me, and I think maybe he does notice but he didn't think I was that bothered.'

'Well I'm glad we've got that settled. They're a clever lot the Irish, and such a way with words. And with looks like that you can see why it works for him, silver-tongued is much sexier than silver-haired, now if I was younger...'

'Gran!'

'And he's clever enough to sort out little Philippa. She needs a man who isn't afraid to handle her properly.'

'She's not a dog or a horse. And what do you mean, sort out Pip? She doesn't even like him.'

'Really? I think I need a proper drink, these bubbles give me indigestion. Catch that man's attention will you dear? The staff seem to have fallen asleep on the job, it's so difficult to catch their eye. In my day you only had to think about it and someone would be there at your elbow with a fresh glass. Ah, and look who's finally heading our way.'

Lottie looked and was surprised to see Dom and Amanda, which was a bit weird. Especially as Amanda had sworn that she wasn't plotting with Dom and, as her and Amanda were supposed to be good friends now, she had assumed that they'd be totally upfront with each other.

'Mother, I think it's time we had a chat.'

'Well past time, if you ask me. I was just telling Charlotte that you procrastinate far too much, Dominic.'

'There's something I need to say.'

Lottie waited. He'd persuaded Amanda to sell, he'd bought the place himself, he'd bought a new horse, forgiven Billy…

'We're getting married.'

'Who is?' This was just too confusing.

'Amanda and I, of course.' Dom had surprised even himself when, during the wedding speeches, between smoked salmon canapés and mini toad-in-the-holes, he'd asked Amanda to marry him. And to hell with the consequences. And when she'd burst into tears and jumped on him, he'd been even more shocked by his desire to drag her upstairs and rip her clothes off. But he hadn't. Just the passing thought of what he had to say to his mother had deflated more than his ego.

'See, that wasn't too painful was it?' Elizabeth, sitting regally on the only chair, with her audience around her, waved her glass imperiously at a passing waiter.

There was a combined intake of air and Lottie fought the urge to giggle. 'Should we have a celebration now, or shall we arrange a nice engagement party for you? I'm sure Amanda could do that, she's quite a capable girl from what I've seen.'

'You knew.' Dominic was slightly annoyed. He'd spent weeks deliberating over whether he could do this. Sleepless nights would have been an exaggeration, as Dom's structured life didn't allow for them. But tortured days he had had. And he was now more than a slightly bit miffed that there was no reaction. He'd been expecting it; worked himself up for it.

'Well of course I knew, Dominic. A mother knows her children.'

'I didn't know.' Everybody ignored Lottie. 'So when I saw you at the yard that day, you *were* up to something.'

Amanda went from a ghostly worried white to crimson in a record time. 'I just went for a chat.'

Dom took Amanda's hand protectively, as though to ward off the questions.

'But why was it such a big secret, oh, I see…' Lottie bit her bottom lip. It all made sense now, the fact that Amanda had turned a blind eye to Marcus's flings, the talk of them splitting up and then trying to devise an arrangement that worked, the fact that Amanda had absolutely no interest in any men in Tippermere, or Kitterly Heath, despite Sam's best efforts (which were pretty incredible) at matchmaking. 'You, him, you were…' Lottie put her hand over her mouth to stop herself finishing the sentence.

'And Dominic thought I would disapprove, didn't you dear?'

'Mother, I know how much this place means to you, and I promised to stay and look after it, and I know you didn't entirely approve when Amanda and Marcus moved into Folly Lake Manor.'

'Well he was rather nouveau riche, rather, what do you young people call it, blingy? Sorry dear, but it's true.'

'I know.' Amanda gave a weak smile, but seemed encouraged.

'And he did do some abominable things to that beautiful house. But I have never said I don't approve of young Amanda here.'

'I didn't want to upset you, I've always tried to put this place first, above what I want.'

'You are so old-fashioned sometimes, Dominic. Duty is such a dated concept.' She patted his arm. 'You're a good boy, you always were.'

'How long have you suspected?' He looked resigned. Facing up to his mother had been difficult. He was master of his horses, but people were a different matter. And he hadn't wanted to cause more upset, not again.

'Suspected?' A smile played across her lips. 'I've known for a long time. Why else would a young married woman who is terrified of horses be sneaking around the stable yard?'

'She doesn't hate horses.' Lottie felt compelled to support her friend as she finally realised why the quaking Amanda had forced herself up onto a horse. It hadn't been a desire to get close to Tom. 'Do you?'

'I'm not that keen, actually, but I am trying. Merlin is very sweet.' Amanda looked straight at Elizabeth, and suddenly saw a very human old lady, not the matriarchal, forbidding figure that Dom had portrayed. 'I've rather cornered Dominic, I'm afraid.'

'That's a woman's job, dear.'

'A few months before Marcus died we had a massive row. I'd said I was leaving him if he carried on his womanising and he made it quite clear a woman couldn't make demands. I was totally pathetic and had run out—'

'You've never been pathetic; you were upset and scared.'

Lottie had never seen her uncle looking like he cared that much, except maybe when his favourite horse had been suffering from a very bad bout of colic.

'And I bumped into Dominic out riding. I begged him to go back with me. And he did.'

That meeting was, he was sure, imprinted on his mind forever. In one short afternoon the impossible had happened; he'd fallen totally, inescapably in love. He should have called someone else, not got involved, but he hadn't been able to help himself. He'd got involved.

Marcus had been calm when they'd returned to the house, no threat to anyone. He'd deflated, his anger gone and never to return, back to the conciliatory and affable figure Amanda had married. But the damage had been done. The bond between Dom and Amanda formed. And each time Marcus was away, Amanda had made her way to Tipping House.

'Just before Marcus died I made the decision to leave him.' Amanda glanced up at Dom. 'Dominic had never made me any promises, and I knew he couldn't. I understood he had responsibilities here and he really thought I should stick it out, but I couldn't. I had to do it for myself. I didn't want to live a lie.'

'I just wanted you to be happy, safe. Sometimes we can't just do what we want.' Dom's voice was soft, but Lottie saw how his hand had tightened around Amanda's.

'That day when you and I bumped into each other,' Amanda looked at Lottie, 'I'd come to a decision. When Marcus died I didn't know what to do really, I didn't feel like I fitted in here, but I had fallen for Dom. And then I decided that if I really was going to make a life and do things for myself, then I had to try it. I came over to tell Dominic that I understood if he couldn't get involved with me, but I was going to stay and try and make a life for myself here. I told him it wasn't open to debate,' Amanda had been quite proud of just how determined she'd been. 'And he did offer,' she gave Lottie a sideways look, 'to help me out if I needed it at Folly Lake Manor. But the renovation was my idea, because I knew that I really did want to stay.' She looked up at Dominic. 'Seeing Tom there and hearing about how it used to be, made me see what it could be like for you and me.' Lottie felt her jaw drop, then snap shut again as Elizabeth's dry tone cut in.

'That boy has his useful side.'

'I couldn't pretend I don't love you, Dominic. And I want to be a part of this place, share our lives properly. And if I have to wait ten years for you to be able to do that then that's fine, but I'm not going to play the victim.'

'I don't want you to play the victim; I never wanted that.' Dom spoke softly. 'I just want to keep my promise.'

'There's no promise to keep, Dominic.'

'Mother, I saw how devastated you were after the accident, and I wasn't going to have you think I would abandon this place. We were just going to keep it quiet until the future was settled here.'

Dom, who had been battling with his conscience for a long time, finally felt the pressure start to lift. At first the relationship had been a secret because it was wrong, Amanda was married, however unhappily. But as time went by, and after Marcus died, he had swung between hope and a complete disbelief that anyone as lovely as Amanda would want to hang around. She'd get bored of him, hate the country life, get tired of waiting for him to fulfil his obligations. He'd tried to be logical, accept that they knew very different lives, accept that the best solution would be for her to move on, go back to the type of life she loved. Not an Aga, welly or horse in sight.

So to come clean, make the relationship public, would have been foolhardy, it would have upset his mother, left the future undecided. And all for what? Within a month, a year, she would have moved on.

Except she hadn't. And in the yard, that day Lottie had bumped into her, she'd declared that she didn't want to return to city life. She'd told him that she knew he had obligations, but she wasn't going to let him push her away. Make decisions for her.

'Silly boy. I love this place, Dominic, it's a responsibility I've always happily carried, but it was never supposed to be a burden on you.'

He grimaced. 'But the inheritance conditions…'

'Nonsense, it's always possible to find a way round these things. You take it too seriously. I've always just wanted you to be happy.'

The hint of a smile chased across his aristocratic features. 'And so why did you encourage every man in Tippermere to land on Amanda's doorstep?'

'I wanted to make you jealous.' She smiled, winked at Amanda. 'Your father was always a jealous man, it was one of his best features. A man can only be jealous if he cares. I thought the best way to settle this was to make you jealous and root you out. And if you didn't do anything, then I'd know it was just a silly infatuation that would die out.'

'Mother! You had the press invade the village, stirred up Billy and damned-near caused him to shoot England's number-one goalkeeper just to make me jealous.'

'Well it worked, didn't it?'

Dominic put his head in his hands. 'Wouldn't it have been

easier to just talk to me?'

'That would have been interfering, and anyway this was more fun. Life can be boring for an old lady.'

'Poor Uncle Dom.' Lottie giggled, then realised she was hopping from foot to foot trying to say something, but there hadn't been a break in the conversation. 'So you really weren't trying to sell the equestrian centre?'

Dom groaned. 'No, in my cack-handed way I thought I might be able to help.'

'But,' Lottie crashed down from her sudden high point as it sunk in, 'if you two are really getting married, then you won't need the Manor. You'll sell up because you've got Tipping House.'

Amanda smiled. 'Oh, we will need it. I love it there now, and I really will learn to ride so I can share it with Dominic. I want to share everything.' She gazed up at him and he gazed back, and Lottie wondered if this was all a dream.

'No.' Lottie felt weak. 'You don't understand Amanda, Uncle Dominic belongs here.' That old word duty leapt into her mind.

'Have you not been listening to a word, dear?' Elizabeth shook her head. 'He was trying to postpone leaving here out of a sense of duty, but—'

'But he lives here. It will all be his one day.'

'No, it won't.' Dominic smiled, then tucked Amanda's hand through his arm. 'But I will be around for quite some time yet. I think we should circulate now that's over, don't you darling? I need a stiff brandy. I will leave the explanations to you, Mother.'

Chapter 27

'What are you lot up to? Wondered where you'd all got to. Guess who I just saw heading into the rhododendrons?' Rory, who had a bottle of Chablis in one hand and a bottle of beer in the other, topped up Lottie's glass with a flourish, and looked expectantly from Lottie to Elizabeth. 'Never say I don't bring you presents, darling. Go on, who do you think?'

'Not Dad.' Please, thought Lottie, not Dad.

'Pip and Mick. Bet you can't beat that, eh?'

Elizabeth nodded, as though she'd expected it all along, which was one of her annoying traits; the ability to be unimpressed and unsurprised whatever happened.

'Oh.' Lottie hardly paused long enough for it to sink in. 'Well, guess who Dom's going to marry?' She had one of her own, which she decided was much more outrageous.

'Amanda.'

'Bugger, how did you know that?'

'She just told me.' Rory grinned. 'Dom was opening champagne and spraying everyone, seemed a bit odd for him.' He took a swig of beer. 'So that's what the riding lessons were about, is it? It must be love.'

'I do believe you could be right.' To an outsider Elizabeth's tone could have seemed dry, but Lottie knew her, it was the closest she was going to get to a display of affection.

An alarming thought suddenly occurred to Lottie. 'Why did he say this place wouldn't be his? You haven't disowned him have you?' What if his engagement to Amanda meant he had to give up Tipping House, that he'd chosen love over money? Romantic thoughts started to fill her head until Elizabeth firmly dashed them.

'Disown him for shilly-shallying with that woman? Nonsense.'

'But—'

'Tipping House never was going to be passed down to Dominic, my dear.'

'What?'

'Well, seeing as you're both here, now is as good a time as any to explain, I suppose. The Stanthorpes never liked to stick to the normal order of things,' she smiled, 'Tipping House is never passed to a male heir, it is inherited by the eldest female. However long you have to wait for one,' her tone was dry now. 'My ancestors were very forward-thinking, and quite sensible when you come to think of it. Women do tend to outlive men, so it seems a jolly good plan.' She waited for it to sink in, watching the puzzled look on Lottie's face be replaced by comprehension, and then doubt. 'If the eldest child is a boy, then naturally they act as guardian until the time is right. Dominic, it appears, has taken his duties very seriously.'

'But he, who…'

'Alexandra should have inherited all this.' Elizabeth put a hand over Lottie's, 'but as she's gone, you are the next in line. If I die before you are ready, then your Uncle Dominic has promised to look after the estate. He feels partly responsible.' Elizabeth had always known that, deep down, Dominic had felt partly to blame for his sister's death, that it was that fact that was the largest obstacle between him and William. Both blamed themselves. Neither had seen clearly. The burden had weighed heavy on Dominic, and his solution had been to wrap himself in a cloak of duty and obligation. But, Elizabeth suspected, it was his chat with Billy that had given him the glimmer of hope that Amanda had opened out into a chink. The timing had been impeccable.

'But he, why couldn't he and Amanda...' Lottie was confused.

'I think the poor man believed that Amanda would never be happy here, that she wanted a very different life. He was torn between staying here and following her. He always was a stickler for doing the right thing. But,' her voice regained its normal brusque edge, 'she appears to be staying, and as I have no intention of expiring any day soon then I don't see the problem. So dear, I'd say your father will be there for quite some time. Right, enough for one night. I'm an old lady, even if I'm not on my deathbed. Don't stay up too late, now will you?' She picked up a fresh gin and tonic and leant forward to kiss Lottie on the cheek, the hint of Chanel wrapping around Lottie's confused senses. 'Oh, you do have to marry to inherit, you know.' And, with what looked like a sly wink in Rory's direction, she was off in a surprisingly sprightly fashion. Leaving Lottie feeling like she was the one who should actually be going to bed, not her gran.

***

'Does that mean you're going to be stinking rich?' Rory, an arm around Lottie's shoulder, and a bottle in his spare hand, took a deep breath of fresh air as the pair of them wobbled off the driveway and onto the lawn.

She giggled. 'No, incredibly poor. Have you never heard of death duties and dry rot? Good innit?'

'I think you're going to have to start talking properly, darling.'

'Oh, it won't be for ages yet, so I can practise. Do you think Pip minds that Elizabeth was using her just so that she could make Uncle Dom do something? I mean, she knew all along that the place wasn't going to be sold off and demolished, didn't she?'

'No, she doesn't.' Pip, in her usual manner, had arrived unnoticed. 'Mind that is. She knew all along that Elizabeth was up to something, manipulating circumstances.' She grinned. 'Besides, I'd rather be on her side than the opposition's.' Pip had always admired Elizabeth, and the more she found out about her the more she liked the old lady. Without Elizabeth, this place just wouldn't be the same.

'Where've you been?' Lottie was staring at her.

'Nowhere.' The grin broadened.

'You've got leaves in your hair.' Lottie gave her the once-over and remembered what Rory had said, a comment that had somehow got lost in the revelations.

Mick plucked the greenery out of Pip's normally immaculate blonde bob. 'I've been educating her about country ways, it's important.'

'Very important.' Pip tried to keep a straight face. 'Is it true about Amanda then?'

'It is.'

'That'll be one hell of an engagement bash. I could really get some press coverage on that one. You know, tortured Lord...'

'He's not a Lord.'

'Whatever. Love-struck widow finding happiness again after heartbreak.'

'You never were one to let facts get in the way of a good story, were you treasure?' Mick, Lottie noticed, had a very possessive hand on Pip's waist and seemed quite mellow. Less threatening.

'Devastated male model who'd sought sanctuary in the countryside being passed over once again.' Pip was in full flow.

'Do you think he minds, Tom, you know, about Folly Lake Manor?'

Pip put her headline manufacturing on hold. 'Not from the look of him, not even you could call him sad, look.' They all followed the direction of her gaze, back towards the stone balustrade that surrounded the terrace at the back of the imposing Tipping House. The crowds had spilled out, to get some air, and the elegant trio stood, model-perfect, glasses in hand. Dom, Amanda and an animated Tom, who, relieved of the task that Elizabeth had set him, felt as though a weight had been lifted off his shoulders. In fact, Lottie decided, he looked happier than she'd ever seen him.

'I should go and find Dad, tell him everything.'

'I'm sure he already knows. And he's busy.' Pip grinned, and Mick chuckled.

'What do you mean? What don't I know now?' Lottie groaned. 'Stop it, you're all doing it again, not telling me.'

'Let's just say I wasn't the only one getting a country education.'

She groaned even louder and put her hands over her ears. 'Shut up, I really didn't want to hear that.'

'You asked, you idiot.' The sight of Billy careering across the lawn, giving the full-bodied Tiggy a piggyback, had been pure Tippermere. They'd been fine until Pip had hollered at them, and then Billy's mistimed attempt at waving back had unbalanced the pair and they'd gone off-piste, straight into the undergrowth. Giggling. 'I'd say he's pretty happy, and they've been in there bloody ages.' She didn't voice the 'crashing about' bit, which was probably too much information to give Lottie. 'Anyway, where are you two sloping off to? I need a drink.'

'Well bugger off back inside.' Rory grinned, but then handed her the bottle that was still dangling from his hand. 'See you later. Come on Lots.'

Oh, she did like it when he was a little bit bossy.

***

A horse nickered as they walked through the old archway, into the stable yard, and Lottie took a deep breath in, of country air, of soft, warm horse smell, of leather and the scent of the roses that rambled up the walls.

'You love it here, don't you?' Rory sat on the edge of the fountain, which luckily was turned off, and pulled her onto his knee.

'I do.' She grinned, suddenly light-headed, his hands burning hot through the thin silk layer of her dress. 'It's always been my favourite place.' And with startling clarity, which she was fairly sure had nothing whatsoever to do with her tipsiness, she knew it was true.

'Is that why you came back?' He looked serious in the moonlight. Serious, slightly drunk. As sexy as she'd ever seen him.

'Well, I reckon I did come back because I love it here,' she traced her fingers through his thick, dark curls, 'and of course there's Dad.'

His firm thumb moved further up her thigh, but he was still studying her closely. 'Of course, who can forget Billy?'

'And I quite like you, too.'

'But if you're serious about the being skint bit, I mean, should I be hanging around with you?'

'Well, if I don't get married I'll be fine. I'll never be skint.'

'Ah, I reckon that might be a problem.'

'Do you?'

'Well what if, and it is just a what if, you meet the perfect man?' His thumb went up higher, and her stomach curled in anticipation.

'What kind of perfect man?'

'The kind that loves you even if he forgets to tell you, the kind,' those fingers were getting very distracting, 'that doesn't always listen, the kind that's only just realised how lucky he is, the kind that never wants to lose you.'

Lottie shivered as his warm hand found its way under the layer of silk, straight to her skin, which had been heating up, but was now covered in goosebumps.

'The kind that will look after you in sickness and health, for richer, for poorer.' Lottie squeaked as his thumb found her swollen nipple.

'The kind that is quite keen on shagging you senseless.' His mouth was on her neck, and Lottie moaned, tipping her head back, forgetting pretty much everything about anything.

'Ah, that kind.' Even she could hear the tremble in her voice. 'That could be a problem.'

'So are you prepared to risk being poverty-stricken?'

'Yep.' It came out on a high note as his hand reached its target.

***

Sometime later, with straw in her hair, and her dress looking like she'd slept in it (but there had definitely been no sleep involved), Lottie stared up at the inky sky, spattered with diamond-bright stars, and squeezed Rory's hand.

'Happy?' His breath was warm against her hair.

She twiddled her toes, wondered briefly what had happened to her shoes, and felt the cool dampness of the grass beneath her heels. She thought how much better this was than twiddling her toes on a beach in Spain.

Lottie grinned. She rolled over and studied the firm, straight lips that had just meandered over practically every bit of her body. What the hell did she ever think she'd find anywhere else? Her feet had brought her straight back to Tippermere, the place that looked like it had everything on offer that her heart could desire...

'Very. But I might be even happier if you could do that thing with your tongue again.'

Rory's rich laugh filled the still air. 'You are so dirty.' And before she had time to react, he'd got her pinned beneath him. 'And so demanding.'

Lottie sighed. She'd come home. To stay.

Acknowledgements

I'm incredibly lucky to be part of two immensely supportive communities – writers and riders. Without them this book would never have been written.

Massive thanks to my wonderful editor, Charlotte Ledger, and to Kimberley Young, who gave me the opportunity and encouragement to write the book I've always wanted to.

To all my talented and supportive author friends, but particularly Téa Cooper, who knew from the start what I should be writing!

Thanks to Helen Shaul, who introduced me to the joys of Jack Russell terriers, and showed me what patience and dedication could achieve with horses. To Bianca Bairstow for introducing me to the world of eventing and teaching me so much. To Pat Mather and John Keleher of the Pickmere Stud who showed me how beautiful a horse could be. To Kate Earthy and Sarah Gummer, who apply harmony to horsemanship so effortlessly, and helped me understand.

And to the many wonderful farriers and amazing horsemen and women who I've learned from and shared fun times with.

In memory of Edmund Frith, a great friend, who is sadly missed and who was a much-loved member of the farming community and village life.

And finally, to the many horses who have taught me well, and to Darcey, a little terrier with a big heart who always was as big a star as the horses and left us far too soon.

Enjoy the ride!